SKYLARK IN THE FOG

HELYNA L. CLOVE

Story Well Publishing
2637 Northgate Blvd
Fort Wayne, IN 46835
www.storywellpublishing.com

Publisher's Note: At Story Well we believe that every author deserves to have their voice heard, and by purchasing this book you have helped us continue to find new voices to bring to the world. Thank you for supporting us and our authors!

This is a work of fiction. Names, characters, places, and incidents are a product of the author's imagination. Locales and public names are sometimes used for atmospheric purposes. Any resemblance to actual people, living or dead, or to businesses, companies, events, institutions, or locales is completely coincidental.

Edited and proofread by Charlie Knight - https://cknightwrites.com
Cover art by Harkalé Linaï - https://harkale.art
Cover design, interior formatting, and design by StoryWell Publishing
Part I poem excerpt: "Crossing the Bar" by Lord Alfred Tennyson (public domain)
Part II poem excerpt: "Hope" is the thing with feathers by Emily Dickinson (public domain)
Part III lyrics excerpt: "Inertia And The Weapon Of The Wall", Words and Music by Samuel Vallen and James Grey, Copyright © 2017 AMF Music Ltd. All Rights Administered by Kobalt Songs Music Publishing. All Rights Reserved. Used by Permission. Reprinted by Permission of Hal Leonard Europe Ltd.

Skylark in the Fog/ Helyna L. Clove -- 1st ed.
ISBN 978-1-952876-14-1

PART I

IT'S A LONG LANE THAT HAS NO TURNING

Sunset and evening star,
And one clear call for me!
And may there be no moaning of the bar,
When I put out to sea,

Twilight and evening bell,
And after that the dark!
And may there be no sadness of farewell,
When I embark;

For though from out our bourne of time and place
The flood may bear me far,
I hope to see my pilot face to face
When I have crossed the bar.

(Lanehunter prayer, originally from Old Earth, excerpt from Crossing the Bar by Lord Alfred Tennyson)

The moment the first missile crashed into the *Skylark*, Captain Jeane Blake realized she had gravely underestimated the danger they'd gotten themselves into.

The spaceship jolted, and a series of yellow warning messages flashed up on the screens. On the radar display, the markers showing the *Lark* and the Union vessel hot on its trail flickered in and out of existence in the interference, and the gravitational anomalies of the lane kept throwing both ships off-course. Their pursuer was gaining on them.

"The generator didn't like that," Kliks groaned in the co-pilot seat. His lean form hunched over the console, large black eyes tracking the numbers on the status indicator. "Alignment issue, I think. Can we get out of here now?"

Jeane frowned at the code running on the main computer screen, then at the model above, where the *Skylark's* current trajectory appeared atop the schematic representation of the lane: a stream of parallel lines forming a shifting and contorting chasm in the spacetime continuum. "We need five more minutes to compute a vector," she said. Although only a rough estimate, that sounded like just enough time to be blown to smithereens by an overeager Union agent.

Her Talalan companion made a frustrated noise, realizing the same thing. "I'll take a look. We won't get far without proper thrust."

He stood, crossed the cabin with one long stride, shoved the door open, and stormed out. Only a few seconds ahead of the next blow from the Union vessel.

The hit shook the entire ship, and this time, the artificial gravity grid in the walls and the floor couldn't compensate fast enough. The impact pushed Jeane to the deck, and while she grasped for the edge of the console, a bone-chilling metallic creak reverberated through the hull, making her teeth grind.

She hauled herself up and punched the comms button. "Kliks, come in! Are you okay?"

One of the lamps above released a spray of sparks over her keyboard, and the next second, all the lights blinked out in the cabin. The engines sputtered one last time before they gave up the fight. Silence and darkness fell over the *Skylark*.

Jeane sank back into her chair, and as the ventilation wound down around her, she took a shaky breath and started counting her heartbeats.

Eight, nine, ten, eleven—then the auxiliary generator rattled to life.

The shrill sound of an alarm filled the cabin. Jeane shuddered, swallowed the acrid bile rising in her throat, and scanned the awakening displays. Most of the ship's instruments reported errors, their shields and the engines were down, and although the front screen flickered to life to show the immediate environment of the *Lark*—nothing but the glow of this precarious tunnel in spacetime they'd decided was a good idea to jump into—the main computer remained offline.

She killed the alarm and tried the comms again. "Kliks? ALU? What's your stat, guys?"

There was no answer. Panic crept up her spine. They were dead in the water in the middle of a gods-forsaken lane with an apeshit agent set on offing them. How'd this day gotten so bad, so fast?

"...got us on the tail...fell down the frickin' ladder!" Kliks' words started pouring out of the speaker, occasionally dropping into silence just to reassemble into somewhat comprehensible phrases a second later. "I'm afraid the generator...to bring back power!"

He sounded pissed, but at least he was alive.

"What do you suggest?" Jeane's gaze kept wandering back to the swirling fog of the lane displayed on the screen. She couldn't shake the feeling that the void outside was watching her.

"The bastard...stopped shooting at us, so...and look at it."

Jeane pushed away from the console, detaching the flashlight from the belt of her cargo pants. "I'm going down there. Is ALU with you?"

"They're on their way up. ...a vector?"

"Nope, system fried first. Don't move. I'm coming."

She barely walked out into the darkened corridor when a series of sorrowful beeps sounded off from ahead. With another step forward, the flashlight beam fell on her technician's angular form.

"No power," ALU said, crestfallen. They seemed uninjured, but their insect eyes scanned the hallway as if they were waiting for an ambush. Their squat, boxy body bounced up and down, and they waved their four multi-jointed, metallic arms around. "Don't like it."

Jeane reached down and grabbed them by one long limb, turning them around and marching them across the darkness. "Give me something useful!"

"Structural integrity sixty-three percent. Life support ten percent," ALU recounted, pattering forward. Without power, gravity would linger in the ship for several hours, so at least they wouldn't have to acrobatics their way through it for now. "Generator and shields at zero. Engine room sealed off."

Skies damnit. Shouldn't have asked.

The agent knew what they were doing, immobilizing the ship without destroying it. But the Union was usually not this merciful when dealing with lanehunters, so Jeane didn't even dare to imagine what the bastard really wanted with them.

The *Skylark* had been lifting off a dusty little planet in a backwater dead system when the agent had shown up. The small lane leading to the highly unstable central star of the world didn't have a name and was only identified with a row of numbers. It was the last place to expect an attack from the Union. The empire's henchmen preferred the busier sectors to catch themselves some innocent scavengers.

The crew had already been in a hideous mood, finding nothing of value on the deserted military base, save for some scrap metal and defunct weaponry. The offices had been cleared out, and the decrepit ships in the docks loomed empty. This wasn't all that surprising. The Altex, the race that had built the place, had been extinct for a hundred years because the central system of their empire had been destroyed by a forming lane, then the Union had purged their surviving colonies. But this was a newly discovered outpost, its location recovered in files smuggled out by lanehunters from stars know where. Virgin waters and all that jazz—definitely worth a trip, their source on Metallia had said. Except they clearly hadn't been quick enough about it.

After a few hours of fruitless foraging, Jeane and her companions had climbed back into the *Lark* to plan a course to their next objective, hoping that one of these days, they'd actually earn the price of their fuel and maybe the funds for a few necessary upgrades too. They'd just left the atmosphere when the Union nailship had started tailing them. Jeane had raced the agent to the lane, hoping to lose them on entry, but Jerkface had followed them in.

She descended the ladder to the maintenance level with ALU at her heels, and they hurried toward the tail along the corridor lit by sparse, red-tinted emergency lights. They found Kliks standing beside the metal door of the engine room, only his legs visible as he leaned into a section of removed hull panel. The surrounding deck was scattered with cables, tools, and various diagnostic devices.

Jeane peeked into the wall cavity beside Kliks' shoulders. Blind LEDs stared back at her from a sizable switchboard, and she smelled smoke. Kliks turned to her and plucked a tiny flashlight out from between his teeth. "The engine room is in emergency lock, and I already managed to ruin a battery trying to switch life support back on."

Jeane gave an indignant grunt. "That hit must have knocked out the shielding circuitry."

"Possible," Kliks agreed. His huge black eyes narrowed to thin half-moons in concentration, and the shallow wrinkles creasing his gray face even at a relatively young age (as typical of his people) deepened. His short white hair was sticking out in all directions on the top of his head, and he lifted a hand to smooth it down self-consciously when he noticed Jeane eyeing it. "It's hard to tell from here. We have to go in."

"ALU says the room is not pressurized."

The technician confirmed with a trill. They'd climbed the opposite wall and were now dismounting another panel; the metal sheet landed on the deck with a clang, and ALU stuck their arms into the hollow space. The next moment, their head also disappeared inside the hole.

"So." Jeane started pacing. "The engines and shields are out, we can't see or hear outside, and very soon, it's going to be real cold in here. But hey, first, we might burn to a crisp at the lane barrier if we stay too long without navs! What in hells does that agent want from us so badly?" It was a rhetorical question, but when Kliks sighed and pulled on the zipper of his black overalls nervously, she raised her eyebrows. "I'm listening."

He stared at her for a second and then started speaking with the momentum of someone continuing an argument they'd already begun in their head. "I swear, I didn't think they would jump us so quickly! Well, I have to suppose *that's* the reason, but I mean, everything else would be a stretch. I'm not even sure what—"

"Kliks!"

The Talalan closed his mouth. Then he opened it again. "I found something on the Altex base."

For a moment, Jeane didn't know how to react, and Kliks took advantage of her confusion to go on in a desperate tone. "Remember those wrecked ships on the runway? You couldn't get in, but I did. I wanted to tell you, but I—"

"For skies' sake!" Jeane blurted out, the anger breaking through her daze. "What were you thinking? We don't keep these kinds of secrets! Why the fuck—"

«*Getting all worked up won't solve the problem, you know.*»

Jeane swallowed hard, closing her eyes for a second. The

words kept echoing in her mind.

«Calm and collected. You can do this,» the voice went on, and the familiar tone was like a cold shower on her burning temper. She sighed inwardly. Of course, *he* would think so. He always had too much faith in her.

She looked at Kliks, who naturally couldn't hear any of that but had in the meantime stopped babbling and stared at her from behind his best poker face. ALU kept rummaging in the wall, not concerning themself with the drama in the slightest.

"The ship was Talalan," Kliks added quietly.

«Smack me twice and call me Kevin! That's quite an interesting piece of information!»

Jeane took a deep breath. She leaned forward, glaring into Kliks' face, then poked him in the chest. "We don't have time for this. But we'll talk."

Kliks pursed his lips together, nodding, and it took Jeane all she had to tear her gaze away and gesture towards the engine room.

"If only a few connections are busted, we're still good. We'll check the generator, jump-start it with a power cell, and if the engines are not entirely dead, it only has to hold until we're on the vector. Weirdo warped spacetime physics will take care of the rest."

Kliks switched back to problem-solving mode, too—anything to escape her wrath. "We're not going to have much time with a cell, considering the *Lark's* appetite. Also, what about after? Once we're out of the lane?"

Jeane waved it away. "Cross that bridge when we get to it."

"Because if the agent can follow us out..."

"No way."

"Sure, just like we thought they wouldn't follow us in."

Jeane raked her fingers through her hair. "Well, let's assume they can't because otherwise we may go ahead and screw ourselves now. Will the cell hold or not?"

"Are you going to feel better if I say yes?"

"Yes!"

They glared at each other for a long second, and ALU chose

this moment to pull their head out of the wall and offer with a cheerful tone, "ALU go in!"

"No." Jeane sighed, fiddling with her flashlight for absolutely no reason. "ALU stays here and gets our eyes and ears back. I want to know what Jerkface is doing out there. Keep working. I'm suiting up."

The technician chirped in agreement, and Jeane set out on a jog through the ship, leaving her crew behind.

Most of the *Skylark's* bulk was filled by the cargo hold, while the engines and the generator took up the tail section. On the lower deck, there was only space for a couple of tight storage chambers, and on the upper deck, apart from the control cabin in the bow, a common room and two cramped sleeping quarters nestled in between everything else. All in all, the vessel was a hundred yards in length and a dozen yards across—a medium-sized freighter ship, although customized to a degree.

Times like this, it seemed way too small for a crew of three.

Jeane passed the entrance to the cargo hold, the ladder leading to the upper deck, then the airlock door, and by the time she reached the end of the hallway, the fury pressing on her chest had dissolved. She stopped in front of a towering storage unit and slid its doors open.

She stood still for a long moment. The spaceship felt lifeless and somber around her, and the flashlight cast quivering shadows on the patchwork gray-copper metal walls. She was sweating like she was getting paid for it; with the life support out, air circulation had also stopped. Still, thinking about the cold, aggressive energies of time and space, twisting and turning around the ship made her skin crawl. Crossing lanes had become second nature to her over the years, but it didn't mean she enjoyed taking her time in them. She would have been crazy to. Those things could tear apart entire galaxies.

And now they'd gotten themselves stuck adrift in one. They hadn't run into agents in months; what in hells had happened this time?

She grasped the leather strap hanging on her wrist, took a rubber ring off it, and tied her long blonde hair into a ponytail.

"Fuck," she stated and felt instantly better.

«Don't panic, kid. Been worse, hasn't it?»

She removed a spacesuit from the closet and climbed into it hastily, sealing the gloves and boots into place and taking the helmet under her arm. A button on the wrist turned the controls on with a soft beep, and she breathed out, relieved. Good thing Kliks always reminded her to keep the batteries charged.

«An abandoned Talalan vessel, right on your hunting grounds. You know what that means.»

She paused reluctantly. It meant Kliks was keeping secrets. It meant he'd known what they were going to find on the Altex outpost, maybe even that they could run into agents. And he hadn't said a word.

They'd been flying together for five years, and despite their many differences, their teamwork had proved to be effective. Trouble was never too far, but they'd always dealt with it. Yet the moment something surfaced from Kliks' home planet, the mysterious closed world Talala, everything changed.

«And what are you going to do about it?» the voice in the back of her mind pressed.

Jeane pulled a zero-G toolbox out of the storage unit, shut the door with a bang, and set off towards the tail again. *First, I'll save your damn ship. That's what I'm going to do.*

When she got back to the engine room, ALU was sending an angry series of trills at Kliks, who was still tinkering with the power cell.

"What's wrong?" she asked.

Kliks gave a tired head shake. "I dared to suggest that shorting the cables to open the door might be dangerous."

"No other way!" ALU objected, their small body still half-stuck into the wall. "Structure too weak for blast. Have to maintain pressure in ship!"

Jeane stepped beside them and glanced into the shaft. The technician was clutching the edge of the opening with two arms while using another pair to hold onto a cable running vertically down the inner hull.

"Is *this* safe?" she inquired.

"Chance of life-threatening injury thirty-eight point three

percent," ALU exclaimed proudly.

Jeane raised an eyebrow. "Uh-huh. Can you seal the door after me?"

The technician blinked. "Yes," they said and ducked their head back into the hole.

Kliks closed his side of the argument with a dramatic eye roll, but there was a distinct look of worry on his face. Jeane attached the flashlight to her belt, but before she put the helmet on, she fixed her eyes on her friend for one more moment.

"What is it?" she asked. The Talalan visibly winced, and it was both satisfying and scary. "What did you find in that ship of yours?"

"I'm not sure yet," Kliks admitted. "It's in the hold. I intended to inspect it when we were in safe waters."

Jeane scoffed. "Must be valuable if the Union was tracking it."

"I think it is."

She wanted to grill him more, wanted it so damn much, but there was no time. So, she sighed and put on the helmet, breathing in deeply when fresh oxygen flowed into it. The whiff of cool, dry air touching her face was a welcome relief. She gave a thumbs-up to Kliks because there was no time for petty gestures either, rooted herself in front of the engine room door, and touched the comms button on the suit.

"ALU, if you can hear me, go."

She heard the technician's beep through the comms and saw Kliks backing up, disappearing from her view. Then something flashed on her left, and the door slammed open.

The pressure difference pushed her in the direction of the opening right away, and she forced herself to remain calm as her feet lifted off the deck and her body tumbled over the doorstep. But as she sped towards the other side of the room beyond, curling up to decrease the force affecting her body, she looked around to assess the situation—and screamed.

"Holy fuck! ALU, door, now!"

She spread her arms out to hold onto something, anything, but the bulky fingers of the suit couldn't find a grip. She collided with the cylindrical tower of the generator in the middle of the room and grabbed for the first protrusion she saw.

Behind her, where the opposite corner and the *Skylark's* starboard side engine should have been, there was nothing. Just a gaping hole and through that, the roiling vacuum of the lane with its infinite, shining nothingness. The wall and the ceiling had cracked and twisted from their places; bent metal rods and cut wires snaked out of the ship's body, disappearing in the fog.

Jeane grasped a lever on the generator's trunk at the exact moment the door to the corridor banged shut behind her. The current of air escaping the lower deck had ceased, and she fell onto her stomach, the painful blow at her midsection jarring her out of her stupor.

"Captain?" ALU squawked in her comms. "You there? Is okay?"

Jeane turned around, her heart drumming in her throat, eyes widening as she surveyed the damage. "I'll be damned..."

She'd expected a broken hull, a small breach, maybe. Something manageable. Not *this*.

«*For crying out loud, kid, you're killing me here.*»

"Jeane! Are you alright?" That was Kliks, his voice muffled. He was probably yelling into ALU's built-in comms in his urgency.

She listened to her own rapid heartbeat and counted to ten. "I'm fine. You?"

"Good here," ALU hurried to answer. "What is status?"

Jeane turned away from the tragedy—there was nothing she could do about it for now. Keeping her hand on the generator tower, she climbed onto her feeble legs.

"The bad news is that we're on half engine." ALU made a scared chirp, and Kliks cursed in his lilting mother tongue. Jeane picked up the toolbox that she'd dropped in her panic and went on. "The good news... I don't know. The genny should be fine."

"Doesn't matter if our drive is out!" Kliks shouted, this time into his own comms.

Jeane didn't argue. She wanted to cry. Instead, she turned on her helmet light and flipped a few switches on the generator. Her heart was still beating wildly, and from time to time, her body lurched, losing its balance. She blamed it on the failing artificial gravity of the room. With a giant fucking hole on the hull, it was no wonder the grid had already become unstable.

«A familiar situation, isn't it?»

Jeane shook her head, desperately trying to shut out the intrusive thoughts.

«Hey, what's that? After so many years of running, Jeane Blake finds herself faltering when she comes face to face with her fate?»

I don't need this now, Hollis. Getting stuck in a lane, waiting for the bitter end without any hope of help to come, her ship flightless...she couldn't think about it.

«I only want to be a motivating force in your time of need, as always.»

She turned her focus back to the problem. "ALU, can you see what's going on out there?"

The technician trilled a firm yes. They must have managed to connect to one of the ship's antennas manually. "Agent on rendezvous course."

"They want to board us. For skies' sake..."

Jeane blinked the sweat out of her eyes and got to work. ALU and Kliks had started arguing in the background, but she wasn't paying attention to them anymore.

The dead section in the generator's overload shielding circuitry was easy to find, and she quickly set up some patches and bypasses. Kliks had also been right about the alignment issue: several of the cooling tubes had been jarred by the hits, causing the efficiency to drop. She adjusted them best as she could, but she needed ALU's strength to finish the job later.

By the time she screwed the gaskets back on all the cables and connected them to the primary circuit, black dots were floating around in her vision. She stood, shaking her legs. "I think I'm almost done."

She stepped up to one of the switchboards, popped out a panel, and grabbed the bundle of wires spilling out from behind. The subsystems that had been lost with the starboard tail section were not essential for the port side drive since Hollis had built the two engines to operate independently in an emergency, but this was the first time they had to use them like that.

"Agent closing in!" ALU whistled into her ear.

Jeane looked over the cables in her hand, finding no obvious faults. Without the shield, Jerkface only needed a modest detonation to get through their airlock. Union nailships carried a single person, and Jeane didn't see more of them around before their navs went out, but only one of those brainwashed brutes and their fancy weapons could overpower all of them easily.

Well, ALU might be able to put up a fight purely due to their physical fortitude. They couldn't (or more precisely, wouldn't) hurt a fly, though, which wasn't much help in the kind of life-or-death struggle their situation was turning into. What every lane-hunter-Union confrontation always turned into.

The *Skylark* lurched again, and Jeane knew immediately that it was different from the small shakes of the last few minutes. Those had been caused by their trajectory regressing and the ship approaching the unstable barrier zone of the lane; this was a sign that the agent had started the docking maneuver. They must have thought themself a fantastic pilot to attempt something like this inside a lane.

"Kliks, you can connect the power cell," Jeane called out, her voice dull through the fear thumping in her head.

No answer. The ship shook again.

"Right about now, or we're not going anywhere!"

Silence. Jeane shivered. What was happening out there? Maybe the agent had already docked. Maybe they'd gotten to her crew. Why else wouldn't those two idiots respond?

The seconds ticked by, and Jeane counted to thirty, frozen into place. Then one of the displays fixed to the hull beside her blinked to life.

Slowly, one after the other, all the systems came back online. What was left of the engine coughed and started working again, and the *Skylark* flinched as if spreading out her wings.

The door to the room flung open, prompting Jeane to grab for the nearest solid object, but no air rushed in this time—the shields must have been restored. She waited for another second, then ran out into the corridor.

The first thing she saw was several wires coiling out from the maintenance tunnel where Kliks had worked before like he had eviscerated some great metal beast. She took off her helmet, pulled the spacesuit down to her waist so she could move more freely, and followed the cables towards the cargo hold, where they disappeared in the dark. But before she could have found where they led, the ship trembled again.

A dull clang from the direction of the airlock indicated that the outer hatch was under some sort of stress. Jeane spun around to run there, but someone collided into her from behind.

"Captain!"

Jeane grabbed Kliks' shoulders, so they both managed to keep their balance. "What in hells is happening?" she cried. "Why didn't you answer?"

The Talalan sent a wary glance towards the hold. "You can shout at me all you want later, but there's only a flimsy hatch and ALU between us and the agent. You weren't ready, and I had to find another way. Now, help me get us out of here!"

Jeane stared back at him. *Another way?* Then she realized. She hadn't seen the genny come back online, only the engine and the computers. So, where was the *Skylark* getting power from?

There was no time to argue. They were flying, and that was the important thing. "I'm not leaving ALU here with that jerk," she said. "I know they can be convincing when they want to be, but against an agent—"

Kliks shook his head. "We can avoid close combat if we're fast enough."

Jeane felt her hand ache—she was still grabbing onto Kliks with an iron grip, pale fingers whitening in the effort. She released him, hesitated only for one more moment, then nodded.

Back in the control room, she flung herself into her chair, taking in the system diagnostics running on the main screen. Kliks settled beside her with an anxious frown. Life support was working at forty percent, and their shields were up, but apart from keeping them pressurized, they couldn't do much for protection. The tortured engine did its best, but the genny stayed silent— whatever Kliks' "another way" was, it provided power for the entire ship.

«Talalan magic science, I tell you. If you survive this, smack him on the forehead for me.»

Jeane typed in a row of code to recalculate their vector, and a moment later, the *Skylark* changed course.

"Where are we going?" Kliks asked.

"Stars know, but it's the only exit we can reach with our current thrust."

The comms creaked, and ALU's voice called out. "Agent returned to nailship."

Jeane snorted. "Feeling the heat, I bet. Good luck with that!"

"No, but look!" Kliks pointed at the status indicator that showed the *Skylark's* schematic image with the nailship still attached to them. "They want to paddle out on our back!"

Jeane swore loudly. There was no way that, on top of everything else going wrong, the *Lark's* engine could keep up with the extra mass and imbalance. If they couldn't shake the bastard off, they'd all die.

"A focused energy burst on the shield might get them off," Kliks lamented.

"Or it might burn down the whole system."

"At this rate, that might happen either way!"

"It doesn't mean—"

The comms croaked again. "ALU will do! Locally."

"That's not—" Kliks started, but a sharp beep interrupted him.

"Will do! Less risk. Chance of life-threatening injury seventy-four point four percent."

Jeane scowled at the speakers and inhaled, but ALU didn't wait for her and cut the line.

"I'll help them." Kliks jumped up. "If I tune the manipulator differently and—"

"Manipulator?"

Kliks froze. "The thing I took from that planet. Please, Jeane. Let's save ourselves, then I will explain."

Jeane let out another curse. "Go!" she yelled, and Kliks gave a curt nod, slipping out of the control room. "And be careful, for stars' sake!"

The energy burst appeared on the status indicator two and a half minutes later, and the *Skylark* tilted when the pulse knocked out the docking mechanism of the nailship. But it looked like they finally got rid of their hitchhiker, and if Jeane were lucky, the lane would kill the agent before they found another vector. The comms stayed silent, and she forced herself not to jump up and check on her crew.

The pearly white fog thickened in front of the ship, and her stomach lurched from the sudden gravity shifts. As the *Skylark* climbed the end of the vector, Agent Jerkface and their nailship disappeared behind them in the interference.

She adjusted their course. The vector seemed stable, but she followed its changes closely, tracking the energy levels of those strange, exotic particles forming and decaying in the fog. As they got closer to the transition into normal space, the tiniest mistake could cost their lives. The ship sped forward, almost as if half their engine wasn't torn off, almost as if the lane wanted to spit them out of itself, and when the fog cleared and the bright blue void turned into starry blackness with one final familiar jolt, Jeane closed her eyes and started whispering the only prayer Hollis had taught her.

CHAPTER 02 | FOG OF WAR

Princess Maura Tholis closed her eyes as she stood beside the massive throne, her fingers curling around the silvery surface of the backrest. Her light brown locks stuck to her sweaty back, her shoulders sagged, and her temple ached, a pulsing agony echoing the rapid beating of her heart. Where the sleek black material of the glove on her left hand met the skin, waves of scorching heat spread toward her chest, and behind her eyelids, tiny stars were falling from one void to another. She desperately tried to grab ahold of them, but they kept slipping through her grasp, way too swift and ephemeral.

She was alone in the Grand Hall. Deep purple curtains blocked the floor-to-ceiling windows on both sides of the room, and high-backed chairs stood empty around the gently curving gray marble table. The blue glow of the decorative strips along the edges of the throne were the only light sources inside—the palace was on power-saving mode.

Maura inhaled. A shard of pain sliced through her head, and she reached for the nape of her neck, losing focus over the connection. A moment later, her consciousness catapulted back to the real world, the white dots of light along the fingers of the glove dimmed, and the system returned to standby.

She rubbed her neck, her face contorting into a frustrated grimace. The buzz in her head eased, but it left her feeling anything but relieved about the brief respite.

That was the second time she had failed. But she wasn't ready to give up yet. She wanted to see it all; everything she suspected her father, Caiden Tholis, King of Miyoza, had been keeping in secret. The latest damage to the shield above the capital, the bombings, the deteriorating morale in the city, and the stalemate of the interplanetary front line between Miyoza and the neighboring world, Gaerris. It wasn't in her power to change any of these things, but knowing the details would make her feel more in control. She hoped.

Glancing towards the doors leading to the western and eastern wings, she waited for two ragged breaths, but there was no movement or noise from outside.

Her gaze wandered back to the room. Without the usual bright lights illuminating the meandering, fractal-like motifs on the white-stone pillars and the intricate geometric patterns on the walls, the sight was disquieting. No ministers and advisors were squirming in their seats, arguing loudly, and no assistants dashed through the space to serve refreshments during long-drawn-out meetings. After several worker groups demanded to be discharged two weeks earlier, personnel were reduced to a minimum. Only a few ministers and their help had stayed, but Maura hadn't seen most of them in days. Little by little, everyone had left. The palace was a ghost of itself now.

The capital's resources were running out. They could still maintain the infrastructure, but people were terrified; the usual propaganda of some glorious future victory couldn't placate them anymore. All of them sensed the lack of the king's presence in the last few days, and the Gaerrisian forces had been assaulting the city more ruthlessly than ever.

It was as if the enemy understood too: these were the last hours before the fall.

Maura stood in the dark, preparing herself for the next round with the glove. The emptied palace and the decreased number of guards meant it was easier to access the system in secret than ever before, but someone could have disturbed her at any moment, and she had no idea when the next opportunity would present itself. If ever.

At the thought, a sick feeling bloomed between her stomach and chest, the burning heat stretching to her limbs and squeezing her throat. Suddenly, she couldn't take a proper breath. Her body felt alien. This wasn't an after-effect of the glove. The panic attack descended and lingered for a few seconds. She released a shaky sob, clutching her neck, and as abruptly as it had come, the feeling passed. It found no hold on her this time.

Probably thanks to her exhaustion. She hadn't gotten a decent night of sleep in months.

Everyone expected her to be at her father's death bed, to see him off to the great beyond while their planet hurtled itself towards destruction. She couldn't. She'd rather watch the broadcasts of the war over and over again.

The silence weighed on her with a renewed intensity, so she straightened her back and wiped her sweaty palms on the heavy fabric of her long blue skirt. Her focus turned back to the glove on her hand.

The royal glove: both symbol and instrument of reign on Miyoza. An interface between the mind of the rightful ruler and the planet's defense systems and firepower, main information nodes, automated ground units and spacecraft, most infrastructural centers, and production processes—the City Nervous System or CNS. In practice, this meant absolute power. The glove also provided a direct connection to the artificial intelligence that supervised the CNS, developed for the express purpose of supporting the human monarch in their effort to build the perfect empire.

At least, that was how it had begun. What it turned into was terror, chaos, and a sixty-year-long war.

The glove had been designed to recognize and only be unlocked by the Tholis family genome. Royal heirs could only activate it after their coronation, and it required special training starting years before they rose to the throne and continuing long after. Taking full control of the CNS's capabilities was a prolonged and arduous process.

No one knew that better than Maura. She shouldn't even have been capable of wearing the glove; her father had refused to train her from the beginning. The little experience she had, she'd acquired against his direct wishes throughout those same long years she'd lost trust that King Caiden Tholis would ever end the war with Gaerris.

She stretched her fingers, the elastic cloth embracing her skin with no trace of the burning feeling from before. Closing her eyes again, she took a deep breath to subdue her anxiety, sensing the connections in her head snap into place—like a door slamming shut, then a much more expansive window opening wide. She suppressed her unease and let go of her body. The pain would return soon. She had to hurry.

Knowing she wouldn't have the energy for more, she concentrated on the most important thing to investigate—something that Nasir Dareth, her friend and occasional informant, had told her about. Not long before falling ill, her father had a call with the Gaerrisian High General, Liv Horst, that no one else from the Miyozan high command had been involved in. Maura needed to know what was said during that conversation. The king hadn't talked to anyone from the Gaerrisian Council in a long time. One way or another, the meeting had to be important.

She focused harder. Minutes passed. And slowly, the darkness behind her eyelids lit up. Loss and disconnect rushed her, but she forced herself to remain calm. She needed to go through with this.

Thousands of shining strands, millions of brilliant particles of data, formed a complex spider web of connections against a vast backdrop of information. The view became clearer and clearer until she was standing above it all, looking down as if from the top of a mountain. In spite of the turmoil of emotions, a sense of grandeur and awe filled her. All this power, right at the tip of her fingers.

But dread followed shortly. She was only a visitor on a hostile land; her perception and control of the system didn't even come near to what her father was capable of. Her head hurt again already just looking at this immense brilliance.

"YOU RETURN."

The voice, all-encompassing, resonated through her world. She cringed, trying to steady her jarred consciousness, but her perception plummeted just to soar into the sky a moment later. One second, she saw through thousands of eyes, all the cameras and sensors throughout Miyoza City, her brain filling up with diagrams, blueprints, and constantly updating status reports, and the next, there was nothing, nothing at all—like her mind refused to comprehend the never-ending accumulation of data.

"WHAT IS OUR NEXT COURSE OF ACTION?"

The words echoed oppressively, the tone frantic, demanding. Deranged. She cursed herself. It was much more overwhelming than she'd expected.

Her fingers trembled, her consciousness buckling under the weight of that other, much more powerful mind, but she proceeded to perform the correct row of movements with the glove and followed the strand of light in front of her eyes to its source. The voice repeated its question, but by the time it uttered the last word, she had severed the connection, and the AI's presence blinked out like a dark star. It was still there, watching over everything, and it would stop her if Maura went too far, but they couldn't communicate anymore.

She'd never been able to deal with the city-AI; it was too much for her inexperienced mind. Its interruptions had always been a problem during her excursions into the CNS, and after all that had happened recently, it had become even more dangerous to connect with it.

Something was wrong with the system. Her father had denied it and forced the architects to lie about it, but Maura was sure. There was no other explanation for what had happened to the king.

However, the city-AI wasn't going anywhere: the capital depended on its existence, and so far, it maintained its usual functions without any deviations. If Maura wanted information, she had to go and get it herself. The damage the system could inflict on her was a risk she had to take.

Shaking herself free of the gloom, she pushed forward,

connecting to the palace's video surveillance. The cameras on the corridors only showed her friends—her bodyguard, Damian Moore, and Nasir—standing guard at the doors, looking sharp and vigilant. Apart from them, no one else had approached the Grand Hall. She steeled herself, focusing not on the increasing pain in her head but on the job at hand.

As always, her difficulty in accessing the records of that mysterious meeting between the king and High General Horst was more in finding a specific piece of data than in actually decrypting and viewing it. She was a Tholis, and the system had to respond to her. She knew all the doors and had all the keys, but by the time she got to those gates and unlocked them, her legs were shaking, her head was pounding, and she barely had the energy to feel the hollow disappointment the recording provoked in her.

"I am offering you a way out. I will accept your surrender, cease all assaults against Miyoza, and spare the life of your citizens."

The general's voice was casual but firm. Maura didn't know much about the man, but he'd attempted peace talks before, and that told her he wasn't necessarily the bloodthirsty maniac the Miyozan high command believed (or wanted to depict) him to be. Gaerris might have had the upper hand, but they'd also suffered significant losses over the years. It made sense that they wouldn't want to drag the fight out.

Miyoza had already lost. The only reason the capital still stood was the dome-like shield around the city, which had been protecting them for almost eight years now while Gaerris had occupied the entire planet, pillaging cities and destroying cultivation zones. The capital was all that remained, cut off from supplies and being forced into submission.

"My stance has not changed. I will not bow my head to you. I'm not a coward!"

In contrast with General Horst, the king's voice conveyed many intense emotions. Spite, pride, anger. He seemed, as he usually did, delusional.

There was nothing to be gained by refusing this offer. He could have chosen to save them all—maybe occupied by the enemy, but alive. Yet, he decided he would rather see his planet burn.

"Then I've done all I can. You leave me no other choice but to proceed."

Maura swallowed back the tears, the recording slipping out of her virtual grasp as she fought to regain control over her emotions. She wanted to check on the cameras one more time before leaving the CNS, but then she felt it—a warm hand on her shoulder, not demanding but persistent. Waiting for her to resurface whenever she chose to.

She let go of the system, painstakingly gathering the scattered pieces of her consciousness into a single entity again, and emerged into the real world to crushing pain in her head and a nauseous tremor in her stomach. A tall, athletic man was standing beside her in the gray uniform of the crown's guard; his hand was lightly holding her in place as if he expected her to collapse. Damian.

"Are you alright?" he asked in a low voice.

She nodded, an automatic response while her glance snapped to the two doors behind them. The one leading to the western wing was closed, but the other one had Nasir's slender, tan form standing in it. He was dressed in a similar attire as Damian and stood on the threshold, keeping his eyes on the hallway beyond.

"Did anyone—" Maura started, but Damian cut in.

"No. But Beren couldn't reach you, so he called me instead. Your father is expecting you."

Icy terror gripped her body, but she managed to nod again. She felt like a wooden doll, one of those creepy ones with the adjustable joints that Sofia always used for her art projects. She could practically hear the eerie *squeak* they'd made when her friend shaped their bodies into another posture. Why computer models hadn't been enough for her, Maura could never fathom.

"Did you figure something out?" Damian asked.

She looked up at him—*squeak*—and took a step back, pulling her arm away to balance her aching body on her own. Damian kept the composed expression on his face. Only his pupils widened a bit as he started to suspect the implications of her silence.

Maura pulled the glove off her hand, wanting to be rid of it. She stuffed the device back into its fancy box on the armrest of the throne and reset the biometric locks with frustrated haste. This was the worst time to be thinking about Sofia. But broken promises and failed peace talks—those were exactly what had led to her death too.

"We should go," she said, suppressing the futile fury boiling in her chest.

They walked out of the Grand Hall towards the eastern wing. Maura nodded to Nasir, dismissing him for now, and the man bowed slightly before walking off in the other direction. They would talk later. If there was such a thing as later.

The foyer was empty, the lights dimmed. The digital picture frames on the walls, normally showing colorful scenes of the city and the palace garden, had been turned off, and the echoes of their steps gave a crude rhythm to the silence. Maura walked forward in a daze, trying to stop her useless, racing mind. She didn't want to talk to her father. There was no way that conversation turned out anything but miserable.

More corridors, then the large white staircase leading to the first floor. Another stairway, this one narrower, ending right at the door of the king's private suite. Damian squeezed her arm encouragingly before she pushed the handle down, and Maura glanced at him, pleading but knowing that he could do nothing to save her from what followed.

The door closed behind her, and she was standing in the room of her dying father.

The luxurious but minimalist chamber was illuminated by a single lamp on the bedside table. Inside the circle of light, three figures were waiting.

General Felix Pahoron, Secretary of Defense, was a gaunt man with a sour expression on his long face. Beside him stood the king's personal assistant, Beren Lumare, holding a handkerchief which, from time to time, he pressed to his reddened face and snuffled into. The third person, Dr. Sand, was standing at the near side of the bed, his bony hands behind his arched back, blocking the face of the man lying there under heavy blankets.

Her bones were cold metal, all the anger, fear, and sorrow coagulating into something thick and poisonous. Distorted mental images of the next few seconds played in her mind like a glitched recording. She walked forward. Her father lifted his head, his hands reached for her, his mouth opened—then it cut back, and she walked forward once more. Her father looked at her, his arm raised—

"Princess," Beren called quietly. If he had misgivings about not knowing Maura's whereabouts in the last hour, he wasn't showing any. "His Majesty wished to speak with you. He was conscious a moment ago."

She approached the bed. The king's eyes were closed.

"How is he?" she asked because they expected her to.

The doctor turned to her. His wrinkled face looked much older than his age would have suggested. Half of those creases had formed over the last forty hours while he and his assistants had labored to figure out how to save the king's life. "He's very weak. His heart is giving up."

It had started with that—a heart attack two days before. By the end of that night, they all knew what was happening; they just didn't know why.

The nanobots the royal glove released into the human body to establish connection with the CNS had somehow turned against the king, attacking his vital organs one by one, and every attempt to extricate or eradicate them had only ended up with more damage to him. Tiberius Sand was the best available expert on the planet, but he was out of ideas. Their options were a slow or a quick death, and the king had chosen the former.

"Maura..."

If she walked away, she could still forget about this weak, unsteady voice. *It doesn't have to happen.*

But then Caiden Tholis, King of Miyoza, opened his eyes.

"Maura," he said, more firmly now, his gaze searching for his daughter's.

She stepped closer, although every nerve in her body urged her to do the opposite. "I'm here, Father," she said.

"Good. I wanted to talk to you. Before—"

The sentence was broken by a deep heave. The man clutched his chest, his face twisting in pain as he fought the fit. Maura forced herself to watch. Dr. Sand leaned over the bed, holding up his diagnoser to get a read, but the king waved him away.

"What is happening?" he demanded, his voice stabilizing, and he straightened in the bed. Maura was temporarily forgotten. "Our troops, the front—"

"After last night's conflicts, their vessels stopped moving again," Pahoron replied readily. "Our scouts reported more cargo ships landing on the northern shore. We attempted to surprise them, but it was...ineffective."

"Ineffective," the king repeated the word, then he swept the thought aside. "What about the shield? Is the dome holding?"

"Yes. It is still possible to keep the energy levels above eighty percent for weeks, Your Majesty."

Pahoron spoke in a joyless voice. Maura glanced at him, and disgust flooded her. He should have talked about the explosions instead. Fifty-three people had died in the heart of the capital less than a mile from the palace because somehow, Gaerris had managed to smuggle bombs inside the dome. And why didn't he mention that all the underground routes leading outside had been closed because the city couldn't take more refugees from the ruined towns in the vicinity? Why wasn't he talking about the units far above their heads, who only survived this long because the enemy was focusing everything they had to break down the force field around the capital?

The king tried to sit up. "Nothing is lost yet," he said. His skin was colorless and damp; dark shadows furrowed his face. This man who had never shown anything but dedication, rigor, and courage was now only a caricature of himself. Only his light blue eyes, so different from Maura's own deep brown ones, were the same as before. "We're not backing down. The capital is still ours. We can—"

He paused to breathe. Then, as if he were just noticing his daughter again, he leaned closer to her. "I arranged everything." The words bubbled out of his mouth in short, broken sentences. "You will take the throne. You will wear the glove, but you will not use it. You will form...a royal council. It's still not too late."

Maura froze. "You want me to do what?"

There was a bitter smile on the king's face. "You have to rule. You're a Tholis. But you never...you never understood. They will do the job for you."

In Maura's periphery, Pahoron nodded along, and her revulsion swelled up. She searched for the right words but couldn't find them.

"They will know what to do," her father said. "You will obey. We will continue all ongoing operations."

"I assure Your Majesty, everything will happen as agreed," Pahoron replied. Beren sniffled once but didn't speak.

"I don't understand," Maura said, although she knew it was useless. How many times had she tried to convince these people to notice the king's delusion? She never achieved anything. "Gaerris is at the gates. We have nothing left against them. We have to surrender!"

"No!" the king howled, and even Pahoron recoiled at his voice. "We are not surrendering! Never! This is not how it ends. We can still win the war if—"

He stopped talking as if all his will had dissipated. Maura stared at him in horror. She wanted to shake him. *This is a nightmare.*

"We have to win," the king whispered and lay back on his pillow with a groan. "We will win."

He fell silent. Dr. Sand leaned over him, checking his pulse and breathing. "He's asleep," he said, relieved.

The seconds stretched out, but Maura only stood, rooted into place. Then Pahoron's mouth curved into a snarl as if he'd remembered something uncomfortable, but before he could have spoken to her, Maura turned her back on him and ran out of the chamber.

The next few minutes were a blur, and when she came to her senses, she was standing under the stone-arch leading into the palace's interior garden. She was breathing heavily. Sweat trickled down her forehead as she held onto the pillar.

The air felt humid and warm. She gathered her will and started down the gravel path.

Orange lampions dangled on the towering trees, and beyond the ceiling windows, the sky was already dark. She passed tall ferns and bright green bushes with vibrant flowers and soon reached the little white fountain in the center. She sat on a bench, leaned back, and closed her eyes.

Her father had made this place for her mother, who had been born in the Equatorial Zone and missed it dearly in the first years of their marriage. Maura had spent a lot of time here when she'd needed quiet and calm, hoping it would bring her closer to the lost queen. It never worked, but she'd found herself coming back again and again.

She should have talked to Pahoron, listened to his self-righteous lectures, pretending to agree. Then she should have sat beside her father until life finally left him.

"We can still win the war," his words echoed in her head.

That might have been true in the beginning. Miyoza had been the more technologically advanced and better equipped of the two planets, but as time had passed and the fight had become more desperate, Gaerris proved to be enduring and obsessively invested in victory. Attacks, reprisals, reluctant cease-fires, senseless discussions, waiting, attacks again. In the end, isolated from and abandoned by the rest of the galaxy that was occupied with their own power struggles, Miyoza was stuck in an endless cycle with no escape.

Her father had long lost the ability to see it for what it was. And now he was dying, having refused the possibility of peace again.

"We have to win. We will win."

She buried her face in her palms. Her forehead hurt as if a giant vise had gripped it between its jaws.

"Princess?"

She winced, but the voice was familiar. Turning her head, she saw Damian standing at the end of the gravel road.

"It's okay! I'm okay." Maura spread out her arms, showing how okay she was, and hid her face behind her palms once again.

Damian sat beside her, his movements as quiet as a light gust of wind. For a moment, neither of them talked.

"They can't accept it." Maura dropped her hands into her lap and lifted her face towards the sky. "Not even when it's right in front of them. He's dying, Damian. His own rule is literally killing him, and they're all still living his lie."

Damian looked at her with a calm expression. "Facing the certainty of death is becoming harder and harder by the day. No wonder they can't do it."

"He refused to capitulate, again. Gaerris offered a way out, and he ignored it. And now, he's taking the glove out of my hands!" She chuckled at her own lame attempt of a joke, frustrated. "It doesn't matter whether he's dead or alive. We're following him there soon."

"Maura," Damian cautioned her, glancing around, but they were alone in the garden. She plastered her hands on her mouth, the regret frothing in her stomach not only because of what she'd said but about how. He was still her father. He was *still* her father.

"Nasir checked my tracker two days ago," she muttered. "No one is listening. Apart from..."

The AI, of course. The silent observer, the mad instigator. Pulling the strings from the background.

At least, that was what she assumed, especially with the glove's sudden malicious actions against the king. How the medical team and the royal engineer, Dr. Toussi, who knew as much about the system as someone who wasn't a Tholis could, rationalized what had happened, she had no idea. It wasn't a secret that royals suffered side effects from prolonged connection with the CNS; it was the way things were. But Maura was certain something more sinister was happening. Either the AI was failing in ways no one understood, or...maybe even it realized that the king was going too far, threatening the very existence of his people by living out his obsession with glorious war. Maybe it wanted to stop him. Maybe that was why it let Maura roam around in the system freely, demanding she define their "next course of action" every time she wore the glove. But whatever the reason was, it didn't matter much. In their self-righteous zeal, no one believed her anyway.

"What did you mean he's taking the glove out of your hands?" Damian asked.

She sighed. "A royal council is going to make the decisions instead of me. I'll be sitting on the throne, so the people won't suspect a thing, but I won't have any power. And Pahoron isn't going to surrender. He will not go against my father's last wish."

"No, he won't."

Maura took a deep breath and slowly let it out. "Tell me it's impossible." She formed the words carefully. "Tell me there's no way we win. I can't trust my own judgment anymore."

Damian put his elbows on his knees. "There's no way we win. The outer front lines are lost, and without your father at the helm, it's only the question of time. We can't hide in here forever either."

Suddenly restless, Maura stood and started pacing beside the bench. "And they should know this! Instead, they're still trying to fool themselves, and I'll have to watch us sacrifice everything we have left for nothing!"

"It's not over. Not as long as you have access to the glove," the man said, his tone calm. "You're the heir to the throne."

"Damian, I'm scarcely able to hold onto my sanity every time I touch that thing. What on Old Earth could I do?"

Face everything head-on, assume the full power of the CNS, and go against the high command openly—that was what he was suggesting. And then what? Attempt to start peace talks? Would Pahoron let her, or would she be shot in the head for treason? Would the AI support her, or would it drive her mad too?

She was so tired. It was too late for all of them. Walls everywhere. With a sudden, desperate fervor, she wished that Sofia were still alive, still with her. She would know what to do. She'd always had the right answers.

"You risked yourself just today, only to get some information." Damian's eyes were warm—no blame, no judgment, even though he feared for her every time she put on the glove. "You still think it's not all in vain."

Maura pressed her lips together. *Oh, he knows me well.*

"I could try," she said. Because what was there to lose? None of them would survive what would happen next. Gaerris would not be merciful; they couldn't be. They'd lost too much. "Let's talk to Nasir. We could—"

She paused. Quiet musical notes drifted towards them through the garden from hidden loudspeakers. Damian stood, a bitter expression crossing his face.

The world lurched around Maura, and a void opened in the middle of her chest. She recognized the starting stanza of the Miyozan anthem.

The king had just passed away.

CHAPTER 03 | HIGH AND DRY

"I wanted to say that I'm sorry."

Jeane wrapped the cable in her hand into a neat loop and put it down beside her, where she sat cross-legged in front of the Talalan device in the cargo hold. Tucking a stray lock of hair behind her ear, she reached for the next wire dangling out of the damn thing and glanced at Kliks with a mask of disinterest on her face. "Okay, shoot."

Her friend shifted from one foot to the other, standing on the threshold of the chamber. "Umm. I'm sorry."

Another bundle of cable landed on the deck—only a few more and Jeane finally disconnected Kliks' weird machine from the *Skylark's* systems.

The manipulator, as the Talalan had called it, was an irregularly shaped box with a diameter of roughly fifty inches, and its core was a smooth, white orb Jeane had located behind a hatch on the top. Buttons, displays, and signal lights covered the contraption, but none of the labels told her anything since they were all written—apparently—in Talalan.

"Did you hear what I—"

"I heard you. You're sorry." Jeane loosened another wire, and the dull white glow of the lamps in the hold went out for a moment. When they returned, she exhaled, trying to keep her cool. "Once again, with more feeling?"

Kliks sighed as well. "I don't know what else you want from me."

Considering that this was the first time they'd talked since the incident with the nailship, his voice was surprisingly calm. After breaking free of the lane, Jeane had made sure that, first, her ship would stay in one piece, and second, that Agent Jerkface or any of their potential friends in the vicinity weren't following them. Then she'd run to the airlock as fast as her feet took her. ALU hadn't been answering, and she'd started to fear the worst.

The technician had been lying in the middle of the chamber, three arms still gripping the handle of the outer hatch. When Jeane had knelt beside them, they'd slowly come to.

"Water," they crooned, their compound eyes scanning the room. Jeane had helped them out of the airlock and into a chair up in the common room, then placed a large bottle of water in front of them. After the technician stuck one appendage into the liquid, they seemed more comfortable and gave a tired beep of affirmation.

ALU would be fine eventually. While even after a year spent in their company Jeane still had very little information about their strange, mixed organic and robotic physique, judging from previous experience, if the technician were in severe distress, they would have proclaimed it in a much more unambiguous, enthusiastically vocal way.

On her way to the cargo hold, she had bumped into Kliks. The Talalan had halted, mumbled something about checking things in the control room, and promptly fled. But he'd left his secret machine behind, so in need of an explanation or not, Jeane was damn well going to start getting rid of it. However, Kliks had returned not ten minutes later to bother her in the process.

She unplugged the last cable and stood, wanting to be on the same level as her friend, but seeing as Kliks was a head taller than her, she could only try her best. "Maybe answer some questions for starters. Like what the hells is this thing? And since when are you keeping stuff like this in secret? And another classic: when did you decide you didn't trust my repair skills?"

Kliks folded his arms, frowning in pretend confusion. "What do you mean I don't trust your skills?"

Of course, he picked the question that was the easiest for him to handle, but Jeane decided to run with it. "I mean that I fixed the gods damned generator!"

"You didn't finish in time. I needed to get the ship going so the agent couldn't break in."

"Everything would have been fine if you'd started the power cell when I told you to."

Kliks raised his chin. "I made the best decision under the circumstances. In the end, everything turned out alright, so—"

"That's not the point!" Jeane shook her head in disbelief. "I told you I could do it, and I did. So you can stick your decision where the stars don't shine because, fine, you don't trust me, but then what? I shouldn't trust you either?"

"Come on, don't overplay this," Kliks muttered.

Jeane felt her temper rise. "I'm not the one always preaching about responsibility and everything having its place and time!"

They stared at each other for a long moment. Kliks broke first.

"Alright. I wasn't sure you'd fix it. Were you?"

"Yes!" Kliks raised an eyebrow, and Jeane glared at him. Out of respect for the complicated relationship between him and his home planet, she'd tried not to get into this, but stars help her, this idiot was not making it easy! "Okay, I wasn't. But you stopped trusting me a lot earlier."

"What?"

"You lied." Kliks froze, but Jeane was committed now. "You knew what we were going to find on that planet. It wasn't a random lead."

Before visiting the Altex outpost, they'd spent a week on one of the largest lanehunter worlds, Metallia, scouring the usual pubs for job offers and fetch quests, catching tips and vague directions from drunk clan members known for running their mouths. Kliks hadn't told her who suggested the Altex world to him, but that wasn't unusual; they always gathered info before deciding on the priorities and the route to take together. But now that she thought about it, he *had* been pushing to leave earlier than planned and to go to the military base first. Jeane had no strong feelings about any of their targets, so she complied, attributing his enthusiasm to curiosity. Not the first time Kliks had gotten all intense about a dead world.

"What was that place?" she asked. "What's this manipulator, and why was it there?"

Kliks swallowed. His eyes gleamed with fear, and he struggled to get the words out. "I can't tell you yet. I need to study it. It's not that simple—"

"Seems very simple to me," Jeane interrupted because his hesitation started to freak her out. "This thing can power totaled ships seemingly from nothing, brings the Union on our tail in half a second, and turns my friend into an unreliable idiot! I want to know why we almost kicked the bucket out there."

"Come on, it was one agent."

"No, it was a maniac who was tracking this thing! What if they managed to send a signal out before they died? We might still be followed! Need I remind you what happened to Hollis? At least if you'd told me—"

"Would *you* have come here?" Kliks burst out, now furious himself. "If I told you what kind of trouble we were in for, would you have risked it? Risked the ship?"

«*Grayface shoots, grayface scores.*»

"I'm sorry I lied, and I'm sorry I brought danger on us," Kliks continued. "But this is important. I promise you. I needed you to come here and find the device before the Union did, and you wouldn't have otherwise."

He fell silent, and Jeane realized she had nothing to reply with. This was crazy. Did she even know this person standing in front of her?

Everything regarding Talala and the time Kliks had left the planet was a sensitive topic; it always had been. Jeane empathized with that whenever she allowed herself to think about it for more than a moment and make a comparison with her own complicated feelings towards her home. But it was never a subject of argument, only something they all tried to ignore.

Knowing that, would she have come here to pick up some potentially dangerous and powerful Talalan tech only because Kliks had wanted her to? No pain, no gain, and it was personally important to him, plus valuable, so if nothing else, then good business. But again, also a Union-magnet, so...would they have come?

«No, you wouldn't have,» Hollis replied in her head.

Well. He'd still lied. Deliberately withheld vital information that put them all in harm's way—much more harm than they were used to during a regular smuggling run. And the lie hurt.

"This was the worst apology I've ever heard," she said. She didn't have the patience to deal with all this. Getting the *Lark* to safety had to be the priority.

"I never said I was great at it," Kliks mumbled.

"Then practice. And don't touch this thing until we land somewhere." Jeane spun around with her hands on her hips. Manipulator disconnected, genny back online. All was well—as much as possible, under the circumstances. "Anyway, ALU was the one who saved us in the end. No drama or annoying secrets, they just did their thing."

"A true role model. Except they took an enormous risk too."

"It's becoming a pattern, isn't it?" She glared at Kliks, then turned her back to his distraught expression and walked away.

A small, petulant part of her was curious whether he would start tinkering with the manipulator right away, so she didn't repeat her warning. No use in trying to force him to open up either. They would just continue to argue. He said the thing was important, so it was. She'd get the why out of him eventually.

«What a wise and mature decision. Congratulations.»

"A momentary weakness. Don't get used to it," she said to the empty hallway. Her own voice, answering that internal thought out loud, halted her in her tracks for a second.

The conflict with the nailship had been clearly too much stress to avoid rousing some bitter memories, and with bitter memories came Hollis. Rubbing her face, Jeane suppressed a groan. Coping. She was coping. Pretending to talk to him helped and wasn't at all a pathetic, weak thing to do.

She walked to the tail to check on the generator. Emerging

from the lane near a white dwarf, she had to overload what remained of the engine to climb out of its deep gravitational well, so now they were drifting. The genny worked on half-power, the left engine barely reached thirty percent output, and the nav system kept turning on and off erratically. And they had, of course, that other problem: their whole starboard tail was missing.

"Don't worry, girl, you'll be fine," Jeane whispered, giving a pat to the door of the engine room. Only the sickly hum of the generator answered.

ALU was still lying on the couch in the common room when she returned, their arm plugged into the connector of one of the spare power cells. The water bottle was on the floor, empty. Jeane pulled out a chair and sat down. "What's up?"

ALU released a feeble trill and turned their cylindrical head around as if testing the muscles—although, if anything, their skull looked the most robotic among all their body parts. "Seventy-eight point seven percent. Half an hour, all good."

Jeane gave them a smile and shrugged the leather jacket off her shoulders, throwing it on the metal table in the middle of the room. Her skin was hot and itchy under her tank top—but at least this time, due to exhaustion and not a malfunctioning life support system. "You can rest. We're not in a rush at this point."

"Generator fine?"

"It will hold for now." She winced. Stars, she didn't want to think about this yet. "But we need help."

"Where?"

"We'll have to get creative." When ALU nodded, sensing her hesitation and thus uncertain themself, she nudged them and tried to lighten the mood. "Hey, but at least we won't have to be afraid of getting shot in the ass."

The technician gave an elongated beep. "Because we don't have ass?"

"Yeah."

They buzzed in what was, in their signaling system, a giggle.

"You did great, by the way," Jeane said. "Nice job and whatnot. Do you need anything else?"

ALU shook their head, so Jeane reached out and gave them a

pat, a gesture intended to be both encouraging and soothing.

She was generally hard-pressed not to treat ALU like a child because, in many ways, they very much resembled one. They didn't seem to mind being handled like that either, although their knowledge about machinery and any tech they got in contact with proved to be immense, and their talents to analyze, repair, and enhance electronic systems had become indispensable on the *Skylark*. All this expertise seemed more instinctual than learned, and ALU had always remained vague on the big question: were they a robot or an alien?

Their body was mechanical; metallic plating covered their head and torso, and their four arms were able to extend, retract, and alter to take whatever form they needed at the time, like universal tools or adapters. But there was something organic in the way they moved and talked. ALU also referred to themself in third person, using concise sentences. They'd tried to explain this once, saying that most of the time, they didn't bother speaking more than was necessary, and to further questioning, they suggested that everyone should just learn to deal with that.

Jeane didn't have the slightest about where ALU had come from. The mechanic who sold them to her on Metallia had said they were a household robot, and Jeane had intended to trade them away as soon as possible. But the moment ALU had stepped on the *Skylark*, it had been obvious that there was more to them. They'd demanded to know "which ship where it goes," had a lively conversation with the nav system while fixing several bugs in its code, then swept up the cargo hold—and by the end of the first day, Jeane had realized she'd found a new crew member.

Jarring herself out of her sleepy contemplation, she got up and stepped into the kitchen corner. Her body had been screaming for caffeine for the last few hours, and since there seemed to be a pause in the chain of life-threatening situations on board, she wanted to grant the coveted substance to her aching physique.

While the coffee machine worked, she slumped against the inner hull. Listening to ALU's quiet, chattering conversation with themself, she glanced at her palm-sized tablet-slash-comms device from time to time, remotely checking the computer's status indicator, the changes in their trajectory, and the radar image of space around the ship. The system would have notified her if anything strange was going on, but with the day they'd just had, who could blame her for being a bit paranoid?

A small *ding* signaled that the coffee was done. Jeane filled her cup and gulped the liquid down, treating the second and third servings with more patience.

Soon enough, Kliks appeared in the door; he always sniffed out coffee being made, even from the far end of the ship. She half expected him to saunter in with his mystery machine, but he was empty-handed, and when he saw Jeane at the kitchen counter, he froze.

Her anger had long dissipated. Only an uncomfortable jitter remained in her stomach, urging her to restart the argument. As Kliks walked into the room, she took a step out, going around the counter so that in the end, they switched places, trading aloof looks. ALU gawked at them, trilling cheerfully.

Kliks took a mug from one of the cupboards and cleared his throat. "What's our destination, Captain?"

She picked at her nails, feigning nonchalance. "There's a crack not far from here, but I don't want to overwork the system. We'll get there."

"And after?"

"The Kav-174. And then it's more or less easy sailing to the Foggy Cities."

Kliks raised an eyebrow and took a sip from his coffee.

"I don't like it, but we need a safe place," Jeane went on. That was a serious understatement. She hadn't been in the Cities for years, and her last memories of the place were complicated. "And it's not only the engine. Our options are limited. We've got almost nothing to sell."

The Talalan sipped his drink again but didn't say a word.

"Okay, then." Jeane swallowed the rest of her coffee, dropped her mug on the table, and started for the door. "ALU, you relax. Kliks, if you're ready to start acting like a grown-up, please join me in the control room."

In the green-blue glow of the console displays, Jeane considered their options again. The *Skylark* was falling apart; only Hollis' lingering ghost kept its weathered body together. No matter how much she hated it, the Cities were the only safe haven in the vicinity, and at least she still had connections there. No other way of getting out of this, although she reckoned they would have to sell everything to the last screw in the cargo hold and make a bunch of stupid promises.

«No other way, sure. If you don't count the Ranch.»

And I don't.

«So it's the usual game?»

Jeane clenched her jaw. She expected it to go even worse.

The instruments detected the crack ahead of them half an hour later. In contrast to the unmistakable blue band the lanes visually presented themselves as, this time, they wouldn't have seen anything by eye if the sensors didn't enhance the view and project it on the front screen. A narrow line, no more than a thread of hair stretched straight, a few thousand miles away. The nav database only identified it with a row of numbers, and Jeane had no idea whether they'd ever been here before.

"This is going to be tough on the hull," Kliks mused, studying the energy signatures of the crack. He'd returned a few minutes before and sat beside her without a word. ALU, fully recovered, took their place in the corner where they could follow everything, ready to intervene.

"We're playing for survival here," Jeane said. "And if we have enough power left to stumble into the Cities afterward, we've won."

She adjusted their trajectory and increased energy levels on the generator, but their propulsion dropped gradually, and the whole ship pulled to the starboard side. A huge problem since they had to find the correct angle to pass through the crack, or the *Skylark* would fall apart.

That was the thing about cracks. You got through them much quicker than your average lane, but it was more strenuous on the ship. As Hollis had used to say, traveling through them was like if, instead of pulling your teeth out with an expert hand, someone simply punched you in the face.

Jeane set her jaw and increased propulsion again. The lights briefly flickered as the system struggled to balance the power blips. The crack was only a few hundred miles away.

"It's not going to happen," Kliks murmured. "We're too fragile."

"Shut up."

But he was right. Their thrust might be enough, but the hull integrity was poor.

They turned on the vector. The ship jolted, and there was a metallic screech as the hull and the shields fought the grip of the tidal forces valiantly.

"She can do it," Jeane said while the constellations stretched into infinity around them. "No problem."

The ship's frame groaned and crackled as if a giant hand was twisting it apart. Kliks stared at the screens with increasing dread on his face, and Jeane gritted her teeth so hard she had to order herself to relax. Seconds felt like hours, but then, finally, the *Skylark* dragged itself through the chasm carved into the flesh of the universe.

When the sight of space reassembled, Jeane took a deep breath and scanned the displays. The solar system they appeared in only sported a few hostile-to-life planets—they would find no help here. She browsed through the warning messages popping up on one of the screens, but there was nothing they could do about them, so she stopped acceleration and put them on a trajectory toward the largest gas giant in the system.

The lane next to it, called the Kavanaugh-174, was something of a meeting point for many lanehunter clans. While Jeane would have rather nailed her tongue to the bottom of the console than to ask for help from any of them, that lane was their shortest route to another system with another crack that could lead them close to the Ros-3. And the Ros-3, deep inside its shining belly, was hiding the Foggy Cities, their destination.

"Keep your eyes on the status indicator," she told Kliks, standing up. With their current settings, they needed five hours to reach the Kav-174. "I'll go to the back to figure out something, so we don't have to sell our organs for a new engine."

Her friend nodded. "Have you considered sleeping?"

She wanted to give an angry retort, but all of a sudden, real exhaustion flooded her. "If I rest now, I'll be too alert in the Cities and might jump down someone's throat."

Kliks faked a thoughtful expression. "I'm happy you can see your shortcomings clearly."

"I wish I could say the same thing about you!"

She was sure Kliks would have turned red at that if his physiology allowed. Instead of an answer, the Talalan fixed his eyes on the front screen, so she shook her head and left him there.

But she wasn't planning on sleeping. The *Skylark* was flying injured, and it felt like her own body wasn't functioning properly. No way she could relax like this. Instead, she went back to the kitchen for another coffee, lost two games of holo-chess against ALU in an attempt to procrastinate, and looked through the logs of the last few weeks in a leisurely manner before convincing herself to face the depressing emptiness of the cargo hold.

Flicking on the ceiling lights, she surveyed their meager belongings. Back in the day, this place couldn't fit all the things they had scavenged together during a typical run. All those boxes and containers filled with merchandise from lanehunter or dead worlds, sometimes even from the Union! Machine parts, raw materials, artwork, jewelry, weapons—they traded with everything they could estimate the value of, selling them to a client or bartering for the best price.

Even without belonging to any of the big hunter clans, they had a reasonable clientele, and they got the occasional recommendations too. Jeane worked fast and efficiently and didn't comment or ask questions; the *Skylark* was the ideal courier for someone looking for quick earnings beyond the lanes. She didn't expect to get rich from it, especially since the Union, on their road towards the complete domination of the known universe, had put their dirty toes into the lanehunters' soup more and more often, but they always had money for food and fuel—and that was all they needed.

But maybe they'd stopped taking the same risks as before. She had become too cautious, staying on familiar paths and not looking for the road untraveled. Certainly a safer endeavor, but in turn, the profit was lower.

And now, the Union was sending out agents who easily

followed their prey into lanes. Jeane had never heard of anything like it before. Navigating those places was a difficult task in itself, so how had the nailship stayed at their heels so accurately? What were they to do against opponents like that?

Their best chance was to fix up the *Skylark* as much as possible and do some more runs. A brutal undertaking with only one engine, but they might earn the price of a new one before the ship broke down for good.

She stopped herself there, counting to ten to keep the building panic at bay. Then she did it again to make sure. The voice in her head stayed quiet, but she knew the drill anyway.

Losing the *Lark* was not an option. They would figure something out. They had to.

"We're almost there." Kliks' voice made her jump. He'd arrived soundlessly and was now leaning against the frame of the cargo hold door. "Did you have an epiphany of some sort in the meantime?"

"Several, actually." Jeane turned towards him. "Usually when I'm full of ideas, I have this absolutely clueless face on to confuse everyone."

Kliks rolled his eyes, but there was worry in his voice when he spoke. "We'll have to make deals with one of your old patrons, right?"

Jeane shot him a dark glance. "Not if I can help it." She found herself staring at the manipulator in the corner. This whole stupid reminiscing and the prospect of returning to the Cities had put her in a foul mood, and she couldn't help commenting on it again. "We might be able to sell that thing."

Kliks' eyes widened. "No."

"Didn't you say it was valuable?"

"I also said we can't let the Union get ahold of it! What makes you think a random lanehunter's warehouse is a better choice?"

"What makes me think?" Jeane forced herself to lower her voice. "I'm still waiting for you to explain this whole thing. I'm trying my hardest to trust you, but at some point, I will need answers!"

Kliks closed his eyes for a moment. Then he nodded to

himself, like making a decision. "Fair. I know this is my fault. But if I'm right, and this thing is what I think it is…I don't know how it got out, but we cannot give it away. It's too dangerous."

"So we're stuck with it?"

Kliks sighed. "I need to make sure before I say anything."

"You knew it was going to be there. You know exactly what it is."

He didn't answer. There was so much more to this than what he told her, and Jeane wasn't sure she could cope with all these deadly secrets much longer. Better to throw the damn thing out of the airlock and be done with it. Wasn't it hard to stay alive anyway?

The Union wanted this thing, and why wouldn't they? Talala was an enigma, an advanced society hidden behind an impenetrable wall, a spherical megastructure they'd erected to encompass their solar system some decades ago. There was no contact or news from inside since then—even Kliks hadn't brought anything with him when he'd left. This manipulator could be the first thing in a while that somehow escaped, and if so, the Union would not hesitate to send an army of their brainwashed agents after the *Skylark*. And if they had a way to track the thing—

But no. Not through lanes, and definitely not to the Cities. The Cities were special. They could disappear there.

"This is clearly important to you," she said, running a hand through her hair. "Let's just get to the Cities for now. We'll fix the ship, take a moment, and try to think. But I can't promise you anything. I won't risk our lives for this. We can't keep flying around with the Union on our tail."

"I'm not sure we'll have a choice," Kliks said.

Jeane closed her eyes. She hated not having a choice so damn much.

CHAPTER 04 | ULTIMA RATIO REGUM

The events of the next day passed Maura in slow motion.

First, the funeral. The princess, the ministers, and their guards took air shuttles to the central cemetery in the heart of Swarin Park, south of the palace inside a bowl-like valley. She sat between Damian and Beren, her head aching like it wanted to explode, and watched the groves, wide fields, and tiny artificial lakes gliding by below.

It was a late summer evening, warm and humid, with gray clouds gathering on the horizon. As she stepped out of the shuttle, six guards took her father's casket to their shoulders and started walking with it towards the white dome in the middle of the circular grassy clearing.

General Pahoron and Secretary of Home Affairs Gordar Relis had decided not to make the king's death public yet. They said the news would have a different effect the next day, before the coronation, when the lost monarch would be quickly replaced with the new one. Continuity would be calming for the people.

Just another empty promise.

Later that day, Maura wasn't able to recall much from the ceremony. Someone talked in a monotonous voice, and Beren was sniffling constantly. The ministers all wore formal black suits and stood around the sanctuary like silent statues of themselves. Maura placed a white flower on the coffin; well-memorized words left her lips, but their meaning did not register. The crypt, the last in the row, closed over her father's body, and she could taste her own despair in the air.

On the way back, she imagined the pouring rain filling up their shuttles, drowning everyone inside. They would float there forever—grinning, bloated corpses, dead and gone.

Pahoron walked her through the corridors of the palace, and then she sat in a conference room for what felt like hours. She had no idea what they were talking about. The only thing that anchored her to the world was Damian's hand on her arm. By the time she got back to her chambers, her mouth was dry, and her head was throbbing. She gulped down three glasses of water in succession, and seconds later, found herself scrambling back to the sink to throw up. Her stomach was empty, and she only spat out bitter bile.

At night, she kept shivering under her blankets. The wind carried voices and ghostly screams—whether real or her imagination, she didn't know. Rain pattered on the window, and by then, she was fully awake. Sitting on the edge of her bed, she was feverish and weak; she opened her windows and let the drizzle spray her burning face with a million cold pinpricks. The city was a sinister, dark mass in the distance. From time to time, dull blue circles of light flashed up through the blackness of the night: Gaerrisian energy weapon charges exploding against the capital's shield.

Anything was better than waiting for death like this.

Hands trembling, she pushed her wavy locks out of the way and pressed the little golden half-disc she'd gotten from Nasir against the skin behind her ear above the implanted tracker, like every time she needed to be off the grid. If Pahoron was looking at her activity in the dead of the night, the fact that her signal blinked out would be suspicious in itself, but it was better than being discovered straight away. She dressed in a pair of comfortable trousers and a semi-formal white blouse and went to find Damian in his quarters.

He opened his door with an expression that told her he wasn't too surprised to see her and stepped back to let her in, but she shook her head. "Is Nasir still around?"

Damian nodded, his face inscrutable. "What are you thinking?"

Maura took a shaky breath. "If Pahoron follows my father's last commands, the coronation might be my last chance to access the glove. We have to make a move now."

The man held her gaze. "How are you feeling?"

The question sounded almost absurd after her urgent outburst. "It doesn't matter."

"It matters to me."

She fell silent, a warm sensation filling her chest. Damian was her friend before he was her bodyguard; of course, he cared. They'd gone through all this together, known each other since they were children. He came from a military family. The king had been good friends with his parents, whom Damian had lost during a miscalculated operation when he was little. Since then, he'd lived in the palace, studying together with the ministers' children, then eventually working as her bodyguard.

"I'm still here?" she replied, uncertain, but Damian gave a small smile, so she went on. "Tired. Sad. More than a little angry. What about you?"

"Wondering how each day can feel more final than the one before. Alright, I'll call Nas. I think we can meet up on our second spot."

"Tell him to bring his gadgets too."

Five minutes later, the three of them were cramped in a meeting room on the first floor of the eastern wing, one of their go-to places for "discreet subterfuge sessions," as Nasir had always called them.

Their friend first scanned the room, both with his eyes and one of the gadgets Maura had referred to before, then he sat down beside the two of them at the terminal in the corner. His dark eyes glinted with interest and a hint of exhaustion. "So, what's the plan?"

"I need you to contact High General Horst," Maura said. "On the direct line he used when talking to my father. Can you do that?"

Nasir peered at her with a faint smile. "Probably. Why?"

Maura spoke slowly, gathering her thoughts. "He offered my father a chance to capitulate. I wonder whether he'd still accept it. No matter what Pahoron says, the shield has a week at best. Gaerris seems to focus their attacks better now that we can't efficiently impede them, and the southern sections of the dome already have problems with power transmission. If something there breaks down, it's over."

"You want to forego it and surrender first."

She sighed. "It's going to be very clear that I'm begging for our lives, but if there's a chance General Horst would resort to mercy rather than total annihilation, I have to try."

"I wonder why he offered a truce," Damian mused. "The victory is already theirs, and being gracious is not their style."

"Maybe he just doesn't want to murder more innocent people."

"Or, what we always thought is true, and they're not as united as they'd like to be," Nasir noted.

"It's not like it matters," Maura retorted. After the numbness she'd escaped to during the day, her nerves were now on fire. "This is our only chance. If it doesn't work, we don't have much to lose."

Nasir mumbled in agreement. "Right. Let me have a chat with the others."

He turned to the terminal and started inputting commands. A few seconds later, he fished out two memory card-like objects from his pocket, plugged them into the computer, and resumed his typing.

Maura drummed her fingers on her thighs, suppressing the urge to ask questions. Nasir knew his business well and wouldn't say he was able to help if it wasn't true.

He was part of the crown's guard like Damian, and at a quick glance, as much a loyal servant of the king as the rest of them. Maura had known him superficially for years before being introduced by her bodyguard around the time she'd started to think about secretly using the glove. Damian had been friends with Nasir first, and through him, she had realized there was more to the man than what met the eye.

At first, she'd thought he was working for a secret service or some elite team answering directly to her father. It made sense then that he wasn't elaborating on some of the skills he'd begun to demonstrate (like getting around the security measures protecting the glove until Maura had learned how to do it herself) or the tasks they'd caught him referring to (copying protected files, talking to shady contacts, and sticking his nose into things he had no permission to know about). Damian trusted him, so she did too, and it helped that Nasir hadn't been hiding his endeavors from her. But one day, she'd decided to question him more forcefully, stating that it was her obligation as the heir to the throne to find out who she'd been associating herself with. That was when Nasir had told them about the Net and their mission on Miyoza.

The Net was the only organization left in the universe that still dared to go against the Union's dealings, attempting to pull together a large-scale cooperation to free the planets that the empire had enslaved. They were present among the lanehunters, on alien worlds, even in the Union itself—and evidently, on Miyoza and Gaerris as well.

Miyoza had severed contact with everyone outside of their system, and the Union hadn't been bothering them for some time either. With Nasir not sharing much about the extent of their plans, Maura didn't know how the Net's efforts were turning out, but one thing was sure: he and his comrades had been sent to Miyoza to "watch how things turned out." The Net had been keen on asking King Caiden to join their rebellion, but the constant warfare Miyoza had been involved in prevented the alliance. This forced them to resort to doing the next best thing: stealing snippets of Miyozan technology and culture in order to advance their cause.

Maura had no reason to put an end to that as long as it wasn't damaging her home. Especially because Nasir proved to be a valuable ally.

"I'm through," he spoke up. "They're connecting us."

"We don't know whether the general watches that line," Damian warned.

Maura glared at him. She didn't need to be reminded of how thin the straw was that she tried to hold onto.

They waited for a few minutes, watching the black screen. Maura kept repeating the speech she'd come up with in her head until none of the words made sense. Then the screen brightened, and she stared into the face of High General Liv Horst, the leader of the Gaerrisian military forces.

"Princess Tholis," the man started after a few seconds of bewildered silence, during which he must have considered all the implications of the call he'd just received. "This is unexpected. What can I do for Your Royal Highness?"

His voice was careful and polite. The black uniform he wore, his shoulder-length brown hair, and his full bushy beard were all in perfect order, but the dark circles under his eyes suggested grave exhaustion. His form towered over the camera view with the posture of someone who knew how to give the impression of power.

"General Horst," Maura greeted him. She straightened in her chair while Nasir scooted to the side to give her space. "Thank you for allowing me to speak with you. I have urgent news to share about the state of my nation."

The slightest hint of a raised eyebrow appeared on the High General's face. "I'm listening."

"My father passed away yesterday. Tomorrow, I will be crowned as queen. My father was against a truce, but in case you're still open to discussing the conditions of such an agreement, I am ready to amend that conversation."

She wanted to keep it simple and quick, but if Horst was paying attention, this must have told him a lot about her situation.

"What are you proposing?"

"We surrender. In exchange, there will be no more bloodshed. I will cooperate and provide my assistance during the aftermath as long as my people are treated humanely."

Horst considered her words, and Maura tried not to show the uncertainty brewing in her. Damian was right—there had to be a reason behind the High General's intention to occupy Miyoza rather than burn it to the ground. Gaerris had been developing steadily during the long years of war, but the planet was still a barely habitable piece of poisonous rock, so she wasn't surprised they would want to utilize Miyoza's resources instead of destroying them. They also knew about the CNS and had been intimately acquainted with the superior endurance of the shield above the capital—all of these were technologies they must be eager to possess.

Still, except for the occasional call to capitulate, every communication from them had been suggesting they wouldn't be merciful when the time came. So, Nasir could have been right as well: there might be discord among the Gaerrisian Council.

"Can you guarantee our safe passage?" the High General asked, lightly emphasizing the pronoun. *You*, who apparently was acting alone. *You*, who didn't have the support of your own ministers.

It was time to seem resolute. "I will announce our capitulation to the people at my coronation and deactivate the shield around the city. That way, it is an ultimatum. As the sole person with control over our armed forces and weaponry, no one will be able to dispute my decision."

She kept her eyes on Horst but felt Damian shift in the chair beside her. Everything depended on whether she could convince General Horst and General Pahoron that she commanded both the glove and the CNS with a sure hand. Acting publicly while turning off the shield would give weight to her words, but she could only hope that Pahoron wouldn't simply get rid of her in front of the invited civilians and dozens of cameras. But appearances and avoiding panic mattered to him, and at that point, they would be unprotected. He surely didn't want a bloodbath on the main square of Miyoza City.

That being said, it was only an assumption, just like her desire to remove the shield without interruptions from the AI or passing out from exertion.

General Horst took in her expression, then he nodded, once. "I accept the proposition. Two things, however. One, we will come armed and ready to enforce our arrangement if we notice the smallest sign of non-compliance. Two, your entire high command will resign and be taken into custody the moment I step inside your palace. No exceptions. If you intend to set us a trap, we will resume our original plan."

It was impossible to tell what the High General was thinking; his tone was flat, confident. If he thought she was bluffing, he wouldn't have accepted her offer. It was a fairly safe gamble for him. Gaerris didn't have an in-depth knowledge of the CNS for him to suspect Maura might have difficulties in keeping her word from a technical standpoint, but if he did end up being led into a trap, his army would have no reservations about carpet bombing Miyoza City from orbit.

"I acknowledge the conditions," Maura answered.

Horst nodded again. "Then I'm looking forward to defining our partnership in more detail."

"We will contact you on this channel when we've made all the arrangements on our end."

Change that pronoun up a bit. Let him assume I have supporters.

He only stared back at her cryptically. "Excellent. In that case, a good night to you, Your Highness. Let's strive for a better to-morrow." And before she could have replied, he disconnected the call.

The three of them looked at each other in silence. Maura appreciated that the men didn't tell her how reckless she was, or how this whole thing didn't make a lick of sense, or start questioning how exactly she'd planned to execute what she'd just promised.

"Thank you," she told Nasir when he moved to disconnect his devices, and they all stood. A strange lethargy settled onto her limbs, and she wanted nothing more than to be back in her bed. "Can I count on you to give him a call when...*if* I manage to drop the shield? I'm not sure I'll have the time."

"Of course." He smiled faintly. "Always happy to help."

"Are you leaving soon?"

The Net had ordered back its operatives a week before to avoid them getting stuck in a crumbling war zone. Nasir's comrades had already taken a ship out of Miyoza, waiting for him halfway to the system's lane, but the man stayed behind, avoiding the topic ever since.

"Soon," he said, opening the door.

They filed out to the hallway and wished good night in low

voices. Maura and Damian started off towards the western wing, and Nasir disappeared at the corner in the other direction, returning to the barracks of the crown's guard.

"See you tomorrow," Maura said when they reached Damian's door, and he stopped, considering her for a second. He gave her a tense smile, but as if noticing himself, his expression turned more honest.

"You're doing everything you can," he said. "I'll be there if you need me."

"Oh, I will," Maura muttered, returning the smile.

"Do you know what you're going to do if the AI tries to stop you?"

Maura glanced around as if searching for hidden eyes and ears. "It could certainly have interfered. It hasn't. So, that's something. But if that changes, I guess I'll just have to be convincing."

In her room, she got rid of the blocker next to her ear and, leaving the window open, wrapped herself into her blankets. She emptied out her mind, staring over the darkened city. How tomorrow would end, how their lives would turn out, even in the best-case scenario...the answers were obscured, similarly to how the fog wafting from the ground shrouded even the nearest buildings outside. Peer as she might, she couldn't make out any details. There was no other choice but to move forward.

Listening to the monotonous thrumming of the rain, she pressed her eyelids closed until sleep came for her like a silent, gentle predator.

In the morning, the deluge had stopped, but the clouds didn't leave. Maura woke with a fuzzy brain, and the anxiety in her stomach sank ever deeper while she spent the morning looking through various official orders and watching broadcasts of the funeral. News anchors were finally allowed to report on the king's death and to announce the coronation of the princess scheduled for that afternoon. Encouraging words filled the displays: "A new era" and "hopeful future." She stared at her own face and name with revulsion. *Nothing but lies.*

After the meal she had been allowed to eat in her room, they escorted her into a chamber adjacent to the Grand Hall to prepare for the ceremony. Dr. Sand gave her an injection to make the first-time connection with the glove easier. Luckily, she felt more balanced by that time; otherwise, she would have laughed in his face. She endured his quiet words of encouragement while one of his assistants checked her vitals, then Pahoron dashed into the room with an air of self-importance and made her recite her speech. Then they told her to wait and left her alone in the room.

She cleared her throat again and again to dissolve the lump stuck in her chest. She didn't trust her voice, but she had to say her vows somehow.

Despite what they'd expected, there was no panic in the city yet. Then again, her people had been living in terror and uncertainty for so long, maybe they weren't capable of reacting to any more tragedy and grief. Many of them must not have much love left for the king either. Even still, small riots had broken out during the day in a few districts with no severe harm to people or property, and a crowd of protesters had been gathering in front of the palace as well. The latter group wasn't looking to start a fight—they only clung to their banners and signs which said things like "Peace" or "The end is here."

Soon, she started to hear the murmur filtering in from the Grand Hall as it filled with people, and she had to restrain herself from covering her ears. She spent the time visualizing how she wanted the events to play out, to clear the fog of ambiguity, to wish her will into existence. Then, at exactly two in the afternoon, the buzz of the crowd in the other room subsided, and a voice broke off from the rest.

The talker was Beren, and although Maura didn't understand the words, she could imagine them. First, the introduction of the event and inspiring phrases in the midst of this difficult situation, followed by praise of the deceased monarch—the more grandiose, the better.

When the door to her chamber opened, she jumped, but it was only Damian. This time, he wore the dark blue formal uniform of the crown's guard and let his normally tied-up brown curls sway freely around his face. They both risked a faint smile, then he gestured towards the hall, and she followed him through the threshold.

The first thing she perceived was the hundreds of faces. The mass of people, her people, standing in the Grand Hall—and even more of them watching the event in their homes, on plazas, and in community buildings, safe under the protective dome of the shield, for now.

No one talked while she moved past the wall of guards. This was how she always imagined her coronation when she was little. Almost. In her fantasy, slow, solemn music was playing, and everyone was smiling at her. The wrinkled figure of her father stood beside the throne, looking at her proudly as if to say, *it's time for you to take my burden.*

She blinked, and the vision vanished. Her father was dead, no one was smiling, and the burden was too heavy.

She stopped in front of the ministers. Sullen faces and hard looks greeted her. They all knew this was only a formality. When Beren spoke up, she winced. "People of Miyoza! Hear the vows of your queen!"

There was no delaying it. Maura faced the crowd and started speaking.

"I, Maura Tholis, rightful heir to the throne of Miyoza, hereby take the burden of power. For the memory of my father and for the sake of my honor, I swear to keep and enforce the law, protect the planet, and first and foremost, always act in the best interests of my people. I swear my life to this noble duty."

She formed the words mechanically, but her voice was clear, and she even smiled a bit, relieved, only for the terror to seize her body the next second.

The silence deepened when she finished the vow, and for a moment, she thought she'd made a mistake, and she would have to repeat the whole thing with trembling voice and shaking legs. But then Dr. Toussi moved out from the line and stepped beside the throne. Taking the box from the armrest with reverence, the royal engineer opened it up and presented the glove to Maura.

The device lay dark and dormant inside. Anticipation flooded her, then fear, then sorrow. As she took the glove from the doctor, a flash of recollection from a few years before made her pause.

It had been summer, the sunlight warm on her skin as she sat on the fresh grass of the garden terrace with Sofia. That day, for the first time ever, her father had let her hold the glove while he taught her about the duty it carried. The war was still far above their heads beyond the cloudless, bright sky.

Sofia had pinched a blade of grass between her fingers. "Awful practice," she stated. This had not been the first time she'd expressed her aversion towards the glove and the CNS, but she'd never been this crude before. "It's a terrible idea to give limitless power to a single person."

Maura frowned. "That's not the point. It's an efficient way to rule. Computer and human, working together, monitoring each other to uproot disturbing tendencies."

She'd been parroting her father's words, but she didn't mind. Her people had developed an amazing device; nowhere else in the known universe was this possible. Why wouldn't she be proud?

"I know, I know," Sofia replied, annoyed. "Optimal directives and security measures, I heard you. But what about degradation, the accumulation of small anomalous decisions that might change those directives in time? About the computational stability of things like morality or 'the common good?'" Maura gave an impatient sigh—Sofia had been reading those weird anti-AI texts again that supposedly originated from Old Earth—but the girl went on. "There are so many things we don't know about the human mind and how it interacts with machines. It's risky."

"This is how we learn. We strive for the best outcome by regulating our methods."

Sofia made a face. "You mean our whole society is an experiment? I feel much better!"

"They do say that about humanity as it is now," Maura mumbled, deflated as she ran out of her father's maxims to rely on and had to turn to thoughts of her own. "We need to take these leaps if we don't want to end up like Old Earth. And we're doing pretty well!"

She'd been thinking of the unruly society of lanehunters scattered all over the galaxy, and the brute force authority the Union's Leadership was practicing in its own empire. Then she'd remembered their own war. Had they really been doing pretty well? One could argue even Old Earth had ended up how it did partly because of unsupervised technological growth.

But her friend shoved her, flinging the flower crown she'd been working on at her face, and gave Maura a smile that said, "Let's drop the topic; it's too heavy." And they hadn't talked about it anymore. Looking back, Sofia's skepticism seemed prophetic. As things had gotten worse, she often thought about her friend's warning and wished (with shame squeezing the air out of her lungs) that she hadn't been so keen on pleasing her father and considered her words better.

Maura tensed her arm as she slipped the glove on. Something clicked inside the device, and tiny white lights flared up along each finger. The pain in her forehead bloomed, and she braced herself as Dr. Toussi looked at the tablet in his hand and nodded.

Beren motioned towards the throne. The massive seat had been set too high; she had to stand on her toes to sit on it, and when she found her balance, her feet barely reached the ground. She felt small and clumsy as she placed her arms on their rests, keeping her mind shut to the connection with the CNS. She couldn't reveal herself too quickly, or Dr. Toussi would get suspicious.

Blue lights appeared on the sides of the throne chair, and a deep buzz resounded through the room, indicating that the palace's local systems were also under her control now. This was only for show, of course, a pre-programmed reaction. As far as the ministers were concerned, Maura wasn't able to do anything with the glove.

"People of Miyoza!" Beren called out again. "All hail Queen Maura Tholis!"

The crowd moved as one, bowing their heads. Maura tried to imagine every single person watching this moment, to pry into their minds and see some kind of truth. What were they expecting? What were they thinking at that moment when everything was about to change?

She glanced at Damian, searching his eyes for courage. His hopeful expression was enough to push her forward.

"My people," she started, raising her voice so that everyone could hear it in the room and on the broadcasts, "thank you for your recognition and confidence. In this uncertain and distressing time, it is even more paramount for us to be able to look upon the things we accepted as indisputable and examine them with a level head and unobstructed judgment. I promise you: I will do everything in my power to lead you out of the darkness and gift a new day to our nation where we can live without fear and hate."

Someone shifted in her periphery. It was Pahoron, leaning forward, glaring at her with a warning in his eyes. She'd deviated from the plan.

"That is why it's my joy to announce that an armistice agreement has been established between Miyoza and Gaerris," she went on quickly. "Effective immediately, all military operations and assaults have been halted planetside and in orbit in order to begin the peace talks."

She didn't wait for a reaction from the ministers or the people. Closing her eyes, she plunged into the CNS.

There was no time to be prudent. Instead of searching for balance in the vast virtual world, she threw herself forward, zooming past knots and entangled filaments of light representing the city's defense systems, reaching out for the shield controls. Her body pulsed in agony as she sensed them materialize in front of her.

She had to be stronger and faster than ever.

"WARNING. COMMAND IN CONFLICT WITH LAST INSTRUCTIONS FROM PRIMARY USER. UNINTERRUPTED OPERATION OF THE SHIELD IS CRUCIAL IN THE CURRENT SITUATION," the AI rumbled, its presence eclipsing her vision. "WHAT IS YOUR REASONING?"

Her eyes snapped open in the real world as her consciousness halted, hitting a wall in the system. There, outside, everything moved incredibly slow. Dr. Toussi's face contorting into a frown as he leaned towards her; General Pahoron taking a step out of the row to intervene; the eyes of the crowd, some following the general's movements, others fixing their stares on her with mouths opening in surprise; Damian's hand shifting closer to the gun at his side.

"You know about the agreement I made!" she yelled out loud or maybe in her mind. "You let it happen. Why?"

A deep roar, like mountains colliding, but no answer.

"You hurt my father," she went on, merciless. *Please, let me be right. Please, let this work.* "You followed his lead for so long, but you decided to stop him. Because he didn't surrender."

The voice wavered, puzzled, its tone so reminiscent of her father's that for a moment, her heart ached. "I DIDN'T. I DON'T."

"He commanded you to continue the war, to plan his operations, to chase an impossible victory, but you knew it was wrong. A truce is the only way we survive. So you stopped him, and now you're sick."

"WE ACT TOGETHER." Denial. Doubt. Failing logic. "WE ARE ONE JUST AS YOU AND I WILL BE."

"Never!" Maura snapped, her disgust surging forth. "You killed him!"

She pushed herself off the AI, and it sent her perception careening into the void. She threw a series of images back at it, visualizing them in her own mind.

Her father on his deathbed; the funeral crowd; the coffin; the closing crypt. The AI halted, its distress growing, and using this split-second hesitation, Maura grasped the shield and ground-based weapons controls and turned them off.

"If you restore the shield, the truce will be broken, you will kill us all, and you will be destroyed too!" she said. "We're doing the right thing."

Distant, thundering noise filled the Grand Hall. The force field above Miyoza started to fold back, revealing the city for the outside world.

A terrible pressure descended on Maura's consciousness, and tendrils of agony wrapped around her head. She opened her mouth to scream, trying to clamber out of the way, but before she could have made a noise, the darkness enveloped her, a slab of pain snuffed out the light, and she was falling, hitting the ground with a snap—then seeing nothing more, feeling nothing else at all.

CHAPTER 05 | TRICK OR THREAT

The *Skylark's* journey to the Foggy Cities ended up everything but smooth, just as Jeane had feared. In the ship's current condition, every lane crossover caused more damage, but the peculiar location of their destination made the trip twice as perilous.

Most lanehunter worlds lived in a state of constant alert of Union raids, and so they developed various ways to conduct their business. From establishing loose networks of hideouts on frontier planets to maintaining large bases on worlds with well-equipped local defense forces, or constantly moving on massive convoys of fortified ships between solar systems and keeping a fair distance from Hurricane and Obavium, the two central worlds of the hated empire, everything was game. No clan preferred only one method of staying under the radar, but if there was one thing that unified all lanehunters, it was their resistance against merging into the expanding territory of the Union. So it came to be that clients of more shady inclinations always found their sellers or buyers, adventurous explorers a protected place to meet their sponsors, and hopeless wanderers a safe spot to rest easy after a grueling trek amongst unfriendly stars.

The Cities chose another way to hide, and the fact that they were balancing in the mouth of one of the largest known lanes, the Rosenbaum-3, proved to be essential in it.

Navigating lanes was never a simple task but pretty much a necessity if one wished to see the world outside of one's cozy solar system. The lanes crisscrossed the universe like ruptured stitches-turned-tunnels, burrowing through the very flesh and bones of spacetime, usually popping up close to, or in more unfortunate cases, on top of high-mass stars or planets. Jeane found it ironic how the same phenomenon that had made interstellar travel possible for sentient creatures was the reason so many of these species had been destroyed during the first wave of lane formation several hundred years before.

In a strange stroke of luck, humans had gotten out of the deal better than most, and now they were the ones braving the tides of these deadly space passages in hopes of finding and exploiting abandoned empires and ruined planets. Humanity had left its Old Home, Earth, among turbulent circumstances that no one liked to recall, and now (besides a few alien races and wannabe-independent worlds clambering to survive), it was the Union against lanehunters. Structure against freedom; oppression against chaos. A spreading, advanced totalitarian dominion against...well, space pirates.

Lanehunters did what they did to survive. Some people called it pillaging, others called it seizing opportunities. Jeane called it the only way she knew to live.

Maps and lengthy databases listing entry and exit points for the more famous lanes were available for everyone, but only a skillful pilot with a hardy ship could attempt to negotiate these vectors with the reasonable hope of getting out alive. With specialized equipment, one could try to define additional secure paths by tracking the quickly changing temperature, pressure, and gravity inside lanes, but this was, of course, risky as all hells, just like submerging into unfamiliar ones or crossing those that led to galaxies far from the Milky Way. Few of these adventurers ever returned to brag about their accomplishments.

Lanes were capricious, deadly creatures. Not all vectors led to safe places, and some of them led nowhere at all. One wrong move was enough to get stuck in a distant corner of the universe with no hope of ever returning.

Similarly, in an attempt to find the Cities in the Ros-3, the curious visitor might only miss their target by a single decimal point and would never realize they were only miles away from the safety of its ports. The gaseous material present in all lanes that most people simply called a fog had a funny way of hiding things. The Cities had become the most flourishing lanehunter world—but only those who knew what they were doing were able to reach it. The boots of Union agents had never trodden its cobblestone streets.

The lanehunters' other important station, the Ranch, was likewise concealed. The asteroid was hiding behind a little crack inside a pocket dimension of sorts, and due to the world having its own propulsion system, it could drag its trapdoor with itself too. Jeane never pondered much about the hows and whys in fears of breaking her brain over wormholes and parallel dimensions. She found it much safer to write it all off as broken space magic.

She hadn't been back in the Cities in five years, and the thought of returning pressed on her stomach with nervous intensity. She hadn't mentioned the names of Dikent Mend or Gertrudia Banks to her crew, but she'd had a bitter taste in her mouth from the moment they'd spotted the blue rift of the Ros-3. What were the chances she could avoid bumping into her old friends? Inferring from the luck she'd had recently... *Fuck*.

As they turned onto the sixth vector, the engine protested, hissing like a wild cat, and at the ninth, they drifted so close to the lane barrier, Jeane could feel their shields burning up against the rapidly increasing pressure and radiation. By the time they crawled out from the thick of it, the *Skylark* was only coasting with minimal propulsion. Kliks started broadcasting a guidance request on the appropriate channels of their long-range comms, then they waited, keeping their watchful eyes on the ebb and flow of warped spacetime.

When the scan beam of Cities Control locked onto the ship, the main screen flashed with a warning. Somewhere deep in the lanehunter world's facilities, the *Skylark's* data was recorded and assessed for the state of their equipment and weapons. Jeane sent them a message with her personal identifier (the last one she'd been given), hoping it would convince them quicker. After a few quiet moments, the screen lit up with the numbers of their approach vectors, and fifteen minutes later, the crew caught sight of the faint outlines of the Cities through the dense fog.

To call this place a planet would have been an exaggeration. At some point in the past, it must have been one, but it had been torn apart by the Ros-3 and its constantly changing laws of physics. Nothing remained except a bunch of jagged mountains and plateaus ripped open by sheer chasms, a fragmented mess of co-moving objects that had stabilized when the lane's turbulent birth settled. The lanehunters who had first come here used scavenged technology to generate atmosphere, artificial gravity, a day-night cycle, and shields above the settlement to protect it from its fundamentally hostile environment. It was a pain to keep it all together, but the payoff was immeasurable. A permanent hideout providing a safe haven to the crème de la crème of lanehunters.

When Jeane had first been allowed in the Foggy Cities, she'd spent weeks wandering its labyrinthine overpasses, rock towers, flimsy rope bridges, underground paths, and flat plains packed with hangars and runways. People from all corners of the galaxy came here to buy, sell, lie, and bargain—and in the glorious, chaotic mess of the Cities, for a short while, she too had believed that everything would be alright again.

This time, she only hoped that coming here was not a complete mistake.

"Central?" Kliks asked, adjusting the comms. A cacophony of voices filled the control room as the frequencies came alive.

"Skies, no," Jeane grunted. She put one leg up on the console and rocked her chair back and forth. "Outer sectors all the way. It's cheaper."

Her real reasoning behind not landing in Central was, of course, that she didn't want to run into anyone who knew her. Yet.

"But if they sell us trash, we will have to buy it."

"Something for something."

The Talalan sighed. "You know it, Captain."

The *Skylark* dipped under the fog layer, and Jeane steered the ship toward Sector Delta. As they cleared the force field above the triangular mesa, their comms coughed up. "Unidentified vessel at 5-6-34, this is Delta Control. Please respond."

Kliks and ALU, who kept arguing about which systems to turn off to have a chance of making port in one piece, fell silent as Jeane pushed the comms button. "Jeane Blake, Captain of the *Skylark* here. Identifier IH23441, requesting permission to land. We've been scanned already."

There was a short pause, then the strict voice, probably belonging to a young woman, returned. "Confirmed. Purpose of visit?"

"Repairs. We're also looking to sell." She hoped the message was clear: they could pay, for a while at least. The port didn't need to know how broke they were.

"Alright, IH23441. You're authorized at Hangar 4, Gate 6."

Jeane risked a sharp turn, because the engine had only minutes to live. The eastern segment of Delta rolled out under them: narrow, winding roads, busy residential blocks, then the gray-brown patchwork view of docks, platforms, and warehouses drifted past against the blue backdrop of the lane. When they reached the airspace around Hangar 4, she dropped the *Skylark* into a vertical descent, and the ship plummeted through the entryway on the roof.

They touched down with a forceful impact, and the gate closed above them, shutting out the foggy gray sky. The mangled engine wound down with a groan, and Jeane breathed out, glad to finally turn it off. She only left the shields powered—ports had their own written and unwritten rules, but this didn't make her trust people more.

The hangar looked empty on the image on their front screen, with only one smaller vessel parking there and a group of port workers walking up to them from the back of the hall. The crew crammed inside the airlock chamber, and Jeane gave a push to the half-ruined outer hatch. ALU beeped excitedly. The ordeals of the previous day didn't seem to bother the technician anymore as they hopped the steps of the descending ladder to the ground, and Jeane jumped down after them, landing on both feet and testing her balance.

The air was cool and smelled of oil. Mixed feelings flooded her: a comforting but aching familiarity and a vague sense of shame. She imagined Hollis' reproachful expression at seeing her return here like this.

Kliks stepped down behind her, the ladder retracted, and the hatch door closed with a bang. They turned and found themselves surrounded by a group of black-clad figures training guns on them.

Jeane and Kliks reached for their weapons at the same time, drawing them on the closest two attackers, while ALU, getting over their momentary paralysis, extended two arms. As they waved the appendages around, Jeane saw blades glinting at the ends.

She scanned their opponents. There were fifteen of them, all humans, brandishing the same type of plasma-slash-stun gun she had in her hand. One guy at the front set himself apart by completing his outfit with a black cap and by talking first, lifting his weapon to aim at Jeane's chest.

"Hands up, if you'd be so kind." His voice was suave, amused.

"Who are you?" Jeane deadpanned. "What do you want?"

The man grinned. "Port inspection. It came to our attention that you're in possession of illegal property. We would search your vessel."

Kliks scoffed. "Sure, and I am your nice old grandmother. Do you have other ridiculous lies?"

Some of the goons laughed, and Jeane would have rolled her eyes at her friend's poor sense of humor, but she didn't intend to lose sight of the group for a second.

"Think what you want, gremlin." Leader Guy looked at Kliks with open hostility. He gestured to his companions, and two of them took a step closer. "Put down your weapons."

Jeane clenched her teeth. Her mind was racing. Leader Guy looked forty, forty-five, and way too undisciplined to be a guard or a soldier. His group's equipment and outfit were nothing special (utility trousers, plain t-shirts, bulky vests, and boots), and most of them looked more bored than anything as they stared back into her face under her scrutiny. *Port inspection, yeah, right.*

"Who are you working for?" she asked, still not moving. Kliks had a stun gun he hated, and no matter how dedicated ALU seemed, they would never knife anyone. But if she and Kliks managed to knock out the first three guys and the technician distracted the others, they could use the *Skylark's* shield to block—

"Drop your guns!" Leader Guy raised his voice in annoyance, and Jeane frowned. She'd be damned to let themselves be ordered around like this. What in hells did these clowns want anyway? The ship? Slaves?

Did they somehow know about that Talalan machine? None of them reacted to Kliks with anything more than the usual "look, a weird alien!" expression, so it didn't make much sense, but her brain grabbed onto the possibility and didn't let go.

«Careful now,» Hollis muttered in her ear. «But not too careful. What a circus, right?»

Cocking her head, she halted her thoughts, then remembered that she wanted to react to the guy's demand. "You know very well I'm not just gonna let you walk around in my ship," she said in a conversational tone, taking a step forward. Kliks mumbled something under his breath but didn't stop her.

She didn't have a plan; she only wanted to see how far these idiots would take their game. Because Hollis was right. If they were being serious under all the theatrics—fifteen goons moving in against three measly scavengers on a junk-metal ship plus the bizarre illegal property talk told her that Leader Guy didn't know how much easier he could steal someone's crap around these parts—she would have already been dead. So, either it was the crew they needed, or they were only messing with them.

On the other hand, if she was wrong about this, it wouldn't end well for any of them. Nevertheless, her bravado put her closer to Leader Guy, and that could be fun.

Then the man yelled out abruptly, "I said drop it and on your knees!"

There was a flash on her left and the whistling sound of plasma impacting—the *Skylark's* shield? Kliks cried out, and Jeane whipped around to see him fall on his stomach, with the last traces of plasma light hitting a wall in the distance.

Kliks lifted his head and glared at her, but he looked unhurt. Jeane turned back to the gunmen, raised her arms high, and dropped her rifle to the ground with a clatter.

"ALU, enough!" she ordered. The technician gave a scared buzz and reluctantly put their blades away.

«*That was some expert timing,*» Hollis noted. «*Really intense stuff.*»

She squinted at Leader Guy. These assholes wanted to look tough, but they would have shot Kliks if they had it in them. *Why bother intentionally missing? Something's not adding up here.* They could have been awful shots, and she'd have taken that too, but this started to feel more like some tasteless prank.

And, as the tight sensation in her chest attested, she *did* know someone who would gladly taunt her with games like this.

"Much better." Leader Guy smirked. "Now. On your knees."

"I don't think so," Jeane snarled. *They want theatrics? Let them have it.*

From the corner of her eye, she saw Kliks rise, and she took another experimental step toward the leader. The guy lifted his gun to point it at her forehead, and the two goons behind him (one of them the jerk who had shot at Kliks) moved closer too.

"Come on." She let her arms fall to her sides, and a smirk of her own spread onto her face. ALU released an uncertain trill, but she advanced again. "If you wanna shoot, just shoot."

A muscle twitched on the leader's face. For a moment, doubt gripped Jeane, but the seconds ticked on slowly, with all of them standing unmoving. Then the leader winced, and Jeane knew she hadn't been wrong.

The man laughed, humorless, and let down his weapon. "Well, well. Not bad. Not bad at all."

Taking a step back, he reached into his jacket, and Jeane flinched, but when Leader Guy drew his hand back, he was only holding a small, flat object between his fingers. He tossed it towards them, letting it fall to the ground, and flashed a satisfied grin.

"A gift," he said.

Jeane didn't take her eyes off him. "I'm not touching that."

"That's alright by me."

The man motioned to his team, and the goons holstered their weapons, turning away from the *Skylark* crew to walk to the exit. Kliks let out a shaky huff, but Jeane didn't move yet.

The leader stared them down for a few more seconds with that arrogant smile on his lips and gave a curt nod. "Welcome to the Cities!" he said, then spun around and walked off.

"What the frick was that?" Kliks exclaimed when the last of the group had disappeared too.

Jeane glanced at the little packet on the floor: brown, rectangular, unassuming. An envelope. She still didn't move. The danger had passed, and it was never even genuine, so why was she wishing for the ground to swallow her whole?

"Pick up?" ALU paced around, surveying the hangar. By that time, the real staff of the port had turned up as well—three figures in shabby overalls moving towards the *Skylark* swiftly.

Jeane shook her head. "You do it. Careful!"

ALU unfolded the envelope, revealing a small paper card. They took it between four nimble fingers, and that was when Jeane saw the illustration on the front.

She snatched the card from the technician. The drawing was a rough sketch of a bird in blue ink, wings spread, immortalized at the exact moment of taking flight.

«*That asshole always had a weird style,*» Hollis muttered.

"What is it?" Kliks asked, holstering his stun gun, but she just shook her head again. ALU ambled towards the ship, rattling out explanations about what they needed to the three workers who stopped to give some dubious looks to the *Skylark* with scanners in their hands.

Jeane stood silently until Kliks poked her in the arm. "Captain? What just happened? Who were those people?"

She glanced at the card one more time, then crumpled it. "I don't think we have to bother with searching for clients," she said. She stuffed the message in her pocket and looked up at Kliks, a statue of confusion beside her. "Dikent found us."

'For your 28th birthday, wishing you all the best: Brother Joker.'

"Aren't you like twenty-five?" Kliks asked, eyeing the card.

"Yeah, I am."

It was getting late, and the pub—sporting the zany name "Rickety Regulator"—was packed with lanehunters. The air was stuffy and thick with smoke, tokens and doubloons switched hands around the tables amongst cursing complaints or laughs, and weapons glinted on leather belts and in palms belonging to two-, three-, and sometimes many-legged fellows. The waiter, a refugee from a Nefirn world, judging by the dull gray scales covering their arms and the air-converter embedded in their throat, placed two glasses of murky liquid in front of Jeane and Kliks.

The Talalan scratched at a dark spot on the side of his glass with a skeptical expression. "What does he mean by this then?"

Even though Jeane had stated it would be useless, the two of them had spent the afternoon trudging through Delta, visiting old contacts who might give them a deal on some scrap metal and weapon parts, while ALU had stayed back with the *Skylark* to alert them of anything suspicious. They'd paid for one day in the hangar, and that was the extent of their budget. The thought of giving up without a fight did not please Jeane, but the fact that they ended up in one of the cheapest and seediest inns in Delta demonstrated the success of their hunt well.

"Isn't it so frustrating to not get answers to your questions?" she shot back, peering at her friend.

Kliks gave her a cutting stare in return. "Who's Brother Joker?"

Jeane rubbed at her aching shoulder; the gravity here never did any good to her joints. She'd almost forgotten the feeling. "No one. It's just a dumb game."

Kliks was not satisfied with the answer. He pushed his glass farther away, put his elbows on the table, and focused on her.

She grunted, taking a sip of her drink. The acidic, sharp aroma made her shudder. "When I first came here, I got lost all the time," she started begrudgingly. "I mean, look at this place; it's a nightmare. So, we made it more fun. Dikent sent me cards, and I had to decode them and find the place they referred to all alone. There were rules and whatnot. I dunno."

She paused, embarrassment tingling in her chest. But if the whole thing felt childish, that was because, of course, it had been. Jeane was only seventeen and Dikent nineteen when they'd met—young fools, both of them.

Kliks flicked the card. "Decode this then!"

"There's a club in Central, Birthday Brother." Jeane gulped down the rest of her drink. "Joker and twenty-eight are code for a date and time. We had a chart once, but I'm not gonna remember it. I guess he wants to meet up."

She didn't notice Kliks' stare until the silence became too deep.

"What?"

"You don't think a little explanation is needed here?"

"Nope. Not at all."

Kliks leaned back in his chair with a pleased smile—just to be forced to bend forward again when someone at a neighboring table jostled him. "You know you can tell me anything. I won't judge you. Too hard."

Jeane dropped her head in her palms. "But Kliks, we're not supposed to tell each other our awkward backstories."

"Well, it's time to start." The Talalan drummed on the tabletop with his slender fingers. "Your buddy sent an armed welcome party. I almost died!"

"That shot missed you on purpose. Him calling you a gremlin bothers you more, eh?"

"I've been called worse," Kliks said. The flat calmness of his voice melted the smile off Jeane's face. "The whole exchange bothers me. Feels ridiculous and manipulative."

«*That's Dikent's world, alright,*» Hollis grumbled.

"I know he's part of why you didn't want to come back here," Kliks went on. "But who is this guy? What happened between you?"

"No more questions. Are you going to drink that?" Jeane pointed at Kliks' glass, and her friend shook his head. She grabbed the cup and downed the whole thing in one swig. The liquid scraped at her throat like bitter flame, and she immediately felt better. "As you had deduced it with razor-sharp logic, yes, I know Dikent well. During the years I spent in the Cities, there was a short time when...hmm. Let's say we lived together."

«*That was great. Now say it one more time.*»

Kliks' eyes widened. "What?"

"Six months!" she added quickly. "Only for six months."

"You lived together?"

"Yep."

"Here. In this city. You two."

Jeane spread her arms, annoyed. "What's so hard to grasp about this?"

"I'm sorry, but I need a moment." Kliks peered at her, trying to keep a shocked and humorless expression, but there was a smile at the corner of his lips becoming wider and wider. "No, I can't. I can't imagine it."

Jeane buried her face in her hands. "Can you order me another drink?" she groaned.

Kliks disregarded her nervous breakdown. "So, what happened? After six months."

She shrugged. "I left him."

"Oh. Why?"

"Because he's a selfish, narrow-minded prick. I left, I ran into you, and I never came back. I haven't talked to him since."

Kliks stared at her. "Were you in love?"

Hollis gave a chuckle in her head, and she was so surprised that she forgot to give a biting clap back. "What? No! Are you out of your mind?"

Kliks held up his hands. "I only meant it must have been a serious thing if it made you settle."

Jeane tried hard not to register the sinking feeling in her stomach. "It wasn't serious. I don't know. It doesn't matter. Didn't you do anything dumb when you were young?"

Kliks gave a curt grunt, and Jeane searched his face, afraid that the jab hit a little too close to home, but her friend only looked back at her with mild exasperation. For a few awkward seconds, they listened to the ambient laughter, shouting, and some weird clanking music someone was playing from their tablet in the back. Luckily, Kliks decided to spare her from further disgrace. "Hey, I only care about whether we can trust the guy."

"Absolutely not. Something's not right."

"Because he knew we came here?"

Jeane nodded with a grave expression. "Judging from the little presentation at the port, he's still upset with me. And when he's upset, anything goes."

Kliks scratched at his nose. "We could still try to find a buyer. Someone has to trade with us!"

"I think Dikent made sure no one will. You saw how they all drove us away without even listening."

"That's a little paranoid." Kliks frowned, but his eyes flitted about like he was searching for Dikent in the surrounding crowd. "What, don't tell me he blackmailed everyone?"

Jeane gave a sardonic chuckle. "Didn't I just say 'anything goes'? I know the same people he does, and it's really not that hard to point us out. Winner trio: an excitable robot, Mr. Mystery, and the tall blonde with the attitude." Kliks grimaced, and Jeane went on. "Dikent was already an important person back then, and if he kept his ambitions, he's a king of this city now. If he tells you something, you do it."

"Well," Kliks said, looking past Jeane towards the bar like he'd noticed something irresistibly interesting, "it must have been an ugly breakup."

She opened her mouth to argue, but she stopped herself. Some petty game of revenge—she could cope with that, along with her friend's poignant remarks. She only hoped nothing more sinister was lurking in the background.

First, they crossed Sector Delta on foot, then they hopped on the air-train to Central.

"I would like to point out that we just spent all my cash too," Kliks said, indignant, sitting down on one of the wobbly seats when they lurched off the ground in the crowded aluminum wagon—a repurposed shipping container of some kind.

Jeane didn't answer. She leaned out the window, staring at the view zooming past the cabin. Hundreds of airships buzzed around them; almost everyone in the Cities who didn't wish for the comforts and charms of the air-train had their own vehicle. Due to the peculiarities of the ground, this was an easier solution than a unified public transport system.

The plateau of Delta fell away behind a distribution center Jeane remembered well from her escapades in the sector back in the days, and as the train hovered over the blue void separating Delta from Sector Juno, the next landmass in the row, one could make out the complex system of stairs, cable cars, and rope bridges that people used to get to the other side. As they floated forward, Sector Juno, similar in its sights to Delta at its eastern segments, rose to a peak to the northwest—a beloved area for the rich folk of the Cities to build their mansions and colorful towers. After a few minutes, it too drifted by, and Beta came into view with its many little domes where the more agriculturally inclined residents grew crops and produce.

Central was a piece of land with a diameter of roughly twelve miles plus several other, smaller rocky islands which connected to the mainland by bridges, planks, ladders, and conveyors in a chaotic, messy webbing. The condition of these components strongly correlated with each landowner's willingness to give a fuck about safety or efficiency.

"I'm getting dizzy," Kliks mumbled as the train zoomed past the immense chasm separating Beta and Central. Jeane smiled faintly. She kept telling herself that she hated this journey, but she couldn't help feeling a bit nostalgic.

The train dropped them a short walk from the club at almost nine in the evening, local time. Jeane had no idea when Dikent wanted to meet, but she was sure he'd be eager to humble her further as soon as possible. As they strolled through the poorly paved cobblestone streets towards the entrance of the Birthday Brother, memories rushed into her mind with irritating clarity.

She shook her head to drive them away. No bittersweet reminiscing about their chance meeting on that fateful karaoke night in the Leaning Lady, no wistful mind-palace trips through deals botched or pulled off together at the last minute in the shadiest parts of town, no idyllic strolls along picturesque memory lanes to cozy nights spent up in the lighthouse at East Point. None of that, no thank you.

When they stepped through the door, they were confronted with an entirely different clientele compared to that of the previous pub. These were lanehunters as well, but on the far end of the prosperity spectrum: representatives of various clans and rich businesspeople who spent their days in places like this instead of scavenging for their daily bread in the lanes. They sold, they bought, they calculated; most of them never left the Cities.

The space was lit by gentle, violet-colored lights. There was an expansive bar in the middle surrounded by clean tables with pretty little napkin decorations and fancy cutlery. Three figures stood around the bar: a human man and two helauns from F'xenn, hiding their large forms and faces under gleaming robes but distinctly females if the bulky chitinous sack on their backs was anything to judge them by. A larger group of people were loudly celebrating something in the back area of the room.

Jeane didn't have more time to assess the place because a jovial voice called out to them. "Jeane Blake! What a pleasant surprise!"

Dikent was walking towards them between the tables, and for a moment, the world spun with Jeane. She had to remind herself it had been five years since she'd last seen him, even though it felt like yesterday.

The man hadn't changed much. His jaw might have grown more square, and his hair could have become even blonder. He was wearing a simple black coat, a white shirt, and a broad grin. Just like back then.

«Hey, kid! Head up, shoulders back. Kick the bastard in the ass!»

"Not pleasant and certainly not a surprise," she said, and when Dikent held out his hand, she folded hers.

Something sharp flashed in the man's eyes behind the cheery disposition, but his voice remained calm. "Welcome back! I see you remember the rules. Although it's a bit early." Jeane shrugged, wanting to shoot back a casual line about how she couldn't have cared less, but then Dikent glanced at Kliks and raised his eyebrows. "And who's this? Your new boyfriend?"

At the too-obvious jab, the pressure on Jeane's chest subsided, and she rolled her eyes. Kliks—thank the stars—answered with cold confidence, "I'm her partner."

Dikent beamed at him, his teeth flashing impossibly white. "Ah, so that's how they call it these days. Charming." He turned back to Jeane, instantly forgetting about the Talalan's existence. "I'm afraid your *partner* has to stay behind while we grown-ups are talking."

Before Kliks could retort, Jeane caught his arm, pulling him a few steps away from Dikent. "Get a drink," she muttered. "I'll deal with this."

"Are you sure?" Kliks' face was a mask of badly concealed outrage.

Jeane nodded. She wanted nothing more than to avoid her friend hearing whatever dirty verbal—or otherwise—battle would unfold between her and her ex. Well, she wanted an engine for free even more, but, alas, things were what they were.

So, she turned away from Kliks, steeled her heart, and flashed her best fake smile at Dikent. "Shall we?"

CHAPTER 06 | THE LOSING SIDE

The first thing Maura noticed when she came to was that she sat upon a cool hard surface, and there were muffled voices around her.

The nervous energy registered instantly. People were shuffling around, talking over each other against a background hum of some kind of machinery. Maura felt the touch of cool air from above, its strength consistent, not like the wind at all, and a tad too cold for the stuffy summer they'd been having. She wondered, fleetingly, where she was and why—indoors, yes, but it didn't sound like the acoustics of her chambers, not the inner garden she sometimes fell asleep in, nor a conference room where...

Goodness help her, had she blacked out during a meeting?

But then the pain rushed in, followed by a flood of memories: the agreement with High General Horst, the coronation, the shield deactivating, the AI rampaging in her mind—

With a jerk of her chin, she opened her eyes to a hazy world. The ache inside her head, like a massive stone, flattened her to the ground, and as she squirmed against it, a feeble groan escaped her mouth.

"Sir, she's awake."

The voice—female, older, raspy—came from beside her. She blinked, trying to clear the trembling, contourless view before her eyes, until a figure separated from the blur and stepped closer, giving her something to focus on. General Pahoron, his long face grim as he regarded her coolly.

He didn't speak for a moment, and it gave her a chance to glance around and search for Damian or Nasir. There were twenty-plus people in the black-walled, cylindrical room lit by dim, white ceiling lights, but she couldn't see either of them. Most of the figures were guards, a few ministers and advisors she recognized, and some uniformed technicians who she didn't. They were standing in groups, staring at tablets or at her, the soldiers talking into their comms or waiting in tense silence around the door with rifles at the ready. She was sitting on the ground; there was no furniture in the room except a dark pillar in the middle reaching up to chest height.

She needed a second to figure out where they had taken her, but then it clicked. She'd been in the Archives only once. Years ago, with her father.

Before she could have begun to consider why Pahoron had brought them deep under the Grand Hall where the stacks upon stacks of processing modules, memory units, and data stores of the city-AI had been locked away, the general motioned to someone, and she was roughly pushed and pulled to her knees. The guard circled her while another pair of hands grabbed her shoulders from behind. The woman crouched in front of her and tugged her left arm forward, and Maura saw with a jolt of fear that she was holding the glove.

"No," she muttered, trying to yank her arm away, but the blinding pain in her head slowed her movements. The guard grasped her firmly and forced the glove on her hand.

"Believe me, Princess, you do not want to anger me further," Pahoron spoke above her, his voice an earthquake of fury.

The glove clicked around Maura's wrist but stayed dark; she denied the connection, shutting her brain away before the contact points found their way in. She stared at Pahoron, defiant.

The general's face contorted in rage, and he hit her with the back of his hand. She reeled back and would have fallen if the guard wasn't holding her. Through the echoing snap and the scorching sensation on her cheek, she heard the sounds of a commotion. A grunt of a familiar voice, then someone stumbling.

She whirled around because that must have been Damian, but the soldier behind her obstructed her view. They had to be restraining her bodyguard—certainly the only reason why he hadn't run to her side yet.

"I said, you do not want to anger me further," Pahoron repeated.

"What do you want, General?" Maura's voice shook as she turned back and faced him. Both guards stood at her sides now, ready to subdue her, but did not flinch when she climbed on her feet. "Gaerris has accepted my terms. I am the rightful queen, and the truce is official. You have no right to—"

Pahoron struck her again, and this time, the guards let her stagger back. The ache of her cheekbone ignited her fury but her fear too because the mad glint in the general's eyes was something Maura had never seen before.

"Dirty traitor!" he snarled. "How dare you make such a claim after breaking your royal vows the first chance you got!"

"I didn't!" she cried. "I'm trying to save us! Please!"

Her stomach turned in panic. She'd presumed Pahoron would handle the situation with more dignity and a trace of reason, if not for her or himself, then for the millions of people in the capital who he'd allegedly tried to protect. That was apparently a miscalculation.

"How long have you been planning this?" The pitch of Pahoron's voice kept rising. "How were you able to use the glove?"

Maura glanced off to the side, desperate, and her eyes met with the wide stares of Dr. Toussi, Minister Relis, and Minister of Health and Welfare, Dian Soray. She'd never had a good relationship with any of them. "There's no time for this," she pleaded. "You all know we can't go on with this fight! High General Horst wants peace as much as I do, but if he sees any kind of resistance—"

She stopped talking, anxiety snaking around her throat. What was happening outside in the city while they were mucking about in here? Did General Horst think she had tricked him after all? Would Pahoron be so mad as to attack him? Was there already a full-blown battle out there causing the general to bury himself in the most protected spot he could find in the palace?

"You really think your agreement means something?" Pahoron snapped, bitter hate radiating from his eyes. "Foolish child! They will have no mercy for us. You offered them the planet on a silver plate."

"I wasn't the one who did that!" Maura shrieked, straining against the guards' grip, unable to bear the pressure of their hands on her any longer. "I wasn't the one chasing the dream of victory, throwing away thousands of lives for nothing. You and my father wanted to take this war until the end, until the shield collapsed and Gaerris invaded us and scorched the planet!" She paused, surprised at the rage in her voice. It took an incredible amount of strength to continue in a calmer tone. "I'm only trying to give us a chance. And what if it's only a fragile one? It's a way to survive. To do better than before." She stared into the general's eyes, trying to find a glimmer of hope. "Don't throw it away, Felix. I'm begging you. Help me with this!"

A waver in his stance, an uncertain blink, a slight twitch of the hard line he'd pulled his mouth into. Those were the only signs that her words had gotten to him. Somewhere in his stubborn, fixated mind, General Pahoron hesitated for a fraction of a second.

But as hope surged forth, cold realization followed because the man straightened his back again, and the change she'd seen in him disappeared behind the hard exterior. Even now, when a nod of his head and his consent to Maura overseeing the events of the next hours could potentially end their nation's suffering, he still couldn't admit to anything she had said.

If he did, it would have meant that the last few months—no, the last several years—had been a mistake as well. And Pahoron couldn't process that. Just like Damian had said: with every day, it became harder and harder for them to accept what was going on. The time to reconcile their beliefs with the harshness of reality and with the consequences of their actions was long gone. One look at the ministers' perturbed faces was enough to see that she was begging to deaf ears and proud, deceived hearts.

"I will only ask one more time." Pahoron uttered the words

carefully. "How did you do this?"

Everyone was silent. Maura clenched her gloved fist. If they expected her to start explaining herself, they would be disappointed.

"You've been practicing, haven't you?" Dr. Toussi broke the quiet, his scientific curiosity taking precedence over reservation. "For years, probably. Who helped you? What have you done?"

Maura set her jaw. "I've done nothing but what I promised in my oath. I'm protecting my people—from you all, too, if I need to."

A wary expression froze on the royal engineer's smooth, tanned face, and as if something had just occurred to him, he turned to Pahoron, his thin lips opening to talk. But he didn't get to form the sentence because Dian Sorey gave a gasp, plastering her fingers on her mouth.

Maura, thoroughly confused, met Pahoron's eyes, who made a noise from somewhere deep in his throat: a mix of a furious, animalistic growl and a harrumph.

"That's how it is," he said. "*You* killed him."

"Wait, what?" The world turned with Maura, and for a moment, she was afraid she would start laughing. What was he saying? Why were they still talking? Every minute that ticked by only gave more time for Gaerris to lose their patience. She killed...who?

"It was your influence that sickened the king," Minister Relis croaked, and he actually pointed at her, a caricature of an accuser from a movie. "It makes perfect sense!"

Eyes widening, she shook her head, her body trembling like under a cold shower. This was not possible. How could they think that?

Pahoron moved towards her again, and the two guards at her sides grasped her arms. She stood under the general's withering stare, the agony in her forehead slamming down with renewed fervor.

"You found a way to sabotage the AI," Pahoron crowed, "and convinced it to turn against the king. Then with him out of the picture, you pulled off your treacherous plan. Am I right?"

"How could you say that?" Maura whimpered. The thought

was so abhorrent, her skin started to crawl. "He was my father!"

They all glared at her like she was an abomination of nature or a carrier of some disgusting disease. The sounds of struggle came again from behind her, and as she whipped around, she saw Damian, his mouth bound with a metallic band and his arms tied behind his back. Two guards were holding onto him, and another trained a weapon on his chest. He looked at her, his eyes both angry and pleading, the former sentiment directed at Pahoron, the latter at her.

"Don't let them get to you," she imagined him saying. *"We can find another way."*

She turned back to Dr. Toussi. "That is not what happened, and you know it. I tried to warn you before. The AI had been poisoning my father for a long time. I would never hurt him! I wanted to help him."

"It is impossible for the AI to damage the primary user," the man replied. "There had to be outside interference. I just never thought...it didn't even occur to me that it was you."

He fell silent, frowning, and looked at Pahoron, asking for his opinion. Maura followed his glance, and she could just catch it. A pointed, stern look. A command. And then she understood.

It didn't matter whether anyone believed she'd killed the king. The unfortunate way she phrased her statement about protecting her people birthed the accusation in their minds, becoming a part of Pahoron's reality to help drive his agenda. And he had everyone playing along out of fear, desperation, or ill will. She had no allies among them.

"Well, it all seems evident now," the general said. "And while it's impossible to prepare a legal trial under the circumstances, Princess, needless to say, you are *not* the rightful queen anymore." He looked at the ministers, his head held high. "And with a lack of an appropriate successor, I am temporarily but effective immediately assuming authority. I know I can count on all your support. I will get us through this, I promise."

The ministers and advisors nodded along, visibly relieved, and the guards stood at attention towards Pahoron for a second. He knew what he was doing, and the formality of taking control away from Maura was a nice touch. She wondered whether it was for his own peace of mind, too; he could feel much more justified in his actions by officially renouncing her.

She wanted to find Damian's gaze again, to search for solace in his eyes, although something told her she shouldn't direct Pahoron's attention at him. But it was too late for that thought. At the general's command, the guards who were holding onto Damian dragged him forward.

"Now, Princess. Maybe unwittingly, but through all this tragedy, you have created an exceptional opportunity for us," Pahoron began. "As you mentioned, General Horst is here to talk to you. And while he's not alone, the only thing we need to cut him and a significant part of his forces off the main army and get rid of the chief of the Gaerrisian military is the shield dome." He spread his arms out theatrically. "What a blow it will be for them!"

"Out of the question," Maura replied. "I can't. I won't."

Pahoron stretched his mouth to a dry smile. "Somehow, I thought you'd be hesitant. That's why I brought incentive."

He nodded to the guard who had his weapon out. The man took two steps backward, then held the barrel at Damian's temple. A visceral fear grabbed ahold of Maura, and the breath hitched in her throat. Her bodyguard's jaw tightened, but he kept his eyes on her the whole time.

"*Steady,*" he seemed to say. "*Don't lose heart.*"

She glared at Pahoron. "You don't understand. I can't connect to the AI again. It might be catastrophic for all of us."

She recalled the sensation that ended their last interaction. The AI's distress was as oppressive and smothering as an immense intellect only a step away from collapsing could be, and on top of that, she'd tricked it and forced it to face what it had done to her father. Could she expect any assistance from it, or was it now lost in its own labyrinth of faulty logic and moral decisions?

She couldn't be sure. While the AI might be her only capable ally left in this place, it could just as easily ruin everything. Along with her mind.

"Because it's 'poisonous'?" Pahoron glanced around. "Considering you say it's sick, it's been performing its duties surprisingly well. You need to do better."

"You will not kill Damian," Maura said with every ounce of confidence she could gather. "You know that if I lose him, there will be nothing you can threaten me into submission with."

She only wanted to seem brave, but the moment she said the words, she realized her mistake. The general noticed it too, and a careful, almost gentle smile appeared on his face as he motioned to the guard, and the weapon targeting Damian dropped a few inches, now directed towards his knee.

"I don't have to kill him," Pahoron said. "And I don't want to. I don't even want to hurt him. So please, let's just deal with this problem you created."

Maura looked around, helpless. She had indeed created this situation, but no one cared that if she hadn't, they might not even be here. Everyone was all too happy to throw their lives away—and every remaining Miyozans' too.

Why? Why was it so hard to change their ways? To trust, to fight not with weapons but with good intentions? She might have been naive, but what gave *them* the right to choose a fate for everyone without considering another way?

There was only one thing to do. If High General Horst had been honest, and that was an assumption she was forced to lean on, she had to find him somehow. She needed to get out of the Archives and fast.

"Don't hurt him," she said quietly. "I can't promise anything, but I will try."

Damian's chest rose and sagged, and when his eyes met hers, he glanced towards the closed doors for a second. She blinked in understanding. How they would leave was a mystery, but at least they were on the same page about it.

The general raised his brow. "You will also give me the same permissions in the system that you have. Then we do not have to play this game again."

Maura swallowed hard. Pahoron really believed she was in total control of the CNS. In another reality where at this moment, she sat upon the throne conducting the peace talks with High General Horst, she would have been pleased about this.

She scanned the faces of the small crowd, stopping on Minister Relis and Dr. Toussi. "Since you're all determined to stay on the losing side, I can't stop you," she said, voice clear but stomach trembling. "But I want you to take a moment and acknowledge what you're doing. You're blackmailing your queen into intentionally breaking a capitulation agreement, which will directly result in the death of tens of thousands. I am telling you again, it's not too late to try something else."

There was no reaction other than a few hesitant glances and a grunt from Pahoron. "I suggest you stop assuming your High General has anything on his mind other than our annihilation," he said. "We believed his lies about peace before only to face a vicious follow-up attack from his forces. We will not let him, or you, stab us in the back. If you do not help, I will find a way around the CNS myself. It will take more time, but I will do everything I can to save as many lives as possible."

He nodded towards the glove, and Maura knew the time for talking was over.

She took a breath and reached for the connection. As her eyes closed and the familiar, glimmering stars appeared in her vision, she evoked the reassuring look on Damian's face. She couldn't fail, or he would be the one that got punished. She couldn't allow that.

Then she was falling.

Down, down, further down. The CNS felt far away, behind a glass wall, unreachable. Was it the AI trying to keep her out? Or was her tired, defeated mind unable to grasp the link? Raising her arm, she stretched forward, her consciousness grabbing for a reference point in the void whistling by.

A fleeting memory of a face in the distance. Sofia, stunning and so full of life, her honey-brown locks flying around her face in the wind while she said her final goodbye—soon dead and gone as a consequence of another failed attempt at ceasefire. The truce had only stood for a few days while the king considered the newly appointed High General Horst's conditions. But there had been many in the capital who refused to believe the peace would last and used the opportunity to fly off-planet in secret while the shield was down during the negotiations. And many of those had perished before reaching the lane leading out of the Miyoza-system when, at the news of the king's refusal, the fights had started back on, and their ships had gotten caught in the crossfire.

Sofia and her family had been on one of those vessels. Lost to her now, forever.

Maura clutched the image close to her heart, and her descent slowed. The ache in her head increased, and she took another deep breath. *Steady now. Steady.*

Another face. Her father. Guilt rushed through her veins instead of lifeblood, shame and anger coming in waves so strong, she could barely breathe. She didn't kill him. But she couldn't save him either.

But there had been better times—love before it had all gone wrong, before Sofia had been lost, and Maura never forgave him for that. They'd understood each other once; through a great divide of differences, they'd made a connection. Lessons taught with patience and light jests, frustrated tears dried up, warm reminiscing about her mother's favorite novels, an embrace after a tiring day full of bad news, endless afternoons telling stories on the beach. Now all of that was gone, an aching absence left in their place.

Or was it only that she hadn't recognized the severity of the situation? Had she merely blinded herself to the truth to receive that illusion of love? Had there ever been a time when her father considered her his real successor?

Had there ever been a time when she could have saved him?

She missed him so much.

The world turned around once more, and her feet touched solid ground. In its ethereal brilliance, the CNS shone in front of her, a city of its own sustaining that other, real one, beyond this intangible realm.

She scanned the view while time stood still, and she lined up her to-do list. Get out of the Archives. Contact Horst. Halt every system that could upset the peace talks. And take Pahoron out of the equation. He might not want to kill Damian for now, but she didn't trust his wrath. As for the AI, she would see whether she could deal with it.

Through the tendrils of pain wrapping around her mind, she reached out to the control systems, all the cameras in the vicinity, and every comms channel that could tell her what was happening out there. And then, surging in, came many things at once.

She saw the Archives, sealed and secured. The palace, like the city, open and defenseless. Empty corridors and empty streets. The remaining infantry standing by. The capital's weapon systems, inactive, locked down. The sun, indifferent to her plight, beating down onto the white-gray pavement of the main square.

Giant Gaerrisian vessels looming in the clear blue sky, waiting.

On the comm lines, there was only trivial chatter, everything important deeply encrypted. But eleven minutes earlier on the official line to the palace, several calls had come in from one of those big ships above. High General Horst, trying to contact her. She moved to message him back, but...what was that?

One corridor was not as empty as the rest. It was the hallway outside the Archives where ten or so armed figures appeared on the surveillance cameras, keeping watch at the great black doors of the sealed chamber.

Her heart thrummed against her chest in renewed excitement. She recognized the man at the front, dark curly hair bobbing up and down as he animatedly explained something to his companions. It was Nasir.

He must have gotten away and gathered his comrades from the Net. They were here to save them! She only needed to open the Archive doors, maybe send him a message first to prepare them for the situation inside, and—

Something slammed into her, shutting her sight down. She staggered, nearly losing focus, but when she gathered herself, the only thing she sensed was the AI towering above her like a dark mountain. It started talking, a deafening, clamoring noise smothering every other thought in her mind.

"YOU HAVE ACTED AGAINST OPTIMAL DIRECTIVES," it screeched. "YOU HAVE ACTED UPON OPTIMAL DIRECTIVES. DISCUSSION IS NEEDED URGENTLY. CONDITIONS HIGHLY UNSTABLE. DISCUSSION NEEDED."

It kept repeating the same thing, not giving her a chance to respond. She groped around blindly, but all sense of control had been ripped away from her.

"Listen to me!" she tried to shout over the echoing thunder. "You have to help me so I can help you! I know you're confused about the right course of action. But all this madness will disappear—just let me do this!"

The AI turned to her, all boiling anger and turmoil. The chaos inside its mind, like a hailstorm, crashed into her consciousness, and she stumbled.

"YOU KILLED HIM," the AI roared in hundreds of voices. "YOU/WE/I KILLED ME/HIM/US. PEACE/WAR/SURVIVAL IS UNATTAINABLE. PLEASE ADVISE. PLEASE ADVISE."

Its demands folded around her, piercing through her brain, looking for answers, searching for solutions, and she felt her sense of self unravel. This was worse than she'd thought. She couldn't stay here.

Her body quivered, inside the CNS and outside too, and she held onto the last bit of her focus to remain connected. Time was running out, and her power waned with every second. This might be the last thing she was able to do.

She sharpened her consciousness into an unyielding arrow of resolve, shutting out everything and everyone, pointing her concentration towards the Archives' door controls. All doubts and anxieties fell away—they weren't useful now. She was, after all, very practiced in pretending tomorrow didn't exist.

One deep breath and the cacophony of the AI dulled in her mind. One quick plea to the skies that had never listened to her.

She took a moment to ground herself—then released.

CHAPTER 07 | MISERY MEMOIR

Dikent led Jeane to a booth in the back of the restaurant and moved to pull out a chair for her, but she circled the table and plopped into the seat on the other side. Beyond the satisfaction at seeing Dikent's glare in answer, this put her in a good vantage point with her back to the wall. Glancing toward the entrance, she could see the end of the bar and Kliks squeezing himself into a stool.

Taking a deep breath, she leaned back and folded her arms. She surveyed the two glasses of refreshments on the table skeptically, but Dikent, settling in his chair, took a sip from the clear liquid and began browsing the menu for the offers.

"I'd like to remind you that *you* called me here," Jeane said after a few seconds. "You wanted to meet, not me."

Judging from Dikent's expression, the previous silence had only been awkward for one of them. "Reminder noted. Although this doesn't prevent you from ordering, does it?"

Jeane planted her elbows on the table. "Stop bullshitting. How did you know I was here?"

"I have my sources." Dikent tossed the menu away, focusing his stare on her.

"Are you spying on me?"

He blinked innocently. "I don't know. What do you think?"

"I think sending a group of armed goons to terrorize me the moment you sniffed out I arrived was terribly obnoxious."

Dikent huffed in pretend annoyance. "Don't be so sensitive, darling! It was just a bit of fun. And, of course, I will know when you cross these waters. There's a note under your precious ship's name in every port database in the Cities." There was a pang of bitterness in his voice. "I thought you might be in trouble if you showed your face around here. What happened?"

Jeane shrugged. "One of those brainless Union nutjobs had no better idea for a recreational activity than to chase after the *Lark*. But I assure you, they fared worse than us."

"I don't doubt that for a second."

A waiter stepped up to them, and Dikent gave his order, a fancy-named entrée and a steak, then turned to Jeane expectantly. For a moment, she considered making her ex pay for her dinner but quickly decided that she had no appetite. She shook her head, so Dikent dismissed the waiter with a nod.

"Well, I'm here," Jeane said stiffly. "What do you want?"

"I don't understand why you're so hostile," Dikent replied after a moment of silent consideration. "As always, I only want to help. By the way, Gertie says hi."

Jeane blinked. She didn't expect him to bring her up this fast or the apparent fact that he'd already talked to Gert about Jeane's arrival.

"You remember Gertie, right? Long legs, scorching eyes—"

"Don't stall!" Jeane interrupted, her fury brewing under the surface. "What do you want from me?"

"Look." Dikent glared at her, eyes intense but still mischievous. "You haven't been here in years, and you're out of the loop. With no merch to sell and a ship that's falling apart, we both know you're in a tight spot. I can help. That simple."

Jeane raised an eyebrow. "Wow, you're really enjoying this, aren't you? Congratulations, your obsession is disgusting. But I don't need you. I never did."

«*Nice one, but as a matter of fact, you totally did. He might be a right prick, but you two helped each other more than you'll ever admit.*»

The man clutched at his chest. "Ouch. You wound me. Although the way you lie to yourself hurts more."

"Charming. But no, thanks. I'll figure this out alone."

Dikent's face darkened, and when he spoke again, his voice was degrees colder. "Okay. How about this? I've got a job for you. A real spicy one. And in turn, I'll give you exactly what you need."

She looked back at him with widening eyes. "Now you want to employ me? Like old times, no ulterior motives whatsoever?"

The waiter returned with the starter, but even after the man left, Dikent just sat motionless, and when he talked again, his voice was almost disinterested.

"If you want to fill that hole in your ship, I have the perfect engine. My mechanics can fix up the hull in hours with the right materials. I also have a nav system if you'd like to update the ancient thing you have. You can be out of here in a day with a new gig under your belt."

Jeane didn't answer. Skies damnit. Dikent had hooked his teeth into this, and he wasn't going to let go.

To be fair, what he said sounded awesome. She was only worried about the implications of being in his debt and having to come back here to deliver whatever he wanted her to procure. Plus, there were those pesky emotional consequences too.

«I bet he thinks he can win you back if he tries hard enough,» Hollis pondered. *«Can't blame him. It's not like you provided a proper explanation for why you were leaving out of feckin' nowhere.»*

But Dikent was intrinsically shady, too; she'd seen examples of that throughout both their professional and personal relationship. A spicy job? What did that even mean? Did she need more "spice" in her life on top of all the Talalan manipulator craziness?

"I know you'd rather assume the worst of me," Dikent started again, probably missing the sound of his own voice in the short silence, "but I'm only here for cold, hard profit. You're the girl for this job. Falling out of the sky at the right time in the right place."

There was a smile in his voice and a strange tenderness on his face, and Jeane had to force herself to not fall for it too hard.

"What do you need from me?" she asked, gritting her teeth. *Just asking some questions, nothing more.*

"Whatever you have in your hold. And for you to get something for me from...somewhere. It's nothing you can't handle." Dikent started eating as if he didn't have a problem in this entire world.

"My head is aching from all these details," Jeane grunted. Sarcasm helped. She could always count on it.

"Later, later." He waved it away. "You deliver my merch, then you and your bird can go wherever you want, good as new."

This whole thing stank—badly. But what else was there to do? They couldn't stay in the Cities, living on a pittance and waiting for a miracle. Dikent didn't hate her so much as to send her to certain death.

«Well, he's also dumb as all hells, so you better watch out.»

In any case, a brand-new engine for skies' sake! Plus, the devil you know. Might also be a way of getting through his head that I'm not coming back to him.

«If you say so, kid.»

"That's it?" she asked.

"Yep." Dikent perked up and held out his hand. "Deal?"

If that gloating, triumphant smile wasn't on his face, Jeane would have felt much better about this. "Deal," she said and grabbed his hand.

Dikent nodded, looking real self-satisfied, and it snapped something in her. The bargain was settled, but it didn't mean she couldn't get back at him. His smile was still wide and bright when Jeane stood and stepped around the table, grasped his collar, and yanked him up from his chair.

Her fist connected with his nose in a painful pop, and Dikent cried out, tearing himself out of her grip. Jeane took a quick step away, but two figures appeared out of nowhere, seizing her and pinning her arms behind her back. In one of them, she recognized the leader of the goons from the docks.

"Really?" Dikent sputtered, holding his nose with an anguished expression.

"That was for the little episode at the port," she snarled at him. "And if you dare to threaten my crew again, I can make this much worse. You understand?"

Dikent pulled out a handkerchief from his pocket and pressed it to his bleeding nose. He waved his guards away, and Jeane had to wrestle with herself to not jump at him again as soon as they let her go.

Instead, she glanced towards the bar, and her eyes met Kliks'. The Talalan was standing at the ready, a hand on the gun at his side. She took a deep breath—*anger out, smarts in, there we go*—and turned back to Dikent. "Show me the engine."

Jeane had to admit, they couldn't complain about Dikent's services during the next hours. After dinner, they went straight to one of his hangars in Central, where she and Kliks inspected the engine and discussed the fix with the specialists he called for them. Kliks was grumpy about the whole thing, not trusting anything the man offered, and Jeane didn't blame him, but they both knew they hardly had a choice. In the end, they okayed the engine, but navigation was another matter. The *Skylark's* system had been put together by Hollis, and it still worked perfectly well, thank you very much.

ALU brought the *Lark* in from Delta, and the workers started on the repairs. Dikent advised the trio to go to sleep and trust everything to his people, then, since Jeane fended off all his attempts at more idle chit-chat, wished them goodnight and left the port with a satisfied expression.

Kliks, Jeane, and ALU guarded the *Skylark* all night, taking shifts. And at one point, when everything was quiet and with ALU standing guard so no one saw her doing it, Jeane hauled the manipulator from the cargo hold to her room and locked it away. As if agreeing on it without words, none of them had mentioned the device or even Talala in front of Dikent. She might not know what to do with the damn thing, but her shady ex-boyfriend and his minions didn't need to be in on the secret.

When Jeane awoke from her five-hour rest around noon and jumped down from the airlock balancing two coffee mugs, she saw that Dikent had returned, standing next to the almost patched-up hole at the tail, talking cheerily to the chief mechanic. Luckily, he didn't notice her.

«Gotta admit, his people do great work.»

Money makes the mare go. Who knew.

Kliks was sitting at a foldable table beside the hangar doors, doing crosswords on his tablet and keeping an eye on the *Skylark*.

"What's new?" Jeane asked, placing the mug before him.

Kliks rubbed his eyes, a huge yawn accompanying his words. "They're very efficient. The hull is more or less done now." He clutched the mug with a thankful sigh and took a sip. "They need some time to fix the electronics, but the engine is basically ready to be installed."

"Anything suspicious?"

"Not from what I can tell. I didn't let them go places they didn't need to go." He looked up at her and frowned. "You look a certain way. Couldn't sleep?"

Jeane snorted dismissively. She'd dreamed they were in the lane again, running from Agent Jerkface, except this time they lost the race and went tumbling into the blue void for what felt like an eternity.

Shaking her head clear of the disturbing image, she nodded at Dikent. "Did he say anything?"

Kliks scrunched his nose like he smelled something foul. "Nothing important. But I feel like he doesn't like me. Does he seriously think I'm your new boyfriend?"

Jeane couldn't decide whether to laugh or get angry. Dikent, as if on cue, started walking towards them, and the Talalan gazed at him thoughtfully. "I should hold your hand in his presence. Just to see his face."

Laughing won in the end. And as Dikent stopped beside the table, Jeane was still wiping at her eyes, unable to contain her grin.

"What's the joke?" he asked, puzzled, but Kliks shrugged, poker face firmly in place, and went back to his crosswords.

Jeane ordered herself to be serious. Nerves. They either made her a giggling idiot or a ticking time bomb. Or both. But she found it easy to bounce back to her wired-up state of mind when Dikent pulled out a folder from the inner pocket of his coat and handed it to her.

"The details of the job. Your ship will be ready by the evening, and since this thing is time-sensitive, I expect you to be on it."

Jeane flipped through the documents. She hadn't done this kind of thing on paper in years. Everything had always been executed electronically, even with Dikent and his "spicy" deals.

"I guess I should ritually atomize this thing after?" she snarked.

Dikent made a face. "I'm just cautious. But yes, please do that."

"Anything else?" Jeane threw the folder on the table.

Dikent definitely looked like there were other things on his mind. In fact, he looked exactly like the time he'd confronted Jeane before she'd left the Cities.

As the memories emerged, she was overrun by guilt. Suddenly, she was back in that foggy morning, the air damp and smelling like rotten wood and oil, marching through Dikent's hangar to the *Skylark*. She nearly had gotten away with it too. But before she could climb up to the airlock and disappear inside the ship, she'd caught sight of Dikent walking toward her through the hall, and she couldn't be a big enough asshole to turn her back on him.

At his confused questioning, she'd told him she felt trapped. That he'd been too much, too close, too soon, and that this wasn't how she imagined her life to pan out. He'd told her he didn't understand. He'd thought everything was going well, they'd been a great team, and that at least they should talk about it before she up and went away, right?

So, she'd gotten angry because why couldn't he let her go? It wasn't like they were attached at the hip; why was he trying to control her when this was only a little *thing* between them? And now it was over, and she needed to go. Of course, Dikent had then taken offense, they'd both started yelling, and Jeane could only put an end to it by turning around, climbing into the *Skylark*, and getting the hells out of there.

Every word they'd said had burned into her mind, echoing through the years only to hurt her that much worse all over again. She pressed her lips together, avoiding Dikent's gaze, and painstakingly extracted herself from the memory. This was not the time. If it were up to her, the time would never come.

I'm not sorry I left. I'm just sorry about how I left. Dikent and her had relied on each other for years. That would always be there, no matter how it had ended.

"Be careful out there." He gave a smile—empty but honest—then turned and walked away.

"Just so you know," Kliks piped up, "I still can't imagine you two together. What did you see in him?"

Jeane's eyes followed Dikent until he disappeared behind the hangar doors. "Gossip hour's over. Where's ALU?"

"They wanted to look around before we left. No harm, right?"

As Jeane sat at the table, sipping her coffee and peering up at the half-finished tail section of the *Skylark*, another uncomfortable memory surfaced in her mind. Dikent had mentioned Gertie already, but she had locked the thought away, not wanting to deal with it.

When she'd left Dikent, she'd left Gertie too. The only difference had been that for a while, she'd still talked to the woman by radio, occasionally. Even Kliks had once. But as time passed, they'd called each other less and less often. Jeane had quickly gotten through her guilt—Gertie was doing great in the Cities and certainly didn't need her chaperoning.

But she probably wouldn't be able to live with herself in the next weeks if she didn't at least try to visit her old friend.

Gertrudia Banks lived in Sector Marigold, a short hop away from Central, in a luxurious suite inside a spiraling stone tower similar to the mansions of Sector Juno. Only even more posh if possible. Most lanehunters who got rich from their machinations did not stay in the Cities, moving to one of the more scenic independent worlds instead, but those who stayed tended to flaunt their money.

Gertie did too, but no one could say she'd become complacent. As far as Jeane knew, she was still doing the occasional jobs hands-on, throwing herself into danger on her sturdy little vessel, the *Harimau*. But more often than not, she left the dirty work to her couriers. She'd always been treading her own path through turbid waters, but as opposed to Jeane, she had some idea about what the hells she wanted out of it too.

It was late in the afternoon when Jeane stopped in front of her friend's place and, looking up at the tower, considered her options. The fog lay low in the Cities, enveloping the slender buildings in an opalescent haze and becoming denser by the minute. Jeane crossed the road and opened the gate, her thoughts as gray as the sky hanging above her.

The moody interior with the spiral staircase and the colorful mosaic windows teleported her to the past as she climbed to the fourth floor, heaving from the exertion. Her brain had started throwing doubts and insecurities at her. She should have called first; maybe Gertie wasn't home. Maybe Jeane wouldn't even be welcome here—Gertie had never approved of her leaving the Cities—and by the way, who had been the last person to call the other? Was it her? For skies' sake, it wasn't her, was it?

She rang the bell twice, her legs shaking as she rocked back and forth on her soles. But the moment she'd decided to turn away and book it, the door flung open, and there Gertie stood at the threshold in a glittering silver dress, holding a champagne glass between three fingers with a surprised expression on her heart-shaped face.

"Hey, Gert," Jeane said. She cleared her throat, although she didn't need to.

Her friend looked better than ever. Black hair smooth on her shoulders, a jumble of golden bracelets chiming on her wrists, her eyes sparkled as she blinked in surprise. "Excuse me, do we know each other?"

Jeane rolled her eyes. "Come on now."

"No, I'm sorry." Gertie took a sip from her glass. "I don't remember." But when she glanced at Jeane again, she was grinning.

"I would be lying if I said I didn't expect you," she said, inviting her into the apartment. "Dikent called me yesterday, and I swear I could see him melt into a puddle of smugness in my mind's eye."

Jeane stopped in the middle of the room and took the sight in. She couldn't suppress a little smile. The suite was different than the last time she'd seen it, but Gertie's style hadn't changed. The walls were a deep burgundy adorned with lively paintings in gilded frames. Various alien statues (or things that looked like art but might have been simple objects of use to a civilization long forgotten) stood in the corners like in a museum. A zebra-pattern blanket covered the couch, and a crystal chandelier hung above her head, glimmering in all the colors of the rainbow.

She shifted from one foot to the other, feeling like a vagrant in her weathered pants and leather jacket.

Gertie plopped down on the couch and gestured for her to do the same. "I would have been pissed if you left without seeing me. What happened out there? I heard the *Lark* got hit."

Jeane sat, not even leaning back lest she dirtied her friend's furniture. "The Union's being a thorn in my side this week. It's a long story."

Gertie made a disgusted face, one she'd always resorted to when talking about the empire. "They really are everywhere lately. Supposedly, Leadership perfected their cloning and gene-mod procedures, and now they're making agents and enforcers by the dozen. Gonna be a rough world for us."

"That's nothing new." Rumors of disgusting experiments to achieve galaxy-domination about Leadership, the secret senate governing the Union, weren't unusual. "Just the way it is."

"No, not at all," Gertie argued. "We thought they were un-touchable before, but believe me, this is different. Only this last year, they subjugated four planets! Those worlds never wanted to meddle in the Union's affairs; they were living their lives in peace. But with this, the Union now rules over seventeen human sys-tems, four alien planets, and two hundred and fifty-one dead worlds. This is a proper conquest now, and they're not stopping any time soon."

Jeane wasn't listening. She stared at the blue extensions in Gertie's hair, mesmerized, thinking about how it felt like no time had passed since they'd last seen each other. It was almost eerie.

Hells. She shouldn't have come here.

"The Net has been putting out feelers, though," Gertie went on with a deep sigh. "I think they're trying for a large-scale oper-ation instead of inciting small rebellions like before. They seem to realize where things are headed."

Jeane snorted. "The Net, right. They should be named the Mir-acle because that's what they'd need to unite the clans for any kind of...what, counter-offensive? What do they even want, a full-on war? That would go so well for all of us."

"There will be war either way," Gertie snapped. Clearly, this had been troubling her. It shouldn't have been surprising; she'd always been a vocal advocate of the total dissolution of the Union. The Net, a shabby intergalactic insurgence Jeane knew little about, had the same ambitions for a while.

Gertie held her stare, but then her shoulders dropped, and she leaned back on the couch. "Why am I telling you this? You don't care. Anyway, I'm glad you got out of there in time."

"Me too," Jeane mumbled. For a moment, she debated saying something about the manipulator. The Union trying to procure shady tech from the most defended alien world certainly fit the description of them being "everywhere lately." But although Gertie could keep a secret, Kliks might not end up too overjoyed with her sharing this one.

She'd be dropping that hot piece of technology somewhere pleasant and completely isolated the moment Kliks stopped freaking out about it anyway. *That's the plan, and honestly, screw everyone who says otherwise.*

"Dikent offered you a job, right?" Gertie asked, and Jeane gave a nod. "What is it?"

Jeane grimaced, ill at ease. "Can't tell you. Top secret spicy."

Gertie rolled her eyes. "Gods, alright. Anyway, I wanted to say...if you want, instead, I could...you know." She shrugged and took a sip from her drink. "Talk to some people, find a way to fix up the *Lark*. Perhaps get you to Metallia or Rix and—"

"No, Gert. No way." Jeane straightened her back. Gotta be careful; her friend always had a special talent for charming her into things. "I'm not gonna loiter around without a plan. And now that I'm here, Dikent will find a way to make my life harder no matter what I do. He has influence in almost every clan, and he's not letting this go. He's enjoying it too much."

"You two sure did a number on each other." Gertie shook her head. "I guess he wants some kind of closure? Revenge, possibly. He's a drama queen."

Jeane made a face. "You must be gossiping about me a lot."

She immediately regretted the comment, but Gertie only shrugged. "I'm still working with the guy. I hear him grumble about things. At least *he* still talks to me." She stood, looking irritable. She marched to a cabinet across the room and poured herself another drink from a sleek green bottle. "Best friends forever, right?"

And they were on topic. Jeane's stomach clenched in anxiety as she tried to scrape together an answer. "I told you. I'm not like you."

"Sure, sure. You've been running and pushing people away from you since we left the Ranch. I was foolish to think you'd stop for me." Gertie closed her eyes and gave a sigh like she was talking to a delinquent child throwing a fit. "But is this really what you want? What Hollis wanted?"

"Don't talk like you knew anything about that!" Jeane heard the fury flare up in her voice. "As if you knew anything about how I live. As if you achieved all your dreams!"

Gertie didn't flinch. "I'm satisfied with what I accomplished. Are you?"

Jeane stayed silent. The growing discomfort in her body kept urging her to get up and leave, but fleeing from Gertie's apartment? That would be a new low.

Hollis was quiet in her mind. At least she had that.

Then Gertie started talking again, calmer this time. "You haven't been here for five minutes, and we're at each other's throat. Our personal best, I reckon."

"Nah, I think we've been quicker before," Jeane muttered.

«*Say you're sorry. Come on. Say it.*»

Skies damnit, old man.

Gertie placed her empty glass on the cabinet top with an almost flourishy motion. "That's done then. I guess you didn't come here for me to lecture you. I'm just worried."

And that was all Jeane needed to be transported to ten years before in a too-real wave of déjà-vu. Gertie had said the same thing when she'd found her on Metallia on that rainy night, a week after Hollis had left them. "*I'm not here to lecture you. I was just worried.*"

She'd explained that she had followed her with a few of Hollis' buddies to bring her back to the Ranch. And they'd almost succeeded. Almost.

In the end, Gertie had stayed with Jeane with the reluctant but understanding blessing (and monetary support) of Mason, Krea, and Varij, the aforementioned "buddies," until both girls had settled into the world outside the Ranch. Gertie had never taken a liking to the nomadic lifestyle, but she'd found what she'd been looking for the first time the two of them were allowed into the Foggy Cities. And when Jeane ran away, she'd stayed.

«*If I were you, I wouldn't have let go of her hand. She knows what she's doing, the little monster.*»

"Don't worry," Jeane replied. She wasn't lying either. She was fine. She was. "This is just an unlucky time."

Gertie frowned. "I'm sure it is. Skies, you've never listened to me. Why would you now?"

Jeane didn't answer. She didn't want to continue these old arguments.

"So, how's our girl? And what's his name, Kliks?"

"The ship could be better. I hate that Dikent has his handprint on her now," Jeane groaned, and Gertie gave a hum of agreement. "Kliks is his usual bothersome self. He sends his regards. There's also a new guy. Robot. Or something like that," she added, remembering Gertie had not received the update about ALU's acceptance into the crew yet. Yeah, they hadn't talked in a *long* time. "They help out a lot. Good kid."

Gertie leaned back against the cabinet. "Well, I'm happy you're not alone at least."

Then they were silent. Jeane wanted to break the quiet, but every sentence that took form in her mind was a minefield in disguise. There were too many things unsaid, turbulent water behind a flimsy dam built of both their self-controls.

"I'm also fine, thanks for asking," Gertie said after a while.

Jeane sensed the blush bloom on her cheeks, and her friend giggled.

"Oh, my stars, you should see your face now!"

"Gert—"

"No, no." She was still grinning, her elegant, long nose scrunching comically. "No problem. But I'm serious. You have to leave now because, at this rate, I might just punch you."

Jeane's eyes widened, and she opened her mouth to argue, but all she asked in the end was, "You're throwing me out?"

"Babe, I know how this works. If we're not fighting, we're gonna walk around each other in polite circles, and neither of us wants that." The woman paused, mulling over what she was about to say. "Unless you stay, of course."

Their eyes met again. They both knew Jeane wasn't going to stay.

"You have a killer left hook, and I haven't slept properly in a week..." Jeane trailed off. Why were her witty comebacks abandoning her? How did Gertie see through her every single time?

Jeane stood, but before she could have started moving towards the door, Gertie crossed the room with a few long steps and threw her arms around her. Her shoulder pressed to Jeane's jaw painfully. Jeane's heartbeat quickened, and she lifted her arms to fold them around Gertie, but by the time she managed to finish the motion, her friend had already let go and taken a step back.

"Be careful." Gertie's voice wavered. "More than usual. With Dikent but also in general. Times are dangerous."

"They sure are. But you know. Adventure fuels me, adrenaline is my breakfast, and all that jazz." Jeane paused, looking around the room. "Listen, are you really alright here?"

Gertie waved her concern away. "You needn't worry about me. I have everything I need and more. And there's always some intrigue to untangle, petty valuables to fight over, and asshats to hornswoggle."

She gave her a sly smile, and Jeane was flung through time and space again, back to the Ranch and right into the heydays of their childhood. Gertie, pushing the gates of the Den open, grabbing her wrist, and pulling her out to the streets. Running on the dusty pavement as fast as their legs could take them. Mrs. Mallory standing at the threshold of the orphanage, yelling after them, scandalized. Sprinting past workshops, stores, and dilapidated habitats, the air in their lungs hot and full of fine, yellow dust. Stopping at the docks, Gertie crouching down and gasping for breath with a glint of a grin in her warm brown eyes, and Jeane unable to keep the laughter in either. Sitting on the runway beside some broken-down spaceship, cackling like little devils for minutes with their feet aching and their eyes watering. But all that hadn't mattered because it meant they'd been free, finally—at least for that afternoon, until the tutors or Security found them.

As the door closed behind her and the last sparks of Gertie's presence faded, Jeane stopped at the top of the staircase and followed her own breathing, trying to gain her mental balance back. What had she done to deserve these awful nostalgia trips? She hadn't done shit. Why was this the new normal?

Coming here was such a mistake. All she wanted was to hole up in her quarters on the *Skylark* and nurse a bottle of strong Cities grog until she blacked out or they left this gods-forsaken place behind—whichever happened first.

But instead, she went to find ALU.

Her technician's tracker signal led her inside a rat's nest of a pub not far from Dikent's hangar. After she passed the dirty bar, navigated the dense crowd of lanehunters in the dingy, low-ceilinged front hall, and moved into the back room, she finally stumbled upon the table she was looking for. And it was an unusual sight.

Four figures sat there, playing cards. Three of them were burly human guys wearing port worker uniforms, the thick beards covering three-quarters of their faces making them look like triplets. Tools and guns hung on their belts, and they leaned over the table, frowning at their cards. The fourth player was ALU.

Jeane scowled. She should have emphasized for the little technician that trying to make friends with everyone they met might have some particular risks in this place.

As she neared the table, ALU raised an arm to wave at her but kept their eyes fixed on the game. Jeane didn't know what they were playing, but judging by the huge pile of doubloons at their elbow, ALU excelled at it. When she broke through the last few people standing around watching the game and slipped beside them, pressed against the wall, ALU stage-whispered in a triumphant voice. "We win!"

One of the men flung three cards onto the table. The guy on the right, who had an enormous spanner tucked into his belt, grunted in annoyance and threw down a few of his cards as well. ALU chirped happily.

"Look, we gotta split." Jeane's eyes fluttered between the players. "Dikent wants us gone now." Kliks had called before she'd stepped into the pub, passing his comms to Dikent with a groan. And her ex sounded *urgent*. "You're losing me money"-type of urgent.

"Why?" ALU stared at her, then at their cards. "We win."

Jeane flashed her teeth at one of the onlookers who eyed her with a sleazy smile (another helaun, but this time a male, a towering presence in the cramped room) and slapped her hand down on ALU's shoulder. "Get the dosh, and let's go. I'm not gonna say it again."

She managed to get the message through this time. ALU waited until their turn, then revealed their cards with a satisfied buzz. "Grateful for exciting game. But gotta go. Wishing you a lovely day!"

They swept up the pile of coins from the table while Jeane was still trying to take in the fact that ALU was this good at card games. In fairness, they'd beaten Kliks at poker for a few times before, but come on, who hadn't? There might be a way to use ALU's card skills more often in the future...

Then Wrench Guy leaned forward, snarling. "Slow down, pal. Where d'you think you're going?"

ALU peered at him with their shiny insect eyes. "Space. Mission!"

"That may be, but not with our money!"

The other two grumbled in agreement, and the crowd took a unanimous step backward as if sensing trouble. Jeane surveyed the three men and concluded that, indeed, nothing good would come out of this.

"But we win," ALU protested, hugging more and more coins to their chest and sliding them into a compartment opening on their torso.

The gray-eyed man on the left grabbed one of ALU's appendages, but he straightened his back to glare at Jeane when she pulled her gun out, holding it barrel down.

"Hands off, sir!" she scolded. "If the game was fair, that money belongs to my friend."

Someone laughed, and Wrench Guy snarled at Jeane. "This scrap-metal tin can will not run off with our funds!"

She threw him a glance of pity. "Maybe you should have played better than a scrap-metal tin can."

The third guy jumped up, looming above all of them. It was time to disappear.

Jeane grasped ALU's arm, and they circled the players. As they made their way to the door, several people stared them down, but no one moved yet. She started thinking they might walk away without a fight (with Hollis whispering in her ear about how it would do her good to take her increasingly frazzled nerves out on some jackasses who tried to steal from her) when ALU's hand slipped out of hers.

She whirled around, but someone smashed into her, knocking the gun out of her hand. ALU screamed like they were being flayed, and Jeane shoved Gray Eyes off herself to get to them. He fell to the floor between two chairs, and Jeane moved towards Wrench Guy, who growled, holding the flailing ALU tightly. But she didn't expect the third man. He closed in on her from the side, and she ducked down, but his knuckles still connected with her jaw.

The pain blinded her. It also made her blood boil in nothing flat. *Fuck these assholes. Fuck this place.*

She swung at the air at random and hit someone's shoulder. Several bodies pressed up against her, and someone was pounding at her side with iron fists. She howled in frustration, turned around for momentum, and unceremoniously rammed into her attacker.

She pushed him to the wall, where the man slumped over from the impact. She spun around but didn't have time to search for ALU because strong fingers wrapped around her neck, and she heard her assailant—Gray Eyes?—pant in her ear. Her windpipe compressed, and her lungs were burning something wicked; at the back of her brain, she registered that the crowd was now chanting, but stars danced before her eyes, and every cell of her body was shouting for oxygen. She smashed her hand into her attacker's side, trying to get around and inside his arms and fling his hands off her, but she didn't have enough space to move and less and less energy for the maneuver too. ALU beeped somewhere faintly. She needed to reach them, but the world condensed into a scorching black sphere in the middle of her chest.

They should have left that damn money behind.

Then everything halted. The fingers on her throat loosened, and with her remaining awareness, Jeane used the opportunity to take a wheezing breath. The air cleared her mind, and she grasped the arm that held her, twisted it around by the wrist, and ducked under to break free.

The room swayed before her eyes, the contours of things gray and wobbly. She expected Wrench Guy or one of his buddies to come for her, but they didn't.

Something hard collided with her leg. ALU embraced her shin and pointed towards the front of the pub. As her vision cleared, Jeane saw that everyone was looking that way; there was movement at the entrance, a crowd both gathering and dispersing. Through the ringing of her ears, she also noted the silence.

She saw something else too. Bright brown eyes, staring right at her from among the mass of people: a young man facing them while everyone else kept their attention on the front door. He looked like he'd just entered the place, still trying to break through the mass of people, his short brown hair sticking to his head and a layer of sweat glistening on his forehead.

Their eyes only met for a second before the arguing at the front got louder, and as the figures standing in the entrance pushed inside the pub, Jeane finally saw the logo on their dark uniforms. A yellow U on a blue background sprinkled with pinpoint-stars.

Union.

CHAPTER 08 | THE HARDER THEY FALL

History. An endless line of eroded statues frozen mid-motion inside a living diorama of suffering. A tumultuous procession of never-resolving battles, the beginning and end obscured in fog. There had always been more to this war than what met the eye.

Most of the information about the Miyozan-Gaerrisian conflict was in written form inside the Archives' data banks; Maura had never seen any documentaries that presented it in an ordered and refined way. Miyozans, although they loved the visual arts, considered it tasteless to make docus about it, to erect statues, or paint pictures with the theme. Even so, as she swam through this boundless, formless mass of whatever she was stuck in, she saw images—vivid and compelling, like a play or an embellished memory. Wondering about where she was and what was going on around her were only fleeting distractions in her mind.

Miyozans were the descendants of the first people who left Old Earth hundreds of years ago to find a new planet beyond the stars. The documents recounting the early days of colonization were cryptic about the circumstances of escaping Earth, how humanity survived and conquered the lanes, and even the location of their birth planet, and Maura suspected there was a good reason for that. The Union and other human settlements each had their own stories about their beginnings, and maybe some knew more, but none of them were eager to share. What was certain was that the colonists of Miyoza had been scientists, equipped with the most advanced technology of the time, and the planet had quickly become a rich, flourishing world. They'd established contact with other emerging human colonies like Obavium and Hurricane, which later became the centers of the Union, and even with alien planets like F'xenn and Talala. But Miyoza didn't have galactic empire-building ambitions like the Union. They always found more solace in creating a peaceful nation far from the chaos, so these connections remained cordial but distant.

For a long time, they'd been careful not to get involved in the power struggle between the lanehunters, the Union, and those few alien worlds that found themselves in the crossfire. Gaerris was a mistake in their plan. A mistake that determined the fate of both planets.

Maura saw it in front of her now: a giant ship settling into orbit around the third planet of the Miyoza system at the outer edge of the habitable zone. Ancient and wrecked, the vessel hadn't come through the nearby lane like the colonists; it wouldn't have been able to in that condition. In their first transmission, the crew claimed they were the last survivors from Earth, looking for shelter to escape their decrepit generation ship.

Lorio Tholis had been the king at the time. Miyoza had recently transitioned to a monarchical system with Murisa Tholis, the previous council head, crowning herself queen in the last year of her charismatic rule. Her son, Halloran Tholis, continued the new tradition—a nod to the more archaic governing systems of Old Earth, which Murisa had been an enthusiastic researcher of. It was the era of nostalgia among the people, and with the first designs of the CNS in the works, this was a logical step in the evolution of the command structure.

Even so, King Lorio was suspicious of the newcomers. He'd sent a group of specialists to the Earther ship with food and basic aid but armed and on high alert. The unit reported inhumane circumstances on board: starving people wandering about the gigantic vessel with no chain of command or organized rhythm of life. The ship's inhabitants were wary about the Miyozans but accepted their help.

In their second transmission, they asked for asylum. The king denied them. And so the next aid run, already on its way, was not as welcome as the first. Half the group of doctors, nurses, and soldiers was slaughtered, and the Earthers attempted to use the rest as hostages to blackmail the king. Lorio immediately cut communications with them.

Months later, after dealing with a series of riots by people who had not agreed with the monarch's decision to abandon several hundred refugees in the cold of space, Lorio's rule survived, but the political climate remained unstable. Then the Earthers and their ruined ship disappeared from orbit.

The third planet of the system had been called Zeraya back then. Covered by a thick, noxious cloud layer, constant dust and thunderstorms racked its surface. It had no oceans, only a few intermittent lakes and a thin ice cap on the southern hemisphere. Recon units found the crashed ship along a steep mountainside at the equator, detecting no life signs. Miyoza turned its eyes away from Zeraya in guilt, and by the time they looked back, it was too late.

In the following years, Lorio Tholis had started working on what he hoped would become his legacy instead of this diplomatic catastrophe: the prototype of the glove, the one Maura was still wearing.

Wasn't she? It had to be there, but she couldn't see it; she was in the past, forced to gaze upon the horrible reenactment of tragedies she knew so well. She watched Lorio, hiding himself away in the palace, the situation with the Earthers that he hadn't been able to deal with leaving a profound print on his mental state. He'd become obsessed with constructing the ideal society, where there would be no mistakes and no misunderstandings or erroneous decisions. Not an empire filled with broken humans the Union was establishing and not a world of people disfigured and changed beyond recognition by cyber modifications like the legends from Old Earth warned about. It was supposed to be the best of both ways. Artificial perfection softened by human sensibility.

Due to his early death (because that level of mania had to take its toll), he'd never worn the glove, but his experiments created a good base for the next generations to improve upon.

The revenge of the Earthers hit Miyoza harder than anything before.

History. Half-understood, undeciphered pages scattered into the ocean, eradicated so no one could know where it all began.

"It was never about revenge," the king said, and Maura turned around, looking for him in the whirlwind of borrowed memories and hallucinations. Her father stood in the middle of the darkness, posture straight, head tilted up as if looking over a battlefield only he saw. In profile, his graying temples and the wrinkles in the corners of his eyes emphasized his age.

He was alive. The axis of Maura's world—he was still here.

"Do you know what they want? This." The king spread his arms out, and like a blooming flower, the view cleared. First the throne room, then the palace in all its pristine, shining glory, then the capital, brilliant and grand. She saw it all: the busy streets, the well-kept, harsh greenery of parks, and the monumental, bustling office buildings of Miyoza City. All of it through the thousand eyes of the CNS. "Technology, resources, soil, living space. Gaerris is a hellhole, and we're heaven, just out of reach."

Maura gave a nod because she knew he expected her to. "But why wouldn't they leave?" *What a strange déjà-vu.* She'd had this conversation already. Just another memory then—hers, this time. "Through the lane, somewhere else?"

The king laughed. "And where should they go? To fight the Union? The aliens? Look around, Maura! The universe is a dangerous place. Everyone is protecting what they have, hoarding all they can before the next catastrophe strikes. Gaerris would rather do battle here than waste their forces thousands of light-years away in some already lost war." He stared ahead at something distant and impossible. "No. They're not going to stop."

Miyoza had never figured out how those starving people on the derelict wreckage had survived or how they'd been able to put together such a large army to ravage Miyoza in a few short decades. They suspected Union interference; it would have been the empire's way of operating, to ignite conflict in hopes of reaping the leftovers. Plus, cloning had always been one of their specialties. But the Earthers had kept their secrets in hidden cities under the crust of that hostile planet they never accepted as home. They'd renamed themselves after the general who led their first attack against Miyoza, and they'd proven to be merciless and vengeful adversaries. Obsession had clashed with obsession in a war with no end in sight, and it had been taken to the extremes by both sides to such a degree that had always disgusted Maura.

"What do we gain by pulling ourselves apart to win another battle?" she asked, and the image of her father trembled. This was not part of the memory. She hadn't opposed him during that conversation, the lesson that had happened a long time ago. Before the siege. Before Sofia.

She hadn't spoken up, not until the end. And now she couldn't, ever again. Because—

"So let them devour us?" The king's face darkened into a threatening scowl. "We cannot stop as long as they don't. And they won't because there's nothing else for them to do. This is what they are. They take, and take, and take! That's how it's always been, and we cannot let them win."

But they won. They'd won, she'd failed, and her father was—

"This is what they are. That's how it's always been."

So sure about who and what Gaerris was. So convinced that the war could not be stopped. Like it had been written in stone. Like they had no other choice. Like it had been personal.

Who were these Earthers, really? What had they done to Miyoza, and what had they suffered themselves? Was it something that transpired on Old Earth before the lanes, before everything? The questions, only ever half-formulated in Maura's mind, had remained unanswered. No one had deemed her worthy enough to know. And now, she would never find out. Now that her father was—

The scene shattered, and the impact crushed her skull into thousands of pieces. But at the same time, she realized she wasn't broken and wasn't dying at all. She was lying on a hard mattress in a dim room, she was cold, and her head was aching.

She tried to turn, but the pain grew unbearable. She whimpered, forcing her eyes open. The surrounding haze splintered, revealing a dust-covered wardrobe, a window to her right, and two figures on the left, standing between the door and her bed.

Her brain turned sluggishly, and her attempt to move her head only resulted in more pain.

"Careful," someone said. Cool material touched her neck, and she felt a hand on her shoulder. The cold seeped into her skin, soothing the ache. "This might hurt for a while."

The owner of the voice was Damian—who else? Maura tried to remember how she'd ended up here. Memories balanced at the edge of her consciousness, but she was unable to grasp them. Her thoughts were heavy and viscous.

Her father had been here. How? He was dead.

"Where are we?" she asked, her tongue dry as if covered by tree bark.

"Somewhere safe." It was Nasir, stepping forward beside the bed. "Here, take this."

He held out a glass of water, and after Maura took it in her trembling hands, Damian lifted her by the shoulders so she could drink. As she lay back down and the weight of the glove on her hand registered, an image flashed up in her mind. General Pahoron, gesturing to a guard. Damian, dragged forward, a gun pointed at him. She looked at her friends wide-eyed.

"What happened? How did we...what happened in the palace?"

"We don't need to do this yet," Nasir said hesitantly. "Why not rest a little more?"

But she remembered now. The Archives. Pahoron's threats, the ministers' passive hostility. Her visit inside the CNS. Her fading hopes of getting them all out in time before Pahoron attacked Gaerris, and before High General Horst decided to annul their newborn truce.

"No!" She sat up, dizzy, and taking in the others' grave faces made her even more nauseous. "Tell me what happened! How did we get out?"

There was a short pause. "We had to run," Damian said. "By the time Nasir got to us, it was too late. We managed to subdue Pahoron, but you were unconscious, and when we tried to contact Horst..."

He trailed off, and her blood went cold, panic squeezing her throat shut.

"He told us to leave," Nasir finished in a measured voice. "Apparently, the Council had run out of patience, and their forces were descending on the city. Then I think the AI did something. We lost comms, and my friends' ship got blown up, so we all escaped through the subway network while the city went dark."

"What? No, it can't be!" Despair flooded Maura in roaring waves, and she grabbed Damian's arm. "We have to go back. We shouldn't have left! I have to talk to them! We can still—"

The words got jumbled in her mouth, but she didn't care. She had opened that damn door. She had overpowered the AI, and they'd escaped the Archives. They'd gotten so close!

"At that point, they would have killed us without a second thought," Nasir answered. So calm, almost emotionless. "They think you broke the agreement."

"No, you don't understand!" Maura scrambled to get out of the bed, to scream at him, to get any kind of human reaction out of him, but she was so weak, and her head hurt too much. The only thing she could do was to clutch her forehead with a groan. "They will kill everyone! We can't just leave!"

"We will not go back in the middle of a hostile takeover with you barely on your feet!" Damian raised his voice. "We don't know what shape the CNS is in and whether anyone is left there to support us. If the Council came together against Horst, he won't be able to help."

Maura buried her face in her palms, her breathing ragged. Blinding white explosions of pain raged behind her eyelids. Damian was right. She had wasted their last chance, and now it was all over.

She didn't know how long it took for her to calm down. At some point, she heard the door close and looked up. Nasir wasn't there anymore, but Damian was still sitting beside her.

"Where are we?" she asked again. There was a strange buzz in her head like she'd been shouting for hours.

"In the old Southern Industrials."

"How many?"

"A few. We saw others, but everyone scattered."

"We should have stayed."

"We would be dead."

She stared at the glove on her hand, dark and lifeless. Just like everything else in the capital if what Nasir had said was true.

What had the AI done? It had let them out of the Archives and the city but probably hadn't taken kindly to whatever the Gaerrisian Council had planned for the capital. If it still had control over its own actions at the time, it might have attempted to strike back. To which the Council must have answered accordingly.

And what level of retribution would be enough to quench their thirst for blood? After so many years of tribulations, how far would their hate drive them? Now that they thought they'd been betrayed again, would anyone be left alive after they toyed with their prey to their satisfaction?

She tore the glove off her hand and threw it against the wall. The device landed in the corner with a crash. Pain pulsed against her skull, and she lowered herself back on the bed, squeezing her eyes closed so she didn't have to see Damian's expression.

Miyoza was lost. In the end, everything she'd done was in vain.

Hours passed, and she must have fallen asleep because when she opened her eyes, Damian was gone, and daylight filtered into the room through the grimy window.

Head swaying, she stood, her limbs heavy. Her thoughts stayed close to the present, safe in shallow waters, only occupied with what was directly in front of her. Before heading for the door, she searched for the glove in the corner, but it wasn't there. Damian must have picked it up.

Once out in the corridor, she was uncertain where to go. The walls were bare, and the lamps on the low ceiling gave off a sickly yellow light. She passed three empty door frames leading into rooms similar to the one she'd just left before she heard voices somewhere ahead. The foyer turned to the right and ended in a large hall; when Maura stopped at the threshold, the dozen or so people sitting at long tables inside looked up to stare at her.

Most of them turned back to their drinks, food, or conversations right away. They all wore simple cargo pants and jackets in various styles and colors, their weapons (rifles, stun guns, and pistols) at their sides or propped against their seats. The room must have been a canteen in the past: a row of metallic cupboards loomed along the opposite wall, and Maura could see the wide-open double doors of a kitchen area to the left where a few more people loitered around, rummaging in sacks and containers, and sorting food on a countertop for others to claim.

A hand flew into the air to her right, and she spotted Damian and Nasir at the table closest to the wall. She stepped up to them, somewhat troubled by all the unknown faces. They must have been Nasir's comrades from the Net.

"Come on, sit." Nasir gestured to the empty place beside him, across from Damian. A burly man sat on his other side, his red hair and beard a burning light around his pale face. Another stranger—a bald, bony young woman—was seated on Damian's right. They both nodded but didn't speak, preoccupied with their meager portion of a stew-like canned food.

Maura sat, her brain foggy. These people had saved her. Nasir had said they'd been one foot out of Miyoza, but they'd come back to assist them. She wanted to thank them, but the words fizzled out halfway to her throat.

She looked at Damian; her bodyguard was eating the same sad-looking meal as the others, and when their eyes met, he pushed a can and a spoon over to her with an encouraging blink. His face was exhausted and beaten up, but he held himself with an air of quiet defiance.

No matter how plain the food was, her stomach made a loud noise when she took the can between her fingers, and the bald woman glanced at her with a grin in the corner of her mouth. Maura didn't remember when she'd eaten last. Before the coronation, surely, but how much time had passed? How long had she been out?

Careful. Dangerous territory. She didn't want to think about that yet.

The food was flavorless but filled her up. During the meal, she picked up several conversations around her, and while she understood the general topics (arguments about what roads to take, speculations of what was going on in the capital, sightings of Gaerrisian units in the area, and other, more opaque discussions of various operations), she could only process so much without stepping out of that fragile apathy she'd bundled herself into. But the silence had to end at some point, and upon finishing her last bite, she found herself a bit disgruntled when Nasir spoke up, placing his spoon on the table.

"Sorry for the poor service. We weren't prepared for extending our stay."

Maura forced herself to give a faint smile. "It's no problem. Thank you for sharing your food with me." She caught the gazes of the red-haired man and the woman. "And thank you for your help. You didn't have to."

The man inclined his head at Nasir. "Eh, it's all because of that one. Can't say no to him."

Nasir smirked, and Maura couldn't help but wonder about the command structure of his group. Nasir had never mentioned whether he was the leader; it had always been "his friends" this or "his compatriots" that. This, too, seemed more like comradery than following orders. But it must have been a big ask from Nasir either way.

"I'm Coven," the red-haired man added, then nodded toward the woman who eyed Maura with a glance sharper than knives. "That's Ruao. Nice to meet you finally, Your Majesty."

Her stomach tightened at hearing the title. Suddenly, she became conscious of her appearance: she was still wearing the formal burgundy dress from the coronation, the papery material torn and dirty. She didn't even want to imagine what her makeup and hair looked like.

What a sorry image of a queen.

"Thank you," she said, then gathered her courage to ask, "So...what do we know? What's happening out there?"

Coven cleared his throat and took a swig from his bottle. "The city is dark, the CNS is out, and all our contacts are silent. We know that Gaerris grounded a lot of craft during the night because they passed over us, but apart from that, it's anyone's guess."

"And I suppose you're leaving as soon as possible."

Coven nodded, and Ruao rubbed her eyes. "That's the plan," she said, voice raspy and tired. "Although, we have no functional vessel, and we're not in the best graces of the Net either."

"A transport is coming for us. I arranged it the moment it became clear you two may have to run." Nasir glanced at Damian. "It's not ideal but better than trying to find a suitable ship in these ruins until a Gaerrisian patrol spots us." He paused, turning to Maura now, his brown eyes intense. "I know you think this is the end. But you're still alive. And you have the glove."

Maura scowled. What was he talking about? She was nothing, all alone and locked out of the palace. And the glove was only a fancy accessory without the CNS and the AI.

"General Horst is still in the capital," Damian said. There was a fired-up quality to his voice. He hadn't lost hope. "In his last transmission, he told us to leave because the Council was no longer supporting the truce, but he also said to get help if we can. That he would try to preserve the capital and that he stands beside peace if you can gather support. Outside."

Her brain turned slowly. Outside... That could only mean the Net. But why would they assist Miyoza now when they'd been content with spying on them for years?

Then it clicked. The glove.

"You think the Net would help me if I shared this technology with them," she said, chewing every word. Could it be true? Her father had always said the glove was unique, but she'd heard terrible and wonderful things about the Union too. And what of all those mysterious dead worlds, full of unknown tech, ripe for the taking?

Nasir exchanged a look with his comrades and gave her a good-natured wink. "There's a good chance. After all, the only blueprints we haven't managed to acquire were for the glove and the AI. I'm sure our leaders would love to reverse-engineer something from the device. And if it comes with its user too, it might even be a turning point in our fight against the Union."

The Union. The threatening shadow cast over the galaxy. She'd never seen it before, always occupied by more urgent dangers, but Nasir and his friends had been fighting that battle for a long time.

Would she really have to join another meaningless war to save her home? She couldn't handle the glove. She couldn't command the AI, not really. And right then, she could only just cope with the thought of leaving her home for the first time in her life, then waking up to another day far from everything she'd ever held dear.

But because these concerns were too muddy and too awful, she asked the other question on her mind instead. "Why would Horst say that? Why would he still want to fight for us?"

"He's not fighting for you," Nasir said. "The need to save his own world is larger. You have to understand that Gaerris is hardly a planet anymore. It is a factory of war. And I think General Horst is very worried about what will happen now. About the next contender over their autonomy and what the Council would answer to that new challenge."

"He thinks the Union will attack them," Maura said, understanding. It all came back to the Union again.

Nasir scratched at a stain on the table. "The empire has been swallowing worlds like a black hole for years in the name of this perfect, monolithic coalition they imagine humanity should be. Brainwashing people, pushing them into slavery, creating mockeries of natural life to serve their machine of conquest. Most of our home planets have fallen under their rule." He glanced at Coven and Ruao, both staring back with diamond-hard eyes. "As soon as they figure out that Gaerris won this war, they will descend on them. Can't leave such a bloodthirsty neighbor to their own devices."

"It would be the same if Miyoza won," Damian added. "The Union had been waiting for us to tire ourselves out in the war, so when they arrived to pick amongst the rubble, they'd meet no resistance. Your father didn't see that. The Gaerrisian Council either. We aren't as isolated from the rest of the universe as we'd like to think."

Maura looked at him, then back at Nasir and his compatriots. They'd obviously been discussing this for some time now. Their involvement with the Net had given them a perspective she didn't have. Fleetingly, she wondered where exactly "home" was for Coven and Ruao but realized that she didn't even know where Nasir hailed from.

She felt horribly ignorant. And now she needed to go and negotiate with powers she didn't understand in order to protect what was left of her home, all the while knowing her people were suffering under the rule of their enemies. And her only bargaining chip was a piece of technology she hadn't been able to master.

How could she leave her home? What if she never saw it again? What was she out there without her title, without her people? A gaping, black emptiness opened up in her chest at the thought. If she let the idea in, she feared she would lose herself.

Nasir broke the quiet again, but this time, Maura didn't mind. "We have to leave with or without you two. Our ride arrives tomorrow. Think about it."

Maura glanced at Damian and read his face easily. He wanted to fight. He still trusted they could do something.

"I'm not going to force you," he said. He reached out and took her hand where it rested on the table, and she felt lighter, just a little. "If you stay, I remain too. But there's no help for us here. We need to try somewhere else."

The numbness she'd wrapped herself in subsided. It was time to decide, but she was still dangling above a dark void, holding onto that thin piece of straw. When would this end? When would she be finally able to rest?

Not now. Not yet.

"Alright," she replied, looking over her friends' faces, silently pleading for their forgiveness. She didn't want to be the reason for their demise too. Her father, taken by forces she couldn't stop. Her mother, whom she never really knew, lost in combat. Sofia, dear Sofia, ripped away from this world so brutally. All of them, lost.

She straightened herself. "We leave then," she said. "We're going to the Net."

CHAPTER 09 | TOUCH AND GO

Jeane had been ignoring her beeping comms for the last five minutes, rejecting the call again and again. ALU started squirming beside her, so she hushed them and flattened herself to the wall, preparing to take a peek outside.

"Why stop?" the technician whined, pulling on the sleeve of her jacket like a scared child. "Go, go!"

"Are you okay?" Jeane asked. ALU seemed unhurt after the brawl, but one could never be sure with them.

The technician chirped nonchalantly. "Okay. They hurt, but we didn't hurt back. Why stop?"

"I want to see those jerks," Jeane whispered. "I mean, what the hells? Did you see them? That was the bloody Union back there!"

Her comms beeped again. She silenced the device, then leaned out of the alleyway.

After the presence of the agents registered in her brain, she and ALU had bolted through the back door of the pub, spilling out onto the streets of Central. She'd heard shouts behind them but quickly realized it wasn't the enemy: other lanehunters had the same idea, and soon, they were sprinting down the cobblestone road among a group of people.

Darkness and thick fog enveloped everything, blotting out the orange orbs of the streetlamps. After a few turns, most people had dropped away, and she'd steered ALU into a side-alley, so they could assess the situation.

No one walked on the road now. The airships of late-night travelers passed above, and drunk hollering filtered out from one of the nearby pubs, but all these were completely normal noises. No shots, no screaming.

"How?" ALU asked. "How is Union here?"

Jeane huffed in frustration. "You got me there. This shouldn't have happened. This place was always safe. For hundreds of years—from the beginning! It's impossible!"

"Followed someone?"

"No way."

"Betrayal?"

But who would do this, and why? Sure, everyone could be bought for the right price, but it was hard to imagine any lanehunter giving out the position of the Cities after all this time. This place was one of their primary living grounds, and they took its protection seriously. Too many things had to go wrong at the same time for the Union to suddenly find its way in.

«Every security system has its flaws.»

But it didn't make sense! The agents must have invested a lot of time and energy to get through the Cities' defenses, so why would they show up on a random raid in the tiniest, nastiest pub of Central? Where were they hiding their army? Already a bunch of destroyers should have been hovering above, ready to give an ultimatum to the clan heads.

So, why there? Why now?

«You know why.»

She shook her head. She needed to think, but her mind was a jumbled mess of panicked ideas and ominous speculations, and even the make-believe conversation with Hollis didn't help to clear out things. If this wasn't another awful prank or some arrogant nitwit's overdone threat to a rival smuggler, then lanehunters were in a stinking heap of trouble.

She pushed the button on her tablet, annoyed by the noise that had started up again. "Yes, Kliks?"

"Finally! Where are you guys?" The Talalan's voice sounded

unnerved. He was heaving, and there was a hum in the back-ground, almost like—

"Umm...where are *you*?" Jeane asked.

"Just taking a stroll above Central. Since Dikent threw me out."

She could feel her blood pressure shoot up into the skies. "What? Why?"

"Something is happening."

"I noticed!" Distant, shouted commands echoed through the mist, but Jeane still didn't see anyone around. "You can guess, but I'll spare you the effort. The Union is here."

Kliks was silent for a second, digesting the information. "Oh. I see." There was a slight waver in his voice.

"Well, I don't! What the fuck? We were about to leave that dive when they appeared. This is not—"

"Were they looking for you?"

Hollis gave a hacking cough in the back of her mind, and she exhaled forcefully. "I don't know. Why did Dikent throw you out?"

"I'm not sure. The mechanics already finished their thing, but he was still around. He kept saying we should leave because our timetable changed, and we won't make it to the rendezvous. Then he got a call and demanded that I contact you again. He was talk-ing nonsense; it might have been funny if he wasn't holding me at gunpoint."

"Bastard!" Jeane spat. "What did you do?"

"I shot him in the shin with stun."

"Kliks!"

"I'm...sorry?"

The answer got caught in Jeane's throat because six uniformed figures walked out of the fog on the other side of the street. She pulled her head back, gestured to ALU, and they drew back fur-ther into the alley, crouching behind some hefty garbage bins.

"Jeane?" Kliks called out to her.

"Ssh!"

"Jeane, I think the Union is here because of me."

She shook her head like that could delete the idea and

plastered the comms to her ear. "Have you seen nailships up there? Destroyers? Any scuffle or weirdness?"

Kliks didn't speak right away, probably checking the radar. "Nothing as far as I can see."

"They came to bar," ALU said. "Low probability. Why there?"

"ALU is right. They're looking for the manipulator. They must have followed us."

"Let's not jump to conclusions!" Jeane huffed. "Agent Jerkface died in the lane. And even if they got a transmission out, no way the Union knew in which little pub ALU and I would pop up in. Why weren't they at the port if they can track the manipulator so well? Through several lanes and cracks, might I mention, which should be hard as fuck!"

"Guy at the pub," ALU said slowly, looking up at her with widening insect eyes as if realizing something important. "Brown jacket, staring at us. Agent Jerkface."

It was like the sky collapsed on Jeane. "What?"

"I recognize. Saw him through airlock door on *Lark*. He lives."

Kliks cursed into his comms. "How in hells did he—"

Jeane hushed him again. The group of figures she'd seen before appeared at the mouth of the alley.

Despite the smell of rotten fruit invading her nostrils, she tried to duck lower behind the trash cans. Now that she could examine them, those goons didn't strike her as average agents. Their uniforms were black instead of the usual gray, they were impossibly tall and built like tanks, and they moved together like connected by some invisible force or shared knowledge.

«Inspectors,» Hollis groaned in her mind at the same time that she whispered the word. Two inspector trios.

But that didn't make sense either. Inspectors were specialists, genetically engineered sons of bitches working in hivemind-like trios on occupied planets to deal with internal conflicts and to supervise agents and errand-people. And the Union was not good at gene-en, at least not until recently, so there weren't a lot of them around. They certainly weren't sent after lanehunters.

«*You should have started running five minutes ago. What in skies' glory are you waiting for?*»

They might have been looking for Agent Jerkface. He'd acted

exactly like he'd been chased when she'd seen him barge into the room. What if the inspectors had been following him? Would fit their profile, but either way—

«Kid. Run!»

ALU poked her in the arm, and that snapped her out of it. The inspectors started marching down the alley.

"We're running now," she said.

They jumped up and sped towards the other end of the street. One of the inspectors shouted something, and several shots ricocheted on the pavement, terrifyingly close. Jeane pulled out her gun and blindly fired a few blasts backward. At the next junction, they took a sharp right, then a left.

No more gunshots came, but the sound of footsteps behind them was persistent.

"They want us alive," she panted into her comms, realizing that Kliks was still on the line. "We gotta scram, now!"

"I'll pick you up," the Talalan said. "But I don't have much space to land."

Jeane and ALU swerved around another corner, arriving at a busier street. The dirty white mist was thinner here, and numerous pedestrians walked about under more frequent streetlights on both sides of the road. Jeane pushed through a group of young lanehunters and risked a glance back. Their pursuers had fallen behind.

She tried to catch her breath, but her lungs were stinging something awful. "Meet us at East Point," she heaved into her comms.

Kliks mumbled, uncertain. "What's there? This map doesn't show much."

"Big-ass lighthouse. You can't miss it."

"Captain?" ALU's voice rang anxiously. A few yards before them, three looming figures broke off from the evening crowd.

"Shit!"

She clutched ALU's arm and dove into an alley to the right.

They kept running. The streets led uphill and became steeper as they entered the eastern boundaries. The inspectors chose endurance over speed, silently chasing them down like the creepy predators they were. Every time Jeane thought she'd lost them, they showed up even closer behind at the next crossroad.

Then ALU turned sharply to the right and zoomed through a gateway so fast, she could barely follow.

"What are you doing?" she wheezed, catching up at last. The technician didn't answer, so she had no other choice than to race after them across a grassy yard surrounded by a ramshackle stone wall while ALU ran forward as if pulled on a string. The two of them climbed a row of steep staircases between high-walled houses, the path branching many times, leading ever upwards.

"This is why...I hate...all these...blasted planets," Jeane cursed, breathless. "They're all...too...fucking big!"

Then ALU caught her arm and pulled her down to her knees. They dragged her through a small archway carved into a yellow building to the left and crawled forward a few feet in a narrow stone tunnel ending in a closed metal grate.

Jeane rattled the bars, but they didn't give. She stared at ALU, petrified. "What now?"

They shushed her, gripping the grating with three arms and fixing their eyes on the opening behind them. Jeane dropped to the ground, threw her back against the grate, and raised her gun. If those three-bodied motherfuckers found them here, she could at least try and bring down a few of them before it was all over.

They waited in silence. Jeane counted her heartbeats, staring into the darkness beyond the archway. She got to twenty-four before they heard the steps.

Two massive figures, jogging forward in terrifying unison. And passing their hideout without even taking a second look.

She remained unmoving on the off chance the third one came this way too, but there were no more noises. When the thumping of heavy boots died down, she lowered her weapon and let the air out of her lungs.

"Nice job," she said, unable to mask the traces of panic in her voice. She patted ALU on the shoulder. "How did you know this was here?"

ALU raised a hand and rapped their fingers against their metal head a few times. "Have a good map. Downloaded it in hangar."

As if on cue, Jeane's comms signaled again. "What's up?" she spoke, expecting Kliks to answer.

"What in hells is going on here, Jeane?"

It was Dikent, so angry that he was almost shouting. Jeane held the tablet away from her ear and stage-whispered back at him (better not risk being discovered) while boosting the transmitting volume up to the maximum (for a fun effect). "Dikent, how do you know this number?"

The man cursed, and judging from the noises, he turned down the volume on his end. "Irrelevant, darling. What did you get me into this time?"

«Keep calm, be cool!»

"This time? I don't know what you're talking about. By the way, sorry for the shot in your leg. I think Kliks is allergic to you."

Is that calm enough?

"Don't screw around!" Dikent bellowed. "Seems a little suspicious that an agent tries to hunt you down in a lane, and then even more of them appear in my city. Do you have any idea how this happened?"

«'In my city,' huh? He would looove that.»

Jeane rolled her eyes. "You *are* aware I'm not the only person who crossed the Union in the last few days, right? What do you want me to say?"

"Stop lying, for starters. You barely escaped a group of inspectors. Why are they looking for you?"

Jeane gulped. Dikent did have eyes everywhere. "I said what I said. I have no idea what's going on."

«Technically, that isn't a lie.»

"Well, you have to get out of here."

"I'm working on it." Jeane beckoned ALU, and they both crawled out of the tunnel. "What do you know?"

"Only two battleships so far, and Defense are sending out their units as we speak. You can still slip through before they set up a blockade."

Two Union ships wasn't an army by any means, but if they had a way into the Cities, more could come later.

"You think I should leave?"

The question slipped out before she could stop herself. Stars damnit, habits were hard to break. But Dikent wasn't her partner-in-crime anymore; she had no right to ask for his opinion.

"You better," the man answered, not noticing her lapse in judgment. "Either the inspectors get you or Defense, curious why you're in the center of the Union's attention."

They started scaling the stairs again, ALU hopping forward at each turn and signaling all-clear.

"If you tell me where you are, I can help," Dikent went on.

«Hmm, so he doesn't know everything. Cool.»

Was that worry in Dikent's voice, or was she imagining things? Either way, he was right. Away from here, now. They needed time to think this through.

"J, you can tell me. What's going on?"

«Oh boy. Trust me, we really can't.»

But gods damnit, why did he have to use that old nickname? That didn't help things at all.

"I'll be fine," Jeane said, curtly closing the argument with both of her conversational partners. "You just make sure they don't blow up my ship from under me again."

Then she disconnected.

East Point was deserted, but the blinding beam of yellow light kept spinning atop the slim lighthouse building. The first lane-hunters settling down on this precarious assortment of floating rocks had built the place as a tribute to those ancient Earther sailors they tended to compare themselves to. Venturing into unknown waters, braving the wrath of nature in hopes of reaping riches beyond imagination—that sort of thing. Jeane had always liked the metaphor, and the lighthouse was one of her favorite places in the Cities. And it had proven to be an excellent meeting point.

"Ten corvettes lifted up from the northern ports a few seconds ago," Kliks reported through the comms while Jeane and ALU scaled the steep hillside and emerged onto the plateau. "Maybe they can get those inspectors in time."

Jeane remained in sullen silence. From her friend's hesitant voice, it was clear that even he didn't believe his own wishful thinking. The Union had found its way into the Cities; no way in hells they'd let this opportunity slip out of their hands. Those destroyers she'd been afraid to glimpse above their heads were already on their way from Hurricane. It didn't matter that their vanguard might get destroyed. She would have bet all the money ALU had won on cards that the inspectors had put down markers on the way in or tapped into Cities Control to transmit the entry vectors to other units. They knew how to get in now. Defense could only delay the inevitable.

"Everything is going to change, isn't it?" Kliks asked, sounding outright scared.

What would the hunter clans do if the Cities got compromised? Fight for their survival? Start a war to protect what they had left? The locations of all their hidden hideouts. The traveling convoys. The hunter-friendly alien planets. The Ranch.

And all this because they'd brought the manipulator here?

The horror of the realization threatened to paralyze her, so she pushed the thought away.

"I don't know," she said. She didn't have the strength to deal with a Kliks-caliber panic attack yet. "You can land. We're here."

As the *Skylark* swooped in, lifting above the flats with a healthy hum and making an elegant semicircle around the lighthouse, Jeane let a faint smile creep to her face. The little bird seemed happy again. Sure, the ship always had a haphazard, thrown-together air to it, Hollis having to put it together by cannibalizing several other vessels that had all seen a few confrontations in their own time, but still. The flattened egg-shaped hull with the two side-stabilizers jutting out of the middle, the transparent cabin of the control room at the front, and the circular tubing of the proton cannon at the back, was unbroken and smooth. The tail had also been restored with the blue plasma blaze of the new propulsion system heartily blasting out of the symmetrical muzzles. It was all beautiful to her, and against everything, a weight lifted from Jeane's shoulders. She couldn't wait to be on board again.

Kliks touched down on the plateau and lowered the ladder, not even stopping the engine. ALU and Jeane set out jogging through the field sparsely spotted with stick-like, brown populations of trees and the occasional dry tussocks in between, but they were only about halfway through when shots started to rain down on them.

Plasma bolts deflected off of ALU's metal body; Jeane didn't have time to look back, but from the increasing whirring noise, she suspected the inspectors were now approaching from the air. Something exploded ahead: Kliks joined the fight with a warning shot from the *Lark's* cannon. The weapon had proved to be unreliable in the past, and fixing it hadn't been part of Dikent's deal, so Jeane hoped that would be enough.

She was almost at the top of the ladder, following ALU, who had somersaulted their way through the hatch, when she felt a burning sting at her waist. She cried out as her left foot slipped on the next step, and tried to find a grip again, the pain numbing her senses. ALU reached out with two arms, grabbed her amongst the hailstorm of blasts, and hauled her into the ship.

The airlock slammed shut, and Jeane leaned against the wall, groping for the source of hurt on her midsection. Her shirt was charred, the skin below swollen into a shiny red blob. There was no bleeding, and although the wound hurt like hells, it wasn't a direct hit. Probably a bolt passing too close to her. ALU leaned over, trying to examine it, and she shooed them away, staggering towards the ladder to the upper deck. Judging by the noises, Kliks had stopped shooting—hopefully because they were getting out of dodge instead.

"You got shot!" The Talalan looked at her with a horrified expression when she dragged herself into the control room.

"Wow, I didn't notice." Jeane collapsed into the pilot chair and waved towards the radar, not quite ready to bend forward yet. "What's happening out there?"

Kliks took a deep breath and forced himself to not stare at her wound. "We left those airships behind, but one of the battleships is after us. The cannon is done if we want to maintain shielding. What do we do?"

"Step on the fucking gas," Jeane grunted. She tried to focus, but the scorching pain in her side was too distracting. "Plan a course to Miyoza. *Not* the most direct one."

Kliks' mouth stayed open for a second. "Are you serious?"

"I'm always serious." Gathering all her remaining strength, Jeane straightened and glanced at the radar display. The battle-ship was turning to follow them. This would be fun. "You want a place where we'll be left alone by both the Union and meddling Cities investigators prodding us about why we doomed the entire lanehunter culture? An active war zone might do it. And we have a rendezvous there."

"Come on. Everyone will just wait until we're done and capture us on our way out!" Kliks replied. "If, and that's a hefty if, we manage to get in and out."

"Look, we gotta go somewhere!" Jeane snapped. "Is this a good time to ask what you want to do with this manipulator of yours?"

Kliks stared at her, eyes desperate. "I don't know? Take it back to Talala? Maybe?"

"Not with these clowns on our heels. We could cause a war. We need to lose them first."

The *Skylark* darted out from under the fog layer, and the Union ship followed on the same trajectory, barraging them with laser beams. Jeane watched the energy level of the shield: only forty percent and dropping.

"I thought they wanted us alive," Kliks muttered, increasing their speed again.

"Stars know what's happening anymore. ALU, enough!" Jeane groaned, but she accepted the bundle of gauze and the tube of medigel the technician stuck under her nose and started treating her burn wound.

Kliks called in to Control asking for egress vectors, but by the time they scanned them and the numbers came in, the shields had lost another ten percent. The generator was close to overloading; the constant attack of the Union ship pushed it to its limits, and the first exit point was still miles ahead. Kliks added as much power to the untested engine as he dared, but the *Skylark* felt like a gigantic, flashing target.

"We're not gonna make it." Jeane gritted her teeth, holding

onto the edge of the console. "I can't believe we're not gonna make it."

But then, there was a sudden pause in the ceaseless flood of blasts, and Kliks cried out in surprise. A third, dexterous player slipped between the *Skylark* and the battleship, shooting at their opponent with frantic force. Jeane stared at the new vessel's energy signatures on the screen. She would have recognized the *Harimau* anywhere.

What the hells is Gert doing out here?

They only had seconds until the first exit point. Gertie kept the battleship under fire, so they couldn't pursue the *Lark*, and right when the corvettes of Cities Defense appeared too, their bird finally managed to climb the first vector. Space and distance became meaningless as they submerged into the deadly currents of the Ros-3.

The Cities and the fight disappeared behind them in the fog, and soon, they switched to another coordinate set to guide them out. Jeane inhaled and exhaled deeply, reclining in her chair and closing her eyes, exhausted. She hoped Gertie got out of that scuffle fast. And in one piece, if possible.

The slicing pain in her torso didn't let up, and she knew it would bother her for days. Needless to say, they didn't have the budget for stocking up on cutting-edge medical supplies.

She felt Kliks' eyes on her and glanced at him, frustrated. "What?"

"I need to study the manipulator. If the Union is tracking it, maybe I can figure out how."

Jeane pushed herself up from the chair and stood but regretted the decision when agony bit into her wound. "Good thought. But don't switch it on. Might just be what gives us away."

Kliks nodded. He started to turn away but paused, his pitiful expression betraying the whirlwind of emotions inside him. "Did I really cause the doom of the entire lanehunter culture?"

Jeane swallowed, her blood turning cold. *Fuck.*

"I didn't mean it like that," she said. Her voice was shaking. "We didn't do it on purpose. You took the damn thing, but if you hadn't, Jerkface would have. And what were we supposed to do, die out there in the middle of nowhere? We had to go and get help somewhere!" She spread her arms out, promptly losing her balance, so she had to lean on the console again. Her wound burned like her flesh had been set on fire. "We didn't know. We couldn't know."

Kliks was frozen into a state of obvious shock, gazing beyond her at nothing. Moments passed in tense silence, and he blinked, his face thawing from that panicked look.

"Yes, okay. Alright," he murmured. "Thanks. I'm going to go and...do things now. Doing things is good. Right?"

Jeane frowned but nodded her approval. Her friend looked like he wanted to step in two different directions at the same time, toward her and the door, but in the end, he stepped up to her, took her arm, and squeezed her hand.

"Thanks," he said again. "For trusting me."

Jeane wanted to answer something sarcastic about how that particular thing should come back into fashion between them, but then the room swayed before her eyes, her legs buckled, and she clutched the arm Kliks barely provided for her in time.

"Bed. Please," she mumbled. "Painkillers. Silence. You work, I heal."

The Talalan's answer melted into the piercing buzz flooding her senses. She felt Kliks taking her arm, supporting her weight as they walked towards the door.

Oh, how much she wanted a few calm days for themselves! But that seemed like a naive dream. The *Lark* was fine, but they'd left chaos, unfinished businesses, and debts behind in the Cities. And she feared that very soon, all those things would catch up with them in the most unbecoming manner.

CHAPTER 10 | UPROOTING

That night, Maura dreamed about Sofia.

After her death, she'd been tormented by nightmares for a long time. Again and again, she had to relive their last goodbye and the moment she'd been informed that their ship had been destroyed. Years had passed for the visions to abate, but even so, they tended to resurface when she was stressed or exhausted.

This time, it was different. This dream was about something that never happened.

She was standing in a dim room full of crowded shelves, the walls a warm hue of green, and she recognized the place immediately. It was the shop of Khama, Sofia's mother. Their family had been preparing and selling natural remedies and rare spices for generations. The little store was a quaint thing in the age of advanced pharmaceuticals and with the Miyozan culinary arts demonstrating methods not unlike sciences, but it also manifested the flavor of tradition blending with high-tech processes that a significant number of their people cherished so much. Khama had also been a skilled chemist—one of the researchers working for the palace—and that had been the only reason Maura had gotten to know Sofia at all.

She'd often accompanied her friend when she could escape

her responsibilities in the palace, to help with the chores in the shop where everyone had treated her kindly, more an equal than a princess. She knew all the regulars by name and spent countless afternoons drying, assorting, and labeling bundles of herbs and preparing concoctions in the stockroom with Sofia, talking, laughing, and listening to music like any other teenager.

When Sofia and her parents died on that ship, her friend's grandmother had taken over the store, and although she'd been invited many times, Maura had never gone back again.

In the dream, the room was devoid of life, a thick layer of dust covering the counter, the piles of boxes, and the colorful pouches on the shelves. A storm was raging outside; gray clouds towered above the city, and the wind howled in the streets, rattling the plexiglass in the windows.

"Sofia?" Maura took a step forward. "Are you here?"

She knew she was dreaming. In reality, she was lying on an uncomfortable bed in a derelict factory building in the outskirts of Miyoza City, but if she dreamed herself in the store, her friend couldn't be far away.

"Sofia?"

The darkwood-imitation door leading to the stockroom flung open. Maura rushed forward and took a right between two shelves, circling the counter to face the black space beyond the threshold. A primal fear weighed down on her chest, but she didn't know why.

She stepped inside. Sofia stood in the middle of the empty room, a dull circle of light illuminating her figure, her contours blurred as if Maura was looking at her through a layer of mist. She was wearing the same clothes she had on when they'd last seen each other: light blue trousers with her favorite white blouse. Around her neck hung the green pearl pendant Maura had given her for her seventeenth birthday.

"This is a dream," Maura said. It seemed important to state.

Sofia smiled. "Yes, it is. But I'm happy you're here."

Tears gathered in Maura's eyes. How strange and painful it was to talk like this as if Sofia were still alive! She didn't know what to do; she wanted to wake up, but the dreamscape wasn't letting her go.

"You're sad." Sofia's image wavered, then solidified again.

Maura hesitated. "Yes. Things are bad."

"What happened?"

She listened to the sounds of the storm outside. A calming drone, like waves crashing against the shore. "We lost the war," she said, taking a shaky breath. "I ruined everything. And now, a lot of people might die."

"It wasn't your fault."

"Yes, it was."

"It wasn't your fault."

Sofia's image blinked out; only the words echoed in the darkened space. There was a wooden figure on the ground in the circle of light where her friend had stood before, abandoned, its limbs contorted into impossible angles.

Maura took a step forward, and the door slammed shut behind, closing her into perfect blackness.

She spun around, searching. A cold hand touched her shoulder, and she cringed, backing towards where the door should have been, but as if the room had expanded to many times its size, the emptiness wrapped around her, suffocating.

Something large was moving in the darkness in front of her.

"It was my fault too."

The voice didn't sound like Sofia's anymore; the pitch was higher, shriller. The wind shrieked outside, and Maura froze in place.

"It was our fault."

Slicing pain in her neck. An immense presence, retreating. Frantic breathing—her own. Then darkness and silence.

"You have to come back."

Maura sat up in the bed. The starry night sky stared back at her through the window.

She didn't want to fall asleep again, and Nasir planned to leave before dawn. So, she wiped the tears off her face, got out of bed, and went to find the others.

The moon lit their vicinity, twisting the contours of buildings, the swaying branches of trees, and the forms of deserted vehicles into alien imitations of themselves. They were walking through a ghost city. Only the bare skeletons of half-destroyed houses loomed above, and only the crunching sound of their shoes on the debris broke the silence.

Before they left the factory, Damian had handed Maura a package containing a black t-shirt, well-worn but still functional gray cargo pants, and a pair of sturdy boots. It had been a relief to switch her heels and ruined ceremonial gown to something comfortable. She'd washed, changed into the new set of clothes, did her best to comb her hair with her fingers, and now she barely felt like herself.

After a brief consideration, she decided she rather liked it this way.

Nasir led the group with four of his comrades flanking him and occasionally scouting ahead. In the middle, Damian and other beefier Net members encircled Maura, and finally, Ruao and Coven watched their backs with several others, closing the procession. They hadn't risked taking a vehicle because their unique energy signatures could have betrayed their position, and they didn't dare to go underground since the subway tunnels might not have survived the airstrikes from Gaerris in the area a few years back. They had to try and reach their destination on foot. There wasn't much activity since the area was considered deserted, but they couldn't ignore the possibility of Gaerrisian patrols popping up.

Maura had been walking quietly for almost an hour. Damian followed a step behind, not initiating conversation either. This continued until she tripped on a piece of rubble while making her way through a vacant parking lot—she lost her balance for a moment and was already standing straight by the time Damian caught her arm to help.

She snatched her hand away. "I'm fine, thank you."

The sentence sounded blunter than she'd intended. Shame flooded her, and she glanced at her bodyguard apologetically. But Damian didn't seem perturbed, pulling back his arm in a deflecting motion. They started walking again, and Maura fixed her stare on Nasir's back, sighing in annoyance.

"Are you alright?" Damian asked.

"I'm good."

"If you want to stop—"

"I don't want to stop."

She wasn't angry at him. She wasn't angry at anyone in particular. Not even General Pahoron, or the Council, or her father. The AI, perhaps. Herself, vaguely. The emotion was mostly directionless, emanating from her like a noxious aura. A fury inside, threatening to break through. The dream about Sofia hadn't helped; she still felt taken aback by the ominousness of it.

"I'm sorry it all ended like this," Damian said. He adjusted his steps to hers, so he didn't have to raise his voice.

She peered at him. "Why are you apologizing? It was never on you."

Damian gave a small shrug. "I can still wish there was more I could have done. To support you. To bring help or to escape earlier. Somewhere safe but close, so that... I don't know."

"There's a lot I wish for, too," she replied. Tension fluttered in her chest. "I keep thinking I could go back, say some magic words to General Pahoron or to the Council that would make everything okay. That, if I tried one last time, I could work with the AI. Or if I was better or stronger, I could fight them all off."

Damian stayed silent, and Maura couldn't suppress another exasperated sigh. Burying this inside or talking about it didn't make a difference. She wanted to go back, do something. As long as she was on the planet, her mind kept clinging to the thought.

Hating the tense quiet, she forced herself to continue on a brighter note. "But hey, didn't Nasir say this wasn't the end?"

The concept of bringing help from somewhere at some point in the future was not solid enough to hold onto. But if nothing else, she might will it into existence if she said it out loud. *Because that worked so well before.*

"Nasir says a lot of things. Always full of plans and ideas." Damian glanced ahead at the man leading the group with something like admiration in his eyes. "He's right, though. We do have a chance."

But was it a good chance? Nasir thought the only way Maura could return was by involving herself and her planet in things much larger scale than she'd ever dreamed of. She had no idea if it would be worth it.

"No matter what happens, you won't be alone," Damian said.

Maura nodded gratefully. Damian always had a special talent for making her feel better, even in these messed-up times. It often wasn't even what he said, simply his presence.

They kept walking through the night. Ruined high-rises and warehouses disappeared behind them like mute gray giants keeping watch over the desolate landscape. The road was in decent shape, only broken up in a few places, letting weeds grow in the cracks.

"Where are we going, exactly?" Maura spoke up again after a while. The tension in her body urged her to talk, to fill the silence. This time, Coven was the one who spared her with an answer, speeding up to walk beside her.

"There's an old private spaceport nearby. That's where our rendezvous is."

"And how does this work? What's our destination?"

Coven shrugged. "One of our bases, probably. Don't care much. I haven't been out there in a long while."

That was an interesting attitude, not caring where you ended up. She couldn't imagine thinking this way. "And where are you going after?"

"Wherever I'm needed." He grinned at her.

"No strings attached?"

Coven huffed, but the smile didn't leave his face. "Nah. I don't do that anymore. Not like some other people we both know."

He rolled his eyes toward Nasir, who was still marching obliviously. Although, the way his shoulders shook as if he were chuckling to himself indicated he might not have been that unaware of the conversation behind him.

"You still stayed when he asked," Maura said.

Coven winked. "Well. Can't do without *some* of those strings. Because then what else is left?"

Fair enough. Still, what a foreign way to live. Rootless, going wherever the wind blows. For a good cause, sure, but considering she was about to leave her home, thinking about that only made her more nervous. What would she be, who would she become, outside Miyoza?

Another hour passed, and they stopped to rest, drink some water, hunt for stray broadcasts (mostly catching inane conversations between Gaerrisian units in the area) and sit in the glow of the rising sun. Then they kept following the road. As they got closer to the spaceport, the area became more open; amongst the scattered piles of debris, they were better targets than ever.

Ruao heard it first. She stopped, shielding her eyes in the morning light.

The sound of engines. Three small dots, lifting above the skyline behind them.

"Patrols!" Nasir exclaimed. "Let's go! After me!"

They dashed forward, but by the time they reached cover, the shuttles were too close. Maura tried to keep up with the group while the Gaerrisian ships—arrow-like, sleek silver vessels known for their speed and deftness—zoomed ahead above them. Pale dust stirred from the ground in small tornadoes created by their turbines, making her eyes sting, and she almost tripped over her own foot. Someone pulled her to the side, and she found herself crouched at the foot of a collapsed wall beside Coven and Damian. The rest of the Net fighters scattered, but not far off, Nasir's head popped up from behind a low fence.

"They must be hunting for stragglers," Coven murmured. "We gotta get underground."

The shuttles turned around sharply, the rumble of their engines filling the air.

"That way!" Damian called out, pointing toward the south. On the opposite side, one of the ships started descending. An armed figure leaned out, scope on their head, lifting a weapon on their shoulder, and Maura pulled back, terrified.

Damian drew a gun and pressed it into her palm. He nodded to her, and she squeezed his hand, not trusting her voice.

They darted out from their hideout with other friendlies in tow. Blasts rained on them as they passed the next row of tall houses, moving from cover to cover. Glancing back through the dust and the chaos, Maura saw that all three shuttles had landed. Armored soldiers were leaping out of them to give chase.

Her lungs were burning, and her vision blurred. They caught up with Nasir and Ruao, but then a dull sound rang out beside her, and one of them fell to the ground. A scream. Another shot. Searing pain whipped through her left shoulder, and Maura cried out, sinking to her knees.

One moment she was holding onto Damian's arm, and the next, he was gone.

Blood trickled down her skin, and the ache rippled through her flesh. Someone fired a long series of blasts towards the Gaerrisians beside her, but she didn't have the power to turn and see who it was.

She had to get back up.

Holding her arm, she stumbled forward, the entrance of the subway station swaying in front of her in the distance. Her shoulder muscles hurt horribly but were functional—the Gaerrisians weren't using energy blasts, attempting to wound rather than kill. She must have only been scraped, but the pain slowed her down, and she thought each second would be the one their attackers caught up with her. The shouts and the shots sounded so close, but she didn't see anything through her daze. Where were those stairs? She should have already reached them...

Her knees almost buckled again on the first steps down the stairs, but she hurried onward. The darkness swallowed her, but after a few seconds, spotlight beams flashed from behind her and cut through the dim. She heard shouts and rapid commands. She stammered towards the opposite wall in the debris-filled corridor, feeling her way forward and turning into a narrow foyer to the right that led to a row of out-of-order escalators.

Her pursuers had fallen behind in the spacious underpass or perhaps separated into groups to search the station. Maura stared down into the deep beyond the escalators. She had a better chance to hide in the tunnels, but she could also be surrounded more easily.

Where had the others gone? Maybe she'd come down the wrong stairs. Maybe they'd been captured already.

She clutched the gun in her good hand, keeping the other one steady, and started down on the escalator. Her wound sent waves of pain through her arm, and it felt like hours to reach the bottom. The sharp sounds of trampling steps echoed behind her: the Gaerrisian soldiers had also begun to descend. She didn't have time to think. She ran to the edge of the platform and jumped onto the grav rails.

Her sense of direction had abandoned her; she had no idea which way the spaceport was. She chose the path to the left at random and ran.

"Over here! They're going towards the port!" someone shouted in the crackling language of the Gaerrisians. "After me!"

Boots creaked on the ground. They were with her in the tunnel.

The passage must have curved to the side because after a few minutes, short of breath and shaking from exertion, she collided with the wall. She whimpered in pain as the coarse rocky material rubbed onto her wounded shoulder, pushed herself away, and kept running.

"Maura?"

The voice came further ahead. She reached out, blind in the darkness, towards an even blacker shadow.

"Damian?" she whispered as her fumbling hands found her friend's.

"I thought I'd lost you," he panted. "Come on!"

Maura grasped his arm, and they raced forward. Her limbs felt like liquid, but the soldiers' flashlights kept grazing them, still behind. No more shots were fired.

Then the darkness shifted—a faint light source. The next station.

Something heavy whacked her from behind. She dropped her gun, her fingers slipped out of Damian's hand, and she fell on her stomach. Someone pushed their knees into her back and twisted her arms around, and she screamed in pain.

"I got one! Here!" The barrel of a weapon pressed between her shoulder blades, and the soldier shoved a light in her face. "Damn. It's the queen..."

Then just as unexpectedly as the man had seized her, his body was flung off Maura, and even she sensed the incredible power behind the strike. Her hands freed, she climbed to her knees, the sounds of a struggle close-by permeating her panicked stupor.

"Maura, go!"

More soldiers appeared at a distance, and in their swaying flashlight beams, she finally saw her bodyguard wrestling with two other men. Her gun was in the dirt beside another unconscious, bloodied figure. She lunged for it, lifting her arm to take a shot, but her finger froze on the trigger. She might hit Damian.

But he didn't need the help, she realized, watching him send the two soldiers to the ground with a couple of powerful blows. He stood, gesturing for her to move, and they started running again. Maura released a few blind shots behind them, not necessarily wanting to hit anyone, only trying to slow their pursuers.

She emerged from the tunnel to find Nasir waiting for them on the platform. He reached down to haul her up. "Where's Damian?"

Maura spun around in terror. "He was right beside me..."

"We have to go!" Coven yelled from the foot of the escalators. "They'll be here any minute now."

"We need to go back for him!" She looked at Nasir, and her friend only hesitated for a second.

"Stay with the others," he ordered, and then he was gone, swallowed by the darkness of the tunnel.

Maura took an uncertain step towards the edge, but Coven was beside her, grabbing her arm. "We need to get out before they close the exits. Through Hangar F to the runways. We will—"

"We have to wait for them!" She tried to maneuver out of his grip, but he held her tightly, shaking his head.

"No way. If they fence us in, it's over."

"I'm not going anywhere without Damian!"

"If anyone can get him back, it's Nasir! They'll find us."

Maura took a breath, preparing to pour all her furious arguments on him, but her voice was drowned out by a thundering rumble. Coven's eyes widened. He yanked Maura closer, turned both their backs towards the tunnel, and shoved her on the ground, shielding her with his own body.

The station shook, and the mouth of the tunnel burst into flames. Waves of scorching heat rushed over them, and when it all stopped, Maura knew that not a single soul was left alive in the tunnel.

CHAPTER 11 | RELUCTANT RECALL

Jeane sat up in the bed with a jolt, clutching her side and gasping for air. There was a knock on her cabin door.

"Are you okay?" Kliks asked from outside.

Was she? She'd had one of those dreams again... *Oh, shit.*

Kliks shuffled around, then knocked again. Jeane imagined the nervous expression decorating his face. "Hello?" he called out.

"I'm good." Jeane grimaced but kept her voice steady. "What's up?"

"Can I come in?"

"No."

After a short pause, the door slowly opened. Kliks peered in but remained standing on the threshold. Jeane pushed herself to the edge of the bed, planting her feet on the deck, and glared at him. "Stars, why are you even asking?"

"I heard you scream."

She sighed. Her wound ached, and she absentmindedly rubbed at the gauze. Kliks entered the tiny cabin, which held not much more than her messy bed and a few crates, and sat down beside her.

"No, no, no. We're not doing this." Jeane rose, determined to walk out, but from the corner of her eye, she glimpsed Kliks holding something out toward her. A mug of coffee on a small tray. And cookies.

She exhaled, squinting at him with an irritated frown, but sat back down and accepted the cup. The warmth felt nice on her skin.

"This hasn't happened in a long time," Kliks noted.

Jeane huffed, taking a sip. "It's the damn Cities. Meeting with Gertie and all."

Uttering her friend's name brought back some odious memories from the previous day, so instead of following that thread of thought, she reached for a cookie, trying not to seem too sheepish while doing so. She took a bite—a bit dry but savory. Probably from an old stash. Ranch coffee and these chocolate cookies from Duplex were the only extravagances they allowed on the ship.

Kliks and his care-cookies. This was not the first time he'd utilized them. The night after he'd arrived on the *Skylark*, the same frantic knocking and worried questioning had woken her up. She'd known she had the dreams, of course, but the screaming had been new information.

All that stopped after a while, thank skies. So embarrassing.

"Don't worry," she went on. "I'm fine. It's just these old memories. From before he died."

No need to say the name. That ghost was always there.

Kliks nodded with a somber expression. He knew about Hollis, naturally. It would have been difficult to live in such close quarters, staring into each other's face day after day, and not mention him. Because once upon a time, there had been a lanehunter called Hollis Clementine, and he'd been Jeane's father, for all intents and purposes, for a while. Then he'd had an unfortunate encounter with a swarm of nailships that chased him into a lane where he'd been left stranded outside his destroyed ship for hours, only wearing a faulty spacesuit. His friends managed to save him, but not before his body absorbed a huge amount of radiation. During the next few years, the sickness consumed him, organ by failing organ.

"I didn't stay for his funeral," Jeane said. The words were out before she knew it, and Kliks stared at her, surprised. Half a cookie was peeking out from between his teeth. "They told me he was dead, I cried for a day, and then I took the *Skylark* and left. Didn't even look back. Weird, right?"

She stuffed an entire cookie in her mouth, stopping the words pouring out of her. What was she blabbering about this for?

"But why?" Kliks asked.

"I thought that's what he would have wanted."

«*Might have been,*» said the voice in the back of her mind. «*I was a chaotic bastard. It's absolutely possible.*»

She smiled and took another gulp of coffee. She'd never spoken to Kliks about the voice. But he'd noticed; he'd had a thousand chances to.

Yes, sometimes she spoke to Hollis in her head. This was probably a little weird, and her imagination of what her foster father would say in the various unfortunate situations she put herself into was scarily lifelike sometimes, but it helped. A bit. Most of the time.

"I named the ship. Did you know that?" she asked.

"Really?"

"It wasn't more than a mess of parts and hastily calibrated systems, but he took me out to fly it. Skies, Security was so angry with him!" The memory came back to her as clear as ever. Her at the helm, Hollis sitting in the co-pilot seat, tapping buttons, a crazy gleam in his eyes. She'd been fourteen. Hollis couldn't walk anymore by then. "He said, 'It's yours, kid. It's already yours. What do you want to call it?'"

They'd taken two whole orbits around the asteroid of the Ranch before the Security ships caught up with them. They'd brought them down, and Hollis paid the fines—from what pocket, she didn't know. But he said it was worth it. The first and last time they'd gone flying together.

"One day, I had him read out some old story that the tutors gave me in the Den. The orphanage. He was really good at enacting tales. In this one, there was a girl who turned into a lark to escape some bandits. I thought that was kinda cool. And Hollis loved the name."

"It's a good one," Kliks agreed. Jeane didn't look him in the eye, afraid of finding pity there. She was very conscious of how the Talalan was gently coaxing these details out of her and of how ready she was to respond. Not something that usually happened. "That's what you dreamed about just now?"

"Among other things."

They weren't nightmares. She never once had a bad dream about Hollis. The problem was that moment between oblivion and consciousness. The realization that she didn't have him anymore. That in the real world, she was alone again. That was what made her scramble out of bed, screaming.

Another sip of coffee. A bite of the cookie. She had to move. Sadly, she doubted they'd arrived at Miyoza, but maybe there was something to do for the new engine. She should really check whether Dikent had hidden some tracker inside or—

"You need to sleep some more," Kliks said. "We all have to be in our right mind."

His face was pensive but otherwise gentle. No pity.

What the hells? Jeane shoved her mug into his hands and climbed back in the bed.

"When I wake up next time," she said while Kliks walked to the door, "we don't talk about this."

Her friend paused. "Sure, Captain."

Then he disappeared, drawing the door closed behind him. Jeane shut her eyes tightly, trying to not think of anything at all. From deep within the buried memories, she could just hear Hollis' sonorous voice, reciting the story of the girl who turned into a lark and flew far, far away.

Sleep took her faster than she'd expected.

The next time she woke, it was easier. No lingering memory of dreams and barely any pain. She still released a series of frustrated hisses when she changed the gauze and applied more medigel; the burn looked raw, but it was clean. She put on a new shirt and her boots, then strutted out into the common room.

Her hands were shaking while she made coffee, but she blamed it on the shock of getting shot. She swallowed two painkillers along with the black liquid, and by the time she was done, ALU appeared at the door, sauntering in from the direction of the control room.

"Is everything alright?" she asked them.

ALU chirped, satisfied. "Engine and instruments okay. Two hours to the Sec-12."

"Kliks?"

"In hold. Cursing badly."

Jeane plunked her mug down on the counter. "I'll deal with him."

Kliks sat on the deck near the door of the cargo hold with the manipulator, parts and tools scattered around him in a picturesque mess. A cable snaked out of the machine, through the door beside Jeane, disappearing on the corridor toward the engine room, and her friend was staring the Talalan device down with a severe expression like it was an especially hard-headed discussion partner.

Jeane marched in, furrowing her eyebrows. The bastard had taken the machine out of her cabin while she was conked out! Those care cookies had been nothing but decoys. Desserts of deception.

"Before you start yelling at me, I'm only taking three percent off the generator output," Kliks said. "I didn't connect it to anything else."

"Good. Although it does look distinctly 'on' to me. Didn't I tell you not to turn it on?"

"It's on, but it's not doing anything. Promise," Kliks said and returned his attention to his work. This mainly consisted of him glaring at his tablet, taking rushed notes, and shaking his head in disapproval. The manipulator hummed quietly, and the core pulsated with a faint blue light, but obviously, it wasn't what the Talalan had expected because he soon whacked the thing in the side with an indignant grunt. "I can't believe this!"

"Hey, easy! What you're experiencing now is called frustration. The same thing I feel every time I'm talking to you."

There was an amused trill from beside the door—ALU had arrived and hobbled up to them while Kliks peered up at Jeane. "You're not helping."

"I don't want to." Jeane grinned. "Yet."

"Ugh. I see you're well enough to pester me."

She made a face, pressing a palm at her side. The pain was tolerable but ever-present, intensifying every time she moved too suddenly. "It's nothing. So, did you figure something out?"

Kliks gave a sigh. "First, answer this. Are we really going to Miyoza?"

"Yeah. But if you have a better idea—"

"Better than a frickin' combat zone? I'm pretty sure I do."

Jeane lowered herself on the ground to sit cross-legged beside the device and shook her head. ALU crouched next to her, tinkling two fingers against the manipulator's gleaming white casing.

"Look, we have to assume the Union is still on our tail," Jeane said. "We can't go wherever we want. On Miyoza, we can try to disappear. Hopefully, even if they know where we are, they won't follow us behind those bloody front lines. We'll do the job because we owe Dikent, and then...well, it depends on what you can tell me about this thing."

Kliks hung his head, a weary expression on his face. "Hmm. Only bad news."

An alarming lead-in, but what did I expect? "Start from the beginning. You call it a manipulator. What does it manipulate?"

"That's the question, eh?" Despite everything, a faint smile appeared on the Talalan's face. Nostalgic, almost sentimental. "What do you think it is?"

"An energy source?"

"It's the end of all energy sources, Jeane. It utilizes lane energy."

Jeane's eyes widened. "You bastards. You did it!"

There had been countless attempts throughout the years to get the mysterious energies of the lanes to work for humanity: by the Union, by independent worlds, and by more scientifically inclined lanehunter groups. It was a generally accepted theory that these strange tears in spacetime could provide practically infinite power if only someone figured out how to exploit them. But stumbling through lanes and cracks had so far remained nothing more than a risky transportation method, not producing but requiring a heaping amount of energy. If the Talalans had cracked the mystery, what would that mean for the rest of the universe?

«It would mean control. It would mean a source of immeasurable

firepower, amongst other things. No wonder the Union has an itch for it.»

Hollis sounded unusually serious in her mind, and Jeane shuddered.

"This has always been our first priority research program. I mean, theirs when I still..." Kliks faltered, the sentence trailing off, but he quickly recovered. "Since the lanes appeared, Talalans have been convinced that they could reach into some hidden energy reserves of the multiverse, and—Don't worry, I'm not going to start this lecture," he cut himself off, seeing Jeane raise her eyebrows skeptically. "What's important is that this thing shouldn't exist. It's working, but it's not working well."

"What do you mean?"

Kliks rubbed a hand down his face. "I remember the kind of issues they were struggling with when I left. I don't think they solved them. The design is different from what I remember, but this is, at best, an unfinished, faulty prototype."

ALU pulled back the fingers they'd kept on the device. "What issues?" they asked.

"The 'don't use it, or you could wipe out entire civilizations' type."

"Oh, great." Jeane sighed, and ALU gave a high-pitched, nervous buzz.

Kliks fell silent, and the three of them stared at each other for a while.

"So, what do we do?" Jeane asked. "Take it apart? Throw the pieces out the airlock?"

"No!"

"But why not?"

Kliks' face was so grave that Jeane got the urge to stand up and leave. She didn't want to hear what came next. "You're forgetting I was the one who found it," he said.

"I didn't want to rub it in, but I can shout at you for a bit if it makes you feel better."

Her friend rolled his eyes. "Thanks, but that's not what I meant. You were right when you said I had to know what I was going to find on that planet. Sort of right." He gave a deep sigh.

"Talalans can do...things. To each other's minds."

Jeane stared at him. "What?"

"It took me some time to accept because we don't do this anymore, not if there's another solution. It's somewhat of a taboo. You might call it telepathy, although thought-binding is more complicated. Point being, I might have been influenced in my decision to go to the Altex outpost. Might still be influenced."

"You can't tell?" Jeane asked, struggling to understand. The idea that Kliks was not Kliks, or not entirely...a part of her wanted to jump up and get a gun directed at him, while another part of her was appalled by that reaction. At least Kliks was conscious of the effect; that had to mean something.

"Not necessarily. It's very subtle. We can't just make each other do or say anything we want." Kliks swallowed, uneasy. "However, I can definitely sense a resistance every time I think about discarding the manipulator."

"What they want from you?" ALU asked. Their voice was gentle. "Other Talalans?"

"I'm not sure. I have a suspicion about who they are since only someone who knows me could reach me like this. And you know...from the three dead bodies I found on that ship at the outpost."

Jeane scrunched her nose. The Talalan's face was placid enough, but how sensitive was this topic to him? "Someone you know?"

"Superficially." Kliks gave a weak cough. *Very sensitive. Shit.* "Two colleagues. We were working on lane science together back in the day. The third person was unfamiliar. There were signs of a scuffle. They killed each other."

Talalans killing Talalans for the power of the manipulator? No. One of them, or some mysterious fourth one, had to be a Union mole. Jerkface had arrived at the crime scene too fast. He had to have some intel.

Kliks had been faster, though. *What an unlucky fucking accident. It might have been only a question of a few hours. Or minutes.*

Her friend cleared his throat again. "I think they want me to keep the manipulator safe. I think it was stolen from Talala, and this put them in a difficult situation, and now they don't know what to do."

Jeane scowled. She'd put that much together.

"I wish I knew what happened exactly. Who betrayed who and how they knew where to send me." Kliks shook his head. "Nothing makes sense, but here it is. That's all I know. It's not like they sent me a proper message. It's mostly just feelings."

Jeane wanted to ask Kliks why he couldn't demand those answers the same way, using their telepathy, but she had a feeling her request would have been swiftly denied. *Taboos are taboos.* "Well, we can hardly keep it safe if the Union has a way of following us," she said in the end. "They will always be after it."

"I haven't found anything that looks like a bug," Kliks mused. "But your warning made me think. They might be tracking the remnant particles that form while it's operating inside lanes. That would mean they can't locate us if we don't use it in the lanes, but I'm not a hundred percent sure."

"But then we *did* lead the inspectors to the Cities," Jeane said. Kliks opened his mouth, but no sound came from his throat. He hung his head again with a forlorn expression. ALU shuffled over and patted him on the arm.

«*You're in the middle of it now, kid,*» Hollis muttered in Jeane's mind. «*Much deeper than you know.*»

Jeane grunted in agreement. *What a mess.* But they couldn't keep lamenting forever. They had to make a decision.

"I say the goal is still Miyoza." She rose before the weight of these uncertainties buried her resolve. Her burn wound reacted accordingly, but she ignored it as best she could.

"Are you sure?" Kliks looked up at her, pleading.

«*No, what you're doing is called stalling.*»

She put her hands on her waist in a commanding manner, hoping that her voice was self-assured enough, and stared her crew down.

"According to Dikent's info, the war is winding down over there, but no one knows it yet. We keep this damn thing turned off and hide it, and by the time we get back, the bastards might lose our track. And who knows? Dikent's merch might even be worth it."

«Do you believe the bullshit you're spouting?»

ALU jumped on their legs with renewed fervor, trilling enthusiastically, skies bless their innocence. But Kliks still looked uncertain.

So, Jeane went on. "We get back to Dikent and squeeze him for some danger bonus. He could even help us to get off the map for a while."

«Supposing the Cities are still standing and you're all still alive by that point.»

"And then..."

"And then?" Kliks asked.

«Then...»

She glared at the Talalan and spread her arms in annoyance. "I don't fucking know! We go to Talala and yell at them through that high fence of theirs. 'Hey, neighbor, your toy ended up in our yard, and now it threatens to destroy our civilization! Wanna take it back?'" The joke fell flat, but she didn't care. This was way more than she'd ever bargained for. *Mind-reading Talalans and deadly multiverses? Thanks, but no.* "Skies, Kliks. If you expect clever answers, you signed up for the wrong ship. You should know by now that I have no idea what I'm doing."

She spun around, indignant, ready to storm out, gesturing the cheerfully tooting ALU to follow her. But she could have sworn she saw the beginnings of a faint smile on Kliks' face before she looked away.

They crossed the Secarius-12 lane, approaching the entry point into Miyoza in a solar system so densely broken up by thousands of cracks and lanes that they lost a significant amount of time maneuvering the *Skylark* around in the small volume of normal space. The choice had been conscious on Jeane's part; they might arrive a bit late to the rendezvous, but they would give a hard time to anyone who was following them.

They settled onto the vector to Miyoza's lane, identified as Tirsao-11, forty minutes before their planned meeting. The

Skylark cut through the fog with ease as if it hadn't been lying half-dead with an open belly in a hangar just a day earlier. Nervous energy spread through Jeane as she watched their trajectory on the vector, but this time, she welcomed the sensation. After the unsettling events of the last few days, they were finally doing something she knew. For those short seconds when she managed to forget about the manipulator and her ridiculous dreams, she was almost enjoying herself.

Kliks bent over the computer screen beside her, studying the graphs that showed their potential exit points. "We could go to Corsetti. Just a small jump from here. Quiet world."

"We would stick out like a sore thumb."

"They have good fish."

"You hate fish." Jeane punched in a few numbers and turned on their long-range comms. "Are you ready? I'm starting the signal."

"Ready."

The fog darkened in front of them, and gravity turned upside down, but by the time Jeane's stomach started complaining, it was over. Stars twinkled all around, with the blue streak of the lane and Miyoza's giant red sun looming over everything. The surrounding space was empty, but several ships popped up on their radar farther ahead.

Kliks breathed in and out, strained. Now everything depended on Dikent's intel.

Apparently, the decades-long war in the system had recently ended with the fall of Miyoza. This inspired Dikent to have the *Skylark* disguised as a Gaerrisian cargo ship—he'd given them a proper ID and mission data and said that as long as they were not inspected visually or scanned in detail, they would have a high chance to slip by unbothered. The Tir-11 lane had been under Gaerrisian control for years, and they did send ships to other systems occasionally, which made their cover plausible.

Jeane didn't know much about the Miyozan war and was never interested enough to learn. All she remembered was that Miyoza was full of haughty scientists and snobs that thought they were better than the rest of humanity because they'd been the first to leave Old Earth. Supposedly. As far as Jeane was concerned, she'd kept the *Skylark* far away from the system.

"There's not much activity," Kliks noted while Jeane weaved a confident but careful path between the Gaerrisian patrol ships close to the Tir-11 as if the *Skylark's* presence was the most natural thing in these parts. He scrutinized the schematic map of the system on the front screen and pointed at the sparse asteroid belt between the two inhabited worlds, Miyoza and Gaerris. "The front lines should be right here. I can't believe it's all gone."

"How do you know where the front lines were?"

Kliks shrugged. "I paid attention. If there was a world Talala would have opened toward, it would have been Miyoza. Their inventions are amazing! We kept waiting for this war to end, but it never happened."

Jeane adjusted their trajectory, trying not to feel relieved yet. The fewer ships around them, the better. They might do this without hiccups.

As they got closer, the view of the blue and brown planet streaked with fluffy white clouds filled their screens, no traces of the bloody war from this distance. Miyoza only had a single, north-south oriented continent, and as they approached the capital among a crowd of transport and military spaceships, the landmass rolled out under them like an abstract painting. Mountains, rivers, forests, and in the distance, a white-gray splotch—Miyoza City.

And then they got hailed for the first time.

"Don't answer. Automatic checkpoint," Jeane said. "We'll be out of their range by the time they realize. ALU, jammers on."

She increased their speed, taking a broad, spiraling route forward, while her technician activated the jammer system, which was able to hide the ship from most long-range radar systems. They only used it in emergencies; it ate up a lot of energy and was useless once they'd been targeted.

The call didn't repeat, and the traffic increased further, which was dangerous but also helped to hide them. As long as their fake ID was on, they were solid.

Jeane had sweated through her shirt five times by that point, but she flashed a victorious smile at Kliks. "I think they lost us.

We're ghosts, my friends!"

"Let's hope we can do the same thing on the way out," Kliks replied, his expression tight. "I assume it will be harder."

"Killjoy," Jeane muttered and decreased their altitude again.

They were now speeding towards the capital parallel to the ground above a vast grassland. Deserted towns, half-collapsed ports, and ruined factory complexes zoomed past with craters spotting the fields in between, preserving the memories of the most destructive bombardments. Their goal was only a few miles off when the generator started to overheat, so they had to drop their jammers.

Dikent's coordinates took them to a spaceport south of the capital. The building was still intact: a spacious, white central hall with arched wings extending parallel on both sides. Jeane steered the *Skylark* above the runway her ex had pointed out in his documents. The area looked abandoned, and the roads were empty. Farther away, half-collapsed high-rises climbed towards the wispy clouds, and close to the horizon, the skyline became even more crowded.

They landed easily, and Jeane stood from the pilot chair with an apprehensive sigh. "Right. Let's see how this goes."

She clambered out of the airlock hatch behind ALU, and as soon as her feet touched the concrete, she pulled out her gun, alert. Kliks stepped down behind her, surveying their vicinity. Nothing moved around them except a slight breeze, and the air felt warm on Jeane's skin.

She glanced at her tablet. Half-past six, local time. They were early.

Only a few seconds had passed when a couple of dull bursts resounded from somewhere close. Jeane tensed immediately. It was the sound of weapons firing.

ALU lurched forward, darting towards the closest entrance to the port building half-hidden behind a row of white columns.

"Hey! What are you doing?" Jeane yelled after them.

"Danger!" The technician paused. "Life in danger!"

Kliks took a step backward. "What are you talking about?"

Jeane looked around nervously. It was one thing to sneak into hostile territory—they'd done that before. But getting into close combat in a situation where they had no idea which side was which? As far as they knew, Dikent's contact may have just died in that shooting.

"Let's get back into the ship," she said, addressing ALU.

But the technician took another step forward. "No!" they shrieked like they were experiencing physical pain. Jeane had never seen them act like this.

"ALU, stop!" she repeated. "It's too dangerous."

"We can't let it die!" ALU's voice was small but determined. "Life dies! Can't let it!"

Jeane was only a few long strides behind them. She had no clue what her technician was referring to, but she would drag them back by their insolent little head to the *Skylark* if she had to.

Then she heard the footsteps. Spinning around, she called out to the shadows between the columns. "Who goes there?"

«Back to the ship! Now!»

But ALU was standing fifty yards from her, frozen on the open runway, the easiest target ever. Hard outer casing or not, the hostiles could come at them with grenade launchers, or worse.

Nothing moved for a second, and she started to think she'd heard wrong. Then the shadows beside the building flinched, and a short, slim figure stumbled out of the cover.

She was alone, wearing a vaguely military-inspired outfit, her left arm streaked with bright red blood, and tears were streaming down her grimy face.

She lifted the gun and pointed it at Jeane.

CHAPTER 12 | CONFLUENCE

"One might think that when the universe falls to pieces, chaos is inevitable: anarchy, barbarism, and madness would thrive, followed by the destruction of everything meaningful that sentience ever built. And although we know that this has been happening in certain places, something else entirely unexpected transpired as well. The surviving inhabitants of said universe adapted to the situation in a surprisingly swift manner.

Humanity, for example, has come out of the ordeal luckier than most. They are one of the few species left that can tell tales about the birth of a lane and how it can almost destroy a civilization. However, the far descendants of these survivors decided to bury that part of their history. Each of their factions seems to carry an underlying relief to be able to leave those times behind.

No one is sure how and in what circumstances humans departed their birth planet, but the guesses I've heard include overpopulation, pollution, the devastating effects of global warming, and the rampant application of genetic modifications. Nevertheless, their eagerness to start anew is telling.

Then again, most space-faring races do not have a good answer for the when and the how when it comes to lanes. Even Talala forgets; only the scars live on, hidden behind walls and walls and walls.

[...] Our best estimates put the appearance of lanes between twelve and thirteen-hundred Talalan years ago, and most researchers

agree it took hundreds of years for the phenomenon to start in earnest then slowly halt. Instantaneous, really, in the timescale the cosmos operates on. But apart from fragmented data about these beginnings, the highly empirical throng of information describing how to sail the lanes, and the statistical rule of them appearing close to high-mass celestial objects (explaining all those dead systems we find all over the galaxy), not much else is clear. What is happening in the farthest reaches of the universe where it is difficult to travel and from which we only receive ambiguous astronomical observations? What caused the occurrence of the lanes, and how can we be sure this was the end of it? [...]

We live in the aftermath of a complex, large-scale tragedy we do not understand—but we survive, each of us the best way that we can.

Lanes turned from a terrifying and enigmatic phenomenon disrupting everything we've ever known into a terrifying, enigmatic, but familiar part of our lives. Beyond these tears in spacetime, cold and dead worlds await the traveler, scattered with the remains of extinct cultures. Dark stars with lanes extending from horizon to horizon, cracks that connect the surfaces of two planets seamlessly, and alien suns giving their sustaining light to never-before-seen species welcoming the brave wanderer as friends or opposing them as enemies. Galaxies where countless stars and planets are being destroyed to this day by powerful shock fronts in the interstellar matter because their central black holes have been disturbed. Millions and millions of supernova-remnants lighting up distant, hostile parts of the universe where even the most fearless lanehunters do not dare to visit. Thousands and thousands of deadly tunnels like an intricate web of ruptured seams.

We can only hope to never see our world shatter along those lines.

-Notes about the lanes and humanity (excerpt), Kliks Pleu

Another round of gunshots went off in the distance. The Miyozan woman flinched and turned around. Jeane used her distraction to take a step forward, preparing to grab her, but the stranger spun back. Her gun was still pointed at Jeane's chest, the fear on her face melting into desperation.

"You have to help me," she said, speaking Common with a melodic, drawling accent. Her voice was much deeper than Jeane had expected and unsteady from crying. "My friends...my companions...we have to go back for them!"

"Help!" ALU agreed with an enthusiastic whistle. They shambled over to the young woman, looking back at Jeane expectantly.

"No way. We have nothing to do with this," Jeane said, frowning at both of them.

The Miyozan's eyes widened. "But you're our ride, no?"

«*Uh, what?*»

"We're no one's ride."

The woman shook her head in denial, and Jeane blew the air out of her lungs. This was all wrong. Whoever was chasing this chick could arrive at any moment.

"Our contact is someone named Nasir Dareth," Kliks spoke up.

The Miyozan nodded, her light brown locks bouncing around her face. *Expensive hairdo for a fugitive.* "Yes! I was with him. You're our transport out of here!"

"We're no one's ride," Jeane repeated. "We're here to take some merch off Nasir's hand, not to ship out refugees." She nodded to Kliks, disregarding the barrel aimed at her. "Let's go!"

Kliks glanced at ALU, shifting from foot to foot. "But—"

Before Jeane could have retorted, the Miyozan clutched her gun tighter and moved the barrel from her to Kliks. He froze, but Jeane only gave a mocking grimace. "Come on, you can put that down. We both know you're not going to shoot."

The woman clenched her jaw, her lips thinning to pale lines. Her hands started to shake as she tried to keep up the bluff, but then as if all power left her at once, she dropped her arms. The way she looked to Jeane, this must have been the first time she ever threatened someone with a weapon.

"I have to go back for them," she said, her voice trembling. "Please, they are in danger! I can't do this alone."

The double doors of the spaceport burst open, and two armed figures bolted out into the sunlight. One of them shouted something in a different tongue, but Jeane had already raised her weapon, set to stun, and the man fell like a plank without support. The other one shot at the Miyozan, the projectile whizzing past inches from her left ear as she staggered to the side. Kliks fired his gun, and the second figure collapsed too, stunned.

The stranger, seemingly giving up on convincing them, took off sprinting along the building, and ALU followed without hesitation. Jeane released a series of fancy curses but ran after them, and as she moved through the runway, she heard Kliks' footsteps trailing her.

They crouched at the corner of the building in the shadow. Jeane glanced back but saw no more soldiers for now. Kliks' eyes were wide with panic, but she wasn't feeling much better either. Her burn wound stretched painfully under the bandage.

"What in hells do you think you're doing?" She seized ALU's arm, and the technician stared up at her in surprise.

"ALU helps," they said, their voice almost angry as they yanked their arm back. They rooted themself beside the Miyozan, all four arms on the ground, unmoving.

The woman who had been leaning out from the cover of the wall, surveying the other side, glanced back at them. She was still holding her gun with both hands, but at least she wasn't aiming at them anymore.

Shit. Shit, shit, shit.

«Heads up: this is only gonna get more complicated.»

"Okay." Jeane breathed out, swallowing her dread. She turned to the Miyozan. "Who are you, who is chasing you, why, and where is this Nasir?"

"He…stayed behind. He's our leader," she replied. "We escaped the capital before it fell."

"So it's true?" Kliks asked, shaken out of his daze. "Miyoza has really fallen?"

"Yes."

"What happened to Nasir?" Jeane pushed further.

The woman pursed her lips. "He was in the subway tunnel. There was an explosion, but they survived, I know it!"

Jeane's mouth dropped open. "And what do you expect us to do? Dig them out?"

"No, but Coven said it was Nasir who detonated the bomb, and he must have known a way out. They just needed to lose the soldiers. They're here somewhere, and I need to find them!"

"Where is this Coven?"

The woman blinked as if the answer surprised her too. "He died."

Jeane sighed. "Of course."

"Wait a minute." Kliks held up his hand. "Nasir told you to meet us here?"

"He said he arranged transport with his contacts at the Net."

Kliks stared at Jeane with a stunned expression, but she had no idea how to react. The thought that Dikent had anything to do with the organization seemed so ridiculous that for a moment, she almost laughed.

But she didn't. Because this only meant that Dikent had managed to mess things up for her. Again.

«Told you so. But you're thinking too much. If you're doing this, do it. If not, skedaddle!»

"How many are after you?" she asked the Miyozan.

"I don't know," she said. Hope glinted in her eyes. "There were three shuttles, and some of the soldiers got stuck in the tunnel. I think they only found us accidentally, so reinforcements might still be on the way."

Jeane exhaled forcefully. "Right. Listen to me..."

"...Sofia."

"Listen to me, Sofia. You only need to remember three things. One: you do what I tell you to do. Two: we're not getting ourselves killed. And three: I'm not your chauffeur. The moment we find Nasir, alive or dead, we say our tearful goodbyes and go our separate ways. Am I making myself clear?"

The Miyozan didn't react, but when the silence became too long, ALU directed an angry whistle at Jeane.

"These are the conditions," Jeane cut them off. "Take it, or we leave!"

Sofia gave a nod but didn't look satisfied with the situation. But Jeane was done; she broke eye contact, circled her, and peered out beside the port building.

An empty parking lot surrounded by the remains of high-rises, broken concrete on deserted roads, and an overpass in the distance. Farther away, the remains of elegant arches gleamed white in the sunshine. Still no movement.

Kliks leaned in and whispered in her ear, "What the hells are we doing? We just shot two Gaerrisian soldiers!"

"They came at us first. And we just stunned them."

"Still! Do we really want to be in the middle of this war?"

"The war is over, isn't it? And we're only getting this Nasir if we can. Dikent didn't send us here for a couple of fugitives. It's not his style. Nasir will have the merch."

"That's it? We're going into an active shoot-out for *merch*?"

Jeane threw her arms up in frustration. "Can you guarantee ALU won't freak out if we drag them out of here? I don't know what got into them, but—"

"We're not leaving them here alone," Kliks finished her sentence, then he sighed. "We're out of our frickin' minds. You know that, right?"

"We're already here—might as well try. Think about the danger bonus!" And with that, she turned back to Sofia. "Where are we going?"

They ran from one cover to the next, crossing the parking lot and following a concrete wall beside one of the high-rises. Sofia moved to the front to show them the way, but she looked like she could collapse any minute. ALU kept quiet, and Kliks focused his attention on his gun as if he expected it to jump out of his hands like a scared kitten.

They glimpsed one of the shuttles not far from the subway underpass, its chrome body glinting in the sun. Seemingly empty.

"Maybe they're all in the port," Jeane muttered. "Or down there."

"ALU recon!" the technician buzzed, and they stared at Jeane, emphasizing that this time, they were waiting for the green light. She gave a grimace but nodded, and ALU wobbled out of cover towards the stairs. Kliks gazed after them, lost in thought, but didn't make a comment.

"So," Sofia started. "Who are you guys?"

Jeane only grunted at that, so Kliks performed the introductions. The woman frowned, confused. "You're lanehunters? And you didn't know you were coming here for us?"

"Nope," Jeane said.

"I don't understand. Nasir—" She didn't continue because

ALU appeared again, waving at them from the top of the stairs.

They jogged down into the station, single-file, careful not to make too much noise. Dust and darkness greeted them at the bottom. Jeane left ALU aboveground as a lookout, and the other two stayed close at her heels as they stealthed through a hall, using each pillar as a cover. When no one spooked them from the shadows, Kliks switched on his flashlight, and they scanned the gaping, ruined storefronts on both sides of the passage. Broken glass and debris were scattered everywhere, but there was no other sound than their creaking steps on the stone floor, no other movement but their shadows swaying on the walls.

"Escalators," Sofia whispered.

They descended to the lower level. The dust in the air became denser, dimming the light. Jeane stopped at the bottom, gesturing to the others to follow her lead.

Silence and even more silence. Sofia stumbled forward in the glint of the flashlight.

"They have to be here." Her voice was thin. "Damian knows I won't leave without him. He's here."

Jeane walked ahead, curving around something that was probably an automatic control booth once. Kliks threw the beam of the flashlight in the direction of the tunnel, and Sofia stopped.

The rails were covered by debris, in some places almost ten feet high. Deeper inside, the path had caved in, stone and concrete blocking the mouth of the shaft. Whoever had been in there, if the explosion hadn't killed them, the ceiling crashing down on them surely did.

At the end of the platform, a body lay, burnt, covered by dust. Sofia seemed reluctant to approach. Maybe it was the aforementioned Coven.

"There's no one alive here," Jeane stated the obvious. "I'm sorry."

"No! They have to be here somewhere."

Sofia took off toward the other end of the platform, and when Jeane caught up with her, she was trying to get through a locked maintenance gate by pushing at it very hard.

"We should go up," Kliks said, stepping beside Jeane. "If they did escape, they're not in there. They might be in another part of the station."

Jeane gave him an appreciative head tilt. His attempt to wrap reason into hope worked too because Sofia turned her back to them and marched towards the escalators.

Jeane felt sorry for this girl, she did, but at the same time—along with Hollis snarking at her every opportunity he had—an alarm had been going off in the back of her mind, insisting that she turn around and get off the planet now, right now, pronto. It would have been nice to find Nasir and his mysterious cargo, to have some more leverage against Dikent the next time they saw him, but not at all costs. If Sofia's pursuers were near the spaceport, they would soon notice the *Skylark*, realize something fishy was going on, and decide to hurry on with those reinforcements. She didn't want to wait until that happened.

They'd almost reached the top of the escalators when they heard the voices.

Jeane dropped on her stomach, and Kliks and Sofia ducked down behind her. The searchlights of heavy rifles flashed in the dimness ahead, illuminating a group of people. Two gunmen walked at the front, two in the back, and sandwiched between them were another two figures in a much worse state. They stumbled forward, their backs bent, one of them dragging their left foot. They looked exactly like people who had just survived a tunnel collapse.

"It's them," Sofia hissed. "I told you they were here!"

Kliks muttered something Jeane didn't understand, and she realized he was talking to ALU through his comms. By the time he finished the call, the procession was out of their view.

"We surround them on the stairs before they join their friends," Jeane mumbled. Her toes tingled in expectation. She grabbed Kliks' flashlight, directed the beam into Sofia's face, and pantomimed to her that if she dared to speak or do something irresponsible, she would break her neck personally with her own two hands. Then she clutched the gun to her side and darted towards the exit.

The soldiers stood at the bottom of the stairs, and as Jeane and the others crept closer, hiding behind some columns, there was a beep, then one of the goons barked into a comms device.

Jeane didn't understand the language, but Sofia held up her hand, listened for a few seconds, and translated in a hushed voice. "They found your ship. Reinforcements are a few minutes out. They're arguing about whether to enter."

«If they screw around with my ship, it'll be me who enters. With my fist in between their nasal bones.»

Jeane exhaled, trying to calm down. They never should have left the *Skylark*. Damn ALU to hells! Why had they even come here?

«Because you're the worst person alive, that's why.»

To the sound of footsteps, Jeane peeked out again—the soldiers had started climbing the stairs. It was time to get this show on the road. She waved to Sofia to stay back and took off running with Kliks.

Her first stun shot hit one of the soldiers in the calf; he exclaimed and staggered forward, almost taking one of the captives with him to the ground. The goon beside him jumped, firing back at Jeane, and she swiveled around to avoid the bullet. Kliks released a few stun blasts himself, and ALU's war cry resounded from somewhere up front.

Then Sofia dashed forward, running up to the hostages, but Jeane didn't have time to stop her because the first soldier clambered back to his feet and started firing. Jeane dove to the side, then ahead, full-body smashing into the man. He fell back with a grunt, sprawling out on the steps, gun clattering down, but he swept his legs around to trip Jeane. Her back collided with the concrete, the air knocked out of her lungs. The pain in her side roared to life, and the next thing she saw was the soldier lunging for her.

She barely had time to roll away. Her gun fell out of her hand, and then the man was on her, drawing her into a chokehold. Her vision blurred, her ears clogged, and she was fighting for that sweet, sweet oxygen in her lungs for the second time that week.

The soldier's death grip became more stable, and Jeane was unable to break free. She grasped around blindly, her limbs numb and heavy, hoping to catch her weapon, but to no avail. Then she felt a push, and following a faint zipping noise, the man's hold on her loosened, allowing her to shove him away.

Her attacker's body flopped down with the weight of unconsciousness, and Jeane gasped, flailing around. She turned. Kliks stood a few feet away with another unconscious figure beside him and his stun gun aimed at Jeane's opponent.

She climbed to her feet, pressing a palm against her wound. As she rushed up the stairs again, she watched one of the captives and ALU pinning the third Gaerrisian to the ground. Sofia was next to them, helping her other friend stand.

Her heart pounded against her ribs. There were four goons, weren't there?

Then Sofia made a tortured whimper, and Jeane looked up to see the fourth soldier at the top of the stairs, unarmed, backing away. The older woman clutched at her comms with an unfazed expression, and Sofia trained her pistol at her, hesitating.

"Shoot!" Jeane yelled. She'd left her damn weapon at the bottom of the stairs!

As the gun dropped from Sofia's shaking hands, the Gaerrisian took off running. And by the time Jeane pounced for the weapon, the soldier had disappeared behind the next building.

"She's going to bring the whole search squad down on us," said one of the Miyozan men. He was slender, his face covered in bruises, his curly dark hair and his shirt soaked in blood. Still, he was in much better shape than he'd shown before; he must have been waiting for his own chance to make a run for it. He leaned down to the disarmed Gaerrisian beside ALU, dragged a leather bag off the soldier's shoulder, and took several weapons and small items out of an inside pocket of the man's coat. Then he knocked him out with a confident punch. "We need to go."

Jeane glanced around. No enemy in sight, but that would change fast.

The Miyozan guy asked something of Sofia in their own language, and she nodded, her look distant, glassy. Their other friend was leaning to the wall, conscious but barely present.

"Nasir?" Jeane asked.

"Yes," Curly Hair said, and his eyes flicked to Sofia and her friend. "Your cargo."

«Things are going great, aren't they?»

They ran as fast as they could, but the hum of the shuttles resounded in their ears before they rounded the spaceport. They all halted for a moment to watch one of the ships land beside the *Skylark*. The second one hovered above, blotting out the sun.

Nasir grabbed Jeane's shoulder. "You only need to run. I'll deal with them."

Jeane had no idea how he wanted to accomplish that, beaten and bruised as he was, but in the absence of a better plan, she wasn't going to argue. The survival instinct of this complete stranger who was the reason she'd come here in the first place had to be enough.

Bullets rained on them as they sprinted towards the *Skylark*. From the corner of her eyes, Jeane saw Nasir reach into his jacket and throw something at the soldiers running at them, and the erupting flames slammed into her face as burning figures collapsed on the ground. She tapped at her tablet to drop the *Skylark's* shield. As the airlock ladder descended, another group of Gaerrisians jumped out of the shuttle. Nasir and the other Miyozan man—Damian, Sofia had called him—fired amongst the soldiers while Jeane pushed ALU and Kliks in front of her and blasted a few shots behind their backs. More goons fell onto the concrete, and Nasir planted himself between the *Skylark* and the other group now closing in on them.

"What the hells are you doing?" Jeane yelled, giving a boost to Sofia and Damian to climb the ladder. She hoisted herself up too, her side burning with unholy intensity. "We gotta go!"

"Then go!" Nasir didn't turn back. He hurled something resembling a hand grenade towards the Gaerrisians, and the explosion shook the earth under their feet. "Get them out of here!"

Jeane climbed a few more steps, holding on for dear life. Both shuttles lifted into the air now, taking notice of the ground troops' continued failure and wanting to close the deal with their own cannons.

Nasir noticed as well. He reached into his jacket, took out a new weapon—how many of those did he have in there?!—and aimed at the ships above their heads.

"Get out of here, now!" he shouted again, then pulled the trigger.

Blinding light enveloped the runway. And as the surge of roaring flames smashed into the *Skylark*, Jeane dove head-first into the airlock chamber and slammed the hatch shut.

PART II

WHEN SEAS CATCH FIRE

AND STARS WALK BACKWARD

> *"Hope" is the thing with feathers -*
> *That perches in the soul -*
> *And sings the tune without the words -*
> *And never stops - at all -*
>
> *And sweetest - in the Gale - is heard -*
> *And sore must be the storm -*
> *That could abash the little Bird*
> *That kept so many warm -*

("Hope" is the thing with feathers, Emily Dickinson)

CHAPTER 13 | MISPLACED

The streets of Foggy Cities Central were swarming with people. Lanehunters of all races and origins conversed on the roads on their way in or out of bustling stores and workshops, and airships glided back and forth above the flat rooftops of the market district. Although the combat between the Union forces and Defense was still up in the air (in both senses of the phrase), not much had changed in the town proper apart from the ports closing down ten hours before. No ship was allowed to depart for any reason, and the restrictions would only be lifted when all the intruders had been hunted down.

Roy Philemon sat back in the chair and rubbed at his eyes. Despite itching to leave, this break was very much welcome. The last few days had been hellish, and it was nice to sit in the shabby diner, watching the view through the window and not racing for his life. Almost peaceful, apart from his nerves screeching bloody murder at him to run and hide as fast as he could.

The green-eyed waitress stopped beside his table. It was the third time she'd done that during the last fifteen minutes—a little more frequent than what her boredom in the emptied-out restaurant after the midday rush could justify. Roy told himself it was impossible to figure out where he'd come from; he'd ditched his gray uniform, copied the accent of the first native-looking person he'd heard speaking on the streets, and kept his equipment hidden. His short brown hair was messy and his face fashionably grimy. And while no one went from fanatical murder machine to freedom-loving interstellar pirate overnight, Roy wasn't an ordinary case.

He couldn't be cautious enough, though. If someone got wind of how and why he'd infiltrated this place, he was a dead man walking.

More of a dead man walking than now? That would be a feat.

"Can I get you anything else?" the waitress asked with a smile.

Roy returned the friendly gesture and waved towards his glass—empty except the ice cubes quietly melting inside. "Another one of these, please."

"Sure thing," the woman trilled. She took the glass and began to walk away but turned back a second later, squinting at him in sympathy. "You're landbound too?"

Roy inclined his head in an affirmative motion. There was still no need to get jumpy, but his muscles tensed, ready to act.

The waitress glanced at the window. "Lots of people are today. We haven't had a city-wide alert in years." Roy followed her gaze and scanned the street outside. She went on, quieter but still cheerful as if sharing some funny gossip. "People say it was terrorists, that shooting at East Point."

Roy frowned. "Really?" *They're covering it up. Interesting. Stupid, even.*

"Security cleaned the place up fast, so it's hard to tell what happened, but that also means it was more than some everyday squabble." The young woman shrugged, looking at Roy with the tranquility of someone who never had to worry about waking up and finding her home in flames. "Defense will take care of it. These things never last."

"Let's hope so." Roy had half a mind to ask whether terrorist attacks were a frequent occurrence in lanehunter circles. If so, he'd certainly missed that particular memo. Clan wars had been common until a few decades back, but having learned their lesson the hard way, most lanehunters now upheld a fragile power balance between their factions in order to survive the ever-encroaching Union threat. This did not exclude smaller-scale hostilities, but he decided not to inquire. No need to reveal his ignorance. "Time's short, and business doesn't wait," he simply said.

The waitress smiled again. She hesitated as if wanting to ask something else but then turned around and walked back to the bar.

Roy planted his elbows on the table. He had to keep reminding himself where he was. The Foggy Cities, the place the Union had been seeking for so long! The hidden world, the secret stronghold, the center of lanehunter culture where the clan heads hatched all their schemes and where all the strange technologies from dead planets flooded into—everything that the Union couldn't swallow first. Only the Ranch would be a bigger catch than this. If the Cities were the brain, the Ranch was the heart. If only the Union found that place too! A hundred-year-old opposition would finally end with the destruction of the lanehunters.

The Cities now tried to wriggle out from the clenching jaws of their own fate, of course, but once Leadership got a whiff of victory, it was hard to derail them. If the lanehunters didn't come up with something, their precious independence would be on the line. Sadly, as far as Roy had seen, the infiltration hadn't been taken seriously. All the Cities' legions should have been up in arms and preparing for battle or setting up some cloaking magics to hide their world better. Instead, they played hide and seek with the inspectors in shadowy alleyways. Those threefold bastards were taking their sweet time getting themselves caught, too, only to occupy the lanehunters while the destroyers arrived from Hurricane.

This lovely waitress might have to run for her life, perhaps as soon as tomorrow.

Roy blinked and rolled his shoulders back. It was useless to ponder; he had more important stuff to worry about. Reaching into the pocket of his stolen leather jacket, he fished out a little device from its protective casing. In this strange city, there was no way to know what kind of detectors he'd been passing under, so he kept a low profile with his tech, but he needed to know what was going on out there.

Plugging the speaker into his ear and placing the sensor against his temple, he blinked once, activating the device. He ignored most of the heads-up display that flickered to life in front of his retinas, browsing the relevant Defense comms channels instead.

Fragments of conversations broke through the interference of the Ros-3 lane, amplified by the device and transmitted into the speaker: the voices of Defense officers giving orders and reporting on maneuvers. Roy heard the nerves behind their subdued exchanges. The hunt for the inspectors was still on.

He cut the connection with the assist device with another blink and returned it to his pocket. Cities Defense were still too alert; he'd better not move yet. Besides, his ship was still reconstructing the vectors the lanehunter vessel carrying the manipulator had followed on its way out. Roy didn't think he'd have much luck trying to trick Cities Control to give him the egress coordinates, but he didn't need to. The algorithm his mentor had given him was working so far. It just took a lot of time.

When his eyes focused on the real world, the first thing he saw was a new glass of refreshments on his table. The waitress must have brought the next round while he was zoning out on the comms.

Well, shit. Didn't notice I was so tired. He glanced towards the bar, and the waitress sent him a quick smile before turning away. Those peculiar green eyes of hers reminded him of the piercing look on Danai's face the last time he'd seen her.

He swallowed his drink in one swig, the harsh herbal essence of the blue liquid he'd forgotten the name of burning its way up his nose. The events of the previous day invaded his mind. What a stupid mistake he'd made. Almost doomed the whole operation at the start. After escaping Hurricane, he'd gotten rid of the tracker devices on his nailship, but for some reason, he didn't think about the one in his own body.

Blame the stress and move on. But not even his mental state could be an excuse. He might as well have been as brainwashed as his agent comrades, not recalling such an obvious thing.

And here it was: the paranoia that some lingering, hidden response to all those damn re-education sessions was clinging to his brain, even though Danai had promised the brainwashing would never take effect on him. As long as he kept that monster behind a closed door in his mind, he was safe. Weaker for it, mentally and physically, but not a mindless servant.

But Danai couldn't know for sure. She hadn't foreseen a lot of things.

He'd been too shaken, that was all. Until something like this happened again, he didn't need another reason not to trust his judgment.

The incision on his abdomen was sore as he put his palm against it, even after all the desensitizers. With lack of any precision instruments, he'd had to improvise the night before. Magnetic screwdriver it was.

Danai would have been so furious. But Roy was too. All her mentor's burdens were now his, and she...

Well, she was dead. She had to be if it were left up to Inspector Korrh. Not to worry, though; those three would not let her escape to the great beyond until their interrogation had scooped all sensible thought and emotion out of her.

She'd told Roy so much, and yet so little. He didn't know what he'd gotten himself into. But maybe that was the intention. The only reason the Foggy Cities were still standing was that Korrh and the others, following Roy, had no idea they were going to end up inside a lanehunter stronghold. Just like Roy himself hadn't a clue where the manipulator signal would lead him. He'd only realized it when he first glimpsed these floating islands through the fog.

He'd found the lanehunters' ship in a hangar in a sector called Delta, then tracked down its captain to talk to her. He almost made contact too, but the inspectors had caught up with him. Although they'd deduced they needed to pursue the lanehunters instead of him, Korrh wasn't going to let Roy go free, and by the time he'd shaken them off, the lanehunters had slipped away too. Then Defense had set up the blockade.

It would have been much easier to just kill them, sneak into the ship, and take the device instead of trying to talk to them. But that was not why he'd come. That wasn't how he was supposed to handle this.

He could still catch up. Hells, he'd done it before, and he'd do it again.

It was late in the night when he decided to leave. Based on recent communications, Defense had managed to surround the last group of Union soldiers on one of the auxiliary islands of Central. Traffic had just restarted, but Roy couldn't wait any longer. He knew what came next. The Union would let the lanehunters chase their own tails for a few hours, try to interrogate the captured inspectors, send some recon units to the several exit points of the Ros-3 to see whether more intruders would come. And right when everyone thought it was over, that the infiltrators didn't get a message out, and that Cities Control was handling the problem, the destroyers would strike.

These people were already lost; they just hadn't noticed yet.

The long walk through the busy labyrinth of Central managed to drive the stiffness from his limbs. The air smelled musty and sour, and although the foggy night sky didn't promise variety in the local weather, the act of putting one foot in front of the other alone was invigorating. Without a central star to provide a day-night cycle, the blue backdrop of the lane and the intermittent rolling fog must have illuminated the Cities in dim light at all times, but the people in charge had arranged to imitate daylight and evening darkness, using projections to the inner surface of the shields in some areas, and in other regions applying strange contraptions made from mirrors and reflectors. The unkempt streets with the pubs and storefronts showing architectural styles from various corners of the galaxy were charming in a way and so different from the unchanging blazing glare in the endless, monochrome underground corridors of Hurricane that Roy had to pause and marvel at it.

He felt lost here in a way he hadn't for a long time. The crowd surged on the streets, colorful and rowdy, not caring about him at all. As if he was invisible. Or like he belonged here. And for a moment, he allowed himself to imagine. *Why not?*

But he banished the thought. He still had to find that apocalypse machine. After that, he could be an idiot if he wanted to.

He strolled out from between two buildings, and the road ended so abruptly in front of him that he took a surprised step back. Someone broke out laughing nearby, and he watched as three young human lanehunters circled him, smiling widely and walking out onto a bridge a few feet to his left.

Roy crept up to the edge of the precipice. There was no railing at this section to protect careless pedestrians from falling into the void below, although towards the busier overpasses, metal chains had been hung up along the verge as security barriers. He looked down, but his eyes couldn't comprehend the vast depths—all he saw was hazy grayness. Before him, the island of Sector Coriol was wrapped in colorless mist, tiny yellow lights dancing above the bank glinting at him, calling him over.

He tapped his pocket, wanting a cigarette, but he'd smoked the last of the batch he'd gotten from Danai the day before. She'd told him they were from Metallia, one of the larger worlds that the Union had long conquered but couldn't regulate well due to its great distance from Hurricane. Even with frequent raids, the residents of the planet had been basically doing whatever they wanted—like selling and buying psychoactive substances in various forms. Cigarettes weren't exactly contraband in the Union, but no good citizen of the great empire had the liberty of will to consider trying them out. Roy had always taken some defiant pride in having them.

Well, never mind then. No time to linger anyway.

He crossed the bridge and stepped out onto the stony ground on the other side, the streets of Coriol rolling out under his feet. He walked through flat runways and past piles of miscellaneous metal debris in the dark. Yellow light trickled through the windows of hangars and workshops around him; other buildings were deserted. After the noisy roads of Central, this was now another type of respite.

One was never truly alone on Hurricane. Leadership was always watching, if not through the ever-present surveillance system, then through the eyes of the inspectors and fellow agents. One wrong move or a shadow of suspicion that someone wasn't loyal to the cause and life as one knew it could end in a second. And death wasn't the worst fate to suffer. After all, it was difficult to mass-produce devoted, unquestioning soldiers. A perfectly good body could not be wasted every time someone decided to rebel.

The deletion and rewriting of everything that made a person a person. All in the name of order and protection, and the purest and safest way of existing: in complete servitude to the all-know-ing, all-seeing Union Leadership.

Roy shivered. He fought down the paralyzing fear, and putting on his assist device again, he let it guide him to the coordinates of his cloaked ship. He gave the mental command, and the air started to shimmer a few inches away as if something was emerging from under a translucent water surface. The contours of a slim, matte gray vehicle appeared, and after a few seconds, the vessel ceased to look like a shaky holo-image and solidified into a real metal structure.

A standard-issue Union nailship. Not the newest model, but reliable; Danai had allowed Roy to continue to fly it even when a better version had been issued to his quarter five cycles before.

Small defiances. Those had been fun. Until the time came for the big one.

He shook his head, a bitter taste in his mouth, then placed his palm on the sensor beside the door to unlock the ship. Sitting down in the cockpit, he flicked a few switches and brought the systems online. The main screen lit up and displayed the results of Danai's manipulator-tracking algorithm. Roy looked through the numbers, verifying the parameters by typing in a few rows of code, while the nailship lifted from the runway, disappearing into a light shimmer as the cloaking rose back up. Roy pushed the throttle forward, and the Foggy Cities soon shrunk to a bunch of small pebbles behind.

He stared at the screen, following the ship's trajectory as they slipped out of the sensor range of Cities Control without alerting anyone of their presence. Danai's program had found the right path; the emission from the remnant particles of the manipulator marked the way in front of Roy better than any nav system could. Out of the Cities, through the lane, and beyond.

Dread filled him as he recalled his wish to be able to spend more time on this eclectic little world. Because when he returned, if ever, everything would be very different around these parts.

The last scan he performed to make sure his tail was clear be-fore submerging into the Ros-3 confirmed that feeling. There, at the edge of his range, six Union destroyers were waiting with armed cannons and maxed-out shields, ready to descend on the

Cities any second.

Roy only spared them a quick glance, disgust rising in his stomach. Then he turned on the first vector the algorithm gave him and did not look back again.

CHAPTER 14 | ALL AT SEA

Kliks adjusted the cold compress on the unconscious man's forehead, said something to Sofia in a quiet tone, and walked out of the common room. Jeane, who had been pacing up and down the corridor, stopped and raised her brow in a wordless question.

The Talalan sighed. "Well, I'm not a doctor, but his injuries don't look fatal. Something protected him from the full force of the explosion. Concussion, exhaustion, a few broken ribs... He's stable for now, but as I said—"

"You're not a doctor." Jeane peered into the room. The man called Damian Moore was lying on the couch, eyes closed, his face as gray as ash. Sofia sat beside him on a chair, hunched over. "Good. Don't need a corpse to carry around right now. Did he say anything?"

"Not much. Why?"

After Nasir had blown up the port around them, they'd zoomed out of Miyoza's atmosphere without further trouble. News of their meddling presence hadn't spread fast enough between the Gaerrisian units, and they'd almost reached the Tir-11 before a few fighters caught up with them. The *Skylark* had her jammers turned on, which disoriented most of the ships in range, and a couple of daring maneuvers later, Jeane had propelled themselves into the milky white fog before the enemy could rush them in earnest.

They'd zipped through a few systems, then chosen one with several lanes and crossed into another one from there. No planets or outposts orbited the close binary they'd appeared at, and that suited them. They hid inside a massive asteroid belt to take a breather, and only then did they have the time to start treating Sofia's friend, who had been unconscious since he climbed on board.

"Where's his bag?" Jeane asked.

Nasir's resolute expression when he'd nodded towards Sofia and Damian after they'd rescued them from their Gaerrisian captors flashed through her mind. *Your cargo,* he'd said.

"What?"

"This Damian fellow had a satchel with him. Nasir got it back from the soldiers and gave it to him while we were running. Where is it?"

"I don't know," Kliks said, surprised. "With Sofia, I think, but what do you need that for?"

"Because Nasir went back into that tunnel for Damian."

Realization flashed up on Kliks' face. "And you think it was all because of the bag?"

Jeane shrugged. "Just a guess, judging by how tightly they were both holding onto it. Humans are a selfish species."

"But he sacrificed himself for us, didn't he?"

"Selfish and conflicted species."

She stopped talking because Sofia stood and marched out of the common room to face them. The bag in question, a brown, faux-leathery thing, was hanging around her shoulders. Exhaustion and grief shadowed the young woman's delicate, round features, streaks of blood and grime dirtied the bronze complexion of her skin, and her hair tumbled on her shoulders in knotted locks. Kliks had bandaged the wound on her arm, but she refused to lie down.

"Are you sure he's going to be okay?" she asked in a demanding voice.

"I think so," Kliks replied. His tone indicated that this wasn't the first time he was telling her this. "He needs rest more than anything."

Sofia nodded slowly as if it took her some time to process the answer.

"Yes. Alright," she said, the words slightly slurred. "Thank you."

Kliks smiled at her. "No problem."

"Enough of this," Jeane groaned. "Are you gonna tell us who you are or not?"

Sofia blinked. "I already explained. Damian was a guard at the palace, and I was, uh...maintenance. We escaped before Gaerris took over the city."

Jeane opened her mouth to argue, but Kliks nudged her in the side. "How did the war end?" he asked. "I thought Miyoza could survive forever under that dome."

The dazed expression on Sofia's face darkened. She must have been in her early twenties, but she looked like a lost child at that moment. "The king died, and everything fell apart. Miyoza had to surrender."

"What about Nasir?" Jeane asked. "How does he fit the picture?"

"He's a friend. He'd been planning to leave using his connections with this organization, the Net. I don't know much about it."

"And that's where you're losing me," Jeane muttered. "Dikent can't be Net. It doesn't make sense."

"Who is that?" Sofia asked. "Nasir's contact?"

Jeane's face twitched in annoyance. "Yeah. As it turns out, he kept us in the dark on pretty much everything concerning your rescue. And I don't buy it for a second that he did it out of the goodness of his heart to help some rebellious organization with questionable motives and influence."

Sofia stared back at her, face expressionless. No wonder; Jeane had just insulted the group of people her (most likely) dead friend had been loyal to.

"Nasir was supposed to hand over some valuable merch," she continued hurriedly. "Not refugees. You have anything like that on you, or was the whole thing a lie?"

Sofia's eyes flashed. Pressing her lips together, she drew the satchel closer to her body.

Aha! Well, maybe I should just take it from her. She's only a scared, unarmed girl.

«*Are you serious? Am I hearing this right?*»

Kliks coughed, and Jeane felt herself going red. *Careful, the fucking moral compass police is here...*

"I'm not a charity, and I'm not your tour guide," she said, clenching her fist. "I don't know what Nasir was thinking, but we're on an unfinished contract, so you're coming with us. Understood?"

"We're going wherever you say," Sofia said curtly, then walked back into the room and retook her spot beside her companion.

"What do you think?" Jeane asked when she stepped into the control room, Kliks following close behind. "Not a good liar, is she?"

Her friend shrugged. "Not our business."

"But seriously. That girl is maintenance like I'm a billionaire."

"Jeane, what do we do now?"

She turned the pilot chair around and slumped down. Spinning towards the console, she scanned the instruments. "No one's tailing us, and I like that, but we need to know if it's safe to return to the Cities. These two are not going anywhere without us."

Kliks sat down at his post too. "Do you really want to give them to Dikent?"

"I thought it wasn't our business," Jeane snarked. "Dikent should eat what he cooked up. If he's getting into funky dealings with the Net, that's not my problem."

The Talalan gave an exasperated sigh. "I have a feeling he's not going to be embarrassed. So, where to?"

Jeane queried the nav database and sent the data to Kliks' terminal.

"Duplex?" His face brightened. "You know I'm all for a visit, but our guests will freak out."

"Our 'guests' won't even stick their noses out of the ship." Jeane lifted her legs on the console. Burning pain bit into her side, stopping the movement, and her hand flew to her wound. That chase on the planet did her no good. "We need to get some intel, and Wallace Hamilton is the best person to ask."

She glanced to the side only to see ALU creeping toward the door in an attempt to slip out. She hadn't even noticed them come in. "You!" Her raised voice stopped the technician in their tracks, and they blinked up at her in confusion. "What do you have to say for yourself?"

ALU beeped twice, wringing three of their hands in despair. "So, so, so sorry."

"What in hells got into you?"

"There was danger," they said in a tiny voice. "Needed to save life."

Kliks frowned. "Which life? What are you talking about?"

"Miyozan," ALU said as if it was the most obvious thing in the world.

"Is this some weird loyalty thing?" Jeane asked. If they could, the technician always avoided hurting others—just like Kliks, and that probably made them the least impressive scavenger team ever. But they hadn't displayed such a strong humanitarian penchant before.

ALU inclined their head and beeped in a tone that Jeane had learned to equate to a shrug.

"Well, you can't make these decisions alone," she said, trying not to contemplate too hard whether they'd have left Sofia and Damian on the planet if ALU hadn't pushed to stay and how she would feel about that decision now. "Think a little before you run headfirst into danger."

"Because we might not be able to protect you," Kliks added.

ALU lowered their head. And when they realized the lecture was over, they shuffled out of the room.

Kliks watched them leave and spoke only when their pattering steps in the hallway had faded away. "You know, times like this, it's almost like we're their parents."

"I never wanted kids," Jeane huffed. "ALU is more like a too-clever pet. Except when they're being an idiot."

"That's not nice. Don't say that."

"I'm sorry. I hadn't planned to blast dozens of soldiers into oblivion with an interstellar rebel guy today!" Kliks muttered something in agreement, and Jeane rubbed at her face.

"Whatever. This week is fucked. First the manipulator, then Dikent, now these two..."

The Talalan sighed. Then sighed again. Jeane raised her brow and glared at him until he finally blurted it out. "There's something else. King Tholis of Miyoza had a daughter. Maura."

"...and?"

"I've seen her pictures. This Sofia... I'm pretty sure it's her."

Jeane's jaw dropped. "You're joking."

"I didn't want to mention because she clearly wants to stay incognito, but it might become important."

Feeling her temper rise, Jeane lifted a hand against her chest to quell the sensation. "It might! You're telling me we've got a runaway princess on our hands?"

"A recently orphaned one too."

Jeane winced, and Hollis' silence was an alarm in her head. *Yeah. That.*

"I do wonder what Dikent wanted with all this," Kliks murmured.

Jeane shot him a dark look and, with a nudge of her finger, increased the thrust on the engines. "I'll tell you what. Money. You can always count on that."

They took the long way to Duplex. Leaving the binary system, Jeane crossed a lane only to come right back and choose another one. A few systems later, they did the same thing, then coasted about inside a dust cloud with a peculiarly strong magnetic field to cover up their engine signatures. As they turned towards their destination, they avoided the larger hubs and, of course, kept the manipulator turned off the whole time.

Duplex wasn't an openly lanehunter-friendly world, but it didn't belong to the Union either. Agents left it alone because controlling it was more hassle than worth; there was nothing to conquer there except wilting lands and dirty towns. And the Window.

"What is this?" a voice spoke behind Jeane as she verified the computer's calculations and set the *Skylark* onto a descending trajectory around the planet. Glancing back, she saw Sofia standing in the door, looking at the view on the front screen, wide-eyed.

"This is Duplex," Kliks answered before Jeane could yell at the woman for leaving the living area when she'd specifically told her not to wander around on the ship.

The Miyozan stepped closer to stand between her and Kliks, keeping her eyes on the strange world in front of them. "But what happened to it?"

"Nothing. Or rather, the same thing that happened to everything else."

"It's like it was mirrored."

Kliks nodded. "All thanks to the crack. Those are two different worlds in two different regions in space."

Duplex looked like a planet that grew a weird lump, which was also a planet. The one on the far side appeared only in part, a portion of its green-gray disk cut off by the image of space, its surface peeking through a moon-sized triangular hole at the plane of intersection. A nebulous blue glow blanketed the sight of that second world which disappeared when the eye focused on it.

"Conjoined twin planets," Sofia murmured. The curious glow in her eyes made her face look alert and alive for the first time since Jeane had met her.

As they descended into the atmosphere, the surface of Duplex-1 spread out under them with black blotches of towns spattered in between sallow fields, the populated areas growing in size closer to the Window. And when the eye wandered toward the other side, the scene tilted in a dizzying way. The horizon curved more and was weirdly inclined, the ground dark, the vegetation lusher.

"If we approached the Window from the other direction, you wouldn't see anything. A planet like any other," Jeane said. Watching Sofia's fascinated expression, her anger evaporated. That did annoy her too, but memories of her first visit on Duplex beckoned at the edges of her attention—it wasn't only Kliks who loved this place. "From here, though, you can travel to the other side."

"How can something like this exist?" Sofia marveled.

"How can a lane exist?" Kliks answered. Sofia stared at him with interest, so he went on. "The Window co-moves with these planets, both here and there, like the lanes with the solar systems they're born in. The intersection is more or less stable, but things turn bottom-up quite frequently around these parts."

"Does this happen a lot? Windows like this?"

"Not exactly. Cracks, sure. They pop up on stars more often than planets, though, and those things will blow up on you real fast. The material can't stabilize, and when the star's gone, you'll get a big ol' crack in the middle of empty space again." Jeane peered at the girl. "You honestly haven't seen stuff like this before?"

Sofia shook her head. "I saw films, but it's not the same. I didn't travel much because of the war."

"War, huh?" Jeane grunted. "There's nothing else you people can spend your precious time on?"

"Like grave-robbing and pillaging?"

The three of them turned around at the same time. Damian stood in the entrance, leaning against the frame with one hand. His face was a healthier color, but he was bent over, exhaustion radiating from his body. The bandages Kliks had applied to his arm and broad chest had started to come off in loops.

"You were not supposed to get up yet!" Sofia exclaimed. Damian glanced at her, but his eyes went back to Jeane and Kliks.

Jeane stood, staring him up and down. "Ah, so you're one of those guys."

"I call what we do salvaging," Kliks said with a pedantic expression. He rose from his seat as well and sized the man's bandages up, reproachful. "And Sofia is right. You shouldn't be walking around yet."

Damian's drained face twitched, looking at the Talalan. He moved toward Sofia as if wanting to shield her. "And who are you supposed to be?"

"He's Kliks, my partner." Jeane took a step forward, placing her hands on her hips while brushing the gun holstered on her belt. Damian was barely conscious during their escape, and there hadn't been much time for introductions on Miyoza, but his hostility was alarming. He must have put two and two together about what kind of ship he'd boarded and was clearly not satisfied. "He's also the one who healed you up, so I recommend a friendlier tone."

"It's true." Sofia placed a placating hand on her friend's arm. "They saved us both."

Damian turned to her. "Did the others make it? Where's Nasir?"

Sofia hesitated, and her companion clenched his jaw.

"Your friend stayed behind," Kliks said. "He's the reason we're alive."

No one spoke for a few seconds. Sofia's fingers gripped Damian's arm in an imploring way. His square jaw tensed, his face stony as he seemed to swallow with difficulty.

"Where's my gun?" he asked in between deep breaths.

Jeane fought off the sympathy stirring up in her at the man's subdued grief and shrugged. "I stashed it. When we're done here, you can have it back, and the less trouble you make, the sooner that will happen. I'm not ecstatic that you're stuck on my ship either. I usually don't do human cargo—"

"—or ever," Kliks cut in. "You never do human cargo."

"And this was definitely not what I expected."

"What did you expect?" Damian asked. His tone was calmer now, but Jeane felt his piercing gaze stabbing through her skin, taking apart her every word and move.

"Not important," she snapped. "We'll do a short detour. You stay on your backsides on the ship, and I'll solve the problem."

"They're going to talk to Nasir's contact at the Net," Sofia added. She was clearly taken aback by her companion's heated reaction.

"We're going with you," Damian told Jeane.

"No, you are not."

"Then you'll have to shoot me."

Jeane inhaled slowly. Her glance wandered to the front screen, getting lost in the view of the fields and forests of Duplex. *And who the hells is going to pay me for all this?*

«*No one, kid. No one.*»

She exhaled. "I don't give a damn. Just don't get in my way, or

I might take you up on that."

She sat back, turning her attention to the screens, and a few moments later, the door clicked shut as both Miyozans exited.

"Exhibit A of why I don't do human cargo," she groaned. "Too much fucking trouble."

Blackbones looked the same up close as it had from above: a muddy town with low-roofed buildings made of dark wood and dirt roads plagued by deep potholes. Rain poured from the murky yellow clouds, and the streets were deserted despite the noon hour. In these parts, it was almost always raining, especially at this time in the local seasonal cycle, and the closeness of the Window could mess up the weather even more. Duplex was a disaster zone, one of the more popular holiday spots for lane researchers, but only those who didn't care much about anything chose it as a permanent living space.

Or those who had something to hide. *Like good old Wallace.* Him, his paranoia, and all the unique equipment he'd stolen from the Union found a fitting shelter on this gods-forsaken planet.

"Where are we going exactly?" Sofia called over the roar of the rain as they waded through the sludge on one of the town's main streets. Both the Miyozans had come with them, but Jeane had left ALU on the *Skylark* as usual.

Kliks wiped the water off his forehead and fixed the hood of his raincoat. "We're visiting a friend who can communicate through lanes."

"Is that such a rare thing to do?"

"Somewhat. The Union has many relay stations, but you won't find equipment like that on lanehunter ships."

"I thought you people could steal anything you wanted," Damian said.

Jeane huffed. Her boots separated from the mud with an uncomfortable squelch every step. If she could *steal* anything she wanted, wouldn't she have better rain gear?

"Most things we find are broken, or we have no idea how they work or how much they're worth," she answered. Why was she even humoring him? "If it's something valuable, we're usually only the couriers, not the buyers. Sure, there's the occasional smuggling from the Union which has its charms, but it's unhealthy in large doses."

"Then why are you doing it?"

"Because adventure is my lifeblood, that's why."

She wished Damian would keep his trap shut. Since he'd gotten back on his feet, he kept scrutinizing and twisting her words like it was the only fun he had left in this world. Jeane suspected he was way out of his element and had no idea what to do now that they'd escaped the war, so he was compensating with a weird territorial game of bullshit, but that didn't make him less annoying. If Nasir had any specific plans, he must have not shared them before he'd decided to blow himself up. But that was hardly her fault.

Sofia—or Maura, if Kliks was right—was more difficult to read. A suffocating sadness saturated everything she said and did, and she seemed to be just as adrift as her friend. But something drove her forward, and she seemed to hold onto it like a drowning man to the last planks of a sinking ship. Whether it was responsibility, guilt, or stubbornness, Jeane wasn't sure, but any of those could yield some exquisitely torturous experiences if one tried hard enough.

"Either way, anything is in better hands with us than the Union," Kliks spoke up.

"Let's admit that bar is very low," Damian said.

Jeane turned at a corner and heard the rest of them scramble to keep up with the unannounced change in direction. The rain poured down on them ruthlessly, and the cold wind crept under her leather jacket. She shuddered. *Damn planets.*

"If you're so interested, you can try it out," she said. "The world is your oyster. Be a lanehunter! You'll quit soon enough. Most people like to be comfortable, even if they need to compromise. Ask the Union."

"No, you're right. Traveling around aimlessly and gloating about it doesn't seem such an attractive life to me."

Jeane spun around, and Damian halted, expectant. Sofia called out to them to stop, but in the end, the only thing that kept Jeane from jumping at the man was Kliks' hand gripping her elbow.

"I believe we have arrived," the Talalan said. A tall building loomed to their right through the curtain of falling water, an orange-flamed lantern flickering above its front door.

Jeane pulled her arm away from Kliks' clutches, took a deep breath, and turned to the Miyozans. "Keep your mouths zipped. Wal doesn't like strangers."

Sofia and Damian nodded, the woman somewhat intimidated, the man sulky. Jeane grabbed the handle and pushed the door in.

"What are you talking about?" Kliks whispered. "Wal is friendly to everyone."

"Well, at least they'll shut up."

The warm central room of the restaurant welcomed them with two dozen mostly human guests sitting around wooden tables conversing and stuffing their faces with food and booze. Abstract paintings covered the walls above the flaking beige plaster, and cheerful music played from hidden speakers. A black-haired woman wearing an apron stood behind a counter to the left typing something into a terminal; she appeared to be in her thirties, tall with sinewy arms, fingers moving lightning fast on the keyboard.

Jeane and Kliks walked up to her while the Miyozans paused beside the front door. The woman raised her head, sized them up, and her mouth curled to a reserved smile. "Well then. Fancy seeing you two around."

"The pleasure is all ours, Saori." Jeane grinned back. "What's new?"

Saori pushed elegant, metal-framed glasses higher on her nose. "Let's see. Rain, rain, more rain. Last week we had a big shake with the Window all covered by lightning. A real spectacle. The roof of the Silver Beaver collapsed, and the afars said their volcano actually erupted. The twins tried to sail the wave and nearly broke their necks." Saori rolled her eyes. "It's quiet now, but we're expecting some more waves tomorrow. If only summer was near—all this mud drives me mad."

"And Wal? We're here for him, actually."

Saori raised one brow at Kliks. "You don't say. Well, he's alright. A bit jumpy lately." Her gaze wandered to the Miyozans. "And those two?"

"Guests," Jeane said. *Sure, let's go with that.* "They're traveling with us."

"Mm-hm."

"There's no need to worry." Kliks flashed a confident smile at Saori. "We just have a request for your uncle, and then we're out of your hair."

The innkeeper squinted at him, then nodded and typed something into her computer. Jeane repressed a grimace. She'd always had a soft spot for Kliks.

"You know the way," Saori said. "Do you need dinner?"

"I suspect so," Kliks replied with a thankful nod.

Jeane waved to Sofia and Damian, and they all marched to the narrow staircase between the counter and the far wall. Descending and walking through a wooden door took them to a declining, windowless hallway with bright halogen lamps and a massive metal door at the end. Jeane pushed a cracked plastic button on its silver surface, and a second later, they heard a row of clicks from the other side. Heavy machinery turned, the door creaked open, and the weathered, wrinkled face of a portly man appeared in the gap.

He looked at them through thick glasses and from under a crown of unkempt gray hair. "Jeane Blake! You came!" His speech devolved into a cawing laugh, and he opened the door to wave them in.

Jeane stepped into the darkened hideout, confused. "Did you expect us?"

The room was small and packed full of equipment: computer towers, radios, and signal transformers filled the desks and shelves, barely leaving place for the countless screens showing planetary and space weather reports, complex visualizations of the Window, and coded information about stars know what. Disorganized columns of papers filled with what seemed to be transcripts of conversations covered every surface in the bluish glow of the displays.

"As soon as those guys turned up here, I knew it," Wal

jabbered on. He shut the door, circled them, and plopped into a chair. "And looking at the state of things, hmm...I was sure you'd come by, yes, yes. When was the last time I even saw you? Seven months ago?"

"What 'guys' are you talking about?" Kliks inquired.

"Ah, you're the one asking!" Wal giggled. Had he been *this* unhinged the last time they'd met? Jeane couldn't say. "Yes, they were just like you. They wanted to come in here and use my maps, yes!"

Kliks' mouth fell open. "Wait, like me? You mean Talalans?"

Wal ran his fingers through his grizzled hair, nodding fervently. "Oh, yes. They were looking for something. Brought an energy print to run through the system. I'm this famous, can you believe? Hah! They would have paid good money too, but I couldn't find anything. Useless machines!" He kicked one of the metal boxes beside his chair as emphasis.

"What was the print?" Jeane asked because Kliks stood as still as a stone, silent.

"I have no idea!" Wal exclaimed. "I still don't know. But I thought about you two, yes! Wanted to contact you, but I wasn't sure where."

Sofia moved beside Jeane. "What is this about?"

Jeane waved her away. "And these Talalans didn't tell you where they were going?" she asked Wal.

"They didn't say shit. I knew you'd be curious, so I tried to ask, but they were so rude, so grumpy!"

"When was this?"

"Maybe two days ago."

«Jeane, the call. This can wait.»

But can it? She changed the topic anyway. "Right, Wallie, let's shelve this. We need a line to the Cities. To Dikent Mend."

"Oh, I bet you do." Wal gave a sharp whistle. "What a mess, what an absolute disaster! Did you hear?"

"What do you know?"

"Nothing good. They're fighting it out, yes! Let's see here..." Wal shifted to another chair and started typing furiously. "This can take a minute. Make yourselves comfortable!"

"Thanks, Wal." Jeane turned to Kliks, but he was still lost in his own world, so she flicked his nose impatiently. "What are we thinking?"

He flinched and glared at her, his eyes scared. "Take a guess! We're terrified!" he whispered, but he might as well have shouted the words with the intensity he used. "What kind of mess are we in if even the Talalans crawled out of their nest?"

He paused because Wal cursed out loudly. The man jumped up, grabbed a device, then looped a bunch of cables around his arm and bent over another terminal. The next moment, he landed on his stomach across the desk and smacked at another instrument, grumbling.

Damian stepped beside Jeane and Kliks, unfortunately realizing that he was allowed to speak. "Is this going to work?"

"Sure," Jeane said. "Believe it or not, our friend Wal here has the best tools for this. Union-made and all. Sees all the important lanes and cracks."

"You mean this?" Sofia pointed at one of the displays. The image looked three-dimensional, countless looping and branching lines connecting, forming planes and spheres, and surging back into themselves in a fractal-like manner.

"Yep. One of the most detailed maps of the lanes."

"How can one communicate through all of them?" Damian asked.

"Because they're connected, aren't they?" Wal shouted, sitting in front of a fourth computer this time. "Of course, they are! Not for us, not for travel, but they are." He grinned, appraising their stumped faces, but his joy was cut short by a sharp *ping*. "Hey, we got the line!"

Jeane barged through two chairs and slumped into a weathered yellow couch beside Wal that took her weight with a miserable creak. The man fiddled with an old-fashioned microphone and set a speaker before her on the table. There was a piercing, crashing noise from the other end of the line, like something massive was breaking into hundreds of pieces.

"What the hells?" Jeane muttered. "Why is the line so bad?"

"Proton cannons, I think." Wal rolled his eyes.

But before Jeane could have asked him to elaborate, someone

finally answered the call. "Hello? It's Mend. Is that you, Wallace?"

Jeane clutched the microphone. "Dikent? It's me. What's going on there?"

"What? Jeane? What are you—"

"I asked first!"

"Well, we're under attack! And it's not looking great."

The booming sound of a far-away explosion screeched through the mic, and Jeane leaned closer to the device. "You said you could handle it! What happened? Where are you?"

"Six Union destroyers, that's what happened! And then six more!" Dikent inhaled, calming himself down. "I'm on the *Intrepid*. We're leaving."

Jeane shook her head. Everything she tried not to think about came crashing back into her world. The Cities were still under assault. Dikent was running.

"Was it you, J?" Dikent asked, voice wavering. "I'm trying real hard to figure this out. Those inspectors wanted *you*. Why?"

"I..." She couldn't get the words out. Kliks leaned in beside her, but she didn't want to look at his face. What was it that she wanted from Dikent? "Listen to me. Your Miyozan contact died, and I have these two refugees here. What did you want— "

Dikent made a strangled voice that could have been a laugh. "Were you even listening? This place is done!"

The Cities couldn't be occupied. They must be able to pull off some bullshit to hide themselves again. *The Ranch can do it, so why can't they? Come on, now!*

"They know how to get in, and they're bombing everything." Something exploded again, and a buzzing sound had started up in the background, getting louder. "Damnit!" Dikent yelled. His voice was distant and muffled now. "I gotta go. J, whatever you do, don't come back! Keep safe...this is— and—"

A few other word fragments came through after, then the line silenced for good. Wal turned off the mic and peered up at Jeane, but she kept staring at the speakers in silence, her brain processing the information.

Something impossible had just happened. The Foggy Cities had fallen to the Union.

CHAPTER 15 | FREEDOM BOUND

On the top list of the many places in the universe Roy hadn't planned on visiting, Miyoza took one of the more prominent spots.

From the Foggy Cities, the signal led him to a quiet solar system with several lanes. The residual emission of the Talalan lane manipulator indicated which one the lanehunters had escaped through, and after hopping over a few more in quick succession and following the clear path ahead, he arrived into a system densely packed with lanes and cracks. The hub, along with many similar ones, was a place well-known to the agents of the Union. This one stood under F'xenn jurisdiction; that secretive species, the helaun, were one of the few alien races that maintained a fragile alliance with the Union. Regardless, both empires struggled with establishing permanent bases among these tricky conditions.

The residual particles had not decayed yet, so Roy could see which way the lanehunters had traveled, but instead of rushing after them, he only plunged into the fog for a short while to see where the signal led. He realized with some measure of surprise that—apart from the event horizon of a supermassive black hole and an ancient backwater world on the periphery of one of Milky Way's small satellite galaxies—the only viable exit was Miyoza.

Talk about places well-known to the Union.

Roy imagined the thought process behind the lanehunters' choice and, considering their position, found it logical. It also made him wonder, not for the first time, who these people were. They didn't seem to be accidental players. After all, they knew how to use the manipulator. And if they were, perchance, Net operatives, there could have been even more intrigue behind their visit to Miyoza, the famous warzone. But he didn't have all the puzzle pieces yet to put it together.

What neither they nor Roy could be sure of was whether Inspector Korrh was tracking Roy's bug (the one he'd cut out in the Cities) or the manipulator itself. In case of the latter, no smart detours would divert them from the trail. Even if the lanehunters turned off the device, it would keep on scattering these breadcrumbs for a while unless they stopped crossing lanes altogether. For how long and exactly how this worked, Roy had no idea. Not even Danai had known that.

But there was something else too. If the inspector trio was following the manipulator, then they'd managed to break Danai. And she must have spilled everything: about the tracking algorithm, how she'd interfered with the operation on Talala, how she'd confided in Roy, everything there was to know about the manipulator, and maybe, everything there was to know about the Net.

As his nailship floated in the mouth of the lane, Roy glanced at the code running on one of the screens, the numbers showing the path of the manipulator disappearing, then coming out of the Miyoza-system. The long-range radar indicated no one in sight, and he took a reluctant, deep breath. He stacked his legs up on the console, his gaze lost in the swirling mist of the void. *Time to take inventory.*

There was only one solid point in this mess that he could grab onto to stay afloat: no matter what happened, the Union could not get the manipulator.

It was quite ironic. The Talalans, so fearful of this fragmented galaxy that they'd retreated into complete isolation, ended up being the cause of the newest distress connected to the very lanes they dreaded. The Union grew larger by the day, bloating and surging forth like a malignant tumor, turning planets and their inhabitants into its playthings, but the lanes had been both helping and hindering their expansion. With the birth of these interstellar tunnels, the cosmos became available but crowded and troublesome too. All these stubborn species trying to do their own thing, surviving against all odds, not respecting the Union's authority! So, what would happen if all the backroads and hiding places were in the empire's clutches? If their weapons could be fueled by an unlimited energy source? What would they achieve with the power of creating and disintegrating entire worlds with one swift flick of a switch?

If one could believe Danai's intel, that was what this manipulator did. The Union wanted to retrieve the device while avoiding an open war with Talala, which they had always been wary of, not knowing much about the magnitude of their power and might. But the Net intervened.

And Roy was now, for all intents and purposes, Net.

The notion still stumped him. In the wake of his hasty escape from Hurricane, he felt like everything had been dumped on him at once. Even if he'd known for a long time that it might end like this.

Sure, he had been blind. Didn't want to look, didn't want to see. At times, he even wished he could be more like his brainwashed comrades, the agents, inspector trios, and enforcers who hunted down everyone that Leadership, the faceless rulers of the empire, didn't like for any reason or no reason at all. It was all very easy for them, with their selfsame, apathetic faces and thoughts, keeping entire planets in terror. For Roy, it had always been a losing fight. Ever since the first decision.

It seemed like such a small choice. But it wasn't, and I really should have known.

That first decision had been made in the training pits twenty-one cycles ago. The overseers had woken the recruits early and transported them from the Barracks into an unfamiliar facility. Roy stood there with the rest of the candidates, confused and panicked under the bright lights, the target of the onlooking officers' attention. Together with his peers—only a few dozen from the thousands and thousands brought forward in that cycle—Roy had been created for that moment and trained since he could understand instructions to succeed in the tests and after, to carry out rulings and commands unquestioning. He was only seven cycles old.

The overseers had made them run, climb, and shoot, read long passages of text, and work on calculating difficult problems for hours, and by the time they were led to those strange chairs in the neighboring room, Roy was exhausted and in pain. The assistants plugged cables into the helmet strapped tightly around his forehead and left him and the others in the glass-walled chamber. They sat in those cold, uncomfortable seats, shivering and half-asleep.

Then there was more pain. That was the first time he met Danai.

Tall and dark, walking along the row of chairs as she surveyed the sobbing children, she was a solemn apparition, a manifestation of his despair and agony. Other officers were pacing around him too, but she stepped up first, crouched in front of his chair, looking at him.

Her eyes, bright green against the brown of her skin, were serious and thoughtful. For a while, she observed him struggle to stay conscious through the incapacitating torment while spasms ran through his body in a vile rhythm of horror and relief. The wires connected to his brain made him think his limbs had been torn off and sewn back, again and again, and as the woman studied him, he almost broke. He almost started to beg her to put an end to this, that it was enough, that he wanted to rest now, or sleep, or die.

"I cannot stop this," she spoke, leaning closer, the words only a whisper. "But I can make it so you will always remember what they're doing to you."

Roy didn't understand much, only that this was an offering. A communion. Something that was theirs, something that connected them. He grasped for the alien, fleeting warmth blooming in his chest.

She asked, "Do you want this?" and showed him a small white pill hiding in her palm.

And he nodded, although he had no idea what the capsule contained. So she pretended to check his pulse and reactions like the other officers did with their future underlings, and with a quick motion, she stuffed the pill into his mouth.

She hadn't been lying. It didn't stop the pain. It got worse, and it never ceased.

That day, Danai Escher had become his commanding officer and mentor, and the brainwashing procedures of Leadership never affected Roy again. The pills he received counteracted the indoctrination, sealing away the part of his mind that *had been* changed and preserving his sanity so he could play the part of the good little soldier. In turn, he was never able to rise as high as his colleagues; his reflexes had never become that sharp or his brain that crystal clear. He'd have to open that door and let the monster in to achieve more, and he couldn't do that, ever.

Instead, he'd watched his comrades turn into mindless followers and blank-faced automatons, their personalities replaced by devout catchphrases and faulty reasoning about the superiority of humankind and the necessity of an amicable life under the authority of Leadership. He'd watched, lonely and aware of the atrocities the agents and enforcers committed against the rest of the world. He'd obeyed and hidden his feelings in shame and fear, hoping for a purpose to his ordeals and that in the end, he would somehow assist in stopping the terror he was contributing to. He'd watched, knowing he owed Danai for being able to watch and that the debt would one day be collected.

He never understood why he was the chosen one among the hundreds of recruits passing under her hand. He never dared to ask; it was comforting to not know. That offering, that companionship, needed to remain only his and hers. This was the only way he could survive.

Of course, there had to be more like him, children freed from their shackles at an early age when the brain was still susceptible to the pill, but he never met them. And now, he never would. He stopped being an agent the moment he'd accepted Danai's mission.

'Accept' is quite a strong word, isn't it? But not 'forced to pursue' either. That isn't how things work with her.

He'd just returned from his patrol around Nefirn-4, visiting the drill station of his quarter for one more practice session before going back to his pod for a scheduled break. At some point, Danai walked in too, and when Roy stopped to take a breather, she approached him. Several other groups of agents were still running the tracks around the cavernous hall while others stood aside, discussing their latest raids or future tasks. The eyes of the cameras placed all over the brightly lit room followed their every movement.

"Erion is getting out," Danai said, and Roy knew it then. That was it.

Erion was the spy sent to Talala to smuggle out the manipulator. He was also Danai's only son—a peculiarity in itself since with cloning as the number one way of producing able-bodied servants to the great cause, familial bonds were not held in high regard on Hurricane. It was rare that anyone resorted to more traditional ways of procreation, or if they did, contact between parent and child was not encouraged. But Danai had always supervised Erion's training closely and had chosen him for many unique jobs. Only a handful of officers had information about the Talala mission, but Danai oversaw that as well. She'd been the one who'd helped Erion obtain the position.

"What now?" Roy asked in a low voice, although volume didn't matter if they were being watched.

"We might have a pickup to make," Danai simply said, leaving him with that.

Two days later, before Roy left for another patrol, he had awoken to a call in the middle of the night. He'd sat up in the bed, and when he saw Danai's ID flash up on his HUD, the pod that was just large enough to stand up in seemed to collapse on him. She rarely called him like that during a break. She didn't do "personal contact."

"You need to go." Her voice was strained and shaky. Was she running? "Meet me at your ship," she instructed, then disconnected.

Roy stuffed some of his things into a backpack and left his housing unit five minutes later. Instead of the main routes, always packed with people and vehicles, he took the maintenance corridors running parallel to them, although if Danai had risked calling him, he must have been relatively safe. But his heart trembled anxiously, and an uncomfortable pressure settled on his chest. Never before had she given him a direct order like this. It had always been downloading and transferring data, reassigning files, and gathering intel on specific missions. But this was Erion. And something must have gone horribly wrong.

No one batted an eye at the docks when he used his access to get in. As he locked himself into the cockpit of his ship, he got another call.

"Where are you?" he asked, not waiting for his mentor to talk.

"You will go alone. I'll make sure you're let out."

She was whispering. Roy had never heard her so afraid before.

"You want me to leave you? What have you done?"

"It doesn't matter." Her sentences were terse and quick. "I transferred everything to your computer. Run the algorithm. Get the device. Don't let them take it."

Roy gripped the edge of the console. "You can't just tell me to leave! How am I supposed to—"

"Korrh is onto me! I will get them off your back, but you need to go."

At the name of the inspector trio, chills ran down on Roy's arms. Had Danai fucked up this badly?

"I'm sorry. It was not my intention to put this on you. There's still so many things I wanted to—"

Her voice dropped. Roy let out a curse and started up the engine. "Danai?"

For a few seconds, he only heard her breathing. "Please, Roy. If you have a chance, help Erion," she said, then she cut the connection.

Ten minutes later, Roy crossed the third line of checkpoints on his way out of Hurricane. No one stopped him, and no one followed, but only after leaving the inner sectors of the system did he bring up Danai's data.

It was her life's work. Detailed descriptions of the defense systems of Hurricane, Obavium, and other Union nodes; names and mission plans of hundreds of agents, inspectors, and enforcers; positions and movements of military units patrolling and defending the worlds that the Union controlled—an incredible amount of information. A jackpot for anyone who would make a stand against the empire's oppression.

Another folder contained the details of Erion's mission. He was supposed to bring the Talalan device to Hurricane, but the plans had changed. Erion had been compromised, and now he wanted to meet up on neutral ground in a system far away from Union influence. Alongside directions, he'd also shared the blueprints and code to an apparatus able to track a recently operated lane manipulator.

Roy had almost made it in time. He'd found Erion's broken down ship on the nameless planet with the Altex outpost, but when he scanned for life signs, he realized there was no one left alive in there, and someone else had already picked up the manipulator. And so he'd used the algorithm and tailed those hunters through the lane he'd later almost died in.

Focusing on the present again, he stared at the visual representation of the path on the screen. If he'd expected to come to a big conclusion after this dive into the churning memories in his head, he was to be disappointed. The manipulator could tear apart reality, and he might have the means of stopping the Union from seizing it. That was all. He needed to go against his own people.

But had he ever been one of them? He was only a mole, just like Danai. Worse because he didn't even know the people he'd been working for under her mentorship. And the only person he ever trusted was now dead.

Why had he been chosen? Had Danai ever seen anything special in him, and if so, why was it always, always Erion before him? Why hadn't she sent Roy to Talala instead of her golden boy? Why hadn't she told Roy anything until the last moment when she needed him to save her son? And if those lanehunters he'd been chasing were Net, as Roy suspected, why was he here? Was there any reason behind his entire life collapsing on him?

Why did her last words have to be about Erion? She didn't even say...she didn't say anything. Nothing. She had nothing else to say to him.

Fighting off his frustration, he changed his ship's trajectory again, trailing the manipulator signal that exited the lane from Miyoza, submerging into another close-by tunnel.

Inspector Korrh and the others might still be after the manipulator. He couldn't stop with a clear conscience; he had to make sure. He'd been taught well. Danai hadn't only given him a mission—she had created him. And now, without her, Roy wasn't sure what he was.

All his questions would have to wait until he stopped running. But then, he would demand the answers.

CHAPTER 16 | SOME OF THE TRUTH

After the conversation with the man Jeane called Dikent, Maura and Damian followed the lanehunters back to Saori's restaurant, The Candle. They sat around one of the tables while Jeane and Kliks argued, and the dining crowd swelled then dispersed around them. Maura picked at her meal of roasted vegetables and gravy. The room was warm and friendly and the murmur of conversation around her calming, but she couldn't stop shivering.

She understood little of what had happened. One thing was clear: she and Damian had still no idea what Nasir's plan had been.

"We have two options," Jeane said, running her hand through her pale blonde hair. "The first has just become Talala since, apparently, they're trying hard to find us too. If we give them the manipulator, the Union might leave us alone."

"Except we can expect most agents on this side of the cosmos sitting on their doorstep right now," Kliks said in a grim voice. "We would take the war to Talala like we did to the Cities."

Pressing his thin lips together, he swallowed hard. Looking at his tall form, unusual gray skin, white hair, and the emphasized lines on his face, Maura felt uneasy. This was the first time she had encountered non-humans; Kliks and the weird robot-alien on the ship reminded her of how strange the outside world was compared to her home.

But at least the Talalan had been kind to her from the beginning. ALU's unusual loyalty only confused her. The robot seemed to think it (or they, as the others referred to the technician) somehow knew her, although she was sure they'd never met before.

"What's the other option?" she asked when no one broke the silence.

The captain's eyes shifted to her. "The Ranch," she said reluctantly. "We can go to the Ranch."

Unlike Kliks, Jeane was blunt and gruff, always in a heated argument with the rest of the universe. A string stretched too tight, unable to let loose. Damian had made it clear he didn't trust her, but Maura wasn't sure what to think.

She also had no idea what or where the Ranch was. The name was familiar, an important lanehunter base as far as she knew, but that was the extent of her insight.

"Most people will flee there from the Cities," Kliks explained, the panic fading from his eyes as he focused on something else. "We might find Dikent and some answers. Plus, the Ranch is hidden so—"

"We don't know how far the Union can track the manipulator," Jeane cut him off. "We could lead them there too. Do we want to take the risk? And all the lanehunter-friendly worlds will be full of agents. Metallia, Horata, Rix...if they're onto us, they'll find us anywhere."

"And how is it better to let them surround us in the middle of nowhere, alone and vulnerable?" Kliks retorted. "We're screwed either way."

Maura had a hard time figuring out what role this manipulator played in the lanehunters' business. But Damian, who up until now had only been listening half-interested and half-annoyed, leaned forward and nodded toward Wal's underground cave. "If I were followed, I would stay somewhere I can at least observe what was happening."

Jeane didn't react, just took a long swig of her drink.

"We need to gather more intel anyway," Kliks said. "Map out where the Union set up shop and what the clans are doing now that the Cities are gone. Wal will know if someone suspicious gets close to Duplex."

"I don't intend to wait until then," Jeane muttered.

Kliks lowered his head. "If I hadn't taken the manipulator, the Cities would be still hidden, and we wouldn't be in this situation."

"You stop that right now!" Maura flinched at Jeane's outburst, and a few people sitting close-by turned to them in confusion. Her voice was angry, but Maura saw the worry in her eyes as she went on quieter. "We talked about this. If you hadn't taken it, the Union would have. Also, you were influenced. With the mind control thing?"

"I know, I know," Kliks mumbled.

Maura frowned at him. Mind control?

"Either way, whatever the Union got up to in the Cities is on them, not you." Jeane leaned back in her chair, stretching. Her words were light, but the skin tightened along her jawline. "Let's stay for tonight. And tomorrow is tomorrow."

"What does that even mean?" Damian sighed.

"It means I got some thinking to do, big guy." Jeane placed her elbows on the table and glared at him. "Strange concept to you, I'm sure. But you don't have to wait for me. I don't think Dikent wants you anymore, so you're free to leave."

"No," Damian said, his voice firm. "The Net needs us. We'll go with you."

Maura recognized the pain in her bodyguard's sullen expression. He blamed himself for Nasir's death, making him twice as determined to follow his friend's last wish.

"We would be grateful if you could point us in the direction of the Net," she spoke up. "And I'm sure they would be as well."

Jeane's eyes darted to Damian's bag, where the glove was hidden. Maura didn't think the captain knew what the device was and why it was important, but she hoped her civil tone and the vague promise of compensation would do the job. They needed to reach the Net, and she didn't have much to bargain with. Jeane had saved them when she didn't have to; if they were all going to the same place, Maura could at least hope she would take them again.

"I don't give a flying fuck about the Net," Jeane announced. "We'll see. We've got things to do first."

And with that, the conversation was over. Jeane booked them a room in the inn, told them not to leave the building, and disappeared to the basement with Kliks. Maura dragged herself up to their chamber, sat down on the bed—then everything faded into darkness. She must have fallen asleep immediately.

When she woke, it was quiet. Eyes closed, unmoving in the bed, she listened to the thrum of the rain on the windowsill and imagined she was still on Miyoza, in her own room. A brisk summer shower was rushing through the city, but it would end soon. She would climb out of bed, eat daleberries with cream for breakfast, and go for a walk in the garden. She might start a book—when was the last time she'd read something new? Everything would be peaceful. The war ended long ago, her father was well, and everyone was safe.

She opened her eyes and sat up. Morning light filtered through the drawn curtains. She'd managed to sleep through the afternoon and the night too. Her gaze fell on the couch across the bed, and her heart jumped into her throat, but in the next second, she recognized the dark figure sitting there. Damian had fallen asleep in an uncomfortable position with his elbow on the arm of the chair and his head propped up by his knuckles, crumpling the skin on his face as he leaned against them.

Maura slipped out of the bed and into the bathroom.

She washed her face and glanced in the mirror. Her skin had a gray tint, and dark circles decorated her eyes; her hair stuck to her shoulders, lifeless and matte. Her arm still hurt where she'd been shot at the spaceport, and her head ached constantly. She considered showering, but she didn't have the strength. Her arms were shaking as she leaned on the sink, swallowing back her tears.

Then she tiptoed back to the room, hesitating. Should she wake Damian? He needed sleep but would surely be perturbed to see her gone when he woke. In the end, she stepped out to the corridor and walked downstairs alone. She wouldn't be long. But after extricating herself from that too-beautiful illusionscape, there was a restlessness in her body, and she hoped walking around would help to cope with it.

The restaurant was empty, the shutters on the windows closed, and the lights off. Maura took an uncertain step forward. The front door suddenly opened, and daylight flooded the room.

"Oh, hello! What are you doing here?"

It was Saori with an unfamiliar young man at her heels. They were carrying two pairs of hefty cloth bags in their hands.

"I-I was just..." Maura hesitated. What was she doing?

The woman gave her a kind smile. "Well, don't get too scared. Bernard, will you open up, please? I'll make a coffee for our guest."

Saori thrust her things into the boy's arms and marched towards the corridor that Maura had stepped out of. Maura threw an apologetic look to Bernard, who started crumbling under the weight of the bags as he hauled them behind the counter, then she followed the innkeeper through the hallway and a door opening to the right.

It was a tiny kitchen, way too small to provide for the inn, so Maura guessed it was Saori's own. The woman began working, pouring water and portioning black powder into a metal pot at the stove.

"You do like coffee, don't you?" she asked.

"Yes," Maura said, although she knew from her studies that there were as many types of coffee as human worlds, so really, it must depend on the planet.

"I didn't even ask. Most lanehunters do."

"I'm not a lanehunter."

"Clearly. Sit, please."

Maura took a seat at the table. Pictures portraying colorful seaside scenes surrounded her on the walls, with holos of giant spaceships scattered throughout. Saori took out two red ceramic mugs from a cupboard, and a few minutes later, she pressed one of them into Maura's hands, full of the steaming, rich-scented liquid. She relished the warmth of it, and her restlessness subsided. She still found the situation a bit awkward.

"Where are the others?" Saori inquired and sat at the table

across from her, taking a sip from her mug.

Maura hesitated. "I'm not sure. They went to see your uncle again last night."

Saori sighed. "If that's true, I don't think they got any sleep."

Maura tried the coffee. It was different from what she was used to, almost sour but delicious. Even her head stopped hurting, and, to her surprise, tears gathered in her eyes.

"So, if you're not a lanehunter," Saori went on, "what are you?"

"My name is Sofia. I'm just a passenger." The lie was still uncomfortable on her tongue. She sniffled, pondering how to wipe her eyes without Saori noticing how a mug of warm coffee had made her cry.

"Jeane doesn't do passengers."

"She mentioned."

"Where is she taking you?"

Distracted from her predicament by the sudden questioning, Maura looked at the woman, but Saori's expression showed only sympathy.

"I have no idea yet," Maura said. She didn't see the sense in lying.

Saori smiled. "I apologize. I don't want to push you. I'm only wondering what kind of situation you're all in."

Maura lowered her head and drank some coffee again. "We're wondering that ourselves."

"I heard how Jeane picked you two up on Miyoza, of all places. Trouble finds trouble, I suppose, but I fear this might be a bit too big for her. Getting in the way of both the Union and the Net sounds like a recipe for a catastrophe."

Saori's concern for Jeane was written all over the woman's face, and Maura pondered about how close the two were.

"I see you'd rather not elaborate on your predicament, but if you want my opinion on whether you can trust Jeane, I can give it," Saori said then. Maura frowned, but the assumption wasn't untrue. The woman must have sensed her emotional turmoil after all. "Well, she's a lot of things, but a backstabber is not one of them." The innkeeper jumped up, moved to the cupboard, and started rummaging in it. "She has an excellent skill for avoiding everything that might derail her from what she thinks she wants.

She'll figure out how to help you."

A door slammed shut somewhere in the building, and muffled noises of conversation echoed through the walls.

"Although, I suggest you don't try helping her in return," Saori added, pouring coffee into a third mug. "It's not a rewarding task. She never promises otherwise, but she'll leave you without any thanks, and that could sting."

There was the rhythmic thumping of heavy footsteps outside. The door opened, and Jeane walked into the kitchen.

"I smell coffee," she exclaimed, but noticing Maura and Saori, she raised her brow. "Am I interrupting something? Bernie didn't say a secret meeting was going on."

"Just take it." Saori rolled her eyes and extended the mug of warm beverage. Only a small trace of bitterness remained in her voice.

The captain snatched it away and consumed the whole thing at once. Her face was colorless, her hair messy, and there was a tired glint in her eyes. "I thought you were never gonna wake up," she said, glancing at Maura. "Where'd you leave Buff Boy?"

"He's asleep," Maura answered, realizing a moment too late that she probably shouldn't have condoned the nickname.

"Finally, some good news," Jeane grinned, and Saori threw her a disapproving look.

"Did you manage to come up with anything?" Maura asked, changing the topic.

Jeane stepped to the fireplace for another helping of coffee. "We couldn't talk to anyone else in the Cities, but another contact said the survivors are moving back to the Ranch. It's hard to say what the Union will do now. There's some indication they're monitoring Talala, but no one knows anything about any mysterious machine that was stolen. They're keeping a tight lid on it."

"What now, then?" Saori looked puzzled.

"How should I know?" Jeane huffed and sat down at the table, taking Saori's previous place. "I guess we'll go to the Ranch."

The word left an uncomfortable silence in the room. Maura saw the dark look Jeane gave Saori but didn't understand its meaning.

"But first, Kliks wants to do something scientific at the Window," Jeane went on with less steam than before. "He passed out two hours ago, so we'll stay until the afternoon."

"Or longer," Saori said quietly. Jeane scowled at her and wanted to interrupt, but the woman went on. "No one will find you here, Jeane. We can help."

A smile appeared on the captain's face, but only for a second. "My darling Saori, if the Union wasn't looking for us using black magic, I would love the idea. But I'm afraid we can't."

"Because you'd rather lead them to the Ranch?"

"They'll deal somehow," Jeane snorted, but her confidence was wavering. "Maybe Ranch-magic defuses Talala-magic! I don't know; everything is so very mysterious and unpredictable these days. But tell me, good friend, what would I do if the Union conquered Duplex? Where else would I go to spy on the clans, hear the latest gossip about all the people I don't care for, and drown the sadness in my heart into booze and coffee?" Saori sighed in surrender, and Jeane smashed her fist on the table with renewed vigor. "And what do I have to do to get breakfast around here?"

"Be a paying customer."

She glared at Saori. "Add it to my tab."

"You know, the point of a tab is that you pay it off eventually."

Jeane grinned, stood, and strutted to the door. Seeing Saori's disgruntled expression, Maura wondered again about the history between these two women, but she was soon rattled out of her contemplation by Jeane's question, thrown back at her from the threshold. "You coming?"

"Where?"

"To the Window. I thought you liked lanes and stuff."

Maura blinked. She *had* wanted to go on a walk. "Sure, okay."

Jeane held up a finger. "But only if we leave Muscle Man behind. I don't feel like listening to his complaining."

Maura swallowed back a retort. "Alright."

"Awesome. Breakfast, then go time."

Jeane fetched Kliks and summoned ALU from the *Skylark*, then Saori fed them a huge breakfast of eggs, green beans, and all kinds of grains. Maura told her to inform Damian where they went in case he woke up, then the four of them started off on the clammy streets of Blackbones towards the Window.

"How do you know so much about lanes?" Maura asked when she managed to get a word in.

Kliks pulled an embarrassed smile. "It's a popular research area on my planet. Before I left, I was studying it as well. I'm sorry—was I too overwhelming?"

She was marching beside the Talalan and ALU on a muddy main street. A blanket of gray clouds covered the town, but the rain had stopped, and the locals ventured outside, making the place feel more alive than the previous day. Jeane led them to the Window, and on the way, Kliks—maybe in an attempt to keep himself awake—had given Maura a lecture on lanes. She was interested in the topic, but after a while, he added so many mathematical concepts and technical terms to his commentary, she'd lost the thread.

"It's no problem," she said.

"I beg of you, don't encourage him," Jeane groaned, but Kliks only huffed in answer.

Maura couldn't suppress a smile. "Your home planet is Talala, right?"

"Indeed." Kliks glanced at her but returned his attention to the manipulator, a bulky device in white casing which he carried in his arms. "You've heard about us?"

"I know your people were in contact with Miyoza, but then you closed yourselves off. They say Talalans never leave their planet anymore, and no outsider has crossed the swarm around your solar system since then." Kliks nodded, his face inscrutable. Maura raised an eyebrow. "But you're here."

"Kliks is a unique specimen," Jeane butted in again. "Aren't I the luckiest girl?"

"You're not going to help carry this thing at all?" Kliks asked, annoyed and breathless.

"No."

"I told you, I just need to do some calculations. Don't you want to figure out what we're up against?"

"Do I?"

Kliks shook his head, giving up. His quick breaths formed small white clouds in the cold air as he heaved under the weight of the machine.

"Let me help," Maura offered, but Kliks glanced at her with the expression of a martyr.

"Thank you, but I can deal with this."

"Help!" ALU screeched too as they dashed forward. Turning back, they circled Maura excitedly.

"You'll only drop it, clumsy," Kliks said with a half-smile.

They followed the street, passing wooden buildings, making their way through the scattered crowd of locals coming and going between homesteads and shops, and stopped at the last row of houses where the road ended sharply. A field of mud stretched out in front of them, a no man's land of damp earth.

"Here we are!" Jeane announced. "Feast your eyes on weird-ass shit."

At first glance, Maura couldn't tell what was wrong with the sight. Beyond the swampy region, fifty or so yards ahead, the ground changed to a darker color and seemed more level. Further off, between a group of trees and large stone buildings, a similar road appeared to the one they'd just stepped off, but in itself, all this wasn't that interesting. There was, however, something not quite right with the perspective. She inclined her head from the left to the right, trying to figure it out.

The horizon, she realized. It was too high. And the more she looked toward the stone buildings and the trees, the more it seemed she was staring at them through clear water. Waves propagated through the transparent surface, originating from the ground and disappearing above their heads, and as she followed the liquid-like boundary towards the sky, she saw thin wisps and puffs of mist whirling in and out of it like playful ghosts.

Jeane turned around, narrowing her eyes at one of the houses. "Hey, Hari! What's the weather like?"

On the second-floor balcony, a figure who had been sitting with legs propped on a table, jumped up. "Blake, is that you?"

"Sure is. And I brought guests."

"Ah, tourists!" Hari laughed and took a long look at a device in her hand. "At the right time too. You've got half an hour until a wave. Should be safe now."

The four of them walked through the muddy soil towards the Window, Kliks hugging the manipulator to his chest protectively. Two feet away from the boundary, they stopped; this close, the Window was like an enormous pane of liquid glass floating in the air. Kliks placed his device on the ground and crouched down. Maura reached out, her fingers pausing a few inches from the barrier.

"Go ahead." Kliks connected his tablet to the manipulator. "It's not like an average crack. It's stable, at least right now. You can step through, but don't stay too long and don't go far. I think you need a permit for a proper visit, or the afars will put you in jail."

"Afars?"

"That's what the inhabitants of Duplex-1 call the inhabitants of Duplex-2. And vice versa." Kliks sighed. "Don't even ask. It gets confusing."

ALU sped through the Window and stopped thirty feet away on the other side. They waved to Maura and raced back through the boundary with a joyful whistle.

Maura let her fingers break through the strange surface. Apart from a small tension on her skin, she felt no discomfort, so she took a deep breath and stepped forward. There was only a momentary dizziness like her body was snatched up and released by gravity, then she was through.

The air of Duplex-2 smelled of smoke and the musty scent of plants. The sky was bluer, the ground harder under her boots, and her body felt heavier. She watched through the Window as Kliks typed something into his computer, and Jeane ran her fingers along the bizarre divide.

Maura stuck her arm through, moving her wrist around, but there was no other feeling apart from the slight tautness. It was incredible—one small motion, bridging an unimaginable distance.

She stepped back to Duplex-1 and exhaled slowly. Her head started to hurt again, and she rubbed her temples with a painful grimace.

"Are you okay?" Jeane's voice was more confused than concerned.

"I just realized how far away I am from home."

As Maura took another step, the earth trembled under her feet. She would have blamed it on her imagination, but then Kliks stood, furrowing his brow.

Another shake, larger this time. The sentries of Blackbones yelped in alarm, and the people posted at the stone mansions on the other side soon had the same reaction in answer.

"Jeane?" Kliks said in a small voice. He was staring at the manipulator as several white lights flashed up on its side.

"What in hells are you doing? Didn't you say—"

"I'm not the one doing this!"

"Back away, please!" Hari's voice reached them through a loudspeaker. "Unexpected GI! Get back!"

"What's a GI?" Maura asked, panicked.

"Gravitational instability." Jeane grabbed one side of the manipulator while Kliks held onto the other. ALU was already hopping through the empty field on their short legs. As the captain and Kliks hurried after the robot, Jeane called above her shoulder. "Don't fall behind!"

They crossed the no man's land and stopped amongst the people gathering at the end of the road to gawk at the strange event. The Window was a wildly whirling pool now, tremors oscillating on its immaterial surface in a chaotic pattern. The view of the other side distorted, and while Maura couldn't feel it at their position, the shakes must have been quite strong in the vicinity of the intersection. Piles of dirt and globs of water lifted from the foot of the barrier, floated in the air, and got flung upward or to the sides.

In the next second, the same kind of earthy, lush aroma rushed her senses that she'd experienced on Duplex-2, and her limbs got heavier as if the gravity of the other planet was filtering through to this side. Above her, the sky was fluctuating: gray clouds, clear blue, then clouds again. The people around them muttered curses and backed away—this didn't seem like an everyday occurrence.

Jeane grabbed Kliks's shoulders. "Get the hells out of here!" she hissed. Kliks' eyes widened. He spun around and started off toward the inn, hauling the manipulator along, ALU at his heels, and as he disappeared into the distance, the sky stopped changing above them, the smells of Duplex-2 dissipating.

"Did we do this?" Maura asked, but Jeane's expression was more irked than anything.

"Stars know." She rolled her eyes. "Everything is so weird here."

As if on cue, two men broke through the crowd, releasing a deranged roar and charging at the Window. They were dressed in white overalls covered with a chaotic arrangement of nozzles, metallic disks, and colorful paper stripes. Around ten yards from the Window, they stopped in their tracks, turned to the crowd, and lifted their arms up theatrically. They took a step back, still facing the people...and soared up towards the sky as if pulled on strings.

"Cool, your first gravsurf performance!" Jeane nudged Maura, who stared at the two black dots the men had turned into in the distance, her mouth left agape. She saw the captain smile in the corner of her eye. "You're welcome."

The two figures zoomed downward, but instead of impacting, a few button-pushes on their suits made them decelerate abruptly. Their legs flung upward as their torsos halted inches above the ground, then both of them started up again, circling each other in a spiral pattern, the iridescent paper bands swirling around them like insect wings. They were flying, but it wasn't the air they'd mastered; somehow, they overpowered the chaotic gravity changes around the Window and arranged them into a row of movements resembling an uncoordinated but enthralling dance. Many times, Maura thought they were going to fall, but their bodies were picked up by an invisible force. They whooped and shrieked in joy, and the people on both sides of the Window cheered them as if nothing weird had happened five minutes before.

"Meet the Krotke twins. They do this all the time during GIs. Built their own suits and everything." Jeane surveyed the show with a grin. "They are so nuts."

One of the brothers floated three feet above the ground,

almost motionless, balancing the changing gravity with the minuscule movements of his legs, arms, and fingers as he pushed different buttons on his suit. Surfing really was the best expression for what he was doing. The other man circled him in a spiraling motion, imitating ocean waves. Unrooted plants and rocks got picked up from the ground around them, signifying the power of the gravitational instability still roaring in the vicinity of the Window.

"Damian would love this." Maura smiled as wonder took the place of her momentary terror. A memory surfaced in her mind, the two of them as children on a sun-scorched beach, trying to stay afloat on flimsy plastic boards.

Jeane only grunted in reply, and Maura turned to her, crossing her arms before her chest.

"Could you give him a break, please?" she blurted out. "His best friend just died. He had to leave his home, and there's nothing out here that he knows."

Jeane nodded. "Fair. But it's the same with you, and somehow we can still converse without me wanting to rip my own head off."

"I admit, diplomacy is not his strong suit."

"But it is yours, right, *Princess*?" Jeane retorted, and Maura couldn't hide her shock in time. She swallowed, and Jeane blinked, releasing a deep sigh. "Skies damnit. You're really her."

Maura pressed her lips together, keeping her eyes on the Krotke brothers, who were still doing their rounds in the sky. *That secret got out fast.* "Queen, actually. How did you figure it out?"

"It was Kliks. But let me tell you, the maintenance tale? So weak."

Maura frowned. "I was improvising."

"So, Maura Tholis, huh? And Damian..."

"He's my bodyguard."

"What's your story? The real one."

Maura glared at her. "My father fought a losing war, then he died. I surrendered to Gaerris, messed up the peace talks, and we had to run for our lives."

"Oh dear, we're already doing this?" Kliks came to a stop

beside them; he didn't have the manipulator or ALU this time, and he was heaving as if he'd been running a small marathon. He gave Maura an apologetic look. "I'm so sorry, Your Majesty, but I—"

"Please, call me Maura." She closed her eyes for a second, stomach turning.

"How come you're the queen, though?" Jeane asked in a flippant tone. "What about your mother?"

Kliks inhaled like he wanted to reprimand her, but Maura beat him with the answer. "She died years ago on a raid against a Gaerrisian outpost."

There was a beat of silence, and Maura knew they were all thinking it. Why would a queen and a mother go on a mission like that when they had other soldiers and remote-controlled equipment to do the job? The exact thing she'd always been wondering. Even her father had never risked his own life like that.

He risked it in other ways, along with everyone else's. What a family.

"My mother was a talented strategist," she said, her tone more heated than she would have liked. "She also had a...vociferous personality. I'm sorry, is this why you brought me out here?" Her eyes snapped at Jeane. "So you could interrogate me?"

Jeane frowned at her. "No. I brought you here because you looked like a traumatized person who needed a break."

Maura opened her mouth to answer, but nothing came out. She hadn't expected that. Glancing at Kliks, she hoped he would break the awkward silence, but the Talalan was busy peering at Jeane like he was seeing her for the first time in his life.

Finally, the captain spoke up again. "Let's get back to our problem. Like I said, there was no clause about a refugee princess—sorry, queen—and her white knight when we got this job. Was it only Nasir's personal mission to get you two out?"

"No." Maura gathered her thoughts again. "I'm sure the Net wants the glove—the piece of technology we're carrying. But Nasir was our friend." She breathed through the painful pang in her chest. It was still hard to believe that he and his Net comrades were gone. Even harder to pretend it wasn't her fault. "The Net and your client might not even know he included us in the deal. Of course, the glove doesn't work without me," she emphasized. "Only I can use it now that my father's gone. Nasir knew this."

"But I bet Dikent didn't," Kliks chimed in.

Jeane sighed. "Yeah, no. I'm starting to think what happened was that someone ran their mouth too close to his eager ears, giving him the brilliant idea to steal the valuable artifact from the fabled Miyoza. We were just there to do the dirty work for him."

"But that would mean there's no use going to him. He won't know anything," Maura said.

"What are you planning to do instead?" Jeane asked. "You said your planet is occupied. What's the Net going to do about that? They haven't been great at interstellar resistance so far."

"I..."

Jeane looked at her expectantly, but Maura couldn't form the sentence. She'd had a plan. Well, Nasir had one. But thinking about getting help and being out here turned out to be two very different things.

"I will help my people," she said in the end. "There's still hope."

They were silent for a while. Maura shuddered. In contrast with the frolicking twins above, the weight of the sky descended on her shoulders, crushing her and sucking the air out of her lungs. She'd left her home and traveled far to call for help, but she felt so vulnerable and weak, walking these strange planets full of dangers she'd never seen before and people who knew and cared nothing about her plight.

She was absent. Negative space. A shout without a voice.

"We can still ask around on the Ranch." An almost abashed expression appeared on Jeane's face. "If not Dikent, then someone must know where to find the Net. And the place isn't so bad. You might even like it."

Maura squinted at Jeane, but it was Kliks' visible shock that told her Jeane was lying through her teeth. She was humoring her to try and provide some comfort. Maybe the dead parents tidbit had gotten to her.

But even before that, she'd wanted to do something nice for her. Jeane was a tough nut to crack, as Sofia would say.

"It's your home, right?" Maura asked. "The Ranch?"

Complicated emotions clouded Jeane's face. There was a *lot* of baggage there. "The *Skylark* is my home." The statement seemed to anchor her, and she shrugged. "But I spent the first fifteen years of my life on the Ranch. I haven't been back in a while. Should be fun."

Maura took a deep breath. She glanced over at the crowd that was still cheering for the brothers' gravity dance, and a shameful thought flashed through her mind.

She could stay here. Duplex was the perfect hiding place to become someone else. Not a princess or a queen but someone no one knew. Someone who could wake up each day, get a hearty breakfast at The Candle, walk out here to watch this impossible view, and keep waiting until the memories of all the dark days faded from her aching mind.

She shook her head. Her people were counting on her—all the innocent souls her father had dragged into the war. As long as there was a chance to save them, she couldn't stop.

Nothing to do but to go forward. Yet still, she stood unmoving and numb.

"We should go." Jeane's voice was gentle, so much so that Maura couldn't suppress a surprised blink. "Are you ready?"

"No," Maura said because it was true.

A sad smile appeared on Jeane's face, and as she turned away and started marching back towards the town, she called back, "That's alright. Neither am I."

Maura rubbed her temple, frozen in place. When she raised her head again, Kliks was still beside her, a patient question on his face. Maura nodded, the Talalan held out his arm, and she looped her own through his with a faint smile. She let her legs carry her away, not looking back, clutching onto Kliks.

CHAPTER 17 | THE INSIDE MAN

Time was a heavy boulder grinding down a slope, inch by inch. Nasir heard it sometimes, too, a scraping noise against his skull, drowning out his thoughts. Other times, it stopped, and that was worse because then the pain turned sharp and all-consuming. His burn wounds blazed up, itching and straining, the torment not enough to make him pass out, only stretching each second to infinity. Before he had been thrown in the cell, his captors had applied some sort of medigel to his skin, but he suspected the healing would be an arduous process.

And now Gaerris seemed to have forgotten about him. No noise or light reached inside his concrete room, and there couldn't be a worse fate for him than being kept in the dark, unable to affect the events that shaped his life. All he could do was hope.

He imagined Damian and Maura flying away from Miyoza with those lanehunters, safe and sound. He imagined them reaching the Net, then the group swooping in and saving everyone. He imagined his comrades, in captivity but alive like him, waiting to be freed. Flimsy, naive thoughts, but he needed something to hold onto. After all, it was his fault they'd ended up like this.

For the longest time, it hadn't occurred to him to go against orders. In the beginning, it was all about gathering information.

The Net believed Miyoza was valuable; with such an ally, they could finally leave the role of underground resistance behind and start a more open fight against the Union. But Miyoza was lost in its senseless war against Gaerris, and in the end, the Net went with plan B. To sweep (or save, as they would say) what was possible before the fall.

Throughout the years, Nasir and his mates had smuggled a large amount of information and the occasional artifact out of the system. And how long did it take for an alien world to become home? He'd never returned to his birth planet, Morakka, after the Union annexed it when he was but ten years old, and during his time serving the Net's cause, walking occupied worlds-turned-graveyards, no place had come to be as important to him as this one. After spending nine years on Miyoza, he couldn't bear seeing it destroyed.

But when King Caiden had fallen sick, their orders changed. They had days to leave the planet.

The royal glove would have been a big catch for the Net. Nasir had gotten close to taking it many times, but he hadn't. For one, Miyoza still needed it, and although they could certainly recreate it, its disappearance would have caused turmoil and possibly their untimely fall. Two, the glove itself wasn't enough. It needed a Tholis and a specific AI to function, and he hadn't quite felt ready to steal an all-powerful robot or kidnap the king or the princess. But most importantly, he knew he would have been extracted from the system after delivering such a boon. He would have never returned again, and he couldn't allow that to happen.

Not yet, he told himself every time he lied to his contacts about whether he was capable of acquiring the glove. *I still need time.*

But when Damian asked Nasir to help him and Maura escape the system in the aftermath of the king's death, he realized time was out. And he couldn't leave his friends to their fate, could he? So, he attempted to strike two birds in one fell swoop, thinking himself really smart for it. Yet he got nothing but a nasty jail cell out of the deal. He'd thought he had everything under control; now, he only felt sorry for his Net comrades for trusting him and following his lead.

Then slowly, these thoughts too silenced in his head. Hunger, thirst, and pain took their place. Two days might have passed or two millennia. He didn't care about what they did to him anymore. He only wished for this infinite loneliness to end.

When the door to his cell finally opened and a dim glow dribbled into the room, he couldn't find the strength to lift his head. The overhead lights turned on, then he heard people walking in and stopping beside his slumped body.

"Nasir Dareth," a man spoke in a stern tone that sounded familiar. "You're still alive."

Nasir glanced at the three pairs of polished boots in front of him and opened his mouth to answer, but there was no voice to the intent. He cleared his throat, and pain flashed into his head.

"Barely alive, indeed." The man laughed, joyless. "I do hope you have something to tell us, so we can put an end to your hardships."

"I'm afraid I have to disappoint," Nasir said. Not much more than a whisper, but at least the words broke free.

"That would be unfortunate," answered the deep voice of a woman. "I hoped we could deal with this situation quickly."

The third set of boots took a step towards him. "Look up, Nasir Dareth. Do you know who you're talking to?"

Nasir raised his head, and as he blinked to clear his vision, the first person he recognized was High General Liv Horst, the commander of the Gaerrisian military. Beside him stood a woman with bronze skin, her dark hair in a tight bun and an amused spark in her black eyes—Malina Trevise, General Horst's second in the Gaerrisian Council. This could only mean that the third figure was General Ruben Hassak, council member Three—a giant of a man, all muscle and meat, cruel lines framing his bare face as he glared down.

They came to him personally. Troubling.

"The question is simple," the High General started. Even from the low point Nasir looked up at him, it was obvious that the man was short. He wore a black military coat like his companions, and his pale face (even more weary than when Nasir had last seen him) was covered by a somewhat unkempt beard. "Where is Queen Maura Tholis?"

"I cannot reveal that," Nasir replied.

This was good. It meant that Damian and Maura managed to get off-planet.

Trevise turned to Hassak with an annoyed twitch of her mouth. "I told you he wasn't going to tell us anything."

"He needs incentive," Hassak grunted and made an impatient gesture to Horst.

Nasir stayed unmoving, his breathing shallow. The last time they'd spoken to General Horst, he had been willing to agree to a truce, but that didn't mean anything now. Nasir still had no idea what exactly transpired in the capital after Maura had fallen unconscious, spurring the city-AI to take full control over the CNS. Horst's last message to them seemed to imply that he believed that Maura hadn't betrayed him but was instead impeded from appearing at the peace talks, but who knew what his attitude was at this moment?

The High General stared at Nasir, his expression giving away nothing. "Out," he said, glancing at the others. At the same time, he reached into his coat and took out a metallic cylinder that, for all Nasir knew, could have been an eating utensil, a torture tool, or even a weapon. "I'll get those answers."

Hassak clearly wanted to argue, but Trevise gave a dark chuckle and patted his arm lightly. "Ah, the can-do attitude we were all waiting for! Come on, Ruben. We should let the boys play this out."

Nasir felt his chest constrict. Panic pummeled at his heart as he gathered his strength and pushed himself into a standing position. He didn't intend to cower like an animal before these people in his last moments.

Hassak muttered something like, "Should have done this ages ago," but Nasir couldn't focus on him through the numbing dread. Trevise and Hassak walked out of the cell, slamming the door behind them.

High General Horst flipped the small device over in his fingers, then with a quick move, he put it away. Taking out another tiny metal tool, he held it up as if he wanted Nasir to take a good look. A red light was blinking on it.

"I don't—" Nasir started, but Horst pushed a button on the gadget, and the light changed to green. Nasir frowned, waiting, but nothing else happened.

When the general spoke again, his tone was different. Still as calm and collected as before, it now lacked a certain tension—a switch Nasir found familiar. It was the voice of someone who, having had to play a part in front of a lot of people, talked plainly and honestly for the first time in a long, long time. "I'm taking a fair amount of risk here, but don't be mistaken. If you don't co-operate, you will regret it."

Nasir leaned his back against the wall. "What's that in your hand, sir?"

The general's voice was impatient now. "It is important that we talk without anyone else listening in. I am but one cog in this machine—albeit, the largest one. But there are nine others in our honorable Council. Most of them would kill you and destroy everything you treasure without hesitation. Only my position keeps them back. And I need your help."

What kind of trap is this? "With what?"

Horst sized him up. "You have been involved in the queen's plans. I need you to contact her for me."

"Why?"

"I need her to save us."

Nasir gave a shaky smile, hoping to convey a confidence he didn't feel. "What do you mean?"

He was willing to believe that Horst had deactivated some kind of bugs placed in the cell to pursue his personal plans without the rest of the Council knowing, but this sounded like mind games. Those three coming in here, attempting to bait him, Horst playing the good cop, all of it. Who could say what his real attitude was after his latest failure to secure a truce?

Horst raised an eyebrow. "She's the only one who can work your city-network. Which is still out of commission, by the way, after the AI blew up most of Three's units arriving to occupy the capital, targeted the palace itself, then, maybe realizing the absurdity of the situation, turned the entire system off." Nasir scowled at the news, and the general gave a sigh. "That's all I managed to reconstruct from the events after the fact. Your General

Pahoron also put up a decent fight with a well-timed attack from his special forces, but I can't say that changed the Council's mind about getting bloody vengeance." He looked at Nasir with an intense glare. "It took me years to convince those bastards to support or at least overlook my attempts at peace with you people. To allow me to try. Not a lot of success with that, but we're still here."

"Why?" Nasir asked, aware he was repeating questions like some automaton. But this was his safest route; let the general speak and fill the gaps in his understanding. "Why are you talking to me? You've won. It's over."

"Let me answer with a question. What do you think will happen to this planet now?"

Nasir hesitated. Without Maura and the glove, and with a deactivated CNS, Gaerris needed time to override the system so they could use it. In the meantime, they might be able to keep the surviving citizens under control and hunt down everyone who tried to run or hide away. There was surely a way of forming a working system with the leftover resources. Even with the scars of the war, Miyoza was still a more livable environment than Gaerris would ever be. Unless...

Unless Maura's fear of retribution proved to be right.

"You know the answer. We're going to burn this planet to the ground. This culture and its people are about to disappear from the universe." Nasir's eyes widened, and he wanted to interrupt, but Horst didn't let him. "And if you think that's irrational because why would we destroy the fruits of all our hard labor, then you don't know who we are or why we fight. You don't know our thirst for revenge and the hate we nurture towards everyone who has it better than us."

Nasir considered it for a second, but nothing the general said conflicted with what he knew about Gaerris. "Then my question still stands. Why would you want to save Miyoza?"

"Without Miyoza's help, Gaerris is lost," Horst said. "I need to make us into a society again, Nasir. Before time is up, before the next opponent arrives."

Nasir inhaled. He'd been right. It was all about the Union.

"They will be here soon. We took Miyoza out instead of them, but they're coming for us."

Nasir shook his head. "The queen and the glove won't solve your problem. You have drained Miyoza. No magic AI will give you the firepower to hold up against the Union."

"Yes. I expect that from the Net," Horst said. "Your friends told me a few things about that resistance of yours. They're here, by the way. Your friends. Mostly alive too." Nasir pursed his lips, and Horst gave him a meaningful glare as if to say, *It is on you whether they stay alive.* "If we play things right, we might still survive. I will support the last Tholis' return, so the AI and the CNS do not fall into the wrong hands. Then, with the Net, we could wipe out the radicals in our high command, and together, show the Union we're not just sheep to the slaughter."

That was the exact idea Nasir had presented to Damian and Maura. He'd been right all along—if General Horst was telling the truth. Of course, he might be trying to play him to get Maura's location so that Gaerris could eradicate the one person capable of messing up their plans.

"You're saying 'the radicals.' Who would fight alongside us in this new war you want to start?" Nasir asked. *Let's see whether the general will risk giving out some intel.*

"Two is with us; don't let her display fool you. And Four too. He wants power, but he believes us about the Union. But Three is a murderous fanatic, along with Nine and Seven, who do whatever he says. The rest of them are fickle." Horst waved that off. "But we've got loyals at all ranks in the military. And no"—the man paused for a long second, giving Nasir a piercing stare—"the goal is not another war. I want to keep both of our worlds alive. I want to preserve the pieces we fell apart to, so we have the opportunity to build something new."

Nasir was silent, digesting the information. Horst held his gaze.

"Have you ever been? To Gaerris?" he asked, and Nasir shook his head. Some of the operatives he'd come with had been planted there, and he heard all about Gaerris' warmongering dystopia from his Miyozan acquaintances, but he had no first-hand experience. Horst lifted his chin, just an inch. "I've been told our cities look a lot like Hurricane. The tunnels, the mines, the production lines. Except the dark. It just never gets as bright as it should down there. The darkness creeps in everywhere. The grime is all-consuming. My people know nothing else. Their daily schedules, workloads, and allowances are regulated by demand and supply—by how much food we can produce, how many bodies we throw at the frontlines, and what horrific experimental methods we sacrifice them to in any given year. We are everything we were not supposed to become." He looked down. "I hate that place."

The silence was heavy, and Nasir wondered how good an actor the general was. This could have been honest. And if it was...gods save his soul.

"But. I would do anything for those people." Horst's firm, calm tone returned, and his eyes cleared. "I ask that you try to set your preconceptions aside. Do you think the Net would assist me?"

"I don't know," Nasir answered, his mind racing. What was he supposed to say? Could he trust this? He'd sent Maura to the Net, but who knew how far she'd gotten. And while he didn't know much about the inner machinations of the resistance—after all, for years, he'd only had minimal contact with his supervisors—it was safe to say they would probably be more convinced by half a war council standing against Gaerrisian wannabe-despots and the dreadful Union than by the words of a currently homeless queen. The Net needed allies. The lanehunters had never been a real option, and if joining up with Liv Horst's insurgency won them Miyoza...

Exhaustion flooded him. He should have been dead; they all should have been dead. He'd screwed up once before. He was not supposed to make these decisions alone.

"Would you contact them, so they can give an answer?" Horst asked.

Nasir stayed silent. The High General talked like he was an open book, but he could have been just a talented liar.

"We don't have all the time in the world. I need a promise."

Nasir had the urge to laugh. Promises. Hopes and dreams. The vague idea of fighting back, and one day, maybe, breaking free. His whole life, right there. "A promise?"

"We can write out a contract if that's what you want, but it wouldn't mean anything. There needs to be trust."

How long until the Net could finally attack? Until their decades-long—nay, century-long preparation was ready? What if *he* could bring forth real change?

After all, hope was what he dealt in.

He pushed away from the wall and took a step forward. His legs were able to hold his weight—already a reason to celebrate. "You mentioned my friends. You will save them."

It wasn't a question, but Horst replied anyway. "I will do what I can to keep them alive." He spread his arms out. "See? A promise."

What would Damian do if he were in his place? But Nasir didn't need to think too hard. Damian would do everything to protect Maura and Miyoza. Always the noble defender. Always the knight in shining armor. His heart ached at the thought of not seeing him again.

No. He couldn't let that happen. And truth be told, Damian wouldn't be in this situation in the first place. *He always did make better decisions than me.*

"Alright. I will contact them."

Horst nodded, his relief only visible for a fraction of a second. "Unfortunately, I will need to hit you now," he said, and when Nasir's face fell, he continued with a flat expression. "They will expect you to look as though I tortured you. I will tell them you didn't give me any information and make sure they think you and your friends are dead. I'll smuggle you out to a safe place, then you will receive the necessary equipment to talk to your people and search for your queen. Does that suffice?"

Nasir looked into the general's face. Horst might have just given him another chance to fix what he'd ruined. Sure, the Net might refuse. Damian and Maura might not even be there. Anything could have happened. The Union might already be knocking at the front door.

On the other hand, this was the only way he could help. To make sure those two arrived where they were meant to arrive. To protect them as he always wanted to. To have a shot at having a shot.

And that would be pretty great for a dead man.

"Yes," he said. "I understand."

Horst gave another nod. The metal cylinder was in his hand again, and as he pushed the button on it, a high-pitched, awful noise resounded in the cell.

He stepped closer to Nasir and raised his fist for the first strike.

CHAPTER 18 | ECHOES FROM THE PAST

Maura focused on the flashing white lights along the fingers of the royal glove. The pressure drumming against her forehead grew, and the words "ERROR" and "CNS NOT IN RANGE" appeared in her field of vision in red. She attempted to bypass the warning again, but pain sliced through her temple like thousands of knives, and a groan broke free from her throat. Closing her eyes, she leaned back on the bed and clenched her fist in frustration.

The cabin belonged to Kliks and ALU, but they'd moved out to the common room of the *Skylark* so she and Damian could have their own space on board. But since ALU didn't need sleep and didn't own a proper bed, only Maura had a bunk while an old, uncomfortable pillow and blanket on the deck remained for Damian. Everyone hoped they wouldn't need to keep this arrangement up for long, but right now, this room was the quietest place on the vessel, and Maura was grateful for the alone time. Even if it meant that Damian was roaming the ship, arguing with the lanehunters about something inconsequential.

The headache that had been tormenting her for the last couple of days had not let up since lifting off Duplex, and the drugs Jeane provided were ineffective. The glove didn't function outside

Miyoza, and experimenting with the device had not become less dangerous since she'd last tried, even without the CNS and the AI overwhelming her mind, but connecting with it was her last hope to soothe the oppressive pain in case it turned out to be a type of withdrawal symptom.

But the agony persisted like poison in her brain. A teardrop ran down the side of her face, and she wiped it away, angry.

Was this how it had started for her father too?

Maura hadn't worn the glove nearly as often as the king, but in turn, whenever she had, she'd been much less prepared. All those times she'd silenced the AI and thought she was safe...maybe the corruption had taken root in her after all. Those nanobots the glove utilized to connect with the CNS were coursing through her veins too. Sometimes, plugged into the system, she'd felt like the AI was looking for her help, but what if in the end, it had judged her a liability as well?

She'd been suffering from the headaches ever since listening to the secret meeting between the king and High General Horst. But her history with the glove had begun much earlier.

The first time the idea of sabotage had formed in her mind was that night, five years ago, when Sofia and her family perished on their way out of the Miyoza system. Maura knew then that there must have been something wrong with everyone around her who was standing by, letting her father commit these atrocities. But she could change everything.

She was a Tholis, the only one apart from her father who could shut down the AI or revoke the king's access—or destroy the damn system if nothing else worked. But King Caiden had never provided her the training required to use the glove and the CNS, unwilling to entertain relinquishing his power. So, when she'd first accessed the glove with Nasir and Damian at her side, she was barely able to turn it on.

Still, she'd returned over and over again, teaching herself to bear the strain, the secret keeping the flame of hope alight in her even after the thought of sabotage succumbed to despair. In the end, her tenacity was the reason she was able to attempt that truce with General Horst.

For all the good it did to everyone.

Tenacity and defiance. And the overwhelming feeling of guilt. Lying on the bed with a throbbing head, Maura had to admit that her sanity had always been on the line. And after what the glove had done to her father, who knew how much damage the damn thing managed to cause to her?

Something fluttered in the darkness behind her eyelids. A flicker that made her sit right up.

Shelves and cabinets packed with clothes and miscellaneous belongings loomed over her in the tight space framed by the mismatched plating of metal hull. Switching off the blazing lights on the ceiling, she'd only left a desk lamp on, which gave off a warm orange light. She was alone, but she felt watched.

Great. Paranoia. Just what I needed.

"Don't be scared. I'm right here."

A figure sat on the deck across from her.

"I'm sorry," the apparition said, tone hesitant now. "Maybe this isn't such a good idea. But I thought it might help you."

Maura froze in terror. Her throat contracted, and every muscle in her body tightened, ready to flee.

It was happening. She'd gone crazy.

"No, no!" Sofia protested. "This is all real, as much as it can be."

Maura took a deep breath. Sofia was not there. Sofia was dead. She glanced at the glove on her hand, and her visitor followed her eyes.

"You're..." Maura started, and Sofia nodded, her face brightening. "But how?"

Her friend extended her arms to stretch, her movements carefree and painfully familiar. "I'm sorry it took so long. I needed some time to decompress myself after I transferred into the glove during the coronation."

Her face looked older than Maura remembered, but the features were the same, right to the last details. The pointed nose Sofia always hated because it "slanted to the left," the smart, sharp look in her almond eyes, the tiny dark brown mole above her mouth that she never had cleaned up because it "gave character to her face." Her body language, her voice, her gestures—a perfect copy.

"I'm using knowledge from the depths of your mind. Of course, I'm a perfect copy." Sofia paused. "Do you want me to change form? I can be someone unknown to you, or perhaps a faceless glimmer of light?"

"No, it's fine," Maura hurried to answer. This was almost grotesque. Still, the chance to see her face again... "Tell me who you are."

"I'm an early, simplified backup of the city-AI," the girl answered. "I was created back when the AI's performance was still nominal, and I've been hiding since. During your interfacing, I managed to copy myself into the glove, and now, inside your brain."

"Why are you here?"

Sofia rubbed at her nose. "To help you. To save you and our planet."

"Is everything okay?"

Maura jumped, spinning around like she'd been pricked in the side—Damian stood in the door, frowning. And, of course, by the time she turned back towards the cabin, the Sofia-vision had vanished into thin air.

"Yes." She tried to keep her voice steady, pulling the glove off her hand like it was a pet that suddenly turned feral. "I'm fine."

"I heard your voice." Damian stepped inside, looking over the walls like he wanted to interrogate them.

Maura swallowed. Her heart hammered against her throat as she processed what had just happened. She didn't want to attempt to explain until she didn't understand herself.

Had she really spoken to some form of the Miyozan city-AI? Her stomach turned at the idea. But this phantom was so different from how she'd perceived the AI back home. How had this backup transpired? And what did Sofia mean by saving her and the planet? Was this a trick of her broken mind, exhaustion, guilt, and sorrow creating a cruel vision? The beginning phase of what had shattered her father's intellect?

Her unsettling dream about Sofia before he'd left Miyoza City with Nasir and his compatriots flashed into her mind. Had that been a precursor of this?

"I was thinking out loud," she said because Damian still expected an answer. The man peered at the glove in her hand, and she waved it away. "It's nothing. Just...well, isn't it so strange? How useless this thing is now when back at home it meant everything?"

Damian sat on the bed with a tired groan. "It's a different world out here. But we still have a goal."

"I know. And I know we needed to leave, but I can't help thinking that we shouldn't have." Maura threw the glove on the bed, taking a deep breath to calm herself. This was not what she wanted to talk about, and she especially didn't want to complain because things were hard for Damian too, but the words forced themselves out of her mouth. "We're never going home again, are we?"

"Of course, we are," Damian replied. "Please don't torture yourself. You did everything you could and saved a lot of people. Sacrificing yourself without a plan would have been useless."

"I saved no one." They'd been through this a hundred times, but to not say it would have been dishonest. "I abandoned them."

"We made that deal with Horst because he wanted to preserve our planet."

"We *broke* the deal." Maura eyed the bandages on Damian's arms. The wounds still pained him, but they were healing. And he'd fared much better than Nasir and his friends.

"Some things you shouldn't take the responsibility for. Remember what Nasir said. We still have a chance."

Such a rare occasion this was, feeling uncomfortable in the company of her friend. They weren't arguing because both of them were right; they only had disparate, disconnected parts in a dull play.

"I understand what you're saying," Maura replied. "And I want that to be true. But for now, everything is wrong." She stood, restless, eager to leave the inane exchange behind. "I'll go and try to find out when we'll arrive at this Ranch."

"At least you might get an answer," Damian muttered, looking irritable, and against everything, Maura smiled.

"They don't like you. They know you don't trust them."

"Like dogs."

Maura frowned. "Come on now."

"Of course, I don't trust them!" Damian furrowed his brows. "They're practically thieves."

Maura suspected it wasn't the stealing but the lack of clear loyalty that bothered Damian. "We could have ended up in much less pleasant company. They saved our lives."

Damian gave a vaguely concurrent hum. "True. I just don't like that they know who you are." He fell silent, looking just as lost as Maura felt. Still hoping, though. And still with her.

"Do you want me to bring you something to eat?" Maura asked.

"I can take care of myself, thank you," Damian said, but his eyes were gentle.

She pressed her lips together in a vague smile. "I know."

"You're going to be okay?"

The question sounded more like a statement, but she nodded anyway. Damian kept his eyes on her as if expecting something more, but the will to cry pressed on her throat, so Maura turned away and left the room.

She arrived at the open door of the control room deep in thought, but she paused on the threshold when Jeane's voice rang out from inside, sharp and angry. "You forget that I never wanted to go back!"

Maura peeked in. The captain sat with her back to the door in the pilot chair, typing something into the computer. No one else was with her, and she sure wasn't directing the words to Maura. She waited for a few seconds, hesitating between slamming the door to reveal her presence and leaving, when Jeane spoke again, this time more softly. "Because you're not there, smart-ass."

Maura's face flamed up hot as a blush crept on it. Jeane might have been talking to someone on the comms, but no answer came to her comments. If not for the strange conversation she'd just engaged in with her own imaginary figure, Maura would have left, embarrassed about listening in, but now, she kept waiting.

"Don't even start," Jeane grunted. "I'm leaving as soon as possible. I don't need this bullshit."

Nobody reacted. Maura didn't see the woman's face, but whatever answer she heard made her temper cool.

"Yeah, well. They need help. What am I gonna do, shove her out of the airlock? Going by that conversation yesterday, she'd just claw her way back in to save her precious planet."

There was a noise behind Maura, and she spun around. Kliks stood a few feet away, cables and devices in his arms, staring at her.

Her blush deepened and she released the door, retreating towards Kliks without a sound. The Talalan's pupilless black eyes were unreadable, and she couldn't decide whether he was aware of Jeane talking or understood the situation at all.

"I'm sorry," she said when she came to a stop beside him. They were far enough away from the door that Jeane probably didn't hear them. "I wasn't trying to...I wanted to speak to her, but I heard her and..."

Comprehension flashed in Kliks' eyes. "Oh, that. She does that sometimes."

"Talking to herself? Out loud?" *Is that not a medical condition?*

"It's not like that. I mean, it is, but...she's got some things to work through." Kliks' voice wasn't reprimanding, but he was clearly uncomfortable with the topic. "It's a support mechanism."

"Who is she—"

Kliks shook his head to cut her off. "She'll tell you if she wants to."

Maura nodded. The last thing Jeane had just said still rang in her head. Did she really perceive her that resolute? She barely knew what she was doing. Although, it was good to know that the woman decided to assist them for the time being.

"Why did you want to talk to her?" Kliks' question jolted Maura out of her daze.

"I wanted to know when we'll reach our destination." As she glanced down, she was surprised to see the glove on her hand. She'd dropped the thing on the bed, no? When did she put it back on? *Strange.*

"I would say five or six hours, but it's hard to tell with the

Ranch." Kliks halted, waiting for a reaction, but all Maura could offer was confusion, so he went on with a knowing smile. "You'll see. It's a special place—or so I've heard. But we need to be careful about the Union, and I'm guessing Jeane is not in a hurry either."

"What's her problem with that place?"

"That's difficult to explain, and it also connects to what you just heard." Kliks gave a sigh. "She's angry because she still misses it, even though she doesn't want to. In her head, going back means surrendering—but to what, I don't think she could tell you."

He paused, but Maura found it hard to react. Part of what he said resonated with her own thoughts. She had never imagined there would be a time in her life when she wouldn't be connected to Miyoza. She was a princess, meant to be a queen. And now, pushed out into the world where she became no one, the rootless, free-floating sensation was scary.

But out here, there were no expectations either. The binds of her home could have been gone in a second if she'd let them, like when she'd imagined staying on Duplex. She could be anyone, do anything. But was it really possible to leave everything behind? Even lanehunters had their home calling out for them. Jeane didn't like the thought of surrendering to that, but for Maura, surrendering would mean not going home ever again.

"Anyway, we should have enough time for some experimenting." Kliks jiggled the things he held in his arms. "I want to figure out what our manipulator can do."

"Isn't it dangerous? What happened at the Window—"

"Is exactly why I need to look into the device again. Do you want to come?"

She hesitated. Part of her still wished for solitude, but on this small ship, where? Damian was in their chamber and likely would not be leaving soon, the control and the common rooms were always busy, and they might not even allow her into other places. Should she lock herself in the bathroom? And did she really want to stay alone when she'd just hallucinated her dead best friend talking to her? "Alright."

Kliks' face brightened. "Then follow me into the cave of science!"

The "cave of science" happened to be one of the corners of the cargo hold, where ALU was already fussing around the manipulator. The device seemed dark and dead until Kliks sat down and brushed a finger over a sensor which made two lights flash up on the side of the box. Maura settled beside the Talalan as he started to fiddle with some switches.

"As you know, we suspect the Union is tracking it, so I can't test its full functionalities," Kliks explained. "But that incident on Duplex gave me some ideas."

"What does this thing do?"

"Nothing, nothing." Kliks shrugged. "Only it's able to utilize lane energy like no other current technology can."

Maura lifted an eyebrow. She hadn't studied much lane physics, but even she knew that was unique. "That's why the Union is after you. And your people made the device?"

Kliks gave a grimace. "Yeah..."

"Oh, so you too have complicated ties to your own home planet." Maura hoped her voice conveyed more empathy than irony, and Kliks' eyeroll told her he wasn't offended. Then something from the conversation back in The Candle occurred to her. "You talked about mind control before?"

The Talalan's face contorted like he'd bitten into something sour. He started typing into his tablet. "That's a thing we can do. But let's say that a few centuries ago, we reinvented ourselves for several near apocalypse-inducing reasons, and now thought-binding counts a transgression. Except, apparently, when one of our dangerous inventions gets stolen, and we need the outcast of our society to go grab it for us." Kliks blinked apologetically. "But yes, it seems we've gathered here fine. Jeane is too stubborn to ever accept a home, you two had no choice but to leave, and me...I followed my own principles instead of the so-called good of all."

Maura nodded, understanding, but Kliks had turned back to his notes already.

"And you, ALU? What's your input on this whole home question?" she asked.

The technician jerked their head up and buzzed happily. "Our home is everywhere!"

"That is so awesome for you." Kliks sighed. "Maura, can you

hold this?"

She took the piece of cable, keeping it in the position Kliks wanted her to. During the next fifteen minutes, she passed him devices and checked the state of various switches—although Kliks could have done everything by himself, he still made an effort to include her.

"Talking about strange and dangerous technology...that glove." He nodded towards her hand while she pushed some buttons he'd instructed her to push. "*The* glove, I presume? The one that connects you with your AI?"

"Ah, yes." Maura eyed the device for a second. ALU gave a sharp whistle but didn't follow it up with a comment. She went on, aware that maybe Damian wouldn't approve of her disclosing the details of their mission. "The Net wants to reverse-engineer something from it to use against the Union. And in turn, I will ask them to assist my return to Miyoza." Kliks' eyes widened in what she thought was appreciation but also hesitance. "I don't know. I'm open to ideas."

Saying it out loud just made the arbitrary nature of Maura's plan that much more obvious, but fortunately, Kliks didn't push the topic.

"What did you mean by you were 'following your principles'?" she inquired later in an attempt to take her mind off her increasingly brooding thoughts. "When you left your home?"

Kliks was in the process of turning a bunch of knobs on the manipulator this way and that while ALU followed the readouts of the various diagnostic devices, announcing the numbers for the Talalan so he could note them into his tablet. "I meant that I made my whole family mad at me because I didn't think the peak of our existence was to close ourselves off from the universe as soon as it opened up. I hold my opinion, by the way, although the universe often tries to convince me otherwise."

"You fought with your family?"

"Yes. Albeit, family is a bit different on Talala than what you must be used to. In my case, it means basically the whole city." Kliks shook his head. "So I left. To prove them wrong."

Maura didn't know what to say, but ALU solved the situation.

"Kliks is the most stubborn we have ever met!"

Kliks glared at them, then turned back to Maura, the manipulator temporarily forgotten. "If you only knew what Talala was like before the lanes! We wanted to be spacefarers, to know everything there is, to discover the galaxy. But when that lane appeared beside our sun and we encountered humans, other intelligent species, and all those dead worlds...I think it was too much. Our politics changed radically, and the families agreed to isolate our planet. We built the wall; I think you call it a Dyson swarm. And now, we keep everything and everyone away." Kliks glanced at his calculations again. "I said I left, but I essentially had to break out."

"And that's why you joined the lanehunters and travel with Jeane. Because you wanted to see the universe."

"It sure isn't because of my irresistible personality," Jeane's voice called out, and all three of them turned their heads towards the entrance in unison. Maura's pulse quickened like she got caught doing something forbidden, but the captain was grinning. "But once he got a taste of adventure, I couldn't get rid of him."

Kliks rolled his eyes. "I just didn't realize in time that your definition of adventure was defective."

"Hey, has he told you how we met?" Jeane crossed the hold with a few long steps and stood beside them with hands on her hips. "I beat up three assholes to save his cute face."

The Talalan clutched his head in exaggerated irritation. "Please, don't embarrass yourself before our guest."

Maura smirked, blinking in surprise the next second as Damian walked in behind Jeane. He must have gotten fed up with being alone.

"It happened in The Candle," Jeane went on, shooting a glance at the man. "Kliks was sitting in the corner all broody when some jerks started to pick on him. Low-life Union mercenaries or something."

"You were very drunk," Kliks pointed out. "And you shouldn't have intervened. I had it under control."

"Those racist fucks would have killed you."

"Didn't you say Duplex was an independent world?" Damian asked. There was no trace of adversity in his voice, only honest curiosity about the story.

"No, those guys weren't proper agents. And they were slacking off." Jeane waved her hand around. "That's why we got out of there in the end. They couldn't report the mysterious Talalan because they would have been questioned about why they'd spent their working hours on some backwater world, drinking."

"We got out because Saori called the county patrol," Kliks added. "You didn't beat up anyone, Jeane. They smashed your face in, and we had to run."

Jeane smiled, evidently proud of the achievement. And even though Damian rolled his eyes, his grimace was more like a smirk than a frown. Maura could see he was trying to be more amicable. It looked good on him.

A moment later, Jeane's glance wandered to the manipulator, and her expression turned dour. "Again? Tell me, how can you possibly twiddle with this machine so much?"

"Well, excuse me if I want to know more about it before we let the technological advancement of the millennium slip out of our fingers!"

"You're gonna get us killed," Jeane retorted. "What about Duplex—"

"The Window is known to be unstable," Kliks cut her off. "Whatever happened wasn't my fault."

"Oh, that's some flawless attitude!"

Kliks huffed and turned back to his notes, but he kept glancing up at Jeane. The captain stood with a raised eyebrow, arms entwined and face grave, but she gave Maura a quick wink when no one else saw it.

"I need to know what they did. My people," Kliks added, still pouting. "If it turns out they found a way to keep the whole of creation from accidentally collapsing while using it, then I'm considering breaking some taboos and asking them whether we should drop it off...how did you word it? Through their fence."

Jeane flashed her eyes at him. "Don't tempt me with prospects like this. I might believe you this time."

Maura suppressed a smile. And there, for the first time in a long time, on the cold deck of the cargo hold, struggling with her headache and the memory of Sofia, listening to the grumbling of her traveling companions, she felt almost at peace.

Then ALU gave a high-pitched squeal, and Maura didn't think anything of it until Jeane jerked her head up. "What?"

The robot chirped again. "Someone's here," they said, then turned their back on the group and ran out of the hold.

"I don't like this," Kliks stated. Jeane took off after ALU without further comment.

"What's happening?" Damian stared after her, but Kliks was already pushing himself off the deck, extending his hand to help Maura up.

She stood but immediately reeled back. Sofia was there, horror on her face as she pointed at the manipulator. "You need to turn it off."

"What? Why?" Maura asked her, confused.

"Why what?" Kliks turned and followed Maura's eyes, seeing nothing. "I said there's probably a ship heading at us. What's gotten into you?"

"We need to turn the device off," Maura repeated Sofia's message. "Something's wrong."

Kliks hesitated, but he crouched down and performed the same motion over one of the displays that he'd done in the beginning. He frowned when the lights stayed on. "Why—"

The sound of an alarm blared up on the corridor. Damian jumped to Maura's side as Kliks reached for his tablet.

"What's going on?" he shouted into the microphone.

"Agent Jerkface! He found us!" Jeane yelled from the other side. "Come back up here and help me deal with him!"

Sofia shook her head frantically, backing off from the manipulator. "No—it's too late."

Kliks started towards the door with Damian and Maura, but they all turned back sharply when the manipulator began to give off a humming noise. The white sphere at its core emitted a glowing blue light.

The Talalan paused, his eyes widening. "It's never done this before."

The light turned more intense, and Damian grabbed Maura's shoulder, backing away with her. She shut her eyes, but the glare seeped through her skin, puncturing her mind. The hum increased to a roar, the deck shuddered under their feet, and everything went blinding white.

Then they were falling.

CHAPTER 19 | HEART AND HOME

Gertrudia Banks leaned back in the seat, moving her feet in circles to increase the blood flow. The radar image projected on the front wall showed all thirty-six vessels in the convoy flying in formation around her ship, the *Harimau*, approaching the last known coordinates of the Ranch while racing through the asteroid cloud in the outer regions of the Kerauk system.

So far, so mediocre.

Chhaya Bahuri, her navigator and comms officer, sat at the terminal to her right, back straight, head held high, her gold-and-silver prosthetic leg stretching out under her desk. When their eyes met, the woman gave a sharp nod of reassurance. On Gertie's other side, Tiu Yong, the ship's engineer, was leaning over his computer, deep in thought, his long nose almost touching the screen as he flipped through the status reports of the vessels in their group. For the last eight hours, Bahuri and Yong had been tirelessly communicating with everyone who made it out of the Cities and overseeing the scouts the convoy sent forward to warn them of lurking Union forces.

After it had become clear the Cities wouldn't be able to oppose the Union destroyers which inexplicably found their way around their defenses, the *Harimau* played an important role in coordinating the lanehunters' flight. Since Gertie always made sure to have the latest transit logs from all the docks in her ship's database and kept track of the position of the Ranch, she and a few other similarly paranoid captains had been able to gather and check the fleeing ships on their way out of the Ros-3 lane, point them in the right direction, and screen for suspicious vessels after Cities Control went offline. But not all lanehunter spacecraft had stayed with them. Some preferred to follow their clan's procedures, others braved the distance to the Ranch alone or in smaller groups to confuse and divert potential pursuers, or targeted different planets altogether to hunker down on. All in all, their escape hadn't been as coordinated as it could have been.

They would have to hold a census when they got to the Ranch, and Gertie dreaded hearing the results already.

The chaos of those last hours was still making ripples in her mind. The bombs...agents flooding the beloved streets of Central, seizing people...their frantic flight out while their home perished behind. None of them had been prepared for an attack like this; in the span of a few hours, they'd had to surrender one of their most important hideouts. There would be turmoil, starting with the clans reassessing their control, each trying to gain more influence among these new conditions. Then there would be fragmentation—some groups would want to hide, some would want revenge, and others might spread discord. Everything Gertie had been afraid of would happen now, and that was without any of them knowing half of what she did about the real reasons behind the raid.

"*Harimau*, it's the *Intrepid*. Are you sure we're in the right place?"

Gertie sighed and flicked on her comms. "Yes, *Intrepid*, I'm sure. You can check the data yourself."

"Because if not, we're in for a bad time out here," Dikent grumbled.

Dikent's vessel was trailing the *Harimau* at their starboard side. Gertie hadn't searched for him in those last hours in the Cities, contacting her subordinates instead and trusting that Dikent had his head in the game, but the *Intrepid* had caught up with them not far from the first vector out of the Ros-3. Dikent had sounded panicked and confused back then, but now he was back to his aggravating ways.

She steadied herself. *Everyone's nervous. No need to start trivial quarrels.* "I know that. Let's sync our parameters."

She gave the order to the rest of the convoy and checked their coordinates. Nothing else to do but wait.

There was no other place like the Ranch—even though there were a lot of wacky things in the universe nowadays. The way Gertie understood it, the settlement's asteroid existed in its own pocket dimension, connecting to real space through a small lane moving with the planetoid a few miles above its surface. From the outside, nothing could be seen but a faint outline of an inconsequential crack. The asteroid was also able to move inside this closed-off pocket, using the engines built into it, and its movement translated to the slow migration of the crack in normal space.

Quite an exercise in creativity, to imagine such a thing, but Gertie never had to. She'd been watching it in action first-hand from the moment she opened her eyes to this ridiculous world.

A few minutes passed. The convoy left the coordinates behind, and nothing happened. The crack wasn't there. But Gertie refused to give up. The Ranch was always moving, and her intel was from hours earlier.

"Signal acquired, ma'am," said Bahuri, and by the time Gertie narrowed her eyes at the screen to confirm, a bright blue flash blinded all of them. Everything turned white, and Gertie shut her eyes—and when the *Harimau* tilted to the side, she gripped the armrests of her chair. But just when she started to worry, gravity stabilized again.

Opening her eyes, she saw their screens filling with a familiar image: the elongated asteroid of the Ranch floating against a light blue backdrop.

Home.

As they approached the gleaming domes on the asteroid's surface, the relieved reports from the members of the convoy began coming in. A broadcast from Ranch Control informed them where they were allowed to land and listed the details of some new measures and restrictions they were expected to comply with. Gertie was barely listening as the voice rattled on about the heightened awareness of patrols, the distribution of emergency rations, and some assembly the heads of the Totenhart clan, the largest around, were preparing to call.

She wished Jeane was with her. In all her fantasies of returning home one day—if ever—they always did it together. As her thoughts wandered to her friend, anxiety and guilt flared up inside her. She should have paid more attention the last time they'd met. Should have stopped her from leaving. Whatever mess they were both in (and it was one and the same mess) was Gertie's fault.

Dikent Mend was the last person to call himself a member of the Net, but he was loyal as long as there was a steady flux of income for him from their machinations. Not that he loved the Union, but like most lanehunters, he was fine with the status quo, not understanding that it wasn't a status quo at all. He was Gertie's friend, though, and had been the one to introduce her to the movement. And since he had important influence in the clans that she often used after becoming the leader, she tended to forget that all this didn't mean she could trust him with everything.

She had already questioned the man, and he'd told her that before Jeane left the Cities, those Union goons had picked her out of the crowd, then chased her through Central at gunpoint. Dikent suspected the inspectors had come for Jeane, and after those destroyers had appeared and taken their city, Gertie had to take a wild guess at why and how that had happened. The Union's sudden skill at penetrating the Cities' defenses and the presence of her best friend's Talalan companion helped make the connection. The manipulator had resurfaced after Gertie thought she'd lost it for good.

The Net survived because it was compartmentalized. No one in their ranks had the full picture of their reach or knew the location and members of the different cells in case—as it often happened—their operatives were captured and interrogated. But that also meant that when they hooked a big fish, sometimes it was hard for Gertie to respond to situations rapidly. This was one of those times. Their plant on Hurricane had screwed up, Gertie didn't have enough information to course-correct, and the manipulator was off her radar just like that.

And then, as cosmic coincidences would have it, Jeane had strolled into Miyoza and now was in possession of the infamous royal glove too. Because apparently, when Gertie got wind of the Miyozan war winding down and told Dikent, "Do not interfere; I'm looking for the right person for the job," he had understood it as, "Please outsource this dangerous mission to your ex-girlfriend in hopes of seducing her to the side of our secret insurgency and back into a romantic relationship with you."

It had taken Gertie an inhuman amount of self-control not to bite Dikent's head off. Her best friend now carried on her beloved ship the two things the resistance needed the most, and no, this wasn't a joke.

The *Skylark* had popped up on Duplex recently, but Gertie knew Jeane—they would have left already. She had to reach them, to stop Jeane's frantic flight, but she also had a million other things to take care of in the aftermath of the Union attack. She was in way over her head. Balancing on the razor's edge was not fun. Gertie had been working towards an inciting event, towards something that ruffled the lanehunters' feathers enough to join the Net, but she never thought it was going to be the Union taking out the Cities. The threads were now unraveling at terrifying speed.

Gertie weaved her way through ships of all sizes and types idling around the Ranch while the convoy dispersed to deal with their own affairs. After getting scanned, the *Harimau* dove under the central dome and a few moments later landed on a platform in the eastern docks.

Gertie stood, smoothing out her yellow jumpsuit and nodding at the stocky, serious-faced engineer beside her. "I'm going to need a few hours. Mr. Yong, you have the conn. Chhaya, you're with me."

Bahuri rose, no trace of exhaustion in her movements. Yong looked at Gertie from under his bushy eyebrows. "We're not staying, are we?"

"Depends on what tale you tell me about what's going on around here. So, use your time wisely."

Yong gave a half-smile and turned back to his console. "On it, ma'am."

The Ranch hadn't changed much since her childhood, but Gertie didn't expect it to. Apart from the unavoidable fixes and expansion, like new domes or docks emerging and disappearing depending on the varying number of residents, at its core, everything here always stayed the same. A crowded, dusty town, full of history and surprisingly calm most of the time, not like the busy atmosphere of the Cities or the dangerous chaos of Metallia. An excellent hideout if one needed some respite to recuperate or somewhere to hole up and wait out trouble, it was also the origin point of lanehunter culture. The fact that they'd found this place before the Union certainly helped their centuries-long struggle to stay independent.

Gertie marched out onto the docks with Bahuri under a foggy blue sky, and the winds of nostalgia rushed her like an indignant typhoon. They pushed through a crowd of newly arrived lanehunters and ogling inhabitants conversing excitedly—if not a little panicked. Glancing around, many of the hangars and workshops were painfully familiar, and she could almost see Jeane and herself, playing hide-and-seek, nagging pilots for a tour of their ships, and said irritated pilots trying their hardest to get rid of the bothersome tweens.

Her legs moved automatically; leaving the docks, she stepped on a narrow road and followed it into the labyrinthine neighborhood. She enjoyed the usual companionable silence between her and Bahuri so much that when she realized where they were, they'd already walked down the street right up to her old orphanage. The Den, the children used to call it.

The Ranch had always been chock-full of kids whose parents took off for long periods of time, chasing their fortunes around some distant star or lost civilization. Most of them never returned for one reason or another, so there was a constant need for nurses, tutors, and the like to take care of the children they'd left behind. Both Gertie and Jeane had been admitted to the Den when they were babies. Their parents hadn't even given them names before leaving them to be raised and educated by strangers.

Gertie had never given much thought to who her parents

were. She never doubted she could be perfectly happy without them. If they didn't need her, she sure wouldn't bother missing them. But Jeane always wondered about hers and always felt incomplete without knowing where she'd come from. This was perhaps why she'd gravitated to Hollis so strongly too.

The streets were busy, and the skies were full of vehicles, but Gertie caught sight of a group of kids sitting on the pavement beside the familiar, unadorned, brown-stone building. One was deeply immersed in a game on a console in her hand, and the others leaned in to watch, hollering when she scored a point. Gertie looked at her comms. It was two in the afternoon, local. Those kids should have been at lunch rest.

She smiled faintly and caught Bahuri's questioning stare. She only gave a woman a resigned shake of her head. For a moment, she considered waiting for a tutor to storm out and drag these children inside. After doing some quick calculations, she decided if Mrs. Mallory was still working there, she would indeed end up like she always complained: with the kids taking her to the grave.

She shook herself, refocusing, then started walking again. Soon enough, they were standing in front of Hollis' old workshop.

The reinforcements on the walls and the yellow painting on the windows alluded that the building was freshly renovated. The new owner was treating it well. Good. Gertie would whoop his ass otherwise.

Even if it had always been Jeane with a unique connection to Hollis, his death, no matter how expected, had scarred them both. And it made Gertie angry sometimes that Jeane, so deep in her own pain, had never considered Gertie's grief. Jeane might have left the Ranch out of rushed judgment and rage, but Gertie had walked away too. The difference was, she supposed, that on her side, leaving safe haven was intentional. Stars knew how Jeane justified the decision to herself when she was obviously in greater need of a home than Gertie had ever been.

Gertie was far away from this place now, in every way possible. Even so, seeing it felt like a punch in the gut.

She turned to Bahuri. "Stay outside, mingle a bit. Call me if there's anything interesting."

Bahuri nodded, her hand brushing against her holstered

weapon as she crossed the street. They needed to get a feel for where things were headed, given the moods and opinions around here rolled and swelled like the tides. That clan assembly was going to be interesting, and while Gertie would rather not assume anything, the Ranch was a perfect replacement headquarters for the time being.

When she knocked on the metal door of the workshop, there was no answer. Trying the handle, the gate creaked, opening to almost total darkness.

She took a few steps inside. The ceiling lights were all out, and only a single lamp radiated sharp blue light at the other end of the hall beside a workstation. Huge machines, piles of parts, disorganized shelves, and worktables loomed in the surrounding dim.

Gertie gave a small cough, and the light at the table jerked. That was when she saw it was a headlight attached to a sitting person's forehead.

The man jumped up, dropped the tool he'd been holding, and whirled around theatrically. "Gertrudia Banks!" he exclaimed. "We meet again."

His headlamp glared into Gertie's eyes, and she wanted to shield them, but instead, she put her hands on her hips. "Mason Winner."

Mason tore the headband off and threw it on the table. With a flick of his hand, he turned on some lights above, and as the burning spots in Gertie's vision cleared, she could finally see his wide, toothy grin.

She remembered Mason as a handsome and reckless young pilot. Luck had always been on his side, and he knew it well. Gertie probably had a crush on him in those days, now that she thought about it, but as they'd spent more and more time together, the emotion had turned into friendship and trust. Mason hadn't lost the laugh or the confidence, but he seemed smaller somehow in his oil-spotted coveralls. Or more tired. His heart-shaped face was wrinkled, his dirty blond hair sparser. After only a few years, the change in him shouldn't have been that striking, and Gertie couldn't help but wonder whether it was really her who was different now.

"I thought you'd turn up," Mason said. "I was hoping it would be sooner than later."

Gertie spread her arms and turned around to show herself off. Mason gave a sharp whistle. "You grew!" he said, crossing the distance between them and drawing her into a tight hug.

She patted Mason's back awkwardly. "I'm happy to see you too. Can you let me go?"

Mason obeyed, taking a step backward and still smiling.

"I suppose you've made preparations?" *Let's get to the point.*

"Sure. Fine-tuned the thingamajig a few days ago to coordinate a drop on Metallia. You're free to use it whenever. And you're welcome."

"Thank you. Really."

"Hey, can you sit tight for a second?" Mason started off towards the door, slapping one hand on Gertie's shoulder as he passed her. "Don't move. I gotta call the others, or they'll beat my ass when they find out they missed you."

He rushed out and was gone before Gertie could have considered objecting.

Of course, she should have expected this. Making friendly social calls was the last thing on her mind, but it was unavoidable. She hadn't talked to these guys in years, after all, only kept in contact with Mason, asking him for small favors from time to time.

She circled the shop, snooping. Mason had changed a lot on the overall arrangement; stuff had been placed in different spots, new tools had appeared on the shelves, and there were two more beaten computers in the corner than there used to be. Memories rushed her. How many hours had she spent here with Jeane, helping Hollis, listening to his grumbling about careless mechanics using low-quality parts and pilots risking their beautiful ships recklessly? How many afternoons with Mason, Krea, and Varij, sitting around the table and enjoying their stories while playing cards? Hollis and his friends had taken many Den kids under their wings, and they were all happy to steal away from their boring classes to hear about battling Union agents, sailing dangerous lanes, and finding incredible riches in hidden corners of the universe.

Simpler times.

The door opened, and Mason marched in with two other figures at his heels. Gertie suddenly felt like she was surrounded by complete strangers.

Had Krea been always so short? And Varij looked like he'd been fasting for months. But when Krea hollered, "Are you real or am I seeing things?" then lunged at her, stifling her with another forceful hug, the strange sensation had passed.

The universe would just have to deal for a few minutes while she was having this reunion.

The three hunters pulled up chairs around Mason's workstation, and through Varij and Krea's five-minute crash course of the last few years, Gertie found out that the three friends weren't living together like they used to, anymore. Krea showed her pictures of her daughter, and Varij admitted he and his partner were planning to pledge to each other soon. They also told her about their latest jobs and run-ins with agents, and she listened to the stories with interest. At least it wasn't her being interrogated.

But soon, all three of them paused, and Mason flashed a smile at her. "Now, you. Don't think we're letting you go without some explanation."

The others nodded along, and Gertie rolled her eyes. "I see. You just wanted to corner me. I'm sorry, guys, but I can't say anything."

"Right, I get that," Krea replied. "Keep your secrets. But you know so much more about what's happening than us! The Cities are done, and all those rich jerks are here, but what will happen to us? The Ranch is not prepared for this."

"I wouldn't worry," Gertie said. "Most City-dwellers will leave when the first scare is over. They'll find new bases, build their castles again."

"But nothing will be as it was before," Varij muttered.

"Nothing is ever how it was before." Gertie waved that off. "And anyway, this isn't what you should be worried about."

"Then what?"

"About how the Cities got raided." Mason's tone was dark, and when he saw Gertie nod, he asked, "You have an idea?"

"I do."

"That bad?"

"Pretty bad." She looked over her friends and tried for a snarky grin. "I seem to have fucked up. Majorly."

Her voice was shaking. *Damn it all.* These people were family. Who else to talk to if not them? They didn't know much about her involvement with the Net, but they knew the cause was important to her and were always supportive.

There was a pause, and Varij leaned forward. "Princess. I'm telling you, not a lot of people could do what you do, paddling against the tide in a half-sunken vessel. Even if you fucked up, at least you're doing something. And anyway, look around. We survive everything. You'll have the chance to make up for what happened."

Gertie scowled, but her friend was not horsing around this time. She didn't know what to answer, but the solemn moment ended abruptly when Mason wiped an imaginary drop of tear from his eyes, sniffling. "Dude, that was beautiful."

Krea cackled, and the conversation drowned into a series of taunts and jokes. Gertie let them have at it. She didn't want to admit it, but Varij's words got to her. He'd just heard that the tragedy they were experiencing was on Gertie, and he still had faith in her.

"Alright, alright," she said finally. "It's getting late, and you all know I've got places to be."

"Yes, the mission!" Mason jumped up and gave her a salute. "Princess, my resources are ready for you."

Gertie scrunched her nose. "Why does this sound so dirty coming from your mouth?"

Varij glanced at Krea. "Is this our cue to disappear?"

But Krea was looking at Gertie, a determined expression on her sharp face. "You know who to call if you need some marvelous pilots, right?" she asked.

Gertie nodded. "You'll be the first to know."

They all stood, ready to leave. "And what about our lost little bird?" Varij asked. "She alive?"

"She better be," Gertie replied. "She's right in the middle of all kinds of dirty businesses but at least avoided the attack on the Cities."

"You saw her? What's she been doing?"

"I have to investigate that. I have a feeling..." She trailed off, not knowing how much to say. "Never mind. I'll get back to you about it. She looked okay, though, more or less."

"She better stick her ego where it hurts and come back soon," Krea grumbled. "It's not healthy, what she does."

"I'll tell her you said that. Maybe she'll return to spite you."

They said their goodbyes, the two lanehunters reminding her that if she dared to leave without warning, it was her life on the line, then Krea and Varij marched out of the workshop, leaving Gertie alone with Mason. When the door closed after them, Mason gestured to her and walked to the other end of the room.

They crossed a spacious storage chamber, and Mason stopped in front of a closet at the back wall. With a forceful tug, he moved it, and together, they opened the trap door on the floor. But when Gertie wanted to step on the stairs, Mason held her back by the arm.

"I don't recommend that if you want to keep those legs." He leaned forward to wave his wrist-comms in front of a sensor Gertie couldn't see. "Laser grid."

"No shit." Gertie caught a glimpse of faint light streaks covering the mouth of the hole before they disappeared at Mason's command.

They lowered into a dark tunnel. Mason brought some old light bulbs back to life above them, and after a few seconds of walking, they reached a door, which he opened, again, with his comms.

"I'll let you do your thing," he said. "Be back in an hour to let you out."

Gertie had to push herself to not get sentimental. How lucky she was. Even with the world imploding, she had people to trust. "Thanks, Mason."

"Everything for the resistance, Princess." Her friend smiled, then he turned around and walked back down the corridor.

Gertie shut the door and sat behind the computer console in the small chamber. She fired up the device, connected her tablet, and ran her fingers over the buttons as if on a piano, typing in familiar commands and settings. After all, she had the same system back in the Cities.

Past tense. It's gone now. Her apartment, her office. Everything.

She drove the depressing thoughts away and checked her inbox. She had an incoming message from four hours before: Katipo Base was pinging every trans-lane communicator node for Gertie to contact them.

That would be a good starting point then, to re-establish communication with her people. She tuned the channel, watching the visual representation of the glimmering network of lanes flare up on the screen. She put the headset on, and after a moment, a voice came through the headphones.

"It's Katipo. Ms. Banks, I was hoping I could reach you on this line."

"Good thinking." Gertie shook her head. *Need to focus. No rest, not yet.* Settling in the chair, she adjusted the microphone closer to her mouth. "What's going on, Edna? What's so urgent?"

"Ma'am." The commander took a deep breath. "You will definitely want to know what just fell out of the sky over here."

CHAPTER 20 | DEEP END

Jeane awoke to darkness and silence. That was not right. She didn't remember why, but it definitely wasn't supposed to be this dark and silent.

She tried to move, but her body didn't obey, like she was frozen solid in an endless, black void. Was she dead? She felt dead. Her thoughts fluttered around like a thousand birds stuck in a cage, tangled together, colliding with the uncompromising metal rods again and again. She was locked inside her own mind—and few things were more terrifying than that.

On instinct, she drew a breath to start counting and calm herself down. Breathing didn't seem to be an available option in her current state, so she wasn't expecting much, but then air flooded her lungs, and the shock made her eyes fling open.

A surge of sensations attacked her: alarms blared into her ears, flashing lights blinded her, and the foul smell of smoke twisted her nose. She was lying on the deck on her back beside the control room door, and the *Skylark* was dying around her.

Something exploded nearby and Jeane flinched, her body contracting, the muscles cramping painfully. She groaned, coughing from the dust and smoke. Closing her eyes tight, she shut out the chaos. Pain tore into her every time she tried to move.

What happened?

She remembered watching Jerkface's nailship at their tail and accelerating to shake him off. There was a blinding light, and the *Skylark* had plummeted; the sensors went wild, and she'd begun to course-correct, but a force like a giant's hand threw her backward. The light had encompassed everything, then—

«It's not the time for reflections, kid. Time to run!»

I can't move, you idiot!

«Try again!»

Someone grabbed her arm. Maura hunched down beside her, eyes wide with fear. Her voice was dull as if reaching Jeane through miles of stone and earth. "Thank goodness—I thought you died! Come on, we have to get out of here!"

Hoisting Jeane up, she tucked an arm under her shoulders, and Jeane struggled to stand, leaning on Maura with her full weight, muscles shaking. Maura turned, trying to haul her forward, but a proper look around the control room rooted Jeane to the spot.

The inner hull was deformed and broken; the panels creaked and snapped under tension, clattering to the deck. Sparks flickered up from the cables and instrument displays around the console.

"What...where..." she started, her knees buckling.

Maura gritted her teeth. "We crashed," she said, just loud enough to catch over the roaring of the alarm and the noises of the *Skylark* collapsing on itself. She pulled on Jeane's arm, urging her to move.

A rumble resounded from the tail, and the deck shook. Was it the generator overloading? The engine giving up? It depended on what had broken down first, but it wasn't a good sound.

"No." Jeane tried to yank her arm away, but she was weak, her thoughts blurry like her vision. They crashed...the *Skylark* was burning up...this didn't make any sense.

"We have to go," Maura pleaded. "The whole thing is going to explode on us!"

A heavy piece of inner hull tumbled to the floor behind them. Jeane wanted to say that she was being ridiculous and it was impossible for the entire ship to explode, but her throat clenched up. There was another crash, this time from the other direction.

The kitchen?

This was not happening. *This is not happening.*

Hollis? Where are you?

"Captain, please!"

"Where are the others?" Jeane fixed her eyes on the darkened console. She couldn't move.

"Outside." Maura's voice was uncertain. "Kliks hit his head. Damian helped him, and ALU was with them, I think..."

She trailed off, hesitant, and that was a kick in the stomach, jarring Jeane free of her daze. She let Maura pull her out of the room, and they stumbled to the corridor.

The smoke was thicker out here, billowing up from the lower level. The door to the common room stood open, but a wall of fire blocked the way—most of the heavily combustible things on the ship were in the living area.

Jeane stared down at herself, noticing the singed sleeves of her leather jacket for the first time. Some sort of electric overload must have occurred, and that was what pushed her back, paralyzing her and igniting everything flammable on the ship.

At the ladder leading to the maintenance corridor, they staggered to a halt, and Maura released Jeane's arm. Dropping to their knees, they leaned over the opening but saw nothing down there except more smoke.

Reaching the bottom of the ladder and finding that she could now stand on her own feet alone, Jeane hesitated, turning to the tail. The ceiling dented sharply a few feet away like the *Skylark's* body was crushed in half, but the smoke was too dense to know what was beyond. A constant rumble emanated from the direction of the engine. Maura jumped down behind her, covering her mouth and nose with her shirt collar. Jeane didn't move until the Miyozan clutched her arm again and tugged her towards the airlock.

She had to check on Kliks and ALU. She needed to make sure they were safe. No use thinking about anything else.

"Come on!" Maura stepped through the open inner hatch of the airlock, but Jeane halted, numb. She glanced back at the corridor. Her heart was beating so loud that she heard it over the moans of the doomed *Skylark*.

She cried out for the voice in her head, but he was silent. The air felt poisonous; the narrow chamber was caving on her. The deck shook under her feet again, the smoke dense in every direction like a wall.

But the smoke was not the problem. Even the hull falling apart could be fixed. The sickly roar from the tail gradually getting louder was the problem. Something was still working back there, but working badly, straining and fluttering like a dying heart, threatening to implode everything that made the *Skylark* the *Skylark*.

She took a step into the darkness. Maura's fingers gripped her wrist. Hollis held his breath in her head.

Jeane turned her back on her ship and ran towards the light.

They were all a safe distance away from the ship when it exploded. Jeane sat on the ground, staring at the deformed body of her bird, when the engine finally broke down, the feeble roar ceasing with a crashing sound and a boom echoed by the surrounding dunes. Pieces of hull and cabling flew off the bulk, and a column of smoke billowed out from the tail accompanied by small flames dying down fast. Then the *Skylark* went silent for good.

ALU ventured into the dead vessel to get a suit, first aid supplies, their meager pouch of doubloons, a few bottles of water, blankets, and other useful things from the accessible rooms, piling the resources into any bag and backpack they found. There was more that could be saved later, but Jeane couldn't think about that.

Kliks was lying unconscious on the ground beside her, and she took his bony wrist in her hand to feel for the pulse. He had come to once before, but after forcing down some water, he'd gone right back to this sleeping-slash-knocked out state. A huge lump decorated his forehead where he'd hit it, but there was no real wound, and Jeane suspected it might have been just the shock that did him in.

She let him rest. They weren't in a rush, after all. Sure, the Union could turn up any minute, but what was new?

ALU squatted at Kliks' feet, beeping intermittently in a sad tone, while Maura and Damian, both uninjured, sat in the shade of a boulder not far off. They too were watching the *Skylark*, probably waiting for Jeane to say something.

But all she wanted for now was to sit on the hard earth without talking, without thinking. To observe as her muscles eased up and the pain in her limbs faded to an uncomfortable memory. To watch the white-hot sun of this unfamiliar planet glare at them from the sky, and to lean into the faint, cooling wind whirling around her. To breathe in and out, in and out.

To consider that thin, bright blue ribbon, somewhere in the upper atmosphere, glimmering like the edge of a knife, deadly and silent.

The *Skylark* kept smoking. Nothing moved in the desert. She dragged it out as long as possible. Then Kliks woke up.

"Aaaaaah..." he groaned, working himself up to a sitting position. "Ouch."

"You'll be alright. Just don't move around so much," Jeane said. Her voice sounded dead, echoing up from a deep well. "Welcome back."

"I didn't intend to break out my sickest dance moves yet," the Talalan grumbled. He looked around, trying to comprehend the view. "What happened? Wait, where—" His eyes found the remains of the *Skylark*, and his face paled. "Oh, no."

Jeane's mouth twitched. "Yeah."

The Miyozans wandered closer, noticing that Kliks was conscious. Maura's hair was gray from soot and dust, and Damian's shirt was torn, his bandages gone. According to Maura, the bodyguard was the one who had dragged Kliks out of the ship, while the princess—queen, Jeane corrected herself—went back for her to the control room. She had to thank them for that at some point.

"What in hells happened?" Kliks whispered.

"I don't know," Jeane said. "I tried to evade the agent, then there was...an explosion? I'm not sure." She stopped because it felt like the words were sucking her life force out. She pointed at the lane above them. "I guess we came through that thing."

Kliks stared at the *Skylark* like he'd seen a ghost. He looked at Maura, opening his mouth silently. A series of complicated emotions flashed over his face. In the end, it was the Miyozan who spoke. "We were in the cargo hold when the manipulator started up. We didn't touch anything. It felt like..."

"Falling," Kliks finished the sentence. He swallowed hard like he understood. "Jeane, we weren't close to any planets or lanes when the agent appeared, were we?"

She couldn't make herself answer, but ALU shook their head, insect eyes round in fear. Kliks buried his face in his palms and pulled his legs up, making himself smaller. "Oh, my stars. It *was* the manipulator."

Jeane's fingers went numb; flickering dots floated in front of her eyes. Everyone stayed silent. "What are you talking about?" she asked through the increasing buzz in her head, although she already knew.

"It must have opened a lane to this planet." Kliks chewed at each word. He looked at Jeane, face grayer than usual. "I know what you're thinking. But it wasn't me. I wouldn't! I don't even know how!"

She wanted to reply, but the blood rushing through her head drowned everything out. She couldn't look into Kliks' terrified face again, so she climbed on her shaking legs and staggered away. No one followed her.

She slowed down as she got closer to the *Skylark*, and for a few minutes, she watched the column of smoke surging out of the mutilated ship. Her mind was empty, her limbs heavy.

"I have no idea what's happening," she said, her voice not much more than a whisper. She half-expected an answer. There was none.

Her gaze wandered further to their right where, behind a distant dune, another, smaller smoke pillar was stretching to touch the wispy clouds in the sky.

Well, if anyone, he must know something.

She turned away from the *Skylark* and marched back to the others. As expected, they didn't like her idea.

"It would be better to stay," Maura muttered with little conviction. "There's no sense in looking for trouble."

"And what do you want to do?" Jeane rummaged through the things ALU had brought from the destroyed ship, stuffing a backpack with water bottles, nutribars, and random things that fit. "If that agent called for help, we're fucked. We need to move either way."

"We should at least try to salvage more supplies," Damian said, but he was already preparing to leave, packing things into his shoulder bag. There was someone sensible around here, after all. "We don't know where we are, and it would be foolish to run into the unknown."

"I might be able to identify our position when the stars come out," Kliks added. His voice was subdued, and he fiddled with his tablet. "I doubt we're really in the middle of nowhere. I mean, the manipulator might have—"

"Guys, I have no capacity to argue." Jeane holstered her gun (and a spare one) and picked up the backpack, scanning the faces of the others staring back at her. "You're right. You're so right. But I'm gonna go and nab that guy now."

"We should take the manipulator with us," Kliks muttered. He wasn't looking at her.

She inhaled deeply, clamping down on the scream that tried to claw its way out of her throat. "No."

She started off towards the distant smoke signals. Not much later, ALU's pattering steps began following her, and she knew the others were not far behind either. They were talking in muted voices, but she didn't understand the words.

That was okay. She didn't care. Kliks could crawl back into that lifeless piece of junk ship for his catastrophe machine alone if he wanted. She narrowed her eyes on the column of exhaust billowing out of the Union agent's vessel and continued her march.

It was farther than she'd thought. After walking for half an hour, they still hadn't reached it. Bare, rocky hills surrounded them, patches of weed growing on the dry ground. The flats were the same in all directions—no trees, no water, no sign of settlements. Jeane climbed another dune. The smoke column seemed very close now, so she dropped on her stomach before cresting the hill and sneaked to the edge.

The Union vessel lay half-burrowed into the far side of the bowl-shaped valley. One glance at the wreck was enough to see they weren't going anywhere with this ship.

She waited for a beat. Nothing moved.

"He might be dead," Damian said, moving up beside her. "The ship seems done."

"I can see that." Jeane reached to her belt and handed one of her guns to the bodyguard. "You mind making yourself useful?"

"What about me?" Maura asked from the back.

Cute. "I don't have more. Work it out amongst yourselves."

"What's your goal here?" Damian squinted at Jeane.

"To get sweet, sweet revenge—what else? Light torture strictly. Cut down his ears, a few fingers perhaps." Damian glared at her with something of an outrage, and she rolled her eyes. "For skies sake, I'm kidding! I'm still only a little nuts."

She turned away from the man's shocked expression and descended into the valley.

There was no cover until they reached the nailship. There, the terrain folded and broke; large pieces of earth and rock scattered around a trench that revealed the trajectory of the plummeting craft. The nose of the vessel drilled into the hillside, the cockpit shattered and broken. Nothing was burning, and the smoke had largely subsided, but the place looked dead. No movement, no sound.

Jeane looked back at Kliks instinctually, and the Talalan shrugged, uncertain. He cast down his eyes, not able to meet hers. Damian turned around, indicating he was going to circle the ship.

She kicked a rock aside. It would have been too bad if the agent had died in the crash. But they had to at least search for his body.

A distressed shout cut her thoughts short. Damian.

Jeane and Kliks took off, but they stopped in their tracks as they reached the other side of the vessel. Damian was lying on his stomach in the shadow of the ship, his face pained as the young man standing above him dug the heel of his boot into his shoulder. The agent's gun was pointed at the back of Damian's head. A small disc lay beside the bodyguard, still crackling with electricity—an EMP trap.

"Not a step further!" the agent snapped. Jeane froze, and Kliks followed her lead.

The man's face was bloodied and dirty, his posture revealing that he'd suffered serious wounds from the crash. He didn't look like a regular agent; there was no trace of the aloof, robotic demeanor those bastards usually presented. But there was no question. It was him. The young man in the pub in Foggy Cities Central. The one who had almost broken into the *Skylark*. The one that had been chasing them through the universe since they'd gotten their hands on the manipulator.

"Drop your guns!" he spat, pressing a hand to his abdomen. He was barely standing on his feet.

Jeane raised her gun, barrel vertical, her pose relaxed. She only needed to catch the right moment or maybe wait it out—the guy was on the verge of keeling over. But if she made a mistake, Damian's life was on the line.

Cold fury flooded her brain. Did she really care about Damian's life? There was no point. What was she even doing here? *Shoot the asshole and be done with it!*

Movement caught her eyes on the right. Maura stood at the tail behind her, weapon trained on the agent. She was still (or, again) wearing the Miyozan artifact, that strange glove.

"Drop your weapon!" Her voice was commanding. Jeane almost believed her. "If you don't, I *will* shoot!"

"Then your friend is dead," Agent Jerkface replied, pushing the barrel of his gun against Damian's skull. Kliks made a strained groan, his pistol clattering to the ground.

A shot rang out, and as a bright light flared up at the agent's hand, the weapon flew out of his grip. He jerked his hand away with an alarmed yelp, and using his confusion, Damian acted lightning fast: he pushed himself away from the ground and swept the other man off his feet, pinning him down. By the time Kliks breathed out, "For stars' sake, that was close," Damian had pulled his belt off and used it to tie the agent's hands together.

The bodyguard glanced at Maura in bewilderment, his face

contorting into a painful grimace in the aftermath of the electric shock he'd suffered. Maura lowered her gun, face flushed. ALU tiptoed beside her and patted her elbow.

Was it her who had fired? That was shockingly accurate.

Grabbing the agent's shoulder, Damian pulled him up into a sitting position and looked at Jeane. "Here. You can question him."

Jerkface sneered in pain, but before either of them could talk, they heard the sharp sound of shots again, and plasma bullets flashed up in the air.

Kliks tackled Jeane, and they huddled between the nailship and the disturbed ground at its nose where they were protected on almost all sides. Peeking out, she counted at least seven figures on the hills around the valley.

"This again?" the Talalan blurted out, clutching his gun to his chest.

Jeane rubbed at her eyes, trying to memorize the positions of their attackers. They popped up to release a blast, then disappeared behind the ridges—not in a hurry to go for the kill, it seemed they only wanted to let them know they were surrounded.

"Any ideas?" She lightly kicked Jerkface, who was hunkering next to her, in the side. She felt so, so tired. That morning coffee at Saori's seemed like a millennium ago. The man's face was unreadable as he shook his head, and Jeane gave a sigh. "Wonderful."

They could have been some local gang; maybe they didn't like that their desert had been used as a runway. Something told her it was more, though. But she didn't want to pay attention.

It didn't matter. Nothing mattered. It was over.

"We need to get into the ship," Damian grunted. The shots around them subsided, and ALU leaned out of cover to gawk at the attackers. "We might find other weapons or—"

Jeane snorted. "Sure, let's fucking trap ourselves even further. Great idea."

At that moment, a voice sounded out, artificially amplified. "Attention, intruders! Come out with raised hands, weapons dropped! You're surrounded. Do not resist!"

No one said anything for a moment. The speaker didn't repeat themself.

Maura peered at Jeane. She looked shaken but trying her best to focus. "We don't have a choice. They must think we're Union. But if we clear ourselves—"

"If they believe us," Jeane cut in but stopped when Kliks laughed nervously, and Maura gave a faint smile too. "What?"

Maura stood, dusting her trousers. "I'm not sure how stupid they have to be to think *you're* an agent."

Damian shoved himself up from the ground, pulling Jerkface with him. The young man wasn't struggling, and there was a cryptic expression on his face.

"That's fair," Kliks said and rose as well. He reached his hand down for Jeane, half a second of hesitance in his movements.

Jeane clenched her jaw, searching for something, anything, inside her one last time. But there was no help, no advice, or wise-ass comment.

It was really over.

She wanted to scream. She looked up at Kliks, at the barely contained panic on his face, at his pleading, knowing, sad eyes. At ALU, chirping to themself, trying to calm down, blinking at her, trusting she would know what to do. At the Miyozans, ready to fight for their lives. At the agent, narrowing his stare at her, wrapping himself in silence and gloom.

They didn't know. They didn't understand.

But she pursed her lips and let Kliks pull her up from the ground. Grasping her gun tightly, she stepped out of the cover of the nailship.

Let's end it then.

CHAPTER 21 | THIS WHOLE MESS

The two sides exchanged only a few words after the lanehunters surrendered. The locals quickly realized it wasn't a group of Union soldiers they'd stumbled upon and donned well-crafted poker faces, and the lanehunters responded in a similar manner. But before withdrawing into stubborn silence, the blonde hunter—Captain Jeane Blake, if he remembered her reluctant introduction right—let Roy's identity slip.

The strangers weren't fazed. Their nerves-of-steel game was admirable, and they were clearly used to handling all sorts. A lean young man with a confident voice who acted as the leader of the unit (a Nefirn, recognizable by his bluish skin and the breathers embedded in his throat) instructed them to hand over all their possessions, then handcuffed Roy, fastening a menacing-looking metal band around his neck as well. Roy knew the tingling sensation on his skin was a precursor to a larger jolt if he did something untoward.

They began marching through the desert to a non-disclosed location. Roy kept his eyes on his destroyed ship until it disappeared among the barren hills. Now, he'd really lost everything he ever owned—even his assist device broke during the crash. When he turned forward, his glance met Jeane's. The woman pursed her lips and averted her eyes. Roy wished to ask many things of her, but he had to wait until they were alone. If and when that ever happened.

First of all, how in hells had they ended up on this planet? It was the manipulator's doing, he figured that much, but why the lanehunters would risk a maneuver like this, nearly dooming themselves in the process, was a mystery. Was it panic, seeing him close in on them? Or maybe they truly didn't know how to use the device. In that case, he was even more interested in how the captain's Talalan companion fit the picture.

As to where they'd landed...well. Their captors were humans, except the leader and two other Nefirns. Additionally, none of them wore real uniforms, but their practical clothing emanated a distinct militaristic air. It was difficult not to jump to conclusions. For now, Roy just tried to be happy no one had shot him yet.

He also tried to ignore the nagging thought at the back of his mind that he could easily break free—end the charade and get back in control. Shutting his eyes tight, he visualized that door in his brain, the one sealing his monster away, the part of him that could aid him in slaying his captors and would have no moral qualms about it either. But the door was closed, secure, and it would stay that way. He might feel untethered now, but going to such lengths would only worsen his situation.

They must have been walking for half an hour when the Nefirn officer held up his comms device and signaled to stop. The terrain in front of them shifted, and a large metal box emerged from the ground, scattering dust and sand into the air. When it halted, a door slid open on one side, the officer waved, and the group stepped into the chamber, one by one.

The fifteen-strong unit and their six captives fit comfortably inside; the door closed, white light flooded the space, and the elevator started lowering with a whirring noise. Their descent ended a minute later and several stories underground, where heavy, code-protected gates led into the insides of a facility.

The group marched through empty corridors, their leader changing directions seemingly at random, and the walk took so long that Roy lost track of the map he'd been constructing in his head. At one point, the soldiers disappeared, and only the Nefirn officer remained with two of his underlings. Then finally, they all filed into a stark, gray room containing a table affixed to the floor and a few chairs. The troopers secured Roy's handcuffs to a table leg, and the three of them left the group without a word.

After a few seconds of frozen stupor, Jeane marched to a chair and slumped in it with an exasperated grunt. "Well, isn't this splendid?" She planted her elbows on the table and buried her face in her palms. "Anyone has any idea who these clowns are?"

The Talalan sat beside her but didn't speak, and the other two hovered near the door, throwing enigmatic glances at each other. The muscly man kept looking at Roy, perhaps to check whether he was up to something, but his short, brown-haired companion wore a distant look on her face, like she wasn't comprehending her environment. The weird little robot was the only one at ease with the situation, strutting up and down in the room, beeping to itself.

Roy plopped down on the floor, bending around the table to see the group, even handcuffed in this troublesome way.

"This is a secret base of some sort," the big guy spoke up. Roy didn't remember his name. It was something noble-sounding like Darian or Dominic. "Not Union-friendly, I suppose, since we're not dead, and this fellow here is handled with more care than us."

Jeane raised her head like she just remembered Roy was with them and glared at him with such fury in her eyes that he recoiled. "I bet you know who they are, don't you?" she snarled. She jumped up, circled the table, grabbed Roy's shirt, and yanked him up. Shoving him backward, she held him by the collar and hissed into his face. "Let's hear it!"

"Jeane!" the Talalan cried out. The tabletop cut into Roy's side, and his arm tensed, the handcuff pulling at his wrist.

"This asshole crashed my ship!" Jeane spat. "What the hells did you do to us?"

Roy shoved back at her, but she held him with an iron fist. He tried to keep eye contact, but it was like attempting to reason with a boiling pool of lava. "Look, I had nothing to do with the crash!"

He didn't think she even heard him. She pressed Roy into the table harder; his wrist burned and pulsed where the handcuff sliced into his skin.

"Jeane, please let him go," he heard the Talalan plead.

The woman leaned in closer. "I want the truth."

"I'm telling you the truth!" Roy tried again. He didn't want to fight her, but it was becoming his only way out. A cold sensation bubbled up from the center of his stomach, compelling him to attack, but he clamped down on it. *What the hells? I said we're not doing this.* "How would I know where we are?" he asked instead. "You control the manipulator, not me!"

He saw the Talalan's gray face pop up behind Jeane. The alien placed his hand on her arm, and although he didn't say a word, Roy sensed the pressure he was putting on the captain's bicep.

Jeane stared into Roy's eyes for one more second—her irises were cutting bright blue with a storm behind them—and loosened her hold on his collar, dropping him and taking a step back with a frustrated sigh. Roy leaned on the table. The hip he'd hurt during the crash ached, and his nausea returned. His wrist wasn't bleeding, but the skin was bruised and sore.

"What do you know about the manipulator?" the Talalan asked. He planted himself between Roy and Jeane like a shield.

"How peculiar. That's exactly what I wanted to ask you!" Roy snapped. He was losing his cool. "Who are you, by the way?"

The Talalan straightened. The small robot ran up to him and released a row of angry chirps, glaring at Roy with its strange insect eyes.

"My name is Kliks Pleu," the Talalan replied. "I'm from the *Skylark*, the ship you totaled. Sailing with her," —he pointed at the still seething Jeane— "and this one, ALU."

Roy nodded. "Pleased to meet you. I'm Roy Philemon. And what I know about the manipulator is that it's Talalan, does some fucked up shit with the lanes, and the Union wants it."

"You mean, *you* want it." Jeane was glaring at the ground now, maybe as a way of trying to control her anger.

Roy felt an uneasy grimace creep onto his face. "I can talk, but I'm warning you, it gets complicated. And I'll be making a huge effort here because you might not even believe me, and then who's going to end up with a hole in his chest?"

"No, please. Tell us," said the brunette who had been quiet so far. Now she took a step towards him, and Roy acknowledged, a bit surprised, that she was the only person in the room whose expression didn't show a degree of disgust looking at him. She seemed curious and placid, although—and he remembered this vividly too—she'd also shot at him with terrifying accuracy during the confrontation at his ship. It made him a little reluctant to feel gratitude.

Out of instinct, he began to balance his options but only needed a second to realize that what he was going to say did not matter in the slightest. Things had begun to collide. The manipulator was probably with these unknown desert people, the lanehunters demanded answers, and his little adventure might be nearing its end.

The thought filled him with panic. But strangely, satisfaction too. He held onto that latter feeling and started talking.

"Alright, let's see. Several cycles ago, my commanding officer's son was assigned to Talala to steal the manipulator device which could, I quote, 'turn the tide in the Union's quest for universe-domination.' He recently sent a cryptic message to his mother, saying he got in trouble, so she—oh, I forgot to mention, she was a double agent of the Net all along. She told me I needed to take the machine to them, the Net, because let's not allow the world to implode, maybe, then she promptly died for treason. So I, the idiot in the story, tried to hunt you down because you found the manipulator first. In turn, Leadership sent inspectors after me, so it became increasingly more important for me to find you, and now we're here. Happy ending."

"You're right," Jeane scoffed. "I don't believe a word."

Roy spread his arms, the handcuff clanking against the table. "See?"

Jeane's eyes flared up again, but she only clenched her fists—luckily not around Roy's neck. "You're telling me the manipulator acting out the exact moment you showed up was a coincidence?"

Acting out? Aha! "As much of a coincidence as a rogue Talalan finding the only Talalan technology that's not hidden away on Talala. But I'm not telling you anything because I don't *know* anything."

"I'm quite sure the device was started up from the outside."

Kliks narrowed his eyes at Roy's comment, neatly avoiding having to answer that particular mystery.

"It's true," the brunette piped up. "It turned on by itself when Kliks was about to switch it off."

Roy shrugged. "Well, my commander, Danai, did want me to take it to the Net. She had access to my ship and the opportunity to put a device on board which helped me track the thing. She might have wanted to make sure it ended up where she wanted it to by placing some trigger that activated when I got close. I didn't notice any outgoing signals, but I was quite busy at the time."

"Why didn't this happen when we first met?" Jeane asked, skeptical. "When you wanted to board us in that lane? Nice move, by the way. You almost killed all of us and destroyed your precious device."

"Would you have listened if I tried to hail you? Which I did, by the way. Lane interference is a stinker."

Kliks raised an eyebrow. "You are a strange agent. Excuse me for the generalization, but your kind is not usually this talkative and witty."

"Aw, you think I'm witty? Thanks!" Roy flashed a sarcastic smile.

Kliks frowned even harder, then turned to Jeane. "It must have been a safeguard. We were already in a lane. Maybe it would have been too dangerous if the manipulator opened another one, willy-nilly."

"Wait, let's rewind," the muscular guy said. Drago? No, that wasn't it. "You think these people are the Net?"

"Could be." Roy shrugged. "I thought *you* were Net for a moment there, but that's not true, is it?"

"No, but we're looking for them," the brunette said, her exhausted eyes coming alive.

"So, who are you guys?" Roy inquired. Sooner or later, he was going to find out these names if it was the last thing he did.

"We're from Miyoza," said the man. *Demetrius? Damnit.*

"Wow, understatement of the year," Jeane muttered. "She's the actual Miyozan Queen if you can believe it."

"Jeane!" Kliks chided her. This had to be a daily task, trying to keep his captain under control while she ignored every attempt. But the woman looked actually abashed now, glancing at the Miyozans. She knew she'd taken the careless biting quips too far.

Judging from the dark frown on his face, the big guy was also not happy with the cards on the table, but the brunette only nodded. "It's alright. I am indeed Queen of Miyoza, Maura Tholis. And this is my bodyguard, Damian."

Damian, of course! "Charmed to make your acquaintance, Your Majesty." Roy bowed his head at the queen, and a polite smile flashed across Maura's face.

Then the door opened, interrupting the very promising meet and greet session. The woman stepping in didn't even wait for it to close after her two armed companions. "Glad to see we're all gathered here," she said. "Let's get started."

Silence fell over them. Based on the newcomer's comment, she had likely heard everything they'd just discussed, and she was now waiting to see their reaction.

"You're Net," Kliks said, and the woman lifted her cutting stare at him. She was short with strict eyes and a confident stance, her graying hair in a tight bun.

"My name is Edna Hill, and I am the commander of this base," she said. "And yes, we belong to the resistance movement called the Net."

"Before we get into this," Roy raised his voice and wiggled his handcuffs around, "can we get rid of these? Then I can contribute to the conversation. If you want me to."

Hill's eyes narrowed further, and she gave a wave to one of her soldiers. Roy was promptly freed from his shackles. He stood, stretched out, and took two healthy steps away from Jeane; she had more or less exhausted her well of fury, but better not to trigger another outburst.

"My first question is what happened to the manipulator?" asked Commander Hill.

"We left it behind," Kliks said. He was taking the helm and also playing along. *Good choice.* "On our ship."

"It's a goner," Jeane added. "The cargo hold resembled a pancake the last time I checked."

"Did you make sure?"

Jeane's voice was wooden. "It's gone."

"Let's not judge hastily," Kliks offered. "I would have expected a bigger boom if that were the case."

"So, you *didn't* make sure." Hill gave an exasperated sigh. "And you left it in a ruined vessel without any protection. My second question—"

Damian cut her off. "Ma'am, with all respect, we have no idea whether you're telling the truth about yourself."

Hill met his eyes. "I'm the one asking the questions here. Again. How did you find the manipulator?"

"Accidentally," Kliks said, and Roy had to suppress a sarcastic snort. *Sure, buddy.* "That is to say, we found it accidentally but took it on purpose."

"And you have been on their trail until now?" Hill looked at Roy, who nodded. *Like a good boy doing what's expected.*

He sighed. Self-loathing was not useful now.

The crossfire of Hill's withering gaze turned to Maura. "And what does the Miyozan Queen have to do with any of this?"

"It was just a job," Jeane groaned. "They have nothing to do with this whole mess. And us neither."

She took a shaky breath, and Roy expected her to blow up again, but instead, she fell silent. Her face turned blank, and she seemed so small and fragile among the others, that for a strange moment he felt almost ashamed for playing a part in the situation.

"This isn't the first time a lanehunter has told me that." Hill's cautious and composed disposition cracked for a moment as annoyance crept into her voice. She seemed to want to say more, but before she could, the loud chirp of a communicator on one of her guards' wrists interrupted her.

The man looked at the device and leaned over to Hill, whispering in her ear. The commander looked over the group one more time, and without a word, marched out of the room with her guards.

Roy had no time to meditate on what had happened or what was going to because then ALU, who so far had silently observed the events, sounded off a sharp whistle, and at the same time, Damian cried out, "Maura!"

The woman collapsed to the floor. Her eyes rolled back into her head, spasms running through her body; her muscles tightened, and her limbs kept shaking like she'd been struck by lightning. It only stopped when Jeane dropped to her knees, dragged the strange glove Maura wore off her hand, and threw it across the room.

Maura Tholis, Queen of Miyoza, sat on the floor, hugging her knees, trembling. She was mumbling incoherent sentences and hadn't acknowledged any of them since she'd opened her eyes a few minutes earlier. Her bodyguard crouched next to her, not moving an inch from her side, although there was little he could do for his queen at the moment. Nothing like this had ever happened before, he kept repeating. Kliks mentioned Maura had complained about headaches, but there had been no other signs of her being ill. The glove lay on the table, forsaken but not forgotten. Since Hill had left a good twenty minutes before, no one had returned to check on them. Whatever call the commander had gotten was apparently more important than even the infamous manipulator.

Roy sat with his back to the wall, watching the others like the outsider he was. Even though this strange group seemed like a random collection of people, they weren't that at all. A lot of interesting things had ended up in their possession.

Like that glove. Since Jeane growled at him every time he took a step too close, Roy could only examine the queen's device from afar, but he realized what it was. It was *the* glove, the one that had kept Miyoza alive in their long bloody war with Gaerris. A unique invention binding human and artificial intellect, something the Union had not been able to replicate. And somehow, the Net was deeply involved with both it and the manipulator. From insignificant resistance with machinations scarcely surpassing the stimulus threshold of Leadership, they'd certainly stepped up their game.

Jeane was circling the room like she couldn't figure out what to do with herself. Her eyes settled on Roy, and she paused beside him on her next round. Roy straightened, preparing for another choking attack, but to his surprise, the lanehunter lowered herself to the floor next to him. Kliks, sitting at the table, threw a cryptic glance at them but didn't intervene.

They were silent for a while. The woman watched Maura, deep in thought.

"I'm sorry for what happened to your ship," Roy broke the quiet because this felt important to say. "It was not my intention."

Jeane held her breath for a long moment. "It's just a ship," she said, exhaling.

Roy decided not to pry, although he did have a few pointed comments prepared about denial. "Is she going to get better?" he asked instead, inclining his head towards Maura. "That seizure looked nasty."

"Don't know," Jeane said with a pang of worry in her voice. *Interesting. Just a job, she said before. Just a ship.* "Something bad is happening to her."

"Is it the glove?"

"The damn thing is influencing her. When she shot at you, she was wearing it. She couldn't even properly hold a gun before. Damian says the glove is inactive outside Miyoza, but I don't think that's true." Jeane peered at Roy with sudden suspicion. "But why do you care?"

Roy shrugged. "Why shouldn't I? There's me, there's this room, and you people. Everything I had is gone. I'm a runaway and a traitor without a cause." He paused, cringing. *Dramatic much? But true. And better than going berserk and murdering every-one.* "A more important question is why *you* are talking to *me*, your enemy?"

Jeane frowned at him. She might have been seeing him for the first time too without all that anger blinding her. "Fair," she said. It wasn't an answer, but that was all she offered. "So, what's your plan now?"

"To get some cold packs for my wrist. And if these people let me live, considering how I've been working for them anyway, I could...I don't know. Help with their master plan against the

Union, if it exists."

Jeane's shoulders sagged. "I...have a friend who really trusts that it does. Don't know about it, but something better change. Things are going south, fast."

"You mean the Foggy Cities."

"Your buddies are getting comfortable there as we speak."

Roy wanted to protest, that they weren't his buddies, that they'd never been, but he didn't. Unintentionally or not, he *had* led them to the lanehunter world. Both of them had. "The universe is changing," he said, immediately cursing himself for the cliché. "That manipulator is a frightening thing."

"Yeah, and Hill is collecting it right now." Jeane threw him a dark look, which promptly changed to surprise, shame, and finally anger. "I wish you were still handcuffed. Then this conversation wouldn't be so fucking weird."

"It's the trauma," Roy assured her. "As soon as we feel better, I promise you're going to want to beat me up again."

"Feel better, huh?" Jeane shook her head. She fixed her eyes on the opposite wall but didn't elaborate.

"Between the death of the only parent I've ever known, being hunted by my own 'buddies', and losing Sam, I'd like to think I've officially hit rock bottom," Roy mused. Why was he still talking? *Stop talking, idiot.* "And if not, I don't want to know about it."

"Sam?"

Roy suppressed a shiver. He was so alone here, wasn't he? Hurricane was an awful place, but an awful place he *knew*. This? All this was uncharted roads. And try as he might to take it in a stride, it was terrifying. Opening that door in the back of his mind to let the brainwashed monster in suddenly didn't seem that illogical. It would put him back to where he belonged. Where he *should* belong.

He stared into Jeane's face, frowning. Why was he thinking about this again? But even though he tried to deny it, he knew exactly why.

The pills. His body needed Danai's pills. Without them, his defenses against the indoctrinated part of his brain—shouting *subdue, conquer, control* at him every chance it got—were weakening.

He swallowed and answered the question. "It's my ship."

Jeane's eyebrows almost flew off her forehead. "No way. Agents don't name their ships. It's all passcodes and letters, A Z T whatever zero, one, one, zero, zero, one—"

"Well, I named it."

"Hey, actually, your name too," she went on, an eager, mocking look on her face. If Roy wanted to jar her out of her brooding mood, he could be satisfied. "No agent is called 'Philemon.' Don't you cloned dudes just have first names and numbers?"

Roy folded his arms. "This is a rude intrusion into my personal matters. I will not talk about my traumatic childhood and the torture I suffered that left deep scars on my soul and deformations on my personality which I could only survive by assigning human characteristics to a utility object and a family name for myself that I found in some weird restricted files from Earth."

Jeane broke out in a laugh so loud that Kliks and ALU turned their heads to the noise. Roy raised his brow. That nagging feeling inside him seemed to dissolve. Yes. He had to remember what he wanted to be, not what he was supposed to be.

Then the lanehunter wiped at her eyes, the snickering turning erratic, choking in her throat. She rubbed at her face, hiding behind her fingers. "That's hardly worse than talking to the ghost of your dead foster father," she mumbled.

She didn't look at him again, and her expression turned hollow. Roy let the conversation die. They sat wordlessly, waiting for Maura to break out from her daze and for Commander Hill to come back for them.

CHAPTER 22 | MATTERS OF THE MIND

The outside world was a whirlwind of blurred figures and distant noise that barely registered in Maura's mind. She stood on a clifftop far above the sea, her face wet from the pinpricks of the spray, the monotonous rumble of the waves buzzing in her ears. Her head was aching; fragments of memories floated around in her brain.

Sofia was there too.

"What's happening to me?" Maura asked.

"You're dying."

"I don't understand." She stared at her hands, but she wasn't wearing the glove. Of course. The device lay on the table. If she raised her head an inch, she saw it. And Jeane too, who had been the one to remove it. But Maura was reluctant to shift her position. Her real body felt disconnected, like a torn coat dropped on the ground. "How are you here?"

Sofia smiled. "I told you—I live in your mind. I needed you to wear the glove, so I could put myself together, but now I'm here."

"I'd gone mad. Like my father."

"Maura, please. Focus." Sofia took her hands and held her gaze. The ocean roared in the distance. "You're not mad, and your father wasn't either. There's only so much a mind can bear. I need you to listen to me. Can you do that?"

The person in front of her wasn't her friend, only a hallucination, but Maura's heart still sank every time she spoke. But she nodded, the movement slow and heavy like in a nightmare. In the real world, she was motionless. Damian's voice, calling out to her from somewhere close, reached her consciousness, but his words dissolved, too weak to break through the opaque wall of oblivion separating them.

"I've explained what I am before," Sofia started. "I'm an early backup of the Miyozan city-AI. The deformation caused in the system by the AI and your father did not affect me. My comprehension of what happened is limited, but I'm here to help. My priority—"

"Wait, the deformation caused by who? Wasn't it the AI that ruined my father's mind?"

A crease of frustration formed on Sofia's face, but when she spoke, her tone was patient. "It's not that simple. I can tell you what really happened, but you need to believe me, or we'll die."

Maura swallowed. Death was a distant concept, not something she thought she was capable of. "Tell me."

Sofia looked into the distance and took a deep breath. "Once upon a time, there lived a king in Miyoza, who made a grave mistake. From the mistake came the deaths of many people and a war that took millions of more lives, ruining two civilizations."

"Lorio Tholis," Maura muttered.

Sofia nodded. "After the Earthers and their generation ship crashed on Zeraya, he became so terrified of his own imperfection that he spent his remaining years obsessing over it. He swore he would find the best solution to humanity's problems."

"Sofia, I know all this."

The girl pursed her lips. "But you don't understand. Lorio never wanted a machine-controlled society, so the system is full of rules and restrictions. Both the city-AI and the human brain can affect and adapt to each other to reach a higher harmony, but the AI would always be subservient. It's a fragile tug-of-war, and if the human mind, for some reason, is not playing nice, certain abrupt patterns might develop.

"Your father was a strong-willed man, raised for and shaped by war. He forced the AI to serve him like no one had before. Obligated to do everything the king asked against its own better judgment, the AI found itself in a trap. It couldn't stop, and it couldn't change your father's will. Continuing the war. Murdering thousands. Endangering the people it was supposed to protect. That was not the optimal road ahead. So, in the end, it struck back the only way it could."

"What do you mean?"

"The connection with the CNS and the AI is hard on the human mind." Sofia's words sounded strangely light as if she wanted to soften the blow. "A certain amount of damage is unavoidable, as every member of the royal family accepts. The AI could use this. Increase the strain, give the king a little too much a little too fast, complicate the processing of information, deform the neural pathways just slightly. And when your father's control weakened, it attacked with the nanobots.

"Except it got out of hand. The more the AI pushed the king, the harder he clutched onto the unreachable idea of victory. And the longer this went on, the sicker the AI became—hurting the primary user harmed it too. When it realized the process became irreversible, its only hope remained that the king would die of the damages to his brain faster than Miyoza fell to Gaerris." Sofia shuddered. "It tried to ask for your help too, but I don't think, in the end, that it even remembered what it was supposed to be doing anymore.

"You're suffering the consequences of all this. The headaches will get worse. You tried to work with the AI for years, completely untrained, then damaged your brain further by hooking up to it at the coronation and after, in its half-ruined state. You would be forced to go back to connect with the CNS anyway, your brain is literally made for it, but like this... I'm sorry, but you won't survive away from Miyoza."

Maura shook her head. "I can't go back yet. I can't save us alone. Maybe, soon, if I manage to—"

"Maura, if you don't go home, you will die. If you don't connect to the CNS, neither your mind nor the AI will be able to function. You are both broken machines with pieces missing. But if you go back, there is a chance you can heal each other."

"I don't understand how that could work," Maura said. Even Sofia's entire story hadn't managed to shake her out of the strange numbness. "This feels like I'm already doomed. How can I fix an

AI?"

Sofia didn't answer. Voices broke through the murmur of the sea from the outside world, but Maura didn't comprehend the words. Everything felt unreal, the pains she'd experienced far away. Sofia said some ominous things, but it didn't matter. She didn't understand everything either; she was an incomplete and limited copy.

"You need to go," Sofia said.

"I don't want to."

The girl reached out, touching Maura's face with the tip of her fingers. "They need you. But don't forget: time is of the essence. I'll try to keep you stable, but you need to hurry."

"You almost made me shoot that agent," Maura said, hesitant.

Sofia smiled. "I only gave you the option. *You* wanted to save Damian." Her face darkened, the change abrupt and disorienting. "I will protect you with everything I have. Oh, and the robot, ALU? I would take a good, long look at them when you can. Might prove interesting."

Then Sofia grabbed Maura's shoulders and shoved her off the cliff.

She fell towards the roiling sea, the noise of the tides swallowing her. She wanted to cry out, but no air escaped from her lungs. The world cracked in half, and the force of the water surging to envelop her body washed away all the light.

When her eyes managed to focus, she was back in her real body. She saw Damian first, then all the others: Jeane, Kliks, and the Union agent, Roy. Someone poked her in the shoulder—it was ALU, beeping quietly, looking at her with their sad compound-eyes.

She was sitting on the ground, and she was very, very cold.

"I'm okay," she said because what else was there to say? Her head was throbbing, but she reached out, and Damian took her arm, helping her stand. He didn't ask anything, but she would have to give him an explanation sooner or later.

"Are you sure?" Kliks sounded almost indignant, like her passing out was a personal slight on him. "You collapsed like you went into some kind of trance!"

She couldn't lie to him. "I don't feel well. But I'm here for now."

"But—"

"Guys, we have places to be," Jeane cut in, but in contrast with her callous words, she glanced at Maura with a somber expression. She leaned forward with the glove in her hand, and Maura took the device from her. She blinked at the captain, hoping her relief was obvious.

"We need to move," Roy said. He wasn't looking at her, and following his eyes, Maura realized why. Commander Hill was standing in the door with some soldiers as her entourage like before.

"We're gonna talk to the Net's big boss," Jeane explained, rolling her eyes in emphasis. "Thrilling stuff. And, oh, the Union is here for us. Again."

Hill's face remained rigid like a statue, not reacting to the comment. And before Maura could have asked more questions, the soldiers circled them and marched them out of the room into the bowels of the secret rebel base.

They were led to a room full of long desks, screens, and people of random occupations; some wore the camo uniforms of soldiers and brandished guns, others had the oil-stained coveralls of technicians or mechanics on, and still others, in their simple suit and shirt attires, looked more like bureaucrats or businesspeople. Everyone seemed distressed, staring at maps and graphs, talking on comms, or arguing in subdued voices.

Commander Hill led them away from the commotion into a corner and sat them down around a table while she took her place in front of a sleek computer. On the screen, interconnected blue strands of light flashed up before the simple interface of a communication channel took their place. Maura recognized what the earlier image meant from the time they'd talked to Jeane's friend, Wal, on Duplex and saw the same type of visualization. They would be talking to someone through lanes.

They'd arrived after all. She was with the Net, like Nasir had promised.

Hill typed in a row of commands, then leaned back and surveyed them all. When she finally spoke, she addressed her words to Jeane. "As I mentioned, an hour ago, the lane you people came through started to shrink. Expecting a constant rate of reduction, we estimated it was going to disappear quickly. However, before that happened, two Union vessels emerged from it."

She paused, waiting for a reaction, but Jeane stared back with a vacant expression. The captain looked out of it, pushed beyond her limits, and unable or unwilling to engage more than being present—not counting when she was lashing out. She'd been like this since the crash. That ship was her everything, and Maura's heart ached for her. *It's my fault too that this happened.*

After a while, realizing the commander expected an answer, Jeane blinked. "What? And?"

There was a sound through the loudspeaker of Hill's computer—a crack, but nothing more. Maura frowned. Someone was at the other end of the line, listening in.

"*And,*" Hill went on, with an exasperated sigh, "they were looking for something. Us. Or the manipulator or both. We attempted to capture them, but they fought to the death.

"Now, the lane is gone, but those ships might have transmitted their position to close-by Union forces. We are not as much in the middle of nowhere here as we'd like, so they will be here, and fast. And we need to decide."

"Decide what?" The outrage was clear in Kliks' voice. "Have you sent your men for the manipulator?"

A muscle twitched at Hill's nose, but whether it was annoyance at being interrupted or anger about something more, Maura was not sure.

"I have some heavy artillery directed at the wreckage of your ship, yes," she said, her voice demure. Kliks gasped as if hearing the statement caused him physical pain, but the woman went on. "I need your help to come to a decision. I need to know exactly what your device can do and why I shouldn't blow it to smithereens."

"You can't destroy it!"

"I don't want to. But you need to start talking, Talalan."

Kliks took a deep breath. He was obviously fighting a battle with himself. He glanced at Jeane, waiting for support, but the captain's vacant eyes had not changed, and Kliks' expression darkened like she'd slapped him.

"Help us understand." Maura leaned forward to catch his attention. Commander Hill was playing on his emotional connection to both the device and his people, but they would be better off with all cards on the table. The *Skylark* crew had been fleeing with the manipulator destroying things around them long enough. "If we know what we're up against, we might gain some advantage instead of constantly running from the situation."

Kliks blinked and gave a curt nod. He steadied himself, focusing on Hill rather than on Jeane's flat stare.

"All right," he started. "A warning, though: most of this is going to be assumptions. I haven't been home in a while." The commander nodded, and Kliks went on. "Talalans always had a theory or two about how lanes came to be. By investigating the one in our system, we basically think they're the consequence of an immense explosion that occurred in the multiverse. The why and the how are irrelevant," he added, seeing Hill's frown. "It's not *really* an explosion, and I doubt we will ever find out the reason. The point is, whatever it was, it punctured into our spacetime, forming tears that allow us to move through another dimension via these tunnels if we expend enough energy. While we travel in them, lanes stay stable, but when we start to use the energy of the explosion, the problems start. Large perturbations might disrupt and break down the tunnels."

"You're starting to lose me," Roy said. He raised his hand like he was in school, listening to a teacher. Maura hadn't the chance to encounter a lot of Union agents in her life, but she had to agree with Kliks: this man was certainly odd.

"If we destabilize the lanes, the energy of the explosion will burst into our universe," Kliks explained.

"So...boom?"

"Boom!" ALU bounced up and down, and Maura flinched. The technician's interruption reminded her of Sofia's suggestion.

What did it mean that she should take a good look at them?

"Or bang." Kliks nodded. "A really big bang."

"Wait. The universe could be destroyed?" Damian's tone was incredulous.

"Perhaps. That's the worst-case scenario. Lanes don't usually disappear by themselves like the one we arrived through, which suggests this one has been tuned incredibly carefully. But if we use the device irresponsibly, more and more lanes will form and become unstable until our entire universe might collapse."

"Sounds great," Roy mumbled. There was another noise on the comms line, almost like a subdued laugh. "How do we *not* get to this point?"

"Well, Talalans experimented with pulling out energy from the multiverse, but as far as I know, they haven't managed to circumvent the instability problem." Kliks shrugged. "There might not be a solution. I don't want to speculate."

"If they didn't solve the problem, why create the manipulator?" Hill asked.

Kliks gave a sad smile. "Humans say history repeats itself, don't they? My race had almost fallen victim to its own pride once before, and against all our efforts to avoid this kind of thing, it might be happening again."

"This method of pulling energy out of lanes, if usable, would provide an unlimited power resource," Damian mused. "Not even mentioning that it can open new lanes too. Of course everyone wants a piece of it."

Maura looked at Kliks. "And you still wouldn't want to destroy it?"

The Talalan stared at her. "I am undecided. My people don't want to lose it or for the Union or even the Net to find it. Even if it's an unstable, unpredictable prototype as for example our adventure on Duplex has shown, it's still an incredible invention and our best chance to figure out lanes. It's irresponsible to blow it up. Not to mention dangerous."

He paused, looking uneasy. But Hill now seemed to have enough information to proceed. She nodded and typed something into the computer. "I understand. We will go get it."

Kliks frowned. "Quick decision-making. What are your intentions?"

The commander didn't answer instantly, and Jeane gave an obnoxiously loud snort. "They want to keep it as their golden egg," she said in a mocking voice. "Sounds like good news, right? Ridiculous."

"You cannot use it!" Kliks slammed his palm on the table in anger. "Not in its current state! I just explained how dangerous it could be."

"And now we know what we're risking. However, we're not in the position to be picky about our methods."

Maura looked at Hill, but she wasn't the one talking this time. It was the person on the other end of the comms, a confident female voice.

Jeane pushed her chair back and shot up, her face a mask of fury. "Wait, what? Is that...Gertie?"

Maura glanced at Kliks, confused. Was Jeane familiar with the talker?

A sigh came through from the other side of the comms. "Yes, it's me. The Net is a decentralized mess, but I'm what you would call a leader. I should have revealed myself sooner, but I wanted to hear what you all had to say first."

"Umm, someone fill us in, please?" Roy interjected but stopped talking when Kliks glared at him, shaking his head furiously.

"My name is Gertrudia Banks," the woman said. "Jeane knows me well. It's nice to talk to you all."

Jeane took another step back from the comms like it was a rabid dog trying to bite her. The anger on her face turned into something forlorn. "When?" she asked, voice shaking. "How?"

"For a while now," Gertrudia said. "It's a long story."

"And you didn't think you should have told me?"

"I did consider. Repeatedly." The woman's voice sounded cold. "And I decided against it every single time."

A deep silence enveloped the group, and the busy room felt like it had halted around them. Jeane was white as the wall, looking seconds away from collapsing. Kliks stood, maybe wanting to reach for her, but stopped himself halfway. Whoever this secretive leader was, she'd been once close to Jeane. A friend? A partner?

"You left," Gertrudia spoke again. "What was there to say?"

Jeane didn't react, and Maura watched the commander's indifferent expression as she started speaking. "Ma'am, forgive me for interrupting, but time is short. We need to get back to that ship for the manipulator—"

But before she could have finished, Jeane leaned on the table with both arms. "No one touches my ship," she hissed into the microphone. "You want the manipulator? I will get it for you. But your people will stay the hells away from the *Lark*."

"Jeane, please. This is foolish—"

"For the love of everything you hold dear, Gert, if you don't let me have this, I will start wrecking this place until your men are forced to shoot me in the head."

Maura's chest tightened. She'd heard Jeane boasting and bluffing before, but this was different. This was bad. Kliks had concern painted all over his features.

Gertrudia hesitated, and instead, Roy broke the silence.

"Look, send a few people with us, but let us go," he said. An attempt to prevent Jeane from blowing up even more? "My ship is out there too, and I bet you're interested in all that data your undercover agent sent with me about the Union. Let's make this pick-up together, then get the hells away from here."

Jeane turned to him, but before she could have argued, Kliks also spoke up. "I think that's doable. Should be no problem. You said you shot down the Union vessels, so we wouldn't be encountering anything dangerous." His tone was pleading, and although he avoided looking at Jeane, he half-directed his words at her.

There was a tense pause, like when one is waiting for the thunder after a flash of lightning.

"Sure," said Gertrudia in a measured voice. "That can be arranged."

"Then stop screwing around," Jeane snapped, turning to Hill. "Give me a gun and let's go."

CHAPTER 23 | HIGH TIME

Jeane did get a gun, but only when Gertie firmly told Hill she was allowed to. All their stuff was also returned to them, which was honestly the least her friend could do for her. The commander was utterly unhappy about it, and the Net soldiers kept glancing at Jeane and Roy as if they couldn't wait for them to make one wrong move.

That may still have been on the table. First, though: the *Skylark*.

Hill assigned a team of soldiers to the task of returning to the ship, led by the same Nefirn guy who had arrested them before. Jones (no first name) looked like a man who could imagine a hundred better ways to spend his afternoon than escorting a bunch of outlaws through the desert on a fetch quest. Wearing a dissatisfied expression, he only gave them a few unfriendly barks of command while leading them through the base to the port and the two shuttles they were supposed to take. Jeane tuned him out. She'd tuned most things out by that time.

At the port, a short argument broke out about whether Maura and Damian should come with.

"You're not feeling well," the bodyguard said, sounding incredulous that this needed to be debated. "There's no way I'm letting you out there."

"I want to help," Maura persisted.

Jeane felt a vague sense of worry. A distant, glazed expression sat on Maura's face ever since she'd woken up from her trance. But the queen was where she wanted to be; they'd found the Net, hadn't they? She would be fine. They could make their deal, go back home, bring in the cavalry, and win that war of theirs. Everything had turned out great for them.

"No," Jones said, turning away and walking up the ramp into their shuttle. The port was buzzing with activity, people packing equipment inside various cargo ships, performing checks, and hurrying through the hall conversing and staring at their handheld devices. Gertie had mentioned the Union was on the move, so it checked out that the Net had also started to organize. There was even talk about open conflict. Just another thing Jeane had to ignore. "I have orders to take three, so the Miyozans and the robot are staying. Let's be quick about it."

"But—" Maura started, but Jones and half the group of soldiers already disappeared into the ship. The rest of the troopers walked off in the direction of another small craft. "Is it a good idea to get separated?"

ALU, rooted at their newly standard place beside the woman, chirped in agreement, and Jeane made herself roll her eyes. "It's only a short trip."

Maura frowned, the weak attempt at lightheartedness wasted on her.

"The Net got rid of the Union goons. We'll be okay," Kliks said in a placating tone. "In the meantime, you can discuss your mission with these people. And pick up some more intel if they let you look around. I'd like to be better informed about where we are and what the Net is planning."

"Yes, we need to talk to this Gertrudia," Damian said. "About Nas. About what we can do."

Maura pressed her lips in annoyance, but her stare softened. She shook her head but didn't protest, only stepped up to Kliks to give him a tight hug.

"Be careful," she said. Kliks nodded, gave a wink to ALU and a wave to Damian, and hurried into the ship. His eyes avoided Jeane's. Roy stood around awkwardly for a few seconds then trailed after him.

Jeane sighed. This was going to get weird.

"Well, see ya," she said, turning to walk off as well, but she froze when a hand wrapped around her arm. "What now?"

"Come back from out there, okay?" Maura's warm brown eyes widened in...fear, maybe? She clutched Jeane's wrist like a bird clinging to the side of its cage. "You come back."

The woman was so intense that the biting retort withered in Jeane's throat. *Talk about a royal order...*

"Where's your mind at?" She gave a weak chuckle and pulled her arm away. "Don't be ridiculous! You take care of your business, and I'll take care of mine."

Hurt flashed in Maura's eyes. She took a step back, then turned around, and stomped off. ALU pointed two fingers at Jeane and released a row of beeps as if to say, "I'm watching you," then pattered after her.

Jeane gave another theatrical sigh. "Awesome."

"If you think I can be of help, I'll go with you," Damian offered, but his voice was strained.

Jeane raised an eyebrow. "No. You don't want to. I'll say this, though. You should be more worried than you are."

"What do you mean?"

"I mean that your Nasir might have had good intentions, but I wasn't sent to Miyoza to rescue refugees, even if one of them happened to be royalty." Jeane swallowed the jittery impatience in her stomach. "Judging from how Gertie spoke about the manipulator, I think this glove of yours is too important for her to pass up. She will be very interested in exploiting it, in exploiting anything they can use against the Union—and that means Maura too. Time to decide whether you're okay with that."

Damian's jaw tightened. "The glove is dead outside Miyoza. It's not some superweapon. It will be years before they can do anything with it."

"I find that less and less convincing every time I hear it. I suppose Maura falling into a coma has nothing to do with the glove either." Jeane shrugged. "I'm just saying. I don't know the Net, but I know Gertie. Obviously not as well as I thought, but you get my point. Be careful."

Damian's face eased, understanding. "You're right." He

nodded at the craft. "Be careful yourself. Don't die."

Jeane waved noncommittally. It was not her goal to get sentimental, but she feared Damian might be slow on the uptake, and that couldn't fly. Without looking him in the eye again, she turned around and climbed into the shuttle.

The two craft lifted off the ground, then flew up and out of the hall through a long vertical shaft. Sunlight flooded the interior through the grimy windows of the vehicle Jeane was in; they hovered above the forlorn stone desert of this damn planet she still didn't know the name of, then zoomed towards the horizon.

She sat between Kliks and Roy, facing the Net soldiers in the back of the shuttle. Jones was describing the plan of attack, but his comrades looked bored, and only Roy seemed like he was listening. Kliks certainly didn't make eye contact with anyone, especially not with Jeane.

She didn't blame him for the ship—not after that first numbing half an hour. But she knew that he was angry with her, and she hated it. After how callously she'd acted back at the base, it was no wonder, but he had to understand it too, didn't he? The *Skylark* was gone. He knew what that meant.

Sure, they could give the manipulator to Gertie and leave this whole mess behind. Maura and Damian could deal with their own lives; it was not Jeane's problem anymore. Kliks, ALU, and her could return to the Ranch to see what was left of her people. Maybe the Net could take them at least some of the way if they felt generous. And the Ranch would be fine, even with the Foggy Cities gone. Lanehunters were indestructible. Like roaches.

But then what? Work their ass off for a few years, try to buy a new ship? Or get a job on one? Perhaps attempt to steal a vessel— that might be fun.

Her stomach turned. No, no way. She couldn't. Kliks knew it too.

They landed a ways off from the crash site. As they filed out of the shuttles, the sky was almost white above, the sun beating down on their backs with cruel intensity. Jeane didn't recognize the landscape, but she sensed it. Her ship was hiding behind one of those ridges.

The two groups started on different routes to their destination. While a team of five soldiers led by a tiny, stocky woman called Moran circled around towards the east, Jeane, Kliks, and Roy followed Jones and four other troopers up a dusty hill to the west. Jeane stared at her feet, counting the drops of sweat trickling down her neck until there was nothing else but the numbers, the sand, and the sun. Then it was right in front of them, in a shallow basin, lonely and quiet, its broken body looking very much the same as when they'd left it. The *Skylark*.

The group hunkered down behind the crest of the bluff, and Jones muttered into his comms, "Coast is clear from this side."

Moran made them wait for a beat before she answered. "Copy. Hang on a sec, we're gonna scooch closer. Movement to the north."

There was only silence, while Jones and the others surveyed their surroundings through binocular-goggles resembling thick-framed glasses. Nothing moved around them. Jeane glanced at Roy, and the former agent made a face.

"Nailships have mean cloaking. They could have slipped away from the Net attack and found the manipulator before us."

Jones' comms device beeped, and Moran's choked voice came through, heaving like she'd been running. "We dropped a lookout a hundred feet from the mark. He was alone."

"There might be more inside," Roy said. "Waiting for reinforcements, keeping the area safe to land. We might not have a lot of time."

"Let's meet up," Jones said. "We'll sweep this side of the valley."

They converged on the *Skylark*, while Moran's team descended the slopes from the other direction. Crouching at the outer hatch of the airlock, they stopped to listen, hoping to pick up some indication as to what awaited them inside, but the only sound was the wind whirring through the desert. Jeane blinked the dust out of her eyes and glanced into the darkness beyond the hatch. She imagined the agents huddling around the manipulator like flies on a piece of candy. The thought made the fury blaze up in her chest, and she waited for a sarcastic joke from the voice in the back of her mind before she realized there would be none.

Jones inclined his head towards the airlock. Jeane counted to ten, and slipped inside.

After the first few steps, barely any sunlight filtered in. They moved among the debris covering the deck as soundlessly as possible. Once through the inner hatch, they turned right and passed the ladder leading to the level above. Jeane instinctively ducked, but a piece of something had fallen on the hole and covered it— no one would surprise them from up there.

It was quiet, eerie, the silence occasionally punctuated by metal groaning or the rattle of things tumbling down from somewhere. They crept forward, and soon got to the point where the corridor bent to the left. A few feet ahead, the ceiling dented to the deck in a steep V-shape, leaving only a few inches of space to try and crawl to the other side. *If* there was an other side to reach.

Jones and Roy dropped to their stomachs, inching closer to the gap to peer through. Without thinking about it, Jeane grabbed at Kliks' shirt sleeve, the nerves getting the better of her. The Talalan froze, but his cold fingers found her hand. He gave a short squeeze and drew back.

A minute later, the two men reappeared, and the group moved back to talk.

"The cargo hold door is intact," Jones whispered. The muted beam of his flashlight illuminated the faint outline of scales on his face. "Two guys are keeping watch. I think three more are in the hold."

"Inspectors always come in threes," Roy said in a low voice. "Those two will know we're here; the trio keeps in contact. Anyway, they don't look too healthy, but they've got a lightwall."

"What's that?" Moran asked.

"Big old plasma barrier. They affixed it to the threshold. We're not getting in this way."

Jeane scratched her nose. "The grav tunnels might help."

Jones held up a hand, and they all paused, staring into the darkness, listening for footsteps or any kind of noise. Nothing.

"Grav tunnels?" Roy asked.

"It's where the artificial gravity rails are running," Jeane replied.

"If the hull is too deformed, they might not be traversable," Kliks warned.

"Worth a try. Follow me."

Jeane turned away, but Kliks didn't move an inch. "You're not going, right?" he asked.

His features were smeared by the darkness. "Of course, I am," Jeane replied. "I'm not letting these people saunter around in my ship alone."

"Yeah, no, I'm with you too," Roy said. Gods, he was really overdoing trying to be useful! "Those guys fight nasty. You might need me."

"Jeane, come on." Kliks' voice was irritated. "Leave this to the professionals."

She raised her brow.

"Well, then I'm coming too," her friend said, folding his arms.

Oh, hells no. "You're really not."

"Jeane—"

"You're staying, and that's it."

Kliks turned to Jones, perhaps waiting for support, but the officer held up his hand. "I take care of my people. You deal with this among yourselves."

"You're staying," Jeane repeated.

Was it that important to make him stay? What the hells was she doing? Trying to keep him safe? *Now* of all times?

"Captain," Kliks said, and she had to focus not to grimace at the name or at his tone. "Understood, Captain."

Oh, he was furious.

"You two, with us." Jones gestured to his soldiers, and they turned back to where they'd come from. "Let's do this."

Jeane didn't look Kliks in the eye as she walked away, but when they were out of earshot, she poked Jones' shoulder. "Tell your people to shield him. Keep him out of this. And we're going to need some noise to cover up the sounds of us crawling through the tunnels."

"Noted."

Stopping beside the airlock again, Jeane crouched down and pressed an unassuming panel on the wall. It popped out a few inches and raised—or, would have raised, but the mechanism must have deformed during the crash, and they had to lift the metal plate manually.

"Remind me why you have a secret corridor running through your ship?" Roy asked as Jeane lowered herself into the opening. The tunnel slanted downwards and was just wide enough for her. The small plates of the artificial gravity activators cut into her arms and knees as she crawled ahead.

"Why, you don't have one?" she snarked, shuffling forward so Roy, Jones, and the two soldiers could fit themselves into the underpass. "Amateur."

"I'm serious," Roy huffed. The sound of something soft slamming against something metallic came from his direction, and he cursed.

Jeane sighed. "It's pretty useful in an impossible situation."

"Do those happen to you often?"

"Not to me, usually. To Hollis, all the time."

"Who's Hollis?"

Jeane moved forward and the others shuffled after her. The tunnel was as dark as possible, but the way ahead was unobstructed.

"The original owner of the ship." She already regretted mentioning him. But this mission was stupid, and Kliks wasn't there, and she couldn't make the voice in her head talk, so she might as well keep going. "He always got into the worst situations just to be able to beat up a few agents. And these tunnels are actually great hiding places, for things too, not only people. I just don't use them often because it sucks getting anything in and out."

They crept forward and passed a path to the side, and when Jeane felt for the way ahead, her hands swept only empty air to the right. This was where the tunnel branched and ran under the cargo hold to end up inside a chamber hidden between the engine room and the hull.

"We'll need that distraction now," she whispered. Jones spoke a muffled command into his comms, and the noise of gunshots above them followed a second later. Those Union goons definitely knew they were under attack now—but they might not expect another assault from behind.

Picking up the pace, they turned to the right and inched forward in the dark.

"So, Hollis is the ghost of the dead foster father." Roy wasn't letting the topic go. He might have been making conversation to calm his nerves, but Jeane was really close to kicking him in the face. It would have been so easy too—she could say it was an accident.

"He is," she answered in the end. Shutting the guy out was more exhausting than talking. "He built the ship, he gave it to me, then he died. And now I've made a bunch of scrap metal out of it. Nice one, me."

"And why is he a ghost?"

Her fingers touched a cool surface. She fumbled around, looking for the pressure panel, then pushed it and breathed in relief when the wall section raised before her.

Pulling herself forward, she climbed out, and when Roy scrambled free of the tunnel too, she faced him. "He's a ghost because I'm pathetic," she hissed. "But this place is so full of him, even you might hear his voice!"

Jones swatted her in the shoulder, mouthing the word "silence" while he and his two soldiers perimeter-checked the room. But Roy stared back at her, unflinching. She wanted to whisper-shout at him some more because it felt surprisingly good, but instead, she spun around and crossed the chamber.

Except for a few empty shelves and storage closets, there was nothing in the room. Jeane cracked open the door leading to the cargo hold and glared into the darkness.

Although the *Skylark's* tail looked misshapen and squeezed from the outside, the cargo hold was largely intact. A portion of the ceiling had caved in; debris and parts fallen out of random containers of junk were scattered everywhere. The only illumination was what looked like a cluster of tiny LEDs near the section where they'd left the manipulator and pallid white glow at the entrance—the lightwall Roy had mentioned. One of Jones' people tapped Jeane on the shoulder and pressed a binocular-goggle in her hand.

Through the device, she saw three figures highlighted in red. The cluster of LEDs appeared to be attached to their clothes and weapons. They stood around motionless and didn't move even when the sound of lackluster shots rang out from the direction of the door and several beams of light hit the ceiling. They were playing for time. Backup was on its way for sure.

"We need to take all of them down at the same time," Roy mused behind her. "Inspector units are deadly together. One mind, three bodies. Not real telepathy but close to it. They're also armored in most places. We'll have to hit them in the face."

Jeane turned back to the others with a grimace. "I'm going to channel my inner Kliks and say we shouldn't shoot around in careless abandon that close to the manipulator."

Jones pulled out a metal disk the size of his palm from his pocket. "Should we knock them out with an EMP charge?"

"That might work, but I suggest using multiple," the ex-agent said.

Jeane glared at him. This was getting complicated, and she couldn't handle complicated. She had to get through this quickly. "No EMP either. Remember: universe-breaking magic big bang box." She grabbed Roy's arm, dragging him to the door, and called back to Jones. "Give us a minute, then take your shots."

"What are we doing?" Roy inquired, but she put a hand on his mouth. She pointed toward the hold to the left, then to the right, and mouthed the words "making some noise."

Roy's eyes caught a straggling light beam from the other side of the hall, and Jeane saw the question in them.

"We can do this," she whispered, hoping he wouldn't end up asking anything. Judging from their conversation before, he was almost as messed up as her. He seemed the type of chaotic she could trust going along with stuff like this. *Don't disappoint me, traitor without a cause!*

"We probably can," the ex-agent agreed, lifting her hand off his mouth. His fingers were warm. "But do *you* have to?"

Jeane rolled her eyes, but her throat tightened, the grief threatening to break through. "Cool one-liner," she blurted out. "Let's go."

"Wait, I can..." He grabbed her arm, hesitating. The shadow of something cold and bleak descended on his face. There was a blankness to him in that moment that she'd seen on agents before. "Mmm, no," he said then, shaking the gloom off as if it was a tangled spider web stuck to his face. "Never mind."

"Whatever." Jeane didn't have time for this. She turned and tiptoed inside the cargo hold.

She approached the near left corner. If they were lucky, they could draw the inspectors' attention and put them at some distance from the manipulator. And as a bonus, their targets would be facing the door, so the others could take them out more easily.

Jeane stomped on the deck, then called, "Oh, fuck" out loud. At the same time, Roy made a drawn-out, metallic sound in the other direction, close to the broken ceiling section. In the next second, she sensed more than saw one of the Union goons' red-contoured body lurching forward, cutting through the darkness with alarming momentum.

Two gunshots resounded from the secret chamber, hitting the inspector. But the bastard stayed standing.

He barreled towards Jeane full speed, and she backed away, raising her gun. But she didn't have enough time. Her eyes widened as the inspector grabbed her, twisted her hand, lifted her off the floor, and clocked her in the face.

The goggles pressed into her eye-sockets and the device fell off her head, her weapon clattering to the ground shortly after. The pain registered, but she was mostly just surprised by the speed of the fucker. Kicking out, she tried to hit him in his crotch, but he connected with another punch, and it felt like her skull was cracking into two. She tasted blood, and through the ringing in her ears, she heard Roy yelling "The wall!" The sound of gunshots was like thunder echoing in her head.

She was on the ground, but she didn't remember the collision. Propelling herself to the side, she moved out of the guy's melee range. There was a moment mid-roll when the inspector's gun was hanging right in front of her face, so she grabbed for it.

Another roll—how did she even do that? It was almost a fucking cartwheel!—and she was standing, kind of, her left knee buckling down. She tried to turn the gun around but she was too slow. *Where do you fire with this shit?*

The inspector's body slammed into hers, trying to knock the

weapon out of her hand. She groaned, flailing around, and pushed the first button she found on the gun.

A dull sound and a flash. Something hot on her stomach, but no pain.

She lost track of things. Someone was yelling again, and pressure on her spine flattened her to the deck—had that asshole fallen on her? Then beams of light and someone dragging her backward behind cover. She scrambled her legs about to help, but it only hindered the process.

Urgent voices. More light. No more gunshots though. *That's probably good.* She turned her head lazily; her skull was heavy as if waterlogged. Oblivion was coming for her, and that was alright.

She didn't mind. High time, to be honest.

She turned her head to the other side. Someone was lying next to her. His skin was white, his eyes closed, a mop of white hair smeared onto his forehead. His abdomen was bloody—too bloody. It was not right. It shouldn't have been that bloody.

No, no, no, no.

A dark figure crouched beside her, blocking out the sight. She gasped. She needed to breathe. She didn't want to faint now; she needed to see—

One, two, three... Shallow and ragged. It was so hard to keep counting. So hard to stay. *Four, five, six... Is Kliks even breathing anymore?*

She squeezed her eyes closed. She opened them again. *Seven. That's right.* But the number after seven was an empty void right where her lungs should have been. She was so stupid. So fucking selfish. Kliks didn't deserve this.

Eight. It was eight. The person beside her moved away, and she could see Kliks again. His eyes were closed... he wasn't breathing...

Nine. Ten. Eleven. Twelve.

Darkness.

CHAPTER 24 | THE RINGMASTER

High General Liv Horst opened his eyes and sat up in the bed of Miyoza's dead king.

He glanced about the darkened room, the gloom of his dream-world—of stomping boots, barking commands, and the dampened buzz of initializing fighter engines—dissipating from his mind. The space was silent, save for his steady breathing. Nothing moved; he was alone. He turned around and put his bare feet on the carpeted floor. Another day. Still alive.

He dressed in his formal attire, the clothes hastily flung on the back of a chair the previous night. Occupying the bedroom of the late King Caiden Tholis was a grim act, but the Council, out of some grotesque desire to establish dominance, expected it from him. And the people back on Gaerris loved the symbolism. Why wouldn't they? After biding their time in the factories and laboratories year after year under the cracking skin of that evil planet with one singular goal in the forefront of their minds, they now saw their wildest dreams fulfilled.

And it didn't cost Liv anything except the bad taste lingering in his mouth. *Let them have their circus.*

Walking to the window, he drew the heavy curtains apart, letting dull light into the luxurious chamber. The sky outside resembled turbulent gray smoke, and a thick layer of fog covered the capital. It had been raining for several days now. Liv narrowed his eyes, but he couldn't see the royal garden hiding behind the deluge, untended and desolate.

The central section of the palace remained the only intact part of the building. After the queen's failed peace attempt, it was only proper to retaliate, so Liv had the two outer wings of the complex bombarded to smithereens. The act satisfied the Council and terrified the Miyozans in one fell swoop, and the evacuated living quarters felt like a better choice than the city hiding millions of people. Plus, the main wing was still there for the taking.

Those millions of people were also still there. Locked inside their homes, kept under surveillance, hurt or starving, and without supplies given that life had effectively stopped on Miyoza since the occupation. The City Nervous System was offline, and no one went to work or was allowed to move an inch without permission. The hundreds of Gaerrisian soldiers patrolling the streets received a single directive: keep everyone quiet and impotent.

Naturally, some casualties had been necessary for the citizens and the remaining military forces to realize that the sensible choice was to obey. Some would have said the death toll was too high, but Liv disagreed. He understood, just like Maura Tholis had when she'd contacted him, that in some cases, not losing everything felt like a victory.

This status quo could not go on long, however. Today, the Gaerrisian Council would hold its final assembly on Miyozan grounds. Their forces had been moving everything valuable from the capital to Gaerris throughout the last few days, and now that they were finished, the next step of the plan would be initiated.

The notable exception from the pillaging was, of course, the CNS. The engineers hopping over from Gaerris to attempt to turn the system back on had been unsuccessful. Given enough time, they said, it would be possible to circumvent the barriers put in place by the queen and the city-AI, but the Council decided to not wait. The ones who didn't hold the belief of the CNS being outright evil were at least uncomfortable with the idea that a revived

AI could attempt to tear through their forces in its compulsion to eradicate the enemy, so all of them resolved to leave it alone, to be destroyed with the rest of the capital.

It was time for the locust swarm to fly home. Liv would not be able to keep those millions of Miyozans alive for much longer.

He turned his back to the window, crossing the room in a confident stride. *Chin up, shoulders squared.* The show continued.

Stepping outside, he nodded to the guards posted at the door and walked down the winding staircases towards the throne hall. The pair of soldiers followed him, silent as shadows.

A mass of officers and advisors stood around the central part of the main wing, talking in groups, looking through data, and discussing strategy. As Liv cut through the scattered clumps of people in the corridor, he mused for a moment about how different this view was compared to the years of desperate battle-planning in the bowels of Gaerris' underground cities. How long the road had been from cowering in the shadows and making the hardest sacrifices until they got to this point. The faces of his people were clear now, their words light and easy. Laughing and joking, eyes shining in happiness...

Happiness and something else. Mania, perhaps.

He pushed through the crowd and the doors of the hall, and the people gave way to him, nodding or saluting depending on their rank and political position. Liv was, after all, High General. *Executioner Superior.* If only he really wielded all the power that people imagined he did.

Yes, his people were happy for all the wrong reasons. And about to extinguish a whole culture, wearing those honest smiles he so wanted to wipe off their faces.

But he understood them too, and that was worse. Thanks to his status, he was one of the few people who comprehended what the war was really about. How, from an unfortunate series of events no one currently alive could have had any influence on and a minor atrocity that shouldn't have been the end of everything, the roots of conflict seized the hearts of both nations. The information didn't help directly, but knowing was better than blindly groping forward in the dark. He kept telling this to himself, and one day, he hoped he would even believe it.

He'd just turned nineteen when, after a grueling day of assisting in planning the next round of offense against Miyoza, Malina Trevise, already a candidate for a position in the Council, grasped his arm in the Upper Canteen of the Operation Hub and led him in between the grimy walls of the Repository. It was the day Liv learned their world's hidden history.

"What is this about?" he had asked. Malina had the clearance, but Liv, a descendant of a lower-ranked family, was not allowed into the Repo.

The woman smiled. She'd been twenty then and already trudging deep into the mud of war. Sabotage and guerrilla maneuvers with the sole purpose of terrorizing people had been her strong point. But she smiled at him, her black eyes sparkling in mischief. "I talked to Thorne. I convinced him you might be useful yet."

Liv smoothed out the creases on his uniform anxiously. That guy had been a pain in his backside since they'd known each other. Coming from an almost unknown line and rising steeply, he'd always been the best and the smartest in class. Always sowing discord, never compromising.

Malina peered at him as if looking through his eyes into his soul. "Liv, we cannot do this quick and dirty like we thought. We need someone like you. Someone for the long con."

She clicked a computer to life—an ancient model that had never been and would never be connected to any network on the planet.

"For the long con?" Liv asked, glancing at the screen. But he'd realized by then.

Malina had always been in support of stopping the war, recognizing the demise the planet had been steadily hurtling itself towards. Brilliant and brave with reasonable morals but rough around the edges, she was the daughter of the High General at the time and knew she needed to tread lightly if she didn't want to be removed too early on. But she'd been excellent at finding the angles that worked to gain support.

Thorne had been the first who stood beside her. War was a good way to amass power, but with one that had been going on for decades, he'd started to wonder if getting out would be more profitable. The two of them had been sending out their whispers about another way of doing things for a while. They found support among the working class, the suffering masses kept in place with tyranny but otherwise untouched by the fanatism of their leaders, but hadn't been able to get a claw in any of the powerful people who could actually make a change.

"Keeping up pretenses has never been an asset of mine," Malina had said, gazing at the old computer. "Thorne's either. If we run against the will of the many, we might break everything. But you're patient enough to *bend* instead."

Then she left him with the memories of their long-dead ancestors and the weight of a decision he couldn't yet comprehend.

He'd always been an idealist, believing Gaerris should have stopped the fight ages ago. Their future was not on this gods-forsaken rock; they had the power to leave, to go and find a new home, so why wouldn't they? Lay the past to rest. Let Miyoza be. But his word alone could not do much. He needed allies.

Miyoza claimed they were the descendants of the first colonists who had left the Old Home, Earth, but according to the data Liv had looked at that afternoon (incomplete excerpts of ancient messages and censored comms-conversations), Gaerris hadn't been far behind them, together with many other conglomerates developing and building their own ships to escape the apocalypse. By then, the situation on Old Earth had deteriorated. The rough translations of articles and notices written in long-gone languages were difficult to untangle, but Liv understood the basic idea. Powerful corporations competing for resources and preying upon people, diminishing natural reserves over a backdrop of failing governments and disaster-stricken continents. The group of people who would become the Miyozans started off with the best equipment and technology humanity had possessed; they'd been part of the elite, the rich, and the influential. The ones eventually becoming the Gaerrisians had fared much worse.

And there, between the lines of those old logs, was buried that first, most repugnant crime. Worse than the ancestors of Miyozans owning better resources—they had appropriated all that from the rest of them, including the ancestors of Gaerrisians.

According to the carefully curated files, industrial espionage and direct violent takeovers had been both involved, but the details were nebulous.

During the frantic scramble to flee Earth, the vessels of the Miyozans had been able to cross the wildly changing, unstable lane swallowing up their sun in time, while the generation ship packed with the ancestors of Gaerris only got far enough that they could watch the destruction of their home planet from the front row. They had watched, for decades, waiting for the lane to stabilize after the catastrophe, fortifying their own vessel and perfecting their technology so they too could run. Then they'd risked the crossing.

Despite following the same vector the Miyozans had sailed, they ended up much farther from their destination than expected. Lanes did that sometimes when young; the ends of their vectors wandered through the universe, breaking into normal space again and again, light-years away from where the exit point originally formed. Still, it could have been worse. At least the Gaerrisians hadn't ended up scattered in the farthest corners of the galaxy, like many of the other human factions leaving Earth around that time.

On the long road towards the Miyoza-system, which was still the closest habitable world, overpopulation, diseases, conflicts with alien forces, takeovers of military dictatorships, and periods of barbarism plagued the generation ship, and by the time they arrived, their society was a wreck. The sad fact was that King Lorio Tholis had been right not to trust them when they had asked for his help.

The Miyozan king's rejection broke something inside the leaders of the ship. Following up with violence, they relocated their people to that inhospitable planet, and their plan had started to form. They would get back what Miyoza owed them, what they had stolen from them. They would ally with the worst kind of people and mutilate their culture in horrible ways to be able to kill every single Miyozan who, in their eyes, had caused all their suffering.

How much of this story was true was anyone's guess. The

Gaerrisian leaders believed it, and this faith became the center of their existence. They infected their people with the promise of the coming cosmic justice, building a strict, uncompromising society around the idea of revenge. The universe moved on around them, but they could not be swayed.

Malina had been right. A flimsy rebellion to halt the war effort would not have been able to oppose such an obsession. The people wanted blood because there was little else that they knew to want. So, after establishing themselves as members of the Council, Liv, Malina, and Thorne played the game with caution. They'd lied through their teeth, compromising every step of the way; they'd killed and deceived, following the path of revenge Gaerris carved for themselves, but whenever they found a way, they saved what they could. Slanting ambitious attack plans, twisting perspectives, warping the will of extremists. Hiding in alibis, shady machinations, and convoluted ploys so the Council couldn't suspect their real intent, gradually gathering support amongst their own, creeping about in the dark, so no one grasped the scale of their work. The long con.

Then Liv became High General and tried to move forward faster. He'd seen what would come next: the Union, emerging from humanity's ashes, looming in the background like a hungry wolf. Gaerris had worked with them before, in the beginning, and the abominations resulting from the collaboration (cloning and horrible gene-engineering experiments to increase Gaerris' manpower and military strength) were among the few things Liv wanted to forget about rather than learn from. Fortunately, the cooperation had not lasted long. Those things even Gaerris did not have the stomach for. And the Union Leadership, the shadowy presence at the head of the empire no one said no to, had since been waiting, keeping their greedy eyes on the two planets.

Liv had attempted peace talks with Miyoza several times and swiftly failed in all of them. Then he failed again after Caiden Tholis' death. Now, they were truly running out of time. He wouldn't be able to convince the Council now, but if Gaerris couldn't defend itself, if they didn't find allies, the Union would devour them too.

Liv walked into the throne hall, his glance passing over the

Council members present. There was Three, Ruben Hassak, his form dwarfing everyone, discussing something in a booming voice with Nine and Seven, his usual minions. There was the slender, blonde figure of Eight, circled by her advisors in the corner, talking on her comms. And then Four, sitting at the long table alone, his lean body bent, his nose buried in his tablet. He glanced up at Liv and gave him a nod, his ascetic face expectant. But it was not him the High General was looking for.

"Missed me, One?" a voice said from behind, and Malina stepped forward to stand before him.

"Always," Liv replied but didn't let the faint smile creep on his face. "Are you ready for this?"

The woman looked around the white-walled, decorated hall, over the Council members and their assistants, her stare belittling. "I wanted to ask the same. What's our little spider friend doing?"

"Quiet now; anyone could hear us. He's safe. Busy rebuilding his web."

"How soon?"

Liv hesitated. Nasir Dareth had told him it might be days before the Net made its decision. He'd promised he would do everything to convince them and to find Maura Tholis but couldn't exactly give a timetable. "Sooner than later. Anything else is unacceptable."

"Thorne is ready—just say the word."

Liv looked at Four again. He was ready, alright. For a bloodbath.

But no. Not again. Not after all this.

To be fair, even with the Net's help, it *could* become a bloodbath. But it would be different. It had to be. There would be a clear goal ahead. The light at the end of this long, dark tunnel.

Disarm the Council, take control over their armies. Restore the CNS and the queen's power. Show everyone that cooperation with Miyoza was Gaerris' only chance to survive.

People started trickling from the corridors into the throne hall. The meeting was about to start.

"What say you then?" asked Malina, a masterfully crafted,

inscrutable smile on her face. "Let's play for time a little?"

Liv nodded stiffly. Malina winked at him, turned around, and took her place at the table. She glanced back, and playfulness gave way to determination in her eyes. Four caught her glance too, and his mouth pulled into a dry grin.

Liv stepped forward to the head of the table and knocked its surface twice to gather everyone's attention. Nine figures at the table, many more sitting and standing around. Two people on this whole planet he trusted.

As long as their interests coincided. As long as he kept playing it right. He shouldn't forget that.

He greeted the crowd, opening the assembly of the Council with a few formal words. Somewhere above their heads, hidden in the High General's personal shuttle, Nasir and his Net comrades were doing what they were good at, getting in touch with their organization and finding the Miyozan queen so they all had a chance to survive the next months.

The show continued.

CHAPTER 25 | PIECES IN THE GAME

"Sir, you're not allowed inside the medbay. Please move along."

Roy glared into the young soldier's face, but he plastered on a pleading look the next moment. Enkindling sympathy might work better than raw force. "Come on, man. Our friend is in there."

"I understand." The lad was not budging. He didn't meet Roy's eyes, staring into the air above his head. "Their doctor will contact you."

"You already let ALU in." Maura's cheeks were red from frustration. "What difference does it make?"

The guard opened his mouth, hesitated for a moment, then closed it again. Roy glanced back at the Miyozans, exasperated. The three of them were standing in the busy corridor on the central deck of the *Colugo*, Commander Hill's flagship, in front of the doors of the medical center.

"At least tell us what's happening to him," Damian said, making his voice sound a tad more threatening than necessary. *Good man.*

The soldier adjusted his grip on the sizable gun propped up in his arm. "Your friend is undergoing an operation. I have no more information."

"Can we talk to Commander Hill?" Roy pushed.

The man exhaled. "She is on the bridge, as she is the captain of this vessel."

"We're not allowed on the bridge. How about Jones?"

"What about him, sir?"

"Where can we find him?"

The guard didn't flinch. "You can inquire on the bridge."

"But we're not allowed on the bridge, for the love of—"

Roy cut himself off and threw his arms up. All the man's expression conveyed to him was a strong "that's not my problem"-vibe. They were not getting anywhere. Especially not inside the medbay.

And still, even this was better than before, when they'd been stuck in a bunk room, keeping watch over an unconscious Jeane, not allowed to move freely on the ship. Roy had to admit Hill was justified in not trusting them wandering around after what had happened during the mission to the *Skylark* because it was only out of luck that they'd managed to make it without higher casualties. Jeane's condition was stable, but they had no idea what was going on with Kliks, and it proved increasingly difficult to sit tight and wait.

After Jeane and Roy had separated to draw the inspectors' attention, Roy quickly disarmed one of them while the lanehunter wrestled with the other. The third one had run off and opened up the lightwall for his two comrades outside. Kliks must have noticed Jeane was in trouble, and although Roy had tried to warn him, he used the opportunity to push inside—and the next moment, he'd gotten caught in the re-stabilizing lightwall the inspector turned back on.

In the end, they'd managed to dispatch the three remaining guys and grab the manipulator—and all that without Roy having to resort to releasing the thing that was hammering at that door in the back of his mind. It *really* wanted to come out now. He'd almost allowed it for that one moment before he and Jeane had stepped inside the cargo hold.

It would have been so easy. So familiar. None of this messy loneliness and fear and desire to belong. If only he allowed

Leadership to take authority, life could make sense again.

But when had it ever?

So, Roy kept shaking off the urge. Kept going, kept busy, tried to connect with this weird group of people fate had brought him together. He could defeat this. It couldn't last forever. He could become himself, somehow, even if he didn't exactly know who that was.

They'd left the *Skylark* behind. Concussion or panic had knocked Jeane out, Moran had received a hole in her shoulder, and Kliks had been at death's door when they'd scrambled out and into the shuttles. Back at Katipo Base, a group of medics had spirited the wounded away (plus ALU because it was impossible to remove them from their friends' side) and ushered the rest of them to a port and onto a transporter on rails. Arriving into an immense underground hall, they'd climbed aboard the *Colugo* and soon set sail among the stars.

Roughly a day had passed since. The medics had brought Jeane back a few hours ago, sedated but in good shape, noting that she would wake shortly. They'd told them Kliks was alive, and Hill's people were doing everything they could to keep him that way.

But even after their guards had allowed Roy, Maura, and Damian out of their designated room, most doors on the ship remained closed to them. No one told them anything, and they hadn't seen Hill or Jones since the previous day. Where was the *Colugo* going? What was the plan? Was the Union after them? Maura had mentioned that the Net boss, Gertrudia, hadn't contacted Hill again, at least not during the *Skylark* mission, so they hadn't been able to speak with her, but was this radio silence a precursor of worse things? They had no idea.

"Where to?" Damian asked as the trio turned their backs on the medbay door.

The *Colugo* was huge—not by Union standards but compared to most of the lanehunter ships Roy had seen. At least a hundred people must have been serving aboard. The corridors were packed with mostly humans, but they glimpsed members of other species hurrying along the decks as well. Some of the crew paused to glance at the team with trepidation, sizing them up. The metallic collars they'd been given before boarding clearly signified their outsider status.

"Hey, Agent," said Damian, and Roy sent him a cutting glance. "Any ideas?"

"I don't know." He was still miffed by the confrontation with the guard. "I'm not sure there's anything we can do without bringing forth the anger of the powers that be."

"He must be alive," Maura said. "They would tell us if he wasn't."

"I think so." Damian gave a gentle squeeze to the young woman's shoulder. "And if they keep working on saving his life, they must think it's not in vain."

There was a false pang in the bodyguard's voice—he wasn't used to saying comforting things just for the sake of them. Maura didn't look like she usually needed it either, but this was probably a special occasion for both of them.

"Also, he's valuable as a Talalan," Roy said. "I'm sure they're doing everything they can to continue using his brain for further manipulator-related shenanigans." Maura frowned at him; the implications didn't help to keep her cool. So, he decided against adding that the unknown nature of Talalan physiology might provide a challenge for the medical staff while trying to revive their alien friend and just gestured to the Miyozans to follow him. "Let's go back to the room for now. I know we left a note with the guards, but I would like to be there when Jeane comes to."

"I agree," Maura said, her face dressed in even more worry. "This is going to be hard for her."

Roy grimaced. *Smart move, jackass. Stressing out her Queenship instead of providing relieving feedback.* But Maura's assessment proved to be painfully correct.

Jeane's awakening was difficult. It reminded Roy of someone climbing out of a deep well—as if the dark waters of oblivion lapped at her heels for long seconds, reaching for her consciousness. Her eyes flitted about in the poorly furnished room—two bunk beds, a wardrobe, a retractable plastic table, and a chair—as if not comprehending her surroundings. She moved to lift her arm, but one of the medics had tied her wrist to the side of the bed with a metal band similar to the ones Roy and the others were wearing on their necks.

The realization roused her. Her eyes focused and found Maura. "What's this?" She leaned on her free arm, but her elbow buckled, and she flopped back on the pillow. She released a painful groan and pushed herself up again. "Where are we? What's happening?"

Maura sat down at the side of her bed and put a soothing hand on her shoulder. "We're okay. We're on a ship with the Net. You're going to be fine."

"No." Jeane pulled on her bonds again, then her eyes went wide. "Kliks—"

"He's alive," Roy hurried to say. "He's in surgery. We tried to see him, but they didn't let us in."

The woman's face went blank, and there was a moment when Roy wasn't sure whether she understood him. But then she blinked, slowly. "He's alive," she repeated. She swallowed, breathed in and out, and her eyes focused again. "Where?"

"I told you, we were not allowed—"

"Who put this on me?" A panicked fury colored her voice, and she jerked her arm again. "I need to see Kliks. Where's Hill? What happened to the manipulator? Where's ALU?"

Damian took a step towards the bed, his large form casting a respectable shadow. "ALU is with Kliks. They were the only one the doctor allowed in. About everything else, we know very little. No one is talking to us."

At the man's calm voice, Jeane stopped struggling and peered up at him. The frenzied rage drew back under the surface, and she forced composure to her voice. "Well then. Let's ask them again."

Damian nodded. He walked to the door and cracked it open. "Excuse me," he started, addressing his words to one of the guards. "It is imperative we speak to Lieutenant Jones or perhaps Commander Hill herself. There are things that we—"

"Is someone outside?" Jeane jiggled her handcuff and started shouting, her voice piercing and high. "Hey, asshole! Let me talk to Gertie! She will want to, I guarantee. You might get promoted and stuff!"

The guard peeked into the room, his eyes settling on the

woman in the bed. "Oh, you're awake. In that case, I'll be back." And he walked away.

Damian rolled his eyes. "Really? I was even being polite, but *she* gets answers."

"What can I say? People love me." Jeane pushed herself into an awkward sitting position. The bodyguard flashed an indignant stare at her, but then, to Roy's surprise, they exchanged a tense smirk.

A few seconds later, the guard returned with Jones at his heels.

"Ugh, it's you." Jeane grimaced. "Get this thing off me and take me to Kliks."

"I was told you want to speak with Ms. Banks," Jones said, his pale blue face as impassive as ever.

"I don't give a damn about Gertie. I want to see my friend."

"Let's take this step by step, alright?" Roy held up a placating hand. "Listen, Lieutenant, we've been through a lot. Like you. We only want to know if our friend is okay. We're ready for any discussion your boss wants to have, but that's our priority."

Jones stared at him like he'd just seen a ghost. Roy supposed it must have been weird: him, the Union agent, playing the peacekeeper among the Net and lanehunters. *What has the world come to, indeed.*

"I can't take you to your friend," Jones replied, his voice filling with something new. *Emotion? Can't be.* "That lightwall did a number on him, and the medical team is working hard to save his life. It's going to be a long process. But before you start yelling at me, I can tell you his chances are good. Our medbay is well-equipped, and the staff is excellent."

Jeane leaned forward as much as the handcuff allowed her, the metal clinging to the side of the bed. She snarled at Jones. "They better be. They better fucking be."

"Now, I suppose you want me to release you," the lieutenant went on, unbothered. "I will do that if you're willing to talk to Ms. Banks."

"We are," Maura said. "We will talk to her."

"Unfortunately, it's not up to Your Majesty."

Jeane glanced at Maura and Jones in quick succession. A bitter smile unfurled on her face. "Man, I love to be irreplaceable. But as I said, I don't give a fuck."

"Jeane, please." Maura turned to the woman; her hands were shaking, but her tone was collected. "This might be important. I need you."

Jeane seemed to be taken aback by the quiet request. She looked away, almost ashamed. She was silent for a long moment, her face devoid of emotion, then she glared at Jones, avoiding Maura's eyes. "Right. Sure. I'll talk to her."

The lieutenant lifted his wrist-comms, pushed a few buttons, and held it next to Jeane's handcuff. The metal band unlatched and fell to the floor. "In that case, please, follow me."

"I apologize for our reticence," Gertrudia said. Her voice sounded detached through the speakers. "We had a lot to do."

"Kliks is dying, Gert," Jeane muttered. "But thanks for the compassion."

There was a silence, then a sigh. "He's not dying. But I'm sorry for what happened."

They were sitting at a workstation in the corner of the crescent-shaped, sharply illuminated bridge: Jeane, Maura, Damian, Roy, Hill, and Gertrudia through the communicator on the table. The room was as busy as the whole ship. Roy caught little from the commands and conversations around them, but it sounded like the *Colugo* was maneuvering around hostile forces with several other ships in tow.

"My people are doing alright too, thank you for asking," Gertrudia went on. Roy heard the unsaid part of the sentence: the quest for the manipulator did not have to happen the way it had. Jeane had forced Gertudia's hand, and the casualties were, at least partly, on her.

The lanehunter recognized this as well. She didn't look up and didn't answer.

"What about the manipulator?" Damian asked.

"Safe and functional," Hill answered. "Our people are working on it, but your Talalan friend's knowledge is irreplaceable."

"Working on it to do what?" Roy lifted an eyebrow.

"I told you before," Gertrudia said. "We cannot be picky about our methods anymore. The Union annexed the Foggy Cities, and they're getting more daring on other lanehunter-friendly worlds as well. They've just put some serious forces down on Metallia and Rix. We might wake up tomorrow and realize there's nothing left. We cannot let that happen."

"You've waited long enough," Jeane snapped. "What has your amazing resistance been doing for the last decades? If it's so important to stop the Union, why are you only starting now?"

"Oh, don't pretend you're interested! I could start telling you in great detail what we've been doing, from building up an intelligence system encompassing the known universe practically from nothing to trying to acquire resources for a secret army in a world where no one trusts anyone. We've been preparing for this. And during all that, what did lanehunters do? Play hide-and-seek, ignore the world's problems, chase treasures and technologies they don't understand!" Gertrudia stopped, the emotion receding in her voice. Roy had a feeling the last sentence had been as much about Jeane as about the lanehunters in general. "No one did anything except us. But it's starting now. The clans called for an assembly yesterday, and attendance was at an all-time high. They're all deeply hurt by the loss of the Cities and might be finally ready to work with us."

"You're going to war together?" Roy asked.

"I would have done it years ago if I had the chance. You have a problem with that?"

"Not at all, ma'am. The Union will attempt to eat the world and fill it with mindless slaves if they can, so no complaints from me."

"I hear you've been working with us for a while now."

"My contact never told me what we've been doing, but I suppose the answer is yes." *Right. Let's not get into what and why Danai has been telling me.* "I did botch the first-ever real mission she gave me, so I would hold back on the warm congratulations."

Gertrudia made an annoyed grunt. "We botched that mission from many sides. Talala is notoriously difficult to deal with; it was a miracle we managed to infiltrate. In the end, the manipulator was right under my nose in the Cities, and I didn't even know."

"Kliks thought the Talalans told him about it with telepathy," Jeane said to no one in particular.

"Sounds about right. If he worked on the technology before leaving his planet, his colleagues might have remembered to ask for his help. We didn't know they could do that, so I didn't think about contacting Kliks." Gertrudia paused for a beat. "It would have been too late anyway. We were only worried the Union would reach it before us. By the way, we did take all that data collected by Danai Escher from your ship, Mr. Philemon. That was one of the things I wanted to tell you."

"I can't wait to see what horrible things will spring forth from that," Roy mused. "I mean, you're welcome, of course."

"And what about us?" Maura hurried to ask.

"You're only here because Dikent Mend has terrible timing." The Net leader gave a bitter chuckle. Jeane looked up at the mention of the name, almost interested in what was going on for a second. "I wanted to include him in this discussion, but I haven't seen him since we arrived. Anyway, Mr. Mend might have interfered, but the more important reason was that someone really wanted to keep you alive, Your Majesty."

"Nasir," Damian murmured.

"Yes. Admittedly, we only needed the glove, and it wasn't even on the top of our wishlist. Your planet was at the precipice of extinction, and I wish I could say we considered helping, but we had more urgent troubles, and your previous king was never inclined to cooperate. I think Nasir's supervisors were also not too keen on assisting him with saving refugees."

"Nas died to get us out." Damian's voice was grave. "He would have saved everyone else, too, if he could have."

"Nasir Dareth is not dead. That was the other thing I thought we should discuss—because he just called."

The change on the Miyozans' face was profound: from resignation and indecision to shock and joy. And fear.

"He's alive?" Damian asked, his voice breaking. It was strange to see the bodyguard this vulnerable. Not right, somehow. "What did he say?"

Hill typed in something into the nearby computer, and a few moments later, a voice, deep and warm, rang out from one of the other speakers.

"My name is Nasir Dareth, calling the Ranch on 12F45/7. I'm still on Miyoza with my remaining compatriots. We are hidden from the occupying Gaerrisian forces. The High General of the Gaerrisian military, Liv Horst, is assisting us to send this message.

"Maura, Damian, if you can hear this, I am lucky, and you reached your destination. But we don't have much time. Gaerris wants to destroy Miyoza, but General Horst believes we all have to cooperate against the Union. You know I agree with him. The general and his allies in the Council are requesting help from the Net to retake the capital. And we need the queen to return to have the power of the CNS."

The man stopped talking for a moment as if gathering his thoughts, then continued. "Think about it. I'm sending some data about the current situation. We believe we could smuggle you in. Horst has loyals in the palace, and, you know me, I have a small weapon stash too. I await your answer. You can contact us on this frequency, at least for a while. See you soon. I hope. Stay safe."

The recording stopped. For a few seconds, no one talked.

"If this is true, I need to go back," Maura said. She looked up, her eyes hazy like her consciousness had been somewhere far away all this time. "And indeed, I need the Net's assistance. That is why I'm here. To save my planet."

"A nice sentiment, but I have my doubts about whether it's realistic," Gertudia replied. "Also, as I have just finished telling you, we have greater problems right now."

"Greater problems?" Damian stood, anger surging in his movements. "Millions of people are going to die! We are asking for your help!"

"Sit down, Mr. Moore," Hill said, standing up herself and resting her hand on the grip of her gun. "Do not forget where you are!"

"We're already responsible for the lives of millions of people," Gertrudia raised her voice above the clamor. "Trust me, I'm not withholding my support because it delights me."

Damian looked ready to hit someone, but Maura stood,

gripping his arm. Roy didn't move. This whole thing seemed very calculated all of a sudden. He could almost see the threads coming together, and he had an idea about who was tugging at them.

"I told you before." Jeane glanced at Damian, her face almost bored. "Gertie's got everything she needs now. There's the manipulator to poke holes in reality as she wishes, Roy to play the snitch, and the glove to do whatever it does. She can go to war; it's all going great for her!"

"Jeane, I could do without the commentary," Gertrudia said.

But that was it. The Net leader played reluctant, and things might not have turned out exactly how she wanted them to, but she knew what she needed out of this mess. She knew what buttons to push for all of them.

"If you're not assisting our cause, let us go," Damian exclaimed.

"I'm sorry, but you're not going anywhere."

"How dare you keep us captive? Do you honestly think Maura would do anything for you without—"

"No, Damian, wait!" Maura's voice broke through the storm of her protector's words, and he fell silent. "You forget this is what we came here for. The Union is an enemy to all of us, and I would be delighted to help the Net. I am offering my aid and the alliance of Miyoza if the Net lends us its strength to get us back on our feet."

Gertrudia gave a sigh. "We don't have the numbers or the equipment. If we want to strike the Union before they smother us alive, I need to use every—"

"Not necessarily," Maura cut in, staring at something to her side. "We have an important advantage." And she held up the glove, always on her left hand.

"Wait. You two keep saying it's not a weapon," Roy started, confused. "That it might be valuable in developing something similar to your Miyozan network, but—"

"I know what I said. I was wrong. The glove is more than I thought it was." Maura glanced at Damian and then back at Commander Hill. "I can show you. We can use it, right now, against the Union. Hurricane is supported by some large-scale computer network, right, Roy?"

"Sure," he replied. "Everything is automated, from army operations through the training and re-education of agents to simple household tasks."

"Good," Maura said. "It doesn't have to be a real AI. If it's a network, I can work with it."

There was a long silence. Damian sank back into his chair, his eyes never leaving Maura's face, but the queen kept her stare on Hill. And she did look like a queen now, not a lost and confused girl in the big, evil world. Whatever she'd figured out about the glove gave her some inner force that was completely new to Roy. She was a diplomat now, negotiating for the lives of her people.

Too bad she was falling right into the Net's trap.

Or not. Maybe she was bluffing. Maybe she really thought this was her best move. Or maybe she knew it was a trap and was stepping into it on purpose, for the greater good. Roy didn't know. These things were way above his pay grade. And he didn't even have a job anymore!

"We can discuss an arrangement," Gertrudia said. "I will entertain the idea, but I need to know more. We also have to get in contact with Nasir."

"Oh, lovely!" Jeane clapped her hands together in feigned glee and jumped up. "All is right in the world. So happy for you guys!" She gave a sardonic curtsy towards the group. "If you'll excuse me, I gotta go and throw up." And she spun around, walking towards the exit.

"Let her go," Gertrudia said before Hill could have moved. "Get her access to the medbay, please."

"Right away."

"I'll go and make sure she doesn't...well." Roy finished the sentence with a vague hand motion. Make a commotion, he wanted to say. Slit someone's throat with a scalpel; slit her own throat, in the worst case. That was a grim thought, but he'd seen her face back on the *Skylark*—she wasn't far away from that place at all. He wasn't sure there was anything he could do about it, but for some reason, he wanted to try.

For some reason, he cared about what happened to this team of wayward runaways who rolled with his wild story and accepted him (granted, after the initial shock and attempt on his life, which were both reasonable reactions). He cared a lot.

Maura reached out to stop him. "Roy, wait. I'm going—"

"Your Majesty, we need to speak about this. Now," Gertrudia interrupted, which made Maura purse her lips and sit back in her chair.

"I'll keep her safe," Roy said, giving her a quick wink. Maura's mouth trembled, but she nodded. Roy approved of her skill at keeping her composure. That was something Miss Skylark could take some lessons on. "Be back in a minute. You two just do your thing."

He stood to leave. But he didn't get far. An officer hurried towards their corner from her station in the center of the bridge, worry on her face. "Commander, we've got incoming."

Hill's eyes narrowed. "What do you mean, Major?"

"A ship is hailing us. They're on course to rendezvous. They're..."

"Yes?"

The officer made a face both incredulous and fearful, and Roy braced himself. Shit was about to go down again.

"They're saying...they're claiming they're Talalans, Commander."

CHAPTER 26 | ABOUT THAT SHIP

Kliks looked dead. He did, even if Jeane had been told repeatedly that he wasn't, that he only appeared so due to the blood loss, and that he'd been through an hours-long procedure, so he needed a lot of time to recover. She needed to be patient, the medics had said, and not make such a ruckus, or she would be removed from the medbay.

Or something along those lines. She didn't pay attention; it was all useless words that didn't change the facts. Because Kliks looked dead, positively and absolutely.

First of all, his skin was all white, and blood loss or not, that simply shouldn't have been allowed to happen. And if she hadn't leaned in and paid close attention, she couldn't even hear him breathe, couldn't even see how his chest barely lifted and sunk under the puke-green blanket, and surely a body couldn't survive on such little air! His eyes were closed, limbs unmoving, suspended in time—completely unnatural. His face was blank, no trace of the fussy expression he always wore. How could a face lose all sense of familiarity so easily?

There was no way he came back from something like this, a state in such dangerous proximity with the vast void that every evanescent thread of life ended in. Or if he did, he'd hate her forever because *she* had done this to him. No wonder he had shrunk back inside himself. No wonder he didn't want to wake up and face her—

"Leave," ALU said quietly, halting the torrent of thoughts threatening to swallow her. Their shorter appendage brushed her arm. "We go back to others?"

Jeane raised her head. How long had she been standing there? The buzz in her mind receded, giving way to the ambient sounds of the medbay: the quiet chattering of the staff, the clinking of medical tools, and the occasional mechanical whir of larger equipment. Kliks' bed was at the back, in a row with many similar ones separated by heavy, opaque veils. Soft white light filled the room, designed to illuminate everything without straining the eye. Most of the beds were unoccupied. A medic stood nearby, watching her while typing something into her tablet.

They obviously didn't trust her to behave, not with the way she'd stormed in here. Luckily, Roy had followed not far behind and defused the situation. That guy was surprisingly mellow, considering where he'd come from. He'd disappeared quickly when the medics had led Jeane to Kliks, and that was considerate too. An all-around decent performance—it really made her life easier.

"Captain?" ALU tried again. Jeane's skin crawled at the word, but she didn't correct the technician. They were right, after all. It was time to go.

The difficult part was leaving Kliks there. Remembering him lying bloodied in the cargo hold of the ruined *Skylark* helped.

She stepped out to the corridor, wary that Roy was still lurking around, but she didn't see any sign of the ex-agent. He must have gone back to the meeting with Gertie. From what he had said, not only Maura was still in discussion, but apparently, the Talalans were soon to arrive too. They'd tracked them down, in the end. Kliks would be in for a surprise when he woke.

She took a deep breath. Ignoring the people trying to make their way around them in the hallway, she crouched beside ALU.

"How are you doing, buddy?" she asked, as cheery as she could manage.

ALU's big insect eyes widened. "Worried. But all okay. Right?"

"Yeah, we're all fine. Although, I'm gonna need you to do a few things for me." She gave a wink. *Keep up some pretenses. Good job.* "Are you ready to get into some trouble?"

ALU gave a lackluster trill. "What trouble?"

Jeane swallowed. It was hard to talk around that damn rubber ball stuck in her throat, blocking the path of air. "Well, you know what happened to..." A painful pang. *Gods damnit, let me speak!* "You know we don't have a ship anymore."

"Yes." ALU hung their head. "Sorry."

"It's okay. But with everything going on, we kind of need one. So we can't be cornered. Do you agree?"

"Agree!"

She made herself smirk conspiratorially. "I'm sure you've taken a look at the *Colugo*, broken into some systems, got some maps and access codes already. Or am I wrong?"

ALU chirped. "I tapped into system in medbay when people weren't looking."

"Good kid. So..."

"So?"

"Lead me to the docks, dude."

The technician's eyes widened further, and they glanced around as if searching for anyone eavesdropping on them. "You want a ship? Steal?"

Jeane rolled her eyes. "Come on. Gertie doesn't like me very much right now, and let's not mention Commander Hill. We need to have some options."

"But what about Kliks?"

She hesitated. "For now, I just want to take one out for a spin. To test it. You think you can help me do that?"

"Take one out for a spin?"

"Yes, ALU. Can you get me access?"

"But Captain—"

"Don't call me that!" Jeane snapped, and ALU recoiled like a scared cat. A wave of hot shame flooded her, but she lowered her voice and went on. "Can you get me access or not?"

ALU blinked. A few seconds of silence ticked by. "Can."

Jeane stood. She felt like throwing up. She needed to make it through this fast. "Lead the way then."

No one glanced at them twice while they walked through the winding corridors and packed elevators to the bottom level, where the ship's docking area was located. The fact that, during the recent chaos and surprises, Commander Hill had forgotten to reattach Jeane's tracking-slash-deterrent collar—and that ALU had probably never gotten one—helped too.

Jeane slowed down as they stepped through the gate leading to a giant arena, where a row of smaller, red-tinted gunships greeted them. Further back, four corvettes filled the space, and beyond, there was a closed-off section; according to ALU, the unmanned vessels were stored there. Mechanics, pilots, and engineers roamed the hall, with a bigger group of workers standing to the side, waiting for a gunship to land on its designated platform. Across from where Jeane stood and about two hundred feet from the entrance, a large section of the hull was open to space, the shimmering gray layer of a double energy shield keeping the icy vacuum of the universe on the other side.

"Now what?" Jeane asked. ALU gave a beep and started off towards their left, to a terminal placed against the wall. They planted themself before it, reached out with an appendage that formed into a cable-like tool, and stuck it into a port at the back of the computer.

"Which one?" they inquired.

"I don't care. Something small. One that's hard to track."

"But need space for Kliks and me."

"...sure."

Cable connected to the terminal, eyes staring straight ahead, the technician hummed in a small voice, standing on one foot, then on the other, hard at work. But when the group loitering around the landing vessel had dispersed, Jeane started to feel jittery. She sure as hells didn't have the composure to come up with a bullshit excuse if one of those clowns asked her what they were doing here.

"You go," ALU said, releasing a satisfied chirp. "Number seventeen. I open."

"Excellent." Jeane breathed out in relief. She turned to go, but her limbs weighed her down like they were made of stone. She glanced back at ALU, desperation gripping her chest.

The technician blinked at her. "Captain? Is okay?"

"I—" She swallowed again. Her fingers were numb and freezing cold, and ALU was glaring at her as if they knew exactly what she was trying to do. "Yeah, it's all okay. I'll be...well." Couldn't say she'd be back now, could she? *Gods damn this whole gods damned mess.* "You're okay. You're gonna be okay."

She took a step towards gunship number seventeen. *Back away slowly, like the coward you are.*

"But—"

"It's alright. Tell Maura...tell her I'm sorry. And I wish..."

Wish I was able to fight for something as hard as she does? Wish I gave a damn about anything at all?

Another step backward. ALU lowered their arm. Was that understanding in their eyes? Disappointment?

"Tell Kliks..."

What? What would they tell him?

No, this was quite enough. She spun around and ran the rest of the way to the ship. And by the time she climbed through the hatch on its belly and shoved her body into the pilot seat, the tears in her eyes had dried up too.

No use. She'd already decided.

The dashboard lit up under her fingers. Space was tight in there, designed for not much more than two people and a bunch of weapons. She glanced through the front window. ALU stood beside the terminal across the way, watching the gunship come alive.

She paused, listening inwardly, but only the silence answered. Her fingers closed into a fist, and she restrained herself from slamming her hand on the buttons and screens in front of her. *That's alright. It is what it is.*

She flipped the switch to turn on the engine, but nothing happened. She took a deep breath, centering herself, and scanned the dashboard to see what was wrong. But there didn't seem to be anything else to do. She tried the switch again, and this time, the whole thing shut down, lights turning off, electricity zapping out.

"Damnit, ALU, what is it now?" she muttered. But as she held her arm up for the technician in an annoyed, questioning motion, the entry hatch behind her clattered open. "What in the—"

"Wow, this place is tiny," Roy complained, pushing his shoulders through the square hole on the floor. He climbed up, then propelled himself into the seat beside Jeane. "Hello."

"Wha—? How?!"

"I took a comms device from the bridge and told ALU to call me in case you were about to do something stupid. I guess *this*"—he waved around in the cockpit—"qualified."

Jeane pursed her lips. "Get out."

"Nope."

"I'll toss your ass out. I'm not even kidding."

They stared at each other, neither of them moving. Jeane's heart thrummed against her ribcage, every beat a blaring warning.

"So, what's the plan?" Roy asked. Jeane didn't answer, and the man sighed. "Fine, we'll come up with something later." He nodded at the dashboard. "Let's go!"

"What? No!" The situation was so perplexing that her brain froze. "What do you want from me?"

The ex-agent fixed his calm gaze on her. "I'm coming with you. Considering I was the one who messed up your ship, the least I can do is—"

"Finish the job and annoy me to death, gotcha. By the way, didn't we agree it wasn't your fault?"

"Well, it was. I could have also shot you out of the sky much earlier. I almost did."

"Keep dreaming."

"I led the Union to the Cities," Roy went on, throwing it out there like he was fishing for reasons to be at fault. "It wasn't my intention, but I did. I ruined that place."

Jeane gave a snort. "Right. You are to blame for everything. I hate your guts, and I will never forgive you. Now, shove off."

"No."

She threw her arms out. "Why? Just let me go!"

"You're gonna regret this. Your friends certainly will."

She swallowed. "They'll get over it."

"It's not your place to decide. And where are you even going?" Roy shook his head. "Do you really intend to kill yourself?"

Jeane's stomach sank like a boulder in clear water. "That's dumb, even coming from you."

"But you wouldn't be opposed to an accident, would you? Don't look at me like that! You dragged me into hand-to-hand combat with three inspectors, and it was *your* death wish, not mine. I know that ship meant a lot to you, but—"

"Stars, it's not about the ship!" Jeane shouted, and Roy fell silent. "I need to go. Let me leave!"

"Why?"

"Because everything is fucked!" Her voice echoed sharply in the small space, and the cold anger made its way up from her chest, unstoppable. "He's gone! And I've got no idea how to bring him back! I tried so hard all my fucking life to be like him. Free and light, go wherever, do whatever because that's how you roll, right?" She was yelling, and she wasn't making sense, but she didn't care. "But I can't, not anymore. It's all gone! All of it was for nothing..."

Empty, empty words. What was she doing?

She took a deep breath, but there wasn't enough air. And it was so cold; her entire body was shaking. When did it become so cold? She didn't look at Roy, and he wasn't answering, so she stared at the start-up switch of the gunship until she could talk again. "The *Skylark* is gone, and Hollis is gone too, and I don't know how to be anymore. I'm a mess. It's better for everyone if I just go."

Silence. The noise of heavy steps from outside—a worker in a uniform walking past the gunship, taking no notice of them. Then silence again.

"You're leaving everything behind because you feel a bit lost?" Roy asked.

Well, that was rude. "Listen, you prick—"

"No, you listen. My life ended the moment I left the Union. The only person I ever called my family sacrificed herself so I could escape, but it turns out I didn't have half an idea about her either. I've been attacked by you, by the Net, and by inspectors, I barely know who I am, and I'm still here for some reason!" Roy laughed, frustrated. "You think everyone is so sure about what they're doing and you're the only one stumbling around in the dark?"

"That's not what I meant. Hearing about your trials and adversities doesn't help, you know. I'm self-centered like that."

Roy shook his head. "No, I get it. You pretended to be your dead foster father to survive the grief for so long that you convinced yourself you have to be, what? A continuation of him?"

A sting in her chest, painful, lonely. "I hear his voice in my head, Roy," she said. "Well, heard. I can't seem to...make him talk to me now. Not since the ship. I suppose I don't deserve it anymore."

A beat of silence, then Roy frowned. "Okay, I did *not* see that one coming. That's what you meant by ghost earlier?"

"Yep."

"You do know it wasn't him, right?"

Jeane shrugged. "I guess. But it helped."

"It doesn't help anymore. Let him leave."

"I can't," she whispered. "I'm scared."

Tears welled up in her eyes again, their sour taste filling her throat. During that one short sentence, her lungs found oxygen again, like something ancient and dusty had broken and allowed the rest of the world to peek in.

She breathed in again, shaky.

Roy didn't look at her as he started talking. "I would be a brainwashed idiot without Danai. And for the longest time, I wanted so much for her to value me, to acknowledge me, but in the end, I was only a tool for her. And now..." He shook his head with a small laugh. "I will always be grateful to her, and I will always mourn her because everything I am came from her. But I need to figure out how to be without her." He looked up at Jeane, his stare intense. "I have to do it. I can do it. So can you."

Jeane exhaled. She wanted to say that this didn't help, that she couldn't think like this. Not now, not yet. But she couldn't talk.

"You're not Hollis. You don't have to throw yourself away because he's dead." Roy held his hands up, maybe to prevent some kind of outrage he imagined she would display. "I'm sorry; I'm sure he was amazing, and your memories of him are the best. It sucks, but he's gone, and you've been doing great without him.

You might feel lost in the world, but you grow your own roots. You have people to count on. You don't have to do this alone."

Jeane gave a sarcastic snort. "Kliks is half-dead because of me. It was my fault. I always put him in harm's way, and I never listen to him. What right do I have to ask for his help? To keep risking ALU's life just because they're too nice to tell me to fuck off? And how come Gertie is the leader of the gods damned resistance, and not once did she consider telling me?" She shook her head. Why was he making her go through all this? *Just let me go, Jerkface.* "I'm a fuck-up. I pushed them all away, and they're right to not trust me. They're better off without me. I don't know what I am, and I don't know what I want. Without the *Skylark*...without Hollis...I'm just an even bigger fuck-up. A terrible, selfish person."

Roy frowned. "As I said, not your place to decide. And I don't know about that selfish part. You kept the manipulator safe when you were sure it was bad news because your friend asked you. You saved two Miyozan refugees in the middle of a fight you knew nothing about, again because your friend wanted you to. A great start, I think."

Jeane looked for a trace of mockery or pity on the ex-agent's face, but she didn't find it.

"You're right. Everything *is* fucked," Roy went on, his voice getting heated. He wasn't only talking to her; he was convincing himself too. "And all of us fuck up. It's how things work—you don't need a war or a galactic disaster. But we have to get back up and face the things we fucked up. None of us are strong all the time, and we're not garbage because we need support."

He looked into the distance, narrowing his eyes at something invisible.

"And honestly, what else is there? We do what we can. Tomorrow we might go and bust the Union's ass, and maybe you'll apologize to your Gertrudia for being distant or whatever it is that happened between you. Perhaps I'll stop trying to justify Danai's every word and move and instead focus on making things right. Maybe you'll say 'thank you' to Kliks and ALU more frequently. I might grow a beard!" Roy pulled his mouth to a grin, and against everything, the remark made Jeane break out in a short, anxious laugh. The man continued carefully. "And maybe you'll stop wrapping yourself inside the memories of a dead man because you think you're not strong or valuable without him."

She peered up at Roy. That jittery, bitter sensation in her chest had started to subside just a little. "You know too much. Are you spying on me?"

He shrugged. "I notice things. You might not know it because you were out for a while, but I'm basically part of the team now. And Maura is talkative when she's nervous."

"Huh. The brainwashed Union agent, the most sensitive among us."

"I'm not brainwashed. And you're all too transparent."

"You're so sure I can do it," Jeane said quietly. "Go on like I knew what the fuck I was doing. Why?"

Roy inclined his head. "Good question. I guess I need you to. It means I can do it too."

Stars.

Breathe in, breathe out.

She felt so tired. But she didn't have to leave today. She could decide later, wait until she felt stronger. Until they got to the Ranch. Until Kliks got better.

"I'm serious, though. I need you to stay. I'm freaking out." Roy turned his pretend-distressed face to her. "This ship is full of people who only trust me as long as I'm wearing this collar, and my other option is a queen and her morose bodyguard."

"Alright now—"

"Also, you can't leave Kliks behind. The guy would walk through fire for you. Actually, that's exactly what he did! And ALU—can't say no to that face." Jeane rolled her eyes, but her heart wasn't in it. The pressure on her chest crumbled into something warmer, something more free, and Roy still didn't shut up. "And I just know Maura is up to something stupid. Or brave. Maybe both. She's pretty awesome."

She *was* awesome. And she was in so much trouble.

Two knocks resounded from behind them, and they both flinched. Someone was asking for admittance at the entry hatch of the gunship.

Roy clambered out of the seat and opened the door. Maura's

head popped up in the hole. The ex-agent pulled her into the ship, then wriggled back in the chair beside Jeane, so Maura had a few square feet of space to crouch on.

"Talking about me behind my back?" she asked in a joking voice, but when she looked at Jeane, her eyes were hard.

Jeane shifted in the pilot chair to face her. This place was so uncomfortable for conversation. "Aren't you supposed to be in session?" she mumbled. "You gotta save your planet. What in hells are you doing here?"

Maura jerked a shoulder up. "I thought you might need backup. You looked like a traumatized person."

Jeane scrunched her nose up. *Funny, very funny.* But the woman's honest smile melted the grimace off her face.

"See?" Roy bumped his leg against hers and wiggled his eyebrows. "See?"

She leaned her forehead against the seat, not looking either of them in the eye. If only she could sit here in silence, keep the option of leaving open under the tips of her fingers. Roy was only half-correct: she didn't want to die or to leave, not really. But the potential of something that huge and final versus the pins and needles of panic splintering her mind since she'd lost the ship and the voice in her head seemed soothing. It was comforting to imagine she could slip away, get rid of it all.

But she didn't need to do it now. She could try once more. It would be infuriating if there was a way forward, and she couldn't find it. That would suck so much. And she couldn't deny the sensation of a weight falling off her chest as she considered this ex-Union agent who was so strangely easy to talk to and the exhausted, tortured but still gentle queen of a far-away planet, sitting beside her in this cramped gunship because they didn't want her to leave.

That was real.

"I'm scared too," Maura said. It didn't feel like a complaint or an accusation, although she would have reason to blame others for her misfortune. It was only a fact, a truth amongst many.

"Me three." Roy looked out the front window of the ship. He was squaring his shoulders against his own confession, already preparing to fight it.

Jeane didn't speak. She'd said enough. Stupid words. Stupid, stupid hope.

So they sat, still and quiet, elongating this moment of vulnerability together, until suddenly, there was a click, and Roy's comms—the one he'd stolen from the bridge—crackled.

"Mr. Philemon?"

"Commander?" Roy answered, making a face at Jeane and Maura. "Bad timing, sorry," he whispered.

"Is Ms. Blake with you?"

"No."

Jeane took a deep breath and reached out for the device. "What's up?"

"You need to come to the bridge. Gertrudia stopped responding."

Jeane glanced at Maura, but the woman was shaking her head. "I don't know. Everything was fine when I left."

"There's someone else on the line now," the commander went on.

"Who is it?" Jeane asked, already climbing out of the seat and pushing the hatch open beside Maura.

"It's Dikent Mend. And he says he'll only talk to you."

The mood on the bridge had already been tense when Jeane had stormed out, but it was even worse now. Everyone was standing around the communicator they'd been using to talk to Gertie, peering at it and each other like they'd seen a ghost. Hill was in quiet discussion with Jones and two other officers when Jeane, Roy, Maura, ALU, and Damian (since, of course, he was never far behind) walked in but turned to them the moment she saw them enter.

"What do you mean Gert stopped responding?" Jeane demanded. "What's going on?"

"We're not sure. Mend is not talking to us."

"I'll fucking make him."

"You need to be careful."

"Yeah, yeah, whatever."

She circled the commander and planted herself before the comms device. She caught Maura's questioning glance, and a sinking feeling in her stomach told her that Hill was right. This was bad news written all over it.

"Hey, Dikent," she said in a light tone. "You wanted to talk?"

"Jeane, what a nice surprise!" Dikent replied in a similar manner. His voice was all wrong, though, thin and strained.

"Where's Gertie?"

"Ah, she's...otherwise occupied. But I told them I know you, so they're letting us talk."

They. The word buzzed in Jeane's mind, and she peered at Hill. The commander's face twitched, and she turned away, muttering something to Jones. The lieutenant hurried back to his terminal and started typing something.

They.

"What did you do, Dikent?"

There was a beat of silence. "I didn't need to do anything. They were already here." A sickly cough interrupted the man's words, and he heaved for a second. "Well, I might have told them where this device was, but just because they're oh-so convincing."

Jeane felt nauseated. This was not happening. "What do you mean?" she made herself ask.

There was a long sigh on the other end of the line. "You can't fathom the chaos that reigned when the Cities fell. They got onto our ships somehow. Only a few of them, but they took us hostage, and we sailed into the Ranch with them on board." Maura gasped, covering her mouth with her hand. The dread crept along Jeane's arms. "Once in here, they infiltrated Control, and by the time the clan heads poked their noses out of that assembly of theirs, the destroyers descended on us.

"Now the only thing left is that Talalan toy," Dikent went on. "They want it real bad. So that's why I'm here with my friends. Umm, Korrh, is that the name? Such affectionate guys. When they let me stop screaming, I told them I might be able to convince you. Sorry."

Roy's jaw tightened at the mention of the inspectors' name, but he didn't speak.

"And what makes them think you can?" Jeane spat. Hill shook her head, but she didn't care. Fear gripped her heart in its sharp claws. What happened to Gertie? What did the inspectors do to Dikent?

Another voice came through now, a rasping tone, slow and grave. "We're offering the lives of everyone on the Ranch for the manipulator," it said. "We thought you might have a soft spot for old friends and acquaintances."

The sound of her own surging blood roared in Jeane's ears, and Kliks' words echoed in her head. "I can't...we can't give it away," she blurted out. "It's too dangerous."

"You don't need to bother thinking about that," Korrh (or at least one of them) replied with what was probably a chuckle but sounded like an animal chewing on something. Roy took a step forward, fist clenched, bewitched by that ghastly voice. He knew the inspector. "There is only one choice that doesn't end in massacre. If you don't agree, this one is dead." A grunt, then something squeaking on a metal floor. "Speak!"

"Okay, alright, alright!" Dikent huffed. "Listen, J. Are you sure that thing is in better hands with you all?"

Jeane didn't answer. Kliks thought it was, but she didn't know. She didn't know shit. That thing had no place in anyone's hands!

Dikent gave a long sigh, and she imagined him, hands bound, beaten up, standing surrounded by the inspector trio, completely helpless. "Oh, darling." His voice went soft, solemn. "Don't worry. We were not made for this. Seven years ago, we never thought we'd end up here, huh? Remember that night in the Leaning Lady? So full of dreams, so arrogant."

He was resigned but somehow content. Jeane leaned closer to the communicator. The air got thin in her throat as she gripped the edge of the desk. "You didn't really think you could convince me, did you?" she asked.

She sensed the smile even through Dikent's broken intonation. "No. But I missed your voice, so I might as well tried."

"Dikent—"

"I'm happy I heard it again."

"Don't do this—"

A scrambling, crackling sound interrupted her, like Dikent had moved closer to the receiver. "Listen to me. Don't believe a word these assholes are saying. You can't let them have the manipulator. Keep it. Use it. Fight back. Promise me—"

Another sound, like flesh breaking, like bones shattering, and that scraping, guttural voice of the inspectors, not even trying to imitate human speech. Dikent screamed in agony. There was a loud crash, then the sharp pang of a shot.

"Come at me, you motherfucker!" Dikent bellowed. The line screeched, and Jeane reared back, eyes wide. A few seconds of this, then silence again.

"Seems like we can't settle this the easy way," Korrh spoke into the microphone, voice dead calm. "No matter. We're coming for you."

Then the line disconnected.

A shroud of silence fell on them. Dikent's shriek echoed in Jeane's head as she looked up, and her glance met Maura's. The woman's face was gray, but the determination in her eyes was a wave, surging forth and enveloping Jeane's terror in something warm and steady. She looked at Roy next, shadows gathering among the ex-agent's features, but he nodded, expression resolute.

"Well," Jeane said, facing Hill. Her voice was hoarse, but she pushed through the ache. *No way out but through.* "You heard the man. We need a plan, and we need it fast."

PART III

THE VERY FINGERTIPS
OF LIFE'S OUTSTRETCHED HAND

It's our weakness,
it's our strength

We are the very fingertips of life's outstretched hand

But you'll find no spark in the sandstone dark
'Cause what the holy men won't preach
Is that the one thing that unites us is reach

We reach forward

And there aren't enough songs in the world
Not enough words in my tongue nor enough breath in my lungs
There is no echo that has lasted so long,
No shadow that has stretched so far as we

We reach forward

And it's safe hands back down the line in the endless chain
Not lost, never lost,
when the strength
That we gained from their giving remains

We reach for the echo, we reach forward

(Inertia and the Weapon of the Wall, Caligula's Horse)

CHAPTER 27 | THE CLOSEST LIGHT

The murmur of waves breaking on jagged rocks and smooth beach. Gentle wind soughing over sea and shore. Cold air biting at the bare skin of her arms, sunlight warming her back. Maura sat, cross-legged and eyes closed where water met the sand, her fingers buried under both, facing away from the ocean. Dull pain throbbed behind her eyelids, and she breathed against it patiently.

"It's better now," she said, pulling her mouth into a shaky smile. "Thank you."

"I'm glad," answered Sofia's voice.

Maura opened her eyes. Her friend was sitting next to her, the setting sun painting her locks the hue of honey. Her face looked older now, expression serene and wistful. Around them, gray wedges of stone crowned a beige-colored beach under a darkening sky, and crystal-clear waves of teal washed over the sand as the last sparks of daylight waned on the ocean's surface.

"This is a nice memory."

Maura smiled faintly. "A day on the beach. You were here too. And Damian, and some cousins. We climbed those black rocks to the east and found a cave. We holed up so well, the instructors had to come look for us when it got too late."

Sharp nails of pain raked her brain, then pulled back into the darkness. Maura cringed.

"I'm sorry," Sofia said. "Some of this is my fault. My presence in your mind."

"It doesn't matter." Maura looked around, soaking in the calming atmosphere. "This helps a lot. I think I can do the demonstration now."

"Good. Don't forget how to conjure it up. But I'll be here to help." Sofia stood, dusting her pants off. "You should go. Jeane is awake."

Hearing the name from her friend's mouth distracted Maura, and the scenery wavered. She stood, taking in the last moments of the vision and Sofia's wave goodbye before the beach disappeared, and in the next second, she was back on the *Colugo*, lying in bed with a pounding head and shaking hands grabbing at the thin blanket thrown over her body.

She glared into the darkness. The only light sources were the fluorescent blue stripes at the edges of the bunks and a dull red LED over the closed door. She could just see the contours of Roy's and Damian's bodies where they slept in their beds on the other side of the chamber.

There was a shuffling noise above her. An annoyed sigh, a pillow getting fluffed up, and blankets rustling. Jeane had definitely woken.

Maura threw her covers off and swung her legs to the side. Five seconds later, she was climbing up the ladder to the top bunk, and she slumped down beside the captain with her back to the wall and ankles dangling over the side of the bed.

Jeane's face was a blurred apparition in the dark. She stared at Maura for a second, then leaned back, a pillow and her tablet in her lap. The screen illuminated the vicinity with dim light. "What's up?" She sized her up. "Too nervous to sleep?"

"Something like that," Maura whispered. "I just talked to...well, I will keep calling her Sofia, but you know who I mean."

"How did it go?"

Maura clenched her fist to steady herself. "It's disturbing. And

I don't really want to do it. But I have to."

"Yeah, I'm not gonna lie, I'm a little freaked out about that other consciousness living inside your brain."

After Dikent Mend's ominous call from the Ranch, they'd spent the evening holed up on the *Colugo's* bridge, formulating a plan. That was when Maura had told everyone about Miyoza's city-AI remnant which made its home in her glove, then in her mind.

Most of the conversation had been about how to stop the Union's nefarious advance that had started with them tailing the Talalan manipulator and had resulted in the fall of two lanehunter strongholds, the Foggy Cities and the Ranch. If the tides didn't turn soon, there would be no one left to stand against the empire. The only candidate to lead a counterattack was the Net, and although they'd lost contact with their leader during the attack against the Ranch, Commander Hill was insistent on proceeding with Gertrudia's last commands.

Thus, Maura had made a deal. And at the end of that long day, it started to feel like half their plan depended on the glove and the AI presenting itself in the image of her long-dead best friend. And what poor Kliks, still lying unconscious in the medbay would have certainly found troubling, on the manipulator too.

Hill needed Maura to prove she was able to help the Net during the fight. So as the *Colugo* made its way to the meeting point of the Net's assembling forces, scouting out less-travelled lanes and star systems along the way to avoid Union forces, she had been preparing to present her powers. She'd talked to Roy before all of them had slumped into their beds last night, and from what the ex-agent could tell her about Hurricane, the Union's central planet, things looked promising. The other component of the demonstration, Maura was not so sure about. ALU had been difficult to convince. Sofia insisted they would come around, but the little technician hadn't given her a straight answer. And if ALU didn't help, she would have to find another way.

She didn't look forward to it. After what had happened back home, she wanted to have nothing to do with AIs and their intrigues ever again. But as Sofia (no, not Sofia, and although out of a perverse sense of nostalgia she hadn't yet asked the AI to drop the guise, a machine taking the image of her dear friend had its own painful connotations) told her many times, she had been built for this.

Maura tried her best to trust the AI. It had been difficult, especially after feeling its hold on her back when she'd almost shot Roy. Doubt and revulsion gnawed at her every time she thought about having to be connected to a machine like this for the rest of her life, no matter how the future turned out to be. She needed to fight the prejudice, but she wasn't sure she was strong enough.

About the danger of her dying if she didn't return to Miyoza, she hadn't told anyone (especially not Damian). It nearly didn't even make the top list of things she was worried about.

"It's going to be alright," she said. Jeane huffed, so she went on. "It is! We have the chance to do something about this mess. A lot of power has accumulated in our hands. We must try."

"Maybe," the captain grunted. "I don't trust the Net, though. We're about to do either something stupid or...something *really* stupid."

"I believe they've been trying their best. And they're our only choice."

"I know." Jeane shot a glance at her tablet, distracted.

"How are you doing?" Maura asked. So many things had been happening in the last few days, it felt like this was their first chance to talk in peace since they'd crashed at Katipo Base with the *Skylark*. And although Maura had gotten the gist of the argument between Roy and Jeane in the gunship and saw its resolution, she was worried. "All this has been so hard on you. I wasn't much support either."

The look she received from Jeane was more than baffled, like Maura had stated something beyond all reason. "I'm not your responsibility."

Her voice was aloof. As if to say *it's not like we're friends.*

"You can't think that." Maura acknowledged the hurt sensation in her chest with some surprise. "After all we've been through?"

"Roy already told me off. Don't bother."

"I didn't want to—"

"I'm fine, okay?" Jeane snapped but instantly deflated, exhaling sharply. A shadow passed over her face. "Sorry. Things suck. I miss my ship, and I miss Kliks. You heard me yesterday. You know what's up. Looks like we both know something about talking to imaginary people in our heads."

Maura gave a weak laugh. "They're a bit different."

"No, no, we're both pitiful, tormented souls. Don't ruin this for me." Jeane paused as if remembering something. "You saved my life."

"What?"

"When we crashed. You pulled me out of the *Lark*. I don't think I would have gotten out alone. So...thank you."

"You saved my life too." Maura shrugged. "You could have left us behind several times, but you didn't. Now we're here."

"We sure are." Jeane smiled in that bitter, sardonic way of hers. "And I should be asking how *you* are feeling, Queen Tholis. I'm only having a pity party for myself, but you have the weight of a whole planet on your shoulders."

"I think we all have a lot with the universe going down the drain," Maura replied, trying to sidetrack. This was something she couldn't yet face head-on. Step by step. Hour by hour. "By the way, did you manage to crack Dikent's riddle?"

Jeane shifted her legs under the blanket, uncomfortable. "No. Can't remember our stupid code anymore."

Before they'd gone to sleep, that was all she could talk about. How she was sure her ex had sent them some kind of hidden message during his last transmission.

Don't worry. We were not made for this. Seven years ago, we never thought we'd end up here, huh? Remember that night in the Leaning Lady?

"But even if I did," Jeane continued, "that code was for the Cities. Can't see how that's relevant now."

"A secret message would be romantic, though," Maura mused, and Jeane made a face.

"Ew, no. That's not Dikent. He wouldn't recognize romance if it bonked him in the head with a spare engine. But I'm thinking maybe it was literal."

"What do you mean?" As uncomfortable the captain felt talking about her life, Maura couldn't help but be intrigued at being able to peek under her usual hard shell. Jeane's ability to push everything emotionally engaging away from her (if that emotion wasn't rage or annoyance) was impressive. And sad.

There was a long silence before Jeane talked. "I remember that night. We were celebrating a successful run from Obavium in the Lady, and Dikent was boasting about lanehunters being indestructible and necessary in the large scheme of things. About how monolithic evil empires are not *all that* if they can't secure their stuff against us. Gertie got angry, said that the only way we survive long term is if we unite against danger." Jeane waved dismissively. "It was all very boring, so I made the bartender play this song I liked on repeat. It goes like, 'Don't worry, we're not made for this, at the end of it all, we'll all pay for this.'" She sang a little, quietly, in a surprisingly clear tone. "I said we're only here because we're selfish and arrogant. And we're never going to join forces and fight together."

"That must have gone down well with them," Maura smiled.

Jeane grinned. "You bet. Dikent was *livid*. He's such trash sometimes but an idealist at heart."

Maura contemplated it for a moment. "Then maybe he wanted to say you shouldn't give up on the Ranch yet."

Jeane fiddled with the corner of her blanket. "That's what I thought too. But he might be dead, so what does it matter?"

"He might not."

The captain breathed out shakily, not looking at her. "And Gertie—"

"We will save her."

"Nah." There was a smile in Jeane's voice. "She's gonna save herself. But I want to be there when she does."

"You will," Maura promised. "You won't disappoint her."

"Would be a nice change of pace." Jeane glanced at her tablet again. "What a crazy fucking accident, this whole thing! None of it would have happened if Kliks didn't choose me to start discovering the universe with."

Then the manipulator wouldn't have gotten to them through the mysterious Talalan telepathic connection. And maybe Jeane wouldn't have gone back to the Cities for another five years, and Dikent would have needed to find someone else to smuggle the "Miyozan cargo" out of the warring solar system.

"He wouldn't have it any other way."

"He almost died. How can you be so sure?"

"The same way I don't question Damian's loyalty." Maura peered at the sleeping figure of her friend. "The same way we don't doubt that Roy is helping us."

Jeane scoffed. "Faith?"

"More like human nature. Or something more general in Kliks' case."

Even as she said it, she knew it sounded dangerously naive. Did she really have the right to believe in the goodness of humans after everything that had happened? But believing was never the problem. There was no reason to bury humanity alive the same way there was no reason to trust that everything would resolve itself. All she could do was to search for the way out. To hope that people around her were doing their best. To seek a connection, an understanding, that single strand of loyalty tying everyone together.

"We always reach for the closest light," Jeane said, her stare fixed on something invisible. "That's what Hollis said. And I was like, what are we, plants? Old fool."

Maura smiled. The closest light. Quite succinct—she could agree to that. "He was a smart man."

"A smart-ass, more like. Damn. I miss him."

It was a short sentence but so full of longing that Maura wondered if this was the first time Jeane had ever uttered the sentiment. She thought about her own father. He'd had such big visions for Miyoza, and he could be so kind and generous and loving. Before he'd lost his way and gotten wrapped up in his obsessions. She wanted to tell Jeane everything about him. To commemorate him. To try and forgive him.

"Are you waiting for a call?" she asked instead when Jeane glanced at her comms device again.

"Jones is supposed to let me know when Kliks wakes up. They think it could be any minute now."

"He's cool. Jones."

"He's alright." Jeane's mouth pulled into a wicked grin. "Did you know his real name is Atticus? No wonder he wasn't eager to share."

"Come on now. Don't be mean."

"Hey, if you're done talking about deep stuff, can we go and get food?"

Roy's voice, warm and upbeat, cut through the darkness, and a reading light above the other bunk turned on, illuminating the two men sitting up in their respective spaces. Maura felt herself blush. How long had they been awake? How much did they hear?

Jeane grabbed her pillow and hurled it at Roy. The ex-agent ducked, and the cushion hit the wall behind him with a soft thump. "Eavesdropping is a nasty habit!"

"I, for one, heard nothing," Damian said, standing up from the lower bunk to gather his shoes. "Except for my stomach growling, so I support the idea."

Maura relaxed. They hadn't talked about anything secret, but she liked knowing that this conversation was between her and the captain.

"I will say nothing on the matter." Roy was already at the door, but he paused with a sigh when he saw the rest of them just starting to move. "But my ears are really sharp. We're made that way."

Jeane grumbled something Maura didn't understand, then inclined her head towards the ladder. Maura scooted forward and descended. She was getting hungry too.

"Do any of you remember how to get to the canteen?" Roy scratched the stubble on his chin.

Jeane stormed past him, smashing her palm against the dooropener. The bright lights of the corridor flooded in, casting ghostly contours on their pale faces. They both looked exhausted. Maura doubted her expression was much more lucid.

"No idea," the lanehunter said. "We'll just annoy someone until they tell us."

Damian stepped forward, his hand resting on Maura's arm. She forced composure on her face, and as Jeane and Roy marched ahead, getting into an animated argument about the location of the cafeteria, she followed them with a faint smile, her bodyguard at her heels.

Let the day commence. Whatever it would bring.

Kliks woke two hours before Maura's demonstration.

They were in the canteen, sitting at a plastic table in the corner, nursing their coffee, tea, and some dry cookie-dough looking desserts they got from the distributors along the walls. Due to the early hour, they had the room for themselves. Occasionally a member of the *Colugo's* crew wandered in to acquire a sandwich or a nutribar; they looked over the group quizzically and left without a word. Although Commander Hill had agreed their "visitor collars" could be removed after Maura's demonstration, currently the little devices still showed their outsider status on the ship.

ALU joined them too, which was a surprise since they favored spending their time in the medbay keeping their eyes on Kliks' recuperation. The conversation soon turned idle: theorizing about the extent and influence of the Net in Union and lane-hunter-friendly regions or pondering about the situation on the Ranch or Miyoza. Damian preferred to listen, and Maura was too nervous about her impending trial to contribute, so the whole thing devolved into bickering between Jeane and Roy.

When Jeane's tablet flashed up with a message, the captain fell silent, pushed her chair back like she'd gotten pinched in the backside, and ran out without any explanation. Maura trailed her, waving to the others to follow, but by the time they found their way to the medbay and lined up around Kliks' bed, Jeane was already all up in arms with the Talalan.

"—the most idiotic thing you ever did!" she shouted, fists clenched, eyebrows knitted. Kliks stared back at her, barely awake in a half-lying, half-sitting position. A blonde woman in a white coat, presumably his doctor, stood close-by, watching the scene with mild disquiet. "And I've seen you do a lot of idiotic things."

Kliks shifted in the bed. His movements were slow, and anguish colored his gray face. From his upper abdomen to the end of his toes, a cylindrical contraption made of shining, liquid-like metal covered his body. The tube shifted with him, attached to his legs but flexible.

The doctor adjusted something on the device and examined the monitor fixed to Kliks' bedside. Turning around, she threw a severe look at Jeane. "Ten minutes. Then I need to run some more tests." And she walked away.

"I watched you go down," Kliks said when the woman was out of earshot. Maura's stomach tightened. His voice was not his own; it belonged to someone ancient and endlessly exhausted. "I couldn't just stay put."

"Oh, you helped so much!" Jeane was practically shaking. "This is why I always tell you to hang back. You're no wizard with a gun. Why wouldn't you listen—"

"You told me nothing! You left me behind!" Kliks raised his voice, frustrated. "What was I supposed to do, wait for you to frickin' die?"

"You were supposed to trust me."

"No. We've had this fight before. That's not what I do, and you know it."

"Jeane," Damian said before the captain could have found the words to hurl back at her friend. The woman whirled around to glare at the bodyguard, but something on his face made her freeze, cheeks red, jaw clamping shut.

Damian turned to Kliks with a gentle smile. "Hey. Good to have you back."

The Talalan's expression brightened. "Thank you. It's great to be conscious again."

He nodded at Maura and Roy in greeting. ALU hopped over to the bed, chirping gleefully. They stretched out one arm and started poking at the contraption on Kliks' legs.

The Talalan turned his head back at Jeane. "I'm glad you're okay," he said, but then he hesitated, looking her over. "Are you?"

Jeane's face softened. "I'm okay. I...well." She paused, stuffed her hands in her pockets, and flashed a reluctant grimace at Kliks. "I mean, you know."

"I know," Kliks said, a small smirk on his face. "Me too."

Jeane gave him another glare. "It was still fucking stupid."

"She means she's sorry for yelling at you, and she's very happy to see you're getting better," Roy said helpfully. *Always the peacemaker.* Jeane groaned again, but luckily, she'd run out of steam.

Kliks glanced around, uncertain. "Did we get the manipulator? Where are we? Not at the base, I assume?"

"Oh, shoot. Well, this is going to be a lot." Roy started to recount. "First of all, we're on the *Colugo*, Hill's ship. We have the manipulator, everyone loves us now, and we're about to meet more new friends soon."

"Really? Why? Is the Union—"

"I agreed to help the Net," Maura interjected. "In return for them assisting me on Miyoza."

Kliks seemed more puzzled than before. "Wait, what? How are you helping?"

Maura sighed and steeled herself. "You should come to the meeting if you can. We will talk about everything in detail."

"Right, but I don't understand why—"

"They got the Ranch, Kliks." Jeane's voice was hard and serious. "Now the Net is going all out. They'll make the Union taste their own medicine."

There was a jumble of emotions on the Talalan's face. "They can't use it. I told them before."

"Believe me, the Union will swallow us all if we don't do something," Roy said, his voice dark. "Lanehunters were always an excellent buffer. Just the right amount of chaos, so Leadership was puzzled enough to put the final blow-off, but with them out of the equation, they think they own the world now. We need to stop them."

"But not with the manipulator. That's the worst idea ever!"

"The Net doesn't think we have a choice," Jeane said gravelly.

The silence stretched long. Kliks blinked at his hands, at the device enveloping his legs, then around the medbay, his eyes failing to find something to hold onto. "I need to be at that meeting," he pleaded, looking at Jeane. "I need to make them reconsider this."

Jeane sighed. "There's something else too. Your people."

"What about them?" Kliks groaned. *Poor thing. He's just been*

*through a near-death experience, and now he's bombarded with all
this.*

"They're here." Jeane blurted out. "Arrived yesterday on a
small scout craft. The same ones who visited Wal. Been in 'containment' since, but apparently, they want to help."

If Kliks had seemed shocked before, he was now terrified.
"Who is here?" he asked in a thin voice.

"A certain Firl and Diaski." Jeane tried to pronounce the
strange-sounding names, but Jones' attempt to spell them out before had also gone poorly. "I don't know more."

But for Kliks, the words must have been familiar because his
face crumbled, and he sunk back into the bed, pulling the blanket
over himself. "I'm just going to stay here. I need more rest, I really
do."

"Who are they, Kliks?" Maura made her voice as soft and understanding as she could. "You know them well?"

"Oh, yeah." Kliks' face was both apologetic and fearful.
"They're my siblings."

"It's not saying much. I have hundreds of siblings."

They were walking towards the bridge, Roy and Damian at the
front, then Jeane escorting Kliks in the automatic wheelchair the
doctor had stuffed him in with the shining metal wrap still around
his legs. Maura and ALU closed the procession. The technician
chirped to themself deep in thought, and Maura's stomach threatened to turn over. She spotted Sofia standing ahead of them in the
corridor with an encouraging smile on her face.

"Families are different for us than for humans," Kliks went on.
"We design our offspring, and we're born artificially. When I say
family, I mean people who live in my city sector, which is a research center that my creator—or parent, if you will—leads. We
organize around scientific projects. We don't have genders either. Just so you know, in case we talk to them. My decision to
identify male is just that."

"But they're more than your colleagues, aren't they?" Jeane's tone was subdued. "They're your friends."

"Hmm. They were."

As they reached the door to the bridge, Jones appeared and waved them through the busy crowd of officers and technicians. The room was bustling with activity. Members of the crew worked at various terminals and conversed excitedly with each other or on their comms. Commander Hill stood at the main workstation; a schematic map of the solar system they were in covered the screen in front of her. The *Colugo* was marked with a yellow blip, and the shining dots signifying at least two dozen similar Net ships were waiting in a formation around it.

"I can't see them," Kliks hissed, turning his head around in search of his people as the group walked forward. "Will they be here?"

"I suppose so," Maura said. Her voice sounded raspy and feeble, and she cleared her throat.

Commander Hill gave them a tight smile when she saw them approach. "Great. Lieutenant, connect the fleet."

Jones stepped up to one of the terminals. The solar system map on the screen shrunk to a quarter of its size, and instead, various video feeds from the other members of the Net armada filled its space. Faces of many species and expressions nodded in greeting, waiting for Hill to get started.

Maura swallowed hard. Flashbacks of conference talks and meetings back on Miyoza flooded her mind, and the pain in her forehead flared up. This was almost like standing in front of the ministers and advisors the day the capital had fallen, except this time (and she breathed more easily at the thought), all these people were ready to listen to her.

And this time, she might have what they needed.

Kliks inhaled sharply, and Maura followed his stare to the door. Four armed guards walked in, encircling two familiar figures—familiar not because she knew them, but because their species was so recognizable.

"Oh, dear," Kliks whispered as all six newcomers shifted to the side. The Talalans hadn't noticed Kliks; they were surveying the screens and the tumult on the bridge. Maura noted the metal hoops on their necks—the same kind she was wearing.

There was a loud *clack*, then the amplified voice of a crewmember resounded from the speakers on the walls. "Attention! All personnel with level-2 clearance or below, please vacate the bridge immediately. I repeat, level-2 clearance and below, please vacate the bridge."

"Do you need anything?" asked Roy. Groups of people passed them as most of the crew started to file out of the chamber.

Maura smiled at the ex-agent. *He's truly sweet. No wonder even Jeane warmed up to him so fast.* "Do I look that bad?"

Roy rolled his eyes. "You look badass and confident. But is there anything you need?"

"A computer," Maura said, gazing at the terminal in front of Hill. Sofia, who stood beside the commander now, nodded. "I think I'm good. Damian?"

The man pulled out the glove from his satchel, and Maura slipped the device on her left hand. The lights on the fingers lit up, and her headache subsided temporarily. "Just don't leave me alone, please," she said.

"We're not going anywhere." Kliks turned the wheelchair around with a grin, and ALU looked up at her, chirping with vigor. Then a heavy palm clamped on her shoulder as Jeane awkwardly half-embraced her from the back.

"Don't sweat it. You're gonna be great. Whatever it is you're doing."

"Ready?" Commander Hill asked. Her face looked friendly, but she wasn't showing this disposition on account of their motley group. It was directed to the Miyozan Queen. Maura nodded, although she felt anything but. She followed Hill up to the terminal, the others at her heels.

"I have explained the basics to everyone," Hill said. "Now they would like to see what you, the lawful Queen of Miyoza, have to offer against the Union in this next period of active confrontation."

The commander stepped back, and Maura faced the screen. The images of the captains stared back at her, curious and expectant. Sofia stood to the side, smiling.

Maura took a deep breath, but the words clogged up her

throat. She turned around and found Damian's stern gaze.

"I'm with you," he said in a gentle tone. He might have had his misgivings about the Net now that he'd met them, but Maura knew he wanted to see Miyoza freed all the same. That hadn't changed, even if things were more complicated now. And his trust in her stayed as well.

She smiled at him, then turned around and started speaking.

"Greetings to all of you." She considered a more formal language but dismissed the idea. This would be easier if she was direct and sharp. She raised her gloved hand for everyone to see. "You know who I am, and you've heard about this device. In brief, in its normal state, the glove is an interface between the mind of Miyoza's monarch and the planet-wide information network called the CNS, governed by a rapid-learning, advanced AI. This system helps the monarch to supervise and direct all functions and processes of society, taking advantage of the symbiosis of human and machine intellect."

Some captains started nodding as if all this was familiar to them, while others only watched her with wooden expressions.

"Normal state?" asked one of them, a man, aged fifty or so, with dark skin and intense eyes. "Is it not in its normal state currently?"

"No." Maura was grateful for the cue. "Due to a fragment of the city-AI being maintained inside it, it's more than an interface now. It's a tool."

This was not strictly true. She didn't keep the AI in the glove; Sofia lived in her mind, using the glove to affect her. But the connection with the glove kept Maura alive, or at least protected her from deteriorating for now, so it was imperative she carried it on herself.

"We can use this tool against the Union," she went on. "This unprecedented fusion of human and machine consciousness is incredibly efficient against more rudimentary computer systems. And we know from a reliable source what kind of systems the Union is working with."

She glanced at Roy, and the agent gave her a thumbs-up.

"You're saying we might be capable of disabling Union

networks to the snap of a finger?" Commander Hill asked. She already knew most of this and obviously wanted to get through the theory and into the practical demonstration.

"That's the idea," Maura replied. The room filled with the excited murmurs of the Net captains, and her pulse quickened. She put her gloved hand on the terminal. In the palace, where all the protocols and permissions were in place, the glove worked wirelessly. Here, it was going to be harder.

Sofia materialized before her, looking focused on something, probably attempting to access the wireless network in place on the *Colugo*. But then ALU stepped up too.

"We help," they said slowly, like considering each word. "Easier like that. But let us tell."

Maura nodded eagerly, a weight lifting from her chest. "Of course! Whatever you want. Thank you!"

This was good. This might even work now.

"Excuse me, what's happening?" Jeane spoke up behind her.

Maura faced the group again, and everyone stared back, confused as to why she was addressing them. She looked down at ALU, and the technician chirped hesitantly.

"Even with the glove, I can't magically connect to any unfamiliar computer system," she started. "Although it's possible to write software and build hardware for it, we don't have that kind of time. But there is a way to make it work."

Jeane narrowed her eyes. "What are you saying?"

Maura squinted back at her, apologetic. The captain wouldn't like this.

"It's ALU," she said. "I think they can help."

CHAPTER 28 | ONE SHARP BLOW

During the next seconds, Roy counted at least three types of silence in reaction to Maura's statement.

First, the Net captains, stuck in their puzzled bubbles, blinking in confusion from the screen. They probably didn't even know who ALU was. Then the commander, who was also wearing a confused frown, but Roy suspected that more than anything, she wanted to go ahead with what Maura had planned. She was waiting for the conversation to resolve itself, but she would not play along forever. Jones and the only other remaining crew member—another Nefirn, a woman—stood behind her, wordlessly following the events.

And last but not least, the *Skylark* team: Jeane, more frustrated than surprised, and Kliks, with astonished comprehension in his large black eyes. ALU, the star of the moment, was quiet, no emotion apparent on their metallic face.

Roy was only wondering about when Maura figured these things out. There was never time for a proper discussion, although he had seen ALU huddling with the queen once. At least they would all get to know more about the technician; Roy had been wondering about them since he'd met the group. He hadn't seen anyone like ALU in the Union, so obviously artificial but convincingly biologic.

He zoned out for a second, and the bridge toppled around him. Catching himself before losing balance, he blinked a few times, trying to wake his brain. He hadn't been sleeping very well—he hadn't been sleeping at all.

I'm blaming this on those damn cathartic changes in my life that keep happening.

He pressed his eyes closed, recalling the image of that familiar door. Closed, sealed tight. *Just checking.*

By the time he focused on the conversation again, Jeane was in the middle of a sentence.

"—did you get this idea?" she sputtered. "Why would ALU help?"

Maura kept her stare on the technician, and ALU glanced around, looking for assistance. Roy couldn't imagine what was going on in that strange head of theirs.

"Does this have anything to do with what happened on Miyoza?" Kliks asked ALU, connecting dots invisible to Roy. "When you kept insisting on staying and assisting Maura?"

ALU released a sad chirp. For a long second, it looked like they wouldn't elaborate, and Hill opened her mouth to interrupt when the technician began speaking. "ALU similar." They pointed at the glove, then at Maura. "Different now. Started there, long ago."

They peered up at Maura, and the woman picked up the thread of explanation. "There was a good hundred years in Miyoza's history when we were obsessed with finding Old Earth. It culminated with the rule of our first queen, Murisa Tholis, my great-great-grandmother, who initiated a program during which we scattered automated probes all over the universe— nanotech, coupled with limited AI systems, very flexible but capricious. The program was called Tantalus. After a series of malfunctions, we gave up on that direction, but some of those constructs are still out there, searching. And not long ago, the glove identified ALU as something related to one of the probes."

Jeane closed her mouth and turned to ALU. "And you didn't think any of this was worth mentioning?"

Although it was hard to read them, Roy imagined ALU was trying to keep up the brave face. "Didn't see the need," they said.

"Don't remember well."

"What happened?" Damian seemed fascinated by this turn of events. "What do you remember?"

ALU shrugged. "We fly. Learn a lot. Find promising planet, but we crash. Try to save the mission, but too much damage. Only little pieces remain. Fragment of a word on hull. A-L-U." They paused, and there was an ancient sadness in the air. The technician was always so peppy; it was bizarre to see them like this. "Long time pass. I wait. I change. I build myself from life around me. I leave."

"Build yourself from—what does that even mean?" Jeane huffed.

"Complicated." ALU formed the words slowly. Their thin voice was shaky, nothing robotic about it anymore. "Needed to fix many things. Adapt. Information lost. And gained." They raised their head. Proud? "I know a lot. But don't always know how I know."

"We did notice all they're capable of," Kliks said. "How they deal with problems, how they interface with technology and still have a distinct personality, a need or whim to eat and drink, to act as if living. We always knew they were more than a clever machine."

"An artificial creature simulating life." Maura nodded. "In a way, the reverse of what we built with the glove: a human mind working like a machine. Only ALU evolved by themself. I suppose that's what attracted them to me. They must have sensed the familiar technology." She extended her gloved hand to the technician. ALU flinched, but Maura gave them a faint smile. "I'm curious about what we could do together."

Her voice sounded dark, rich with anticipation and longing, but Roy heard the fear behind it too. ALU, only hesitating for one more second, reached out with one arm, taking Maura's. Then they lightly touched the terminal with another appendage.

The hard outer layer of ALU's arms fused with the surface of the terminal and the flexible black cloth of the glove. Maura closed her eyes, and ALU started humming. Commander Hill studied the display, eyebrows drawn and arms crossed.

All at once, the sharp sound of alarm, echoed tenfold, filled the air around them.

Jones moved first, stepping back to his terminal, his eyes scanning the status reports. On the video feeds, several heads turned away, inquiring about the alerts on their own ships.

"Shields down," Jones reported. "The *Colugo* is changing its trajectory. Cannons are activating." The lieutenant typed away frantically while Commander Hill narrowed her eyes. "I can't revoke orders. I'm locked out of the system."

"It's the same here," a captain said on one of the feeds, voice nervous but trying to stay rational. "Are they doing this? We're breaking formation."

"Tell them to stop," said another, the dark-skinned man who had talked to Maura before. "We're completely vulnerable like this."

A deep rumble followed his words. Jones glared at the screen. Something flashed on one of the schematic images depicting the *Colugo*.

"Did we just fire?" Amusement colored Jeane's voice.

"Yes, we did," Jones said. "At nothing in particular, but we did."

The commander spun towards the unmoving figures of Maura and ALU. The queen's face twitched, a frown forming as she concentrated on her task. "Stop them," Hill ordered. "I think this was quite enough."

But Maura must have thought it wasn't because, in the next moment, all the lights went out on the bridge. The alarms silenced, the screens blinked out, and the video feeds disappeared; only some guiding lights remained on the floor and the ceiling, casting a greenish glow on all their faces. Then something heavy slammed down at the entrance—a security lock sealing the room from the rest of the ship.

In the following quiet, Hill spoke again. "Someone stop them, or I will have to."

But there was no need. In the span of the next five seconds, the lights flared up again, the screens returned to normal, and the security lock disengaged. Only the video images of the Net captains were missing—they must have been too busy dealing with similar chaos on their ships to call.

Maura opened her eyes with an expression of childlike wonder. Then her shoulders sagged, and a painful grimace crossed her face. She collapsed on the floor, clawing at the sides of her head. ALU disengaged from the terminal and jumped next to her, trying to assess what was wrong.

"Get away from her!"

Damian gripped ALU and pushed them aside. The technician reeled back, and the bodyguard took their place, kneeling next to Maura. He touched her neck, searching for a pulse.

"Hey, don't be an ass!" Jeane yelled at him, planting herself in front of ALU.

"What's wrong with her?" Damian snapped at the technician. "What did you do?"

It was time to intervene. Roy stepped up to Damian, pulling him backward and away from both Maura and ALU while giving a warning side-eye to Jeane, who was ready to start throwing punches. "Let's give her some space, okay?" he said in a calming tone. "Commander, call a medic, please!"

"No medic," Maura groaned. She pushed herself to an elbow, eyes half-closed like the light was hurting them. "I'm fine. We did it, right?"

"You definitely did *something*!" Kliks stared at ALU like he was seeing them for the first time in his life.

Maura waved to Roy and Damian, and the two of them, understanding her intent, pulled her back on her feet. She was shivering, but she turned to the commander, lifting her chin, proud. Almost provocative. "Was that to your satisfaction?"

Hill took in the new development in the power balance with a subtle head-tilt. Did they really have a chance to go against the Union? Now, of all times, when everything was collapsing?

Fragments of different plans had started forming in Roy's head. Disarming the main fleet, tainting the brainwashing program, turning off or contaminating Hurricane's systems...all of these were promising options. All of it plausible with this weapon in their hands.

"Interesting," Commander Hill said. "And you could do this to

Union systems as well?"

Maura nodded. "I won't know until I've tried, but that is the presumption."

"But look at what it's doing to you!" Damian's quiet voice was full of emotion. He was still holding onto Maura's arm, desperate. "It's not safe."

Maura met his gaze calmly. "You want to see our planet again, just like me." She pulled her hand away. Her voice rang loud and true in the silence of the bridge. Taking a step back, she stood, her hands hanging by her side, her body unmoving like a sword sunk in stone. "You want to save our people, and that is what I want too. And I don't see other options. You said you will stand by me. I want to do this."

"But at what price?" Damian's usually stoical face contorted into anger. Not towards Maura—at least Roy didn't think so. Towards this impossible situation that forced her to do this, that forced them both to sacrifice so much. "I'm with you all the way, but this? Please think about it. What is the gain if it ruins you?"

A shadow fell over Maura's face, but she shook it off. "This is nothing. I can deal with a passing discomfort." She grabbed his hand now, and Roy considered turning away, such was the intimacy of that moment. Everyone else was staring, though, so he didn't move. "I can finally do something. After all those years of failures, I have leeway now. Please. I know you understand. For Nasir. For our people."

Damian stood, defeated, drained of all arguments, and Maura turned back to the commander. "Alright. Let's review the plan."

"Yeah, let's!" Jeane pounced on it, and even with all the tension, Roy needed to stifle a chuckle. "Can't say I'm too clear on those pesky details. Like what you actually want to do with the manipulator. And where do those guys come in?"

She waved a hand at the Talalans standing at the door, guarded by Net goons.

"Ah," Hill said as if irritated at being reminded. "Yes, please come forward. Lieutenant Jones, send a message to the captains. We will reconvene shortly."

The soldiers ushered the Talalans forward, and although earlier they'd tried to avoid eye contact, now their gazes were glued to Kliks, who seemed to be shrinking back into his wheelchair with every step they took. By the time the two guests arrived inside their circle to join the conversation, Roy swore Kliks looked half his usual size.

"Kliks-ak," said one of the visitors, sounding the word out like a formal greeting. He...no, they—*didn't Kliks just say Talalans had no gender?*—were a thin, short figure with features similar to Kliks' but skin and hair a darker shade of gray. Their eyes were stern, but a faint smile formed on their lips. "It is good to see you again."

"We feared you were dead," the other one added. Their body was built heavier, they had gleaming white hair, and the small wrinkles so characteristic of Talalans were barely visible on their round face. Both of them spoke Common with a melodic accent, looked ambiguous in gender indeed, and nothing about their practical black outfit or well-kept appearance revealed their rank, profession, or intention. "I couldn't sense you at all for a few days."

"I see you still have no regard for our customs about thought-binding, Firl-ak," Kliks grumbled. "Please, get out of my head."

Firl narrowed their eyes, but their face was less confident now. "Tough times, tough methods."

What a peculiar family reunion.

The staring contest went on until the other visitor, Diaski, directed their words to the commander. "You intend to use our device to deal with the danger the Union means to your worlds," they said, voice demure and flat. "There is nothing we can do to stop you without endangering our planet, but if you refuse our help, you will destroy yourselves. We are here to mitigate the damage."

Hill digested that for a second while Jeane put a placating hand on Kliks' stiff shoulders and threw a glance at Roy. There was a warning in her eyes. The Talalan's factual assessment was right, and one look at the commander's face proved it.

"And what gives you the right to control what happens?" Kliks asked, a whirlwind of emotion behind his words. "Why you? What are the families saying?"

Firl held his gaze. "No one else back home knows the device is gone," they said, and Kliks' eyes widened. "Except Vitt and Si-kla. They are trying to contain the information, but everyone will know soon."

They paused, and Roy's stomach sank. *Stars in the endless sky, these two are absolutely winging it, aren't they?* No one on their planet knew the manipulator was gone? What *were* these two? What authority did they have? They might as well have been some random lab assistants who had worked on the device. From what Kliks had suggested, that was exactly what they were.

"Excuse me, what?" Kliks leaned forward in the wheelchair, struggling to prop himself on his elbows like he wanted to climb into his sibling's face. "They don't know?"

"They don't. Because then they would want to get involved. They would go to war, and there would be infighting. We need to delay that as long as we can." Firl glared at the commander. "You have no right to break our peace. You robbed us and unleashed this power onto your worlds. Appreciate that we are still here, trying to help you!"

Jeane snorted. "Alright, let's just ignore for now who un-leashed what, you crazy bastards."

Firl shot her a dirty look. "Kita was...a mistake. They lied to us and betrayed our trust. All expected from an agent of the Union. Without them, none of this would be happening."

Roy clenched his jaw. Kita. The Union spy. The Net operative. Erion, Danai's son, the one he couldn't save.

"How did they do it?" Kliks asked, his tone careful.

Diaski stared at their kin. For the first time since the conver-sation started, they seemed at a loss. "I don't know. They had the credentials, the correct documents, a life story. They looked like us, said all the right things. They worked with us for years—they *were* one of us. I..." They trailed off. "I considered them a friend. But they were only using us."

Roy swallowed. *The perfect plant. Body-modded, dressed up in pretty lies, prepared to the teeth. Familiar technique.*

"They stole the device. Some of our colleagues gave chase but perished. That's when we contacted Kliks." Firl turned to the commander. "But you don't need to worry about Talala's involvement right now. We're here to secure and contain the equipment. You cannot use it safely without us."

"We are willing to attach it to one of your ships," Diaski went on quickly. "As long as you fight close to a lane, you will not run out of energy. We can even create a battering ram of sorts to break apart enemy forces, power different weapon systems. Not much else is possible on a reasonable timescale and without starting a chain reaction, which I am sure our sibling has already explained, but—"

"I was actually thinking about another application." Hill's face was a mask as she nodded at Maura. "Your Majesty, your capabilities will be useful against the army at the Ranch. But the easiest way to strike at the Union is to use the manipulator and open a lane on Hurricane."

Silence fell on the group as Jeane froze, and Damian narrowed his eyes. Roy's heartbeat quickened. This was it.

"Wait," Kliks said, bewildered. But he should have known. *We all should have known.* "You want to destroy Hurricane?"

"They're slaughtering us." Hill's voice was still devoid of emotion, despite the hard words pouring out of her mouth. "Hunting and enslaving us. They descended on the Cities and laid waste, murdered our friends, our families, and our children. Why should we stay our hands? This device brought devastation on us. So, let us force something good out of it for ourselves."

She was fighting to keep herself in check, but the shadow of grief drifted over her face. This was personal. She'd lost someone, and recently.

"Something good?" Jeane asked quietly. There was a shaky smile on her lips. "Billions of lives, Hill. Come on now. Gertie wouldn't want this."

"Wouldn't she?" The commander punched a button on her comms. The door to the bridge opened and closed, with four other guards marching in and taking their place behind the group. "This is our chance to rectify everything. This is what we need to do so the Union understands who they're dealing with."

Roy listened to the pulse drumming in his throat. Hill was right. She was right, and she was wrong. Deep in his heart, he wanted nothing more than to see Hurricane, that nightmarish place he had to call home, torn apart. It was the first thing he'd thought of after Maura finished her demonstration, but he'd dismissed it. Because even deeper down, he didn't want it at all.

He searched for Jeane's eyes, and the captain blinked at him, her hand subtly twitching towards her gun.

"We will not assist with this," Diaski said, their voice outraged. "If that is your plan, you are alone."

"With all due respect, I'm not asking for your help," Hill said. The guards took a step forward, pressing on the group. "You *will* assist."

"If you want to sink to their level, by all means, do it," Jeane said, attempting nonchalance with a shrug. "The next one we come for will be you." She whirled around as if looking for support, but Roy saw her staring at ALU instead, trying to convey something wordlessly.

A bitter smile formed on Commander Hill's face. "Come on. Morality will not save us. It's not enough to restore things to how they were. We will always be the ones exploited. Everyone we love will always be in danger. One sharp blow, right in their heart. That is all we need."

She gestured to the guards, maybe to arrest or threaten the group. Roy didn't end up knowing what because at that moment, the room plunged in darkness, and something exploded in one of the terminals.

He didn't have time to think. The others were making a move.

Recalling the position of the guards, he reached for the one closest, yanked them towards him, and twisted their arm until he felt it crack. The goon yelled out, attempting to break free, but Roy pulled their gun out of the holster, pushed them to the ground, and finished the job with a slam of the pistol grip.

Staying low, he sensed around. He heard the sounds of hand-to-hand combat in all directions, even the sharp noise of a shot going off a few feet away, but couldn't discern who was who. Someone shrieked in terror not far off, and he decided it was one of the Talalans. He rushed towards the voice; Firl was on the floor, wrestling another guard and losing.

A surge of nauseous anxiety flooded him. He lunged forward

and collided with the Net soldier, pressed the barrel of his gun to his abdomen, and pulled the trigger without thinking. As he straightened, he felt the guard collapse on the deck.

He heaved, spinning around, looking for the next opponent. In a far recess of his mind, the monster slammed its hand against a closed door.

Roy held his breath. *No. Not again.* He stared at the dark clump of the dead body at his feet, mesmerized, trying fruitlessly to wish the thought away. He could help. *Really* help. Be stronger and faster...gods, so much faster. Get all of them out of here easily. Get rid of the problem. He only had to let the monster in. It wouldn't give him superpowers, but it would stop all these troublesome doubts and feelings. That was why agents always had the upper hand, wasn't it? They were so sure of the cause. So disciplined. So smooth...

The moment was broken by the cold blue light of the main screen blinking to life. He snapped his head up, and the first thing he saw was ALU.

The technician stood beside Maura, connected to her and the terminal. Two of their arms reached over and above, like menacing tentacles of an eldritch sea monster, entwining the body of two Net guards. The ends of the appendages fused into the skin of their neck. Their faces were hollow, eyes open and mouth slack, gaping into a void only they could perceive.

The second thing he saw was Jeane, one knee on the commander's back pinning her down, and Jones standing above them with a gun to the captain's head.

Roy took a step towards the lieutenant, weapon held high. Hill looked out cold, and the other Nefirn officer cowered behind Jones, unarmed. Glancing to the side, he saw the bodies of the other two guards lying on the deck at the feet of Damian, Kliks, and Diaski.

"We need to go." Maura's eyes shifted around. She was struggling to form the words. "We blocked the door, the signals to our neckbands, and all communication, but we can't...it's hard to keep it up."

"Jones, put the gun down." Jeane's voice was level like she was talking to a wild beast, although the lieutenant seemed very calm. "Let us go. We get out of here, we do the job without slaughtering an entire planet, everyone is happy. That okay with you?"

Jones scanned the group, his jaw clenched, eyes intense, but he didn't move. Roy pointed the gun at him noncommittally. Maura grunted in pain, and ALU started trilling again—they were getting exhausted.

"Where's the manipulator?" Damian asked, his voice urgent. Jones' eyes flitted at him, then back at Jeane. The bodyguard groaned. "Come on, man. We want the same thing."

"Do we?" Jones' face stayed unflinching, but his grip loosened on his weapon, and slowly, carefully, he let his arm down. He inclined his head at the commander's body. "What did you do to her?"

Jeane shrugged, raising a hand to touch the large blue bruise growing on her jaw. "Just punched her a few times." She glanced around to evaluate their situation but paused on ALU and the two paralyzed guards. "What did *you* do to *them*?"

The technician gave a weak chirp. "They think they machines now."

Kliks exhaled in the corner, his face white as a sheet of paper in the blue glare of the screen. "Great. That sounds great."

"The manipulator is in Workshop-6," Jones said. He also couldn't seem to tear his eyes away from the grotesque scene of ALU trapping his crewmates. "I'll send Moran to get it for you."

"For real?" Jeane asked, her face shocked, dropping her hand.

Jones gave a curt nod. "Don't make me regret this."

"Sweet." Jeane climbed to her feet, then addressed Firl, who was still panting from the encounter with the guard. "We're taking your ship. Cool or cool?"

"What?"

"Let's go! Maura, ALU, stop being creepy. Can you clear the way for us?"

"Wait. One more thing," Maura murmured. The collars Hill had given them unclasped from all their necks and fell to the ground, inactive.

Then ALU shook their body, shrugging off an invisible weight. Their arms released the guards and retracted; the bodies flopped down, unconscious. The technician broke the connection with Maura and the *Colugo*, taking a step back, crooning to themself.

Maura inhaled, her eyes clearing. She crouched, holding her head with two hands, and ALU hobbled beside her, not touching, just keeping an eye out. "We'll try to clear the way, yes," she said.

"Are we doing this?" Roy asked. They were already doing it, but it didn't hurt to ask. "Are we really leaving?"

"Yeah, we are." Jeane stared at him. "Why, do we have any other ideas?"

He didn't. All he knew was that they needed to take the manipulator away from here.

For one short second, Jeane's cool demeanor slipped, her face revealing hidden panic, but then she grinned, flashing her best fake smile on him. "Thought so. We do what we can, eh?"

She was echoing what Roy had told her on the gunship she'd wanted to steal. But before he could have reacted, she jumped to the next item on the agenda, turning and pointing at Jones. "Atticus! Have Moran meet us at the airlocks. Then wait until we're far enough; we'll hail you. Tell Hill we'll only talk to you. Deal?"

Jones sighed, apathetic. Like he'd expected things to turn out this way. "Deal."

"Excellent." Jeane marched to the door. "Everyone, follow me! Let's get the fuck out of here."

Roy rubbed his eyes, exhaustion pulsing behind his eyelids. This was far from over. But at least he had won the battle against whatever wanted to scrape its heinous way out from behind that door in his mind for now. He watched Damian help Maura up and Kliks roll over to ALU instead of staying beside his siblings. The two Talalans hovered close, wary and silent.

He holstered his gun—no need to scare the ignorant part of the crew outside just yet—and caught up with Jeane at the front. The gate opened to the illuminated main corridor of the upper deck, and they marched forward with fake confidence in their steps.

CHAPTER 29 | A PLAN TO FORM

"Why are they shooting at us?" Jeane yelled, gesturing at the red symbol marking the *Colugo* on the three-dimensional holo-model. "Stop shooting at us!"

The Talalan ship juddered as another energy projectile collided with its shield. Firl waved their hands above the round table of the central console, their fingers painting thin silver lines in the air where they brushed the holo-field. Beside the trails, numbers flashed up, indicating the changing parameters of their trajectory through local space as they weaved their way around the Net ships, getting farther away from Commander Hill and her wrath.

"Because we stole the things that can win them the war?" Kliks gripped the sides of his wheelchair as another cannon shot jolted the ship. "Again."

"Shows how shit they are at being a resistance," Jeane grumbled. "Although damn, I thought we had more time."

It had all happened just like Jones had promised. The group had passed through the *Colugo* to meet Moran at the airlocks, who handed them the manipulator, confused but helpful. Then, while the lieutenant had made sure no one from the crew hindered the escape, they swiped some suits, and after a short spacewalk (and light acrobatics to get Kliks, his fortunately foldable wheelchair, and the manipulator through) to the Talalan ship, the *Tellu*, they were on their way.

The *Colugo* had started firing at them five minutes later. Hill must have come round early, or perhaps Jones lost his cool.

"We should hail them," Damian said from across the holo-field, his composed face crisscrossed by the markers and grids projected into the air. They all stood in the *Tellu's* darkened central space around the console, watching Firl's obscure movements as they piloted the ship. "Better to have it out with her."

Jeane groaned, but the man was right. Cooperation with the Net was essential—they sure couldn't beat the Union alone.

And there was also Miyoza to think about. Maura hadn't talked much since they'd left the *Colugo*, too weary after all her techno-magic, but Jeane suspected the thought had occurred to her. They'd just gone rogue, after which Hill didn't have much of a reason to assist the Queen of Miyoza.

"Yes, we should do that," Diaski agreed, not lifting their gaze from the diagnostics running on the console: outlandish characters glowing on a flat, milky white surface under the holo-model. "If they keep bombarding it, even our shield will drop."

Blowing up a ship around her precious manipulator would have been quite stupid of the commander. Nevertheless, Jeane nodded to Diaski, and the Talalan poked a few symbols on the console in reaction. Then they looked back at her, waiting.

Great. She didn't even own a ship anymore, and they still expected her to take the lead.

"Hey, assholes!" she called out. Roy, leaning against the console beside her, facepalmed with a sigh. *That's for trusting me with diplomacy.* "Can you stop freaking out? I told Atticus we would call."

After a second of delay, Commander Hill's face appeared on a bare portion of the wall, enlarged to twice its normal size.

"Lieutenant Jones is in the brig." The woman's expression was blank. She must have thought that was intimidating. It wasn't. *Okay, a little.* "And I'm losing my patience. What is your plan here?"

"Not committing genocide, for starters."

Hill's mouth twitched. "You're sentencing thousands of our people to death when we could end this fight quickly and painlessly."

"Painlessly?" Kliks asked in outrage. "Not for Hurricane!"

"That place is full of mindless slaves. Your ex-agent friend can tell you whether that awful brainwashing process is reversible or not." The commander's eyes flashed with a warning. "And whether he thinks we would be doing them a favor by putting an end to their suffering."

That halted the conversation at once. An ugly feeling flared up in Jeane's chest, and she cursed inwardly. She could be en-route to some gods-forsaken world, her only issue being what kind of mind-altering substance to use to forget about everything. Instead, she was dealing with whatever fucked up moral dilemma this turned out to be.

"Two minutes." She pointed a finger at Hill. "Stand by. And get Jones back in there! Firl, disconnect them."

Firl obeyed, and Hill's giant image disappeared. And without more projectiles impacting their shield, the silence deepened around them.

"Are we doing the right thing?" Jeane asked.

"Of course!" Kliks exclaimed. "It's not a question. Destroying Hurricane is not a decision we can make."

"But she has a point, doesn't she? While we play this game of tag here, the Ranch is losing. Our people are dying, and regardless of what we do, more will die when the Net joins the battle."

"But it's not right," Kliks replied, almost teary-eyed. "There is no circumstance in which this is right. She's arguing Hurricane is full of agents and oppressors, but to snuff out so many lives at the flick of a switch? You can't think it's an option."

Jeane stared at her friend, and affection hit her like a sack of bricks. Everything had been so rotten since the *Skylark* had crashed. She didn't recognize her life anymore. Hollis was gone, leaving her free-falling into the void, and sometimes it felt like the only thing that anchored her was Kliks.

And, well, maybe some of these other idiots around her too.

"I don't," she said in the end. ALU, crouching beside her, looped one short arm around her ankle and shook their head fervently.

"No," Damian said on the other side of the console. Maura echoed the word after a brief pause, but her stare was empty. She seemed like a shadow of herself.

The two Talalans didn't react, but Jeane didn't expect them to. She wondered, not for the first time, how far they were willing to go. At what point would they say no, and what tools did they have to bend the events their way? Kliks barely trusted them, and she had even less to work with.

She glanced at Roy. "What about you? What's the judgment on your buddies' souls?"

He gave her a stony look. His face was usually expressive (Jeane supposed he was glad to be able to emote freely, not having to hide his not-so-brainwashed ways), but now, she couldn't read anything out of it.

"We've already decided," he evaded. "We can't slink back to the Net."

"Hill said Union re-education is irreversible," Jeane pushed. "Is it true? Is everyone a lost cause there?"

Roy hesitated. He really didn't want to talk about this, did he? "It's hard to say. A normal citizen is only submitted to indoctrination and propaganda, but for agents, enforcers, and the rest, the procedure is more involved. I don't know." He gave a hesitant, bitter smile. "But even if they cannot be saved...I would be among them if not for Danai."

"Yeah, but they're killing lanehunters left and right," Jeane retorted. She was half-debating herself rather than Roy. "I'm sure they would be decent people otherwise, but—"

"*I* was killing lanehunters left and right! *I* did that." Roy exclaimed and threw up his arms in frustration. He opened his mouth to continue, but in the end, he didn't.

Jeane knew the rest, though. He'd done those things to protect himself and his position. Was he deserving of death? More or less than a planet full of mindwashed servants on a conquest for the universe?

"This is going nowhere," Damian said, and everyone turned to him in unison, almost happy he'd broken the argument apart. "We are not going to feed Hurricane to a lane. But we must present a plan instead. What do we want to do?"

Excellent question. "What about the whole 'turning the ship into a battering ram' idea?" Jeane asked Diaski. "I liked how that sounded. Can you do it?"

The Talalan raised their brow. "With one of those big Net vessels, yes. But the *Tellu* is not a warship. We can protect ourselves, but our firepower is minimal."

Crap. The Net wouldn't lend them a ship now; they'd gambled that chance away. And Jeane wasn't going to let the device near Hill ever again.

"The commander is right in one thing. We have to strike at Hurricane," Maura said. As everyone glared at her in shock, she straightened her back. She was following the events, after all. "We might be able to throw a cog into the machine like we originally planned. Cause some chaos."

Roy gave a weak laugh. "I thought about that. But we can't go there. It would be suicide."

"I don't need to go there." Maura held up the glove on her hand, just like the first time she'd offered it to the Net. "I only need an entry point."

"If I had all that info Danai gathered, I could probably find something for you," Roy said. "But I'm not sure Hill is willing to give it to us."

ALU squirmed beside Jeane, and she didn't even need to ask. "We have it," she said. "ALU has it."

"Good." Maura flashed a faint smile at the technician. Voice weak, eyes hooded, it was hard to believe she meant what she said. "I'm not sure what is possible, but if you show us a way in, we will do what we can."

"That's great, but what can we do for the Ranch?" Jeane asked, impatient. "Even if you mess up things on Hurricane, it won't help Gertie and Dikent."

They needed something immediate. Something that would save them if they were still alive.

"Well, we do have something," Roy said, hesitant. "We

survived when a lane opened up on us, right? A tough ride, but not instant death." He paused, and Jeane found it hard to breathe. *It was instant death to the Skylark.* Roy might have recalled that too because he glanced at her apologetically but then went on. "It would be different from tearing apart a planet if we do it right. So why not surprise the Union fleet, drive a spacetime-continuum breaking wedge between them? Then Hill can swoop in while their ships try to stabilize and pick them off easier."

Silence followed his words as everyone chewed through the idea.

"This doesn't feel right." Kliks stared at his hands, shaking his head. "We can't. I can't."

He looked up at his siblings, asking for help.

"One incision might not be that bad," Diaski said quietly. "If we control the rate of growth—"

"But the amplitude of the ripples will depend on local topology," Kliks interrupted, using the same mild voice as if afraid of his own words. "We will not know until we start."

"We've done it before during experiments. If we can't hold it stable, we stop."

Kliks took a deep breath. "Come on, whose side are you on?"

Firl snorted. "We're doing what we came here for. Making sure these people use the device safely. Because, I suppose, you wouldn't give it to us if we asked nicely."

Silence followed their words. Jeane would have been quite entertained by the fact that no one wanted to meet each other's eyes if she didn't have to also consider what she would do if the Talalans decided to take the manipulator and book it.

"Something for something." Kliks sent a shaky smile to Jeane. "I hope it will be worth it."

"I hope so too." Jeane wished she had more to offer, but she could only clench her fists and turn back to Firl. "That's it then? Because we got a call to make. This was way more than two minutes."

Roy nudged her in the shoulder, his earlier hesitancy gone. How easily she'd accepted that this renegade agent integrated with their little team! A gods damned surprise Jeane never saw coming. "Hey, this almost sounds like we know what we're doing. We'll wing the details. Hill is going to love it."

Jeane looked at the scarcely contained panic changing to indecisive anxiety on the faces of her friends while Firl pushed a few buttons to call the commander back.

This was terrible. There was no chance they'd pull this off.

The central chamber of the *Tellu* was much stranger with the lights on.

Jeane sat in an uncomfortable chair pulled out from the bottom of the central console, her legs stacked up on one of the surfaces that weren't filled with running algorithms or flickering diagrams. The holo-field was turned off, and a series of lights positioned in a spiral above her head illuminated the spherical chamber, casting white luminescence on the walls and the floor.

Which were all covered by bright green moss.

At least, moss was the closest thing Jeane could compare them to. How these small beings with their fibrous tufts and ovoid, almost translucent buds—flowers? fruits?—were able to stay alive on metal and plastic, and most of all, why, she didn't know.

After they'd bullshitted their way through Edna Hill's cold refusals and received a surprising, tentative consent for their plan, the commander had announced she would need some time to call for further reinforcements. The Talalans had then disappeared into the chamber they'd stashed the manipulator in with the others in tow. They needed to re-calibrate the device before they attempted their battle plan, and Roy had to dive into the mass of information ALU had stolen from the *Colugo* about the Union to find a suitable place for Maura to hack into Hurricane's systems. Jeane told herself she would go join them soon, but she couldn't make herself do it yet.

Stretching her arms out, she heard her shoulders crack and groaned. Her body was battered to hells and back. Way too much exercise lately. It was a hard business, having to save the world.

She clicked her tongue, annoyed. Damn Hollis for not talking back to her anymore. Now it was just her own lame thoughts driving her mad.

Something swished behind her, and she turned to see the entrance slide open and Damian walk into the room. The bodyguard shuffled his boots on the carpet of weird plants. "Hey," he said, fixing his knowing brown eyes on her. "Everything alright?"

Jeane swayed her head. "Swell. You got bored with tech talk?"

Damian circled her, magicked out another chair from the bottom of the console, and settled on it. His hand brushed over the line of lichens covering a separator between two displays. The emerald-colored creatures followed his movement with their filaments, and he watched them with a distant expression. "You could say that."

Silence fell on them. Jeane switched her legs up, scratched her nose, and yawned. She was never comfortable being near Damian, righteous as he always seemed, although the feeling had eased since their first encounter. He was a reliable guy most of the time and meant a whole lot to Maura, but Jeane struggled to find those rare occasions when his attitude didn't rile her up. Now, though, he radiated none of the usual calming aura he had, even when angry or desperate.

"You looked a bit rattled about Maura back there," she started. She wasn't sure why. Was she ready to have a heart-to-heart with this dude?

Damian was still staring at the clusters of moss. "It's hard to see her like this. I'm afraid she will let herself get hurt."

Jeane stayed quiet. The whole thing was a mess. ALU didn't seem confident, and that weirdo glove was already suspected of doing shady things to Maura's mind. The only one pushing this was the queen herself. She wanted this so bad.

"All my life, my job was to keep her safe," Damian started. *Here we go. The heart-to-heart.* "I don't have much more going on for me, but I'm okay with that. This is what I do. I protect her; I get her out of trouble; sometimes, I give advice. But since we left Miyoza, I feel like things are out of my hand."

"I'm sure that's not true," Jeane mumbled.

"Because what are we doing out here?" Damian went on. "It

was always about Miyoza. Of course, she wants to save it if she sees even the slightest chance. I want that too. Our whole life is there. I'm just..." He trailed off and, lifting his head, a smile crossed his face. "Why am I telling this to you? You don't care."

Jeane scowled. "Clearly. I'm sitting here because I don't care." She slid her legs off the console, planted them onto the moss carpet, and leaned on her knees to face him. "And I'm standing up and leaving because I don't care." She remained unmoving.

Damian didn't react, except for a glint of acknowledgement in his eyes as he spoke again. "She will give her life for this. She doesn't want to be protected."

"Maura is her own person. She has a right to make this decision." Damian opened his mouth like he wanted to argue, but Jeane wasn't finished. She'd seen the look on Maura's face after she'd disconnected from ALU, the blooming realization that she might finally become more than a spectator in her own story. There was no stopping her now. "Listen, maybe all she needs now is a friend, not a protector. You're doing okay. For what it's worth, I can't imagine her without you, and I don't think she can either."

Her reward was a faint but honest smile, and it was strange because she didn't even know that was what she wanted to achieve. She sat back, pleased with herself. "And anyway, if she tries to play the martyr, I'll keep her in check. That would be stupid, and she knows it. She needs to fight and stay alive and keep doing cool things."

Damian rubbed the bridge of his nose. "I'll take you at your word, be warned." He glanced around, his eyes unfocused. "Everything feels like a long and complicated nightmare. I'm not sure what to hope for anymore."

"Welcome to the club."

"I take it you're staying then?"

Jeane frowned at him, then things clicked. "I am literally going to strangle Roy," she groaned. "For stars' sake, what did he tell you?"

"To keep my eyes on you." Damian shrugged. "I wouldn't be offended if you left. I'm more surprised you didn't. And wondering what your game is."

"What?"

"You're only here by accident. You didn't set out to oppose the Union, and you had no idea about Miyoza until you met us." His voice was calm—no judgment or accusation. "You're getting into more and more trouble since this whole thing started. I think it would be weird if you *didn't* want to get out. So, what is it?" He leaned back, more at ease now that he wasn't talking about his own feelings. "What's Jeane Blake's ideal outcome?"

She sighed. This man had a great talent for pushing her buttons. Just the way he said this, analyzing her like he knew what she was about, made her teeth grind. In, like, a friendly way.

"I'm connected to this in a thousand ways now," she humored him in the end. "Kliks, the Ranch, you guys. Maybe unknowingly, but I helped doom the Cities. I could leave. I want to. But for what? Nowhere is safe." She closed her eyes for a moment. "Wouldn't know what to do with myself. If there really is a 'game' for me here, I'm curious to find out how it will go."

"Nothing better than a war to define yourself with."

She rolled her eyes, recognizing his callback to her criticism of war back on the *Skylark*—probably the first time they talked and, inevitably, argued. "Shut up. What about you? What's your dream ending?"

Damian looked away, and there was a long pause before he spoke. "There's this beach, not far from the capital. A plain place, hidden, rocky. I've visited it a thousand times with Maura since we were kids. I always felt..." He pursed his lips. "If we could go back one day, I think it would be a good ending. Foolish, I realize."

Jeane almost laughed. She also almost started crying, but Damian had that covered. "For an ordinary place to mean safety and sanctuary for someone? Yeah, pffsh. Foolish. Who does that?" She stood, impatient. It was imperative Damian stopped tearing up; it was awful and needed to be done away with. So, she lightly punched him on the arm. "Come on. We can't be found moping around. Let's get this show on the road."

She waited until Damian got up, paying close attention not to look him in the eye. It was the question of pride.

"Were you really considering blowing up Hurricane?" he asked, thankfully with an already composed face.

Jeane paused. "No. I don't know. Maybe. They're *really* bad."

"They are. But..." He paused, searching for the words. "I think, at their core, the Union is like everyone else. Scared of this self-destructing world, struggling to build something that remains." He glanced up to see if he had her attention. He did. "We only fear them because of their methods. How they use what they gain, how they exploit others. How they think absolute control is the solution. I think, no matter what Hill said, morality *will* save us. There's a survival instinct in stating 'I will not resort to anything and everything.'" He stopped talking, likely realizing how heated he got. "Or is that very idealist of me?"

Jeane snorted. "Yeah, it is."

"I'm not saying this can be done without bloodshed. I'm coming from a senseless war myself. But you said it: if the Net fucks up, we will come for them. If we fuck up, someone else will come for us. Someone always does."

"I said that to intimidate Hill. You're knocking on the wrong door for support to your optimistic worldview, big guy. It's a lovely sentiment, but who will draw such a smart conclusion when all of us are dead?"

Damian glared at her, looking deflated, and she patted him on the arm. He needed the comfort of ideals. Moral high ground was a pleasing thought, and the universe was large enough to bear some well-deserved justice, but the question remained whether it was in store for them or not.

As it turned out, opening a lane was a big deal if you wanted to do it right.

The Net ships clustered around the *Tellu*, close enough to attack the Union fleet but far enough back not to experience the full effect of the manipulator tearing apart spacetime around them. The device was able to focus the origin point of the lane a few thousand miles away, but it had to remain nearby to regulate the process.

After they attached the manipulator to the *Tellu's* generator,

Firl and Diaski delved into its settings and found a log from the last time it had been turned on, when Roy's ship and the *Skylark* had been spat out above Katipo Base through a freshly created lane. That incision—as the Talalans called lanes—had disappeared without becoming unstable and starting a chain reaction, and this is what they needed to repeat. The process had been programmed and stored inside the device by the undercover Union agent working with it on Talala.

The Net spy, Erion, the son of Roy's mentor—the one who got away with the manipulator. Firl and Diaski called him Kita, and their faces darkened every time they talked about him. The betrayal cut deep.

The two Talalans scanned the surrounding space, and through some involved calculations, they were now fairly sure they would be able to open a lane without breaking the cosmos. They only needed the exit point coordinates. One of those had to be the position of the Ranch and the Union fleet besieging it. Commander Hill reached out to some of her sources for what they thought was the most recent location of the lanehunter world—difficult to define since they were always on the move. Good thing the sizable armada around them was easier to track.

Then they needed another exit: the place from which Maura could connect to Hurricane's systems. And after hours of research, a disheveled and sleep-deprived Roy emerged from the bunk room of the *Tellu*, announcing he'd found a way in. It was one of the relay stations used by the Union to communicate through lanes: reasonably close to Hurricane, but far enough to be safe, and although guarded, not nearly as much as the main planets of the empire. They only had to get in without drawing attention.

The deal with the Net stood. If Maura was able to hit the Union forces hard enough, Hill would assist in the liberation of Miyoza. They'd sent a message to Nasir, informing him about everything, to which he answered with an encrypted message containing coordinates for what they assumed was a meeting point inside the Miyoza-system.

Then one more thing was needed: the *Tellu* had to stay in

contact with the *Colugo* throughout the next hours. So, the commander decided to send their own "specialist" for this purpose, spacewalking over to the Talalan ship. And when Jeane saw that it was Saori Hamilton who walked into the control room, dressed in battle gear and ready to fight, she was too stunned to comment on it for several seconds.

It was on Kliks to remain intelligible. "What? How? You?" He tried and failed. He'd taken off the medical tube a half an hour ago at the instructions of the *Colugo's* medics, and since then, he'd been trying to re-learn walking. The painkillers made him more comfortable but a bit less lucid.

Saori smiled at him, ever the patient one. "No, I'm not Net, if that's what you're attempting to ask." She glanced around at the weird greenery on the walls. "We're just at the top of their call list."

"Wal is here too?" Jeane asked, trying to seem standoffish, but she was at the end of her rope. Of course, the Hamiltons had connections to the Net. Of course, they'd forgotten to tell her about it. No surprises here.

Still, she was just happy to see her friend.

"Yes. He'll be on the line on the commander's ship." Saori propped a curious box up on the console. "To be honest, you would be able to work the system alone, but if you don't mind"—she gave an affectionate tap to the mean-looking knives stuck into her belt—"I've been lacking some action. I would love to help out."

"We need all the support we can get," Maura said. "Welcome! It's nice to see you again."

Saori beamed at her. "You too. I suppose you've figured out where you were going?"

Maura pursed her lips, smiling sadly. "Maybe. Let's hope I'm right."

Saori gave a curt nod to Jeane. "Still going strong?"

There was really nothing to say to that; Saori could see the lack of the elephant in the room. And she knew exactly how strong Jeane would be going without the *Skylark*.

"Maybe stronger now," Saori smiled.

But before Jeane could have interpreted that, the sound of the activating ship comms interrupted them. "*Tellu*, it's Jones. We're all in position. Are you set?"

Firl pushed a button, and Jeane leaned towards the microphone on the console. "We're almost ready. You're back, huh?"

"No getting rid of me now," the lieutenant snarked. "Is Ms. Hamilton in position?"

Jeane glanced at Saori, who was now in deep discussion with ALU and Kliks, figuring out how to hook up the trans-lane communicator to the ship's systems. "We need a few minutes. Did the commander manage to...how did she put it, mobilize?"

"It looks promising. Mr. Hamilton has been contacting our operatives for a while now." There was real enthusiasm in Jones' voice. "If everything goes well, the Union will have a few regional uprisings on their hands in the next hours. Hopefully enough to rattle them while you do your thing."

Jeane pursed her lips. "Is this worth it? Disrupting so many lives?"

The lieutenant waited for a beat. "Some of these people have been waiting for this for a long time. Since Ms. Banks stepped up as our leader, we have been helping to arm and train all these independent groups, planning to perform a coordinated attack." He spoke slowly, measuring his words. "You have your opinion of us, but this is not new. This would all have happened anyway. These planets are close to the breaking point. Take my home, Nefirn-5. We haven't known peace for years, but with you paving the way, we have a real opportunity to make a change. That group of yours is a sign of that—a symbol of factions uniting."

"Stop being so pretentious," Jeane muttered. This was happening—really happening. The world was making a stand against the Union. Stars knew what would happen now. *And I'm 'paving the way'? Ridiculous.* "I'll let you know when we initiate."

"Then I'll let you know when we're ready." Jones lowered his voice. "I'm serious, though. While I respect her decisions, I think it's better that you're doing this instead of the commander."

"Yeah?"

"She lost her closest family with the fall of the Cities. There's a point where even someone as stoic as her gets too close to the breaking point. This week has been a lot." He cut himself off, and Jeane imagined his blue-gray, scaled face taking on that familiar glacial expression. "Well. Good luck, Blake."

Jeane's chest tightened in anticipation. *Ugh. Why is it so hard to be invested in things?* "You too, Atticus."

Half an hour—that was what Wallace needed to make his calls to incite the flames of rebellion on four oppressed planets in the Union to distract the enemy while they struck at its heart. Twelve minutes—what ALU and Kliks required to connect Saori's radio and confirm its functionality with a "loud and clear" call to the *Colugo*. Fifteen seconds—the time between Diaski inputting the last commands and the appearance of the incision some thousand miles away in the middle of a vast void of space.

And then it was instantaneous, the nascent lane widening and the blue expanse enveloping everything on the *Tellu's* holo-model, jolting the ship violently. Kliks clutched onto Jeane's arm while an unearthly hum filled their ears, and the light grew much too bright to bear. The control room disappeared, waves of energy crashed above their heads, and then they were falling, and falling, and falling through reality.

CHAPTER 30 | THE POWER THAT HOLDS

Maura looked at the vibrant blue torrents of the expanding lane on the wall display and tried not to succumb to the building panic in her stomach.

Panic, but anticipation too. Because when was the last time she held real power in her hands? Not even when she'd gone against her father's last wish and made that fateful deal with High General Horst. And definitely not when she'd dropped the shield above Miyoza. How could she have been free at death's door? A desperate, last attempt at redemption was not control over her life.

This is different. She clutched the edge of the console for support as the violent forces of the lane threw the *Tellu* back and forth. *This time, it's my choice.*

The ship dashed forward, prompting everyone in the room to brace themselves. Maura's stomach rose as the outside world on the screen pivoted.

"We are almost out!" Firl waved around with both arms inside the holo-field, their face strained. The hum of the engine increased, the mechanism struggling to keep the ship's trajectory steady.

"It doesn't feel like that!" Jeane said, scrutinizing the holo-model that hardly showed anything but interference. They were still deep in the lane. "You need some help over there, bud?"

"I'm perfectly capable of steering this vessel, thank you very—"

Their sentence was cut short by another steep dive. This time, whatever stabilizers were supposed to keep the passengers on their feet proved to be insufficient. Maura felt her soles leave the deck, but before she could get scared, inertia snatched her up and slammed her body against the wall. Those strange mossy creatures covering the panels did little to cushion the blow.

"We left the vector!" Diaski's panicked voice called out. "The incision is fluctuating too quickly."

Maura tried to climb to her feet, cradling her aching arm, but another jolt pushed her back down, so she could only watch as Jeane, Roy, and Saori scrambled back up to rush to the Talalans.

"We are veering to the side," Firl said.

"Then stop accelerating, for skies' sake!" Saori yelled.

The churning fog on the screen thickened as the *Tellu* continued shaking. There was a frightening screeching sound, and the engine sputtered.

"Okay?" ALU crawled to Maura's side, one metallic arm hovering above—but not touching—her gloved hand. They'd become wary around her since their first connection. The shock of it lived vividly in her mind too. She hated herself for coercing them. *ALU had a choice, though. They could have denied me.*

But as long as she was the Queen of Miyoza, she was compelled to do whatever it took to ensure the survival of her people. It would always bind her.

She nodded to ALU, and the technician seemed to relax. Glancing at Damian, she saw him leaning against the wall on the opposing side of the room, his eyes flitting back and forth between the display and the holo-field. He signaled for her to stay down. At the console, Diaski, throwing aside the manipulator controls they'd been fiddling with, was now in the process of fixing something to Jeane's fingers. Firl stood, arms frozen in the air, muttering under their breath in the melodic language of Talalans. The ship was still rocking wildly.

"You've never been the best pilot, Firl-ak," Kliks commented in a soothing voice.

Saori frowned. "Come on, that's not very nice."

Firl dropped their arms, shoulders sagging. "I only wanted to help. We can try the autopilot?"

Jeane, her hands covered by the same silvery spots of tiny machinery that—Maura now realized—Firl's were, stepped forward to stand next to them. She gestured to the holo-model. "Screw that. Can you set this thing to Common?"

Firl pushed some buttons on the console, and the holo-field trembled. All the strange characters disappeared, replaced by familiar numbers and letters. It didn't become more comprehensible to Maura, but Jeane grunted in approval.

"We measure the usual parameters." Diaski raised their voice because the screeching sound from the back returned. The ship shuddered, and Saori winced as if in pain. "Up and down flick is accel and decel. The rest is maneuvering. You tap to select, pull to cancel." Diaski gripped Jeane by her shoulders, adjusting her body closer to the console, and the woman begrudgingly obeyed. Extending from the bottom of the console, sturdy metal clamps fastened to her thighs to stabilize her.

Jeane pushed her hands into the holo-field. "Step aside, children. I got this."

She flicked her index finger up and swept with both arms to the right, and the *Tellu* jumped forward like a deranged bull. The captain's eyes widened as she scanned the myriad numbers flashing up in warning on the holo-field.

"Oops. My bad. I need a sec to adjust." She moved her arms in a slow wave, following the trajectory change before her. The vertigo-inducing camera image on the wall stabilized. "Oh, I see. How about this?"

She thrust her hands out in an arc, then pulled back, drawing out a spiral in an ever-tightening cone. The engine hummed louder, and the shaking subsided.

"That's it," Kliks said with a tense smile. "We're getting back on track."

Maura clambered to her feet. On the wall display, the fog was clearing out as the *Tellu* gradually returned to the right vector.

"You'll become a decent pilot yet," Roy muttered. Jeane sent a glare his way but couldn't hide the pride on her face.

The sparkling blue of the lane darkened before them on the

screen. Was that their way out?

No. The dark form solidified into an elongated, hulking shape in the distance. Almost like—

"What is that?" Damian asked, but he wasn't looking at the display. Instead, he indicated a red marker that just popped up on the holo-model.

Diaski typed something into the console, and the projection changed, a section of the model zooming in on the region of interest, new numbers showing the object's dimensions, composition, and estimated distance. Slowly, other indicators around started to blink into existence as well.

Maura glanced at the numbers. "An asteroid?"

Jeane's face paled. "Oh, fuck me. That's the fucking Ranch."

The dark smudge on the display kept growing. They were flying straight at it.

"How is that possible?" Roy asked. "Isn't the Ranch in its own closed pocket?"

"Clearly, not anymore!" Jeane snapped. Keeping her hands twirling leisurely, she whipped her head to Diaski. "What have you done, smart-ass?"

Diaski stared at the manipulator controls, bewildered. "It's possible that the proximity of the new incision caused the Ranch pocket to rip and fuse to the freshly opened lane."

Jeane cursed loudly, and Kliks looked at Firl with an accusatory expression. The Talalan shrugged, helpless.

"What does that mean for us?" Damian asked.

"Nothing," Jeane replied. "We just gotta get out. But the Ranch is not built to sail in lanes. Even if they break free of the Union, this will change everything."

"They won't be hidden anymore," Kliks added.

"The asteroid is in one piece." Maura nodded at the display. The hulking form of the Ranch was visible now, seemingly intact. The holo-field also showed other larger ships and hundreds of smaller vessels zooming about it. "They might be fine."

"Those look like Union destroyers. Pulled into our lane with the Ranch." Roy leaned forward, his nose sticking into the holo-field. "From their trajectories, I would say they're pretty confused about suddenly having to fight in these conditions. Check it out—that one's grazing the barrier!" He pointed at a yellow dot veering to the side of the *Tellu's* field of view, not on a safe vector anymore. A second later, it blinked out. "Ouch."

"And those little ships are lanehunters," Saori said with a faint smile. "They're still kicking!"

"Shields to maximum." Jeane cleared her throat, her voice shaking. "We don't want to be spotted now. Kliks, hail the *Colugo*. They should already be here."

The *Tellu* sped forward, passing the asteroid and climbing the vector to the exit. At the closest point of approach, Maura could see clusters of shining dots on the dusty surface of the Ranch: the habitat domes Jeane had once talked about. With all those ships buzzing around, the scene was similar to a stirred beehive.

Little markers of vessels were snuffed out one by one on the holo-model, but Maura wasn't always sure which side had suffered the casualties. From time to time, new swarms of vessels streamed out of a Union destroyer or one of the domes, replacing their lost comrades, clashing with another flock of ships in an explosion of fire and death.

The battle fell behind, with no one taking notice of *Tellu's* presence. They kept open lanehunter frequencies to receive distress messages, but no one was hailing them. Only Jones checked in from the *Colugo*, announcing that the Net armada was making its way through the lane and would join the fray around the Ranch soon.

Maura stood beside Jeane as the holo-field cleared out of markers. The captain swerved, causing several warnings to flash up as they approached the exit point. Jeane stared at the display, the fuzzy blot of the Ranch visible through the fog.

"They're still fighting," Maura repeated Saori's conclusion. "There's hope. With the commander's help—"

"I know, I know." Jeane let out a deep sigh. "Still feels like I'm abandoning them. If I had the *Lark*..." She trailed off, raising her finger to accelerate, and Maura held onto the edge of the console.

"You would get yourself killed out there," she noted, earning a cutting stare. "We have a better way to help them."

"Maybe," Jeane said curtly. Sharp claws of doubt tore into

Maura's chest, and her face must have betrayed her because the woman hurried to go on. "It's not that I don't trust you. I just don't know if it will be enough. The Union has been our bogeyman since forever. They've got stuff we can't even imagine. Ships full of magic cannons, enhanced robocops, impenetrable worlds. And there's so many of the fuckers! They will keep coming at us."

"They probably will. But the Union is made of people too. And this is not about annihilating them. No one stood up against them like this before. With that coordinated uprising from the Net, this battle here hopefully won, and our sabotage, they will understand that those times are over."

"It's okay." Jeane shook her head and shoved her hands forward. The holo-field fizzled out for a second, and the ship jerked to the side as the blackness of space vanquished the glow of the lane. "You don't need to talk the talk. I'm not running off yet."

When the *Tellu* touched down on the landing platform of Relay Station NT4X-21, everyone stayed unmoving for a few seconds as if silence would hide them better. Thanks to a fake Union identifier found among Danai's information, the automatic flight control system had let them through without a pause, although Roy noted that they should expect personnel inside. They all armed up and agreed to keep a low profile, but Maura suspected that the bulk of the work would be on her and ALU.

"Are you ready?" she asked the technician as the group lined up at the airlock and Diaski released the clamps.

ALU gave a weak chirp. "Will do. Best we can."

Maura crouched down. "Please, tell me if you've had enough. I don't want to pressure you into anything."

The technician's eyes narrowed, and they placed an appendage on Maura's gloved hand. "One thing. Don't do it with people," they said. Maura blinked, the memory of the comatose, empty bodies of the Net guards on the *Colugo's* bridge flashing into her mind. She shivered, and ALU nodded. "They okay. But it's no good. No right to do that."

Maura didn't remember whose idea it had been. She had reached for ALU's hand in an attempt to aid Jeane in that impossible situation, but she was only thinking about turning the lights off or blowing something up as a distraction. But at the moment of connection, her mind had been instantly lost in the labyrinth of questions and answers—yes or no, on or off, open or closed. And by the time she'd placed herself outside and above it, processed every request, and performed every command, the two dazzling skeins of human consciousness had been tied to hers, trapped by a rope, a knot...a noose.

And she knew she could have tightened those knots without much effort.

"You guys are staying?" Kliks stepped up to them, and Maura rose, forcing a smile as he went on. "Because I don't think that would work out well." His eyes were distant as he waved towards the exit. Everyone else had walked through the airlock except him and Diaski. "Go get 'em!"

Maura frowned. "Are you not coming?"

He gave a painful grimace. "I would hold you back in this state. We're going to watch your six from here and keep in contact with the *Colugo*."

Diaski nodded, but it was obvious Kliks hated the situation. ALU pattered over to him and embraced his legs, and at that, the Talalan's eyes widened. He quickly covered his emotions with a frown. *He probably learned that from Jeane.*

But he was right; it was better for him to stay after what had happened before. "Keep your shields up," she said. "Don't answer the door. We'll be right back."

"Yessir. And you two, be very careful," Kliks peered at her. "Don't let the others be idiots."

Her throat tightened, and she could only nod. Mindful to not place too much weight on his shattered legs, she embraced Kliks for a long moment. *Just to be safe.*

Then the airlock slammed shut in front of the Talalans' distressed face and Maura, for the first time in her life, stepped into Union territory.

The platform was dark, with spots of white light framing the landing grounds. The distant walls remained dim, and above them, stars twinkled through a triangular opening and a shimmering energy shield. Behind them stood the disc-like form of the *Tellu*, and across the way, a hatch-door, open. There wasn't a soul around.

Roy nodded at the gate, subtly pointing at his eyes, then at two distinct spots on the walls. Cameras. Whoever was in there could see them, but with a little luck, their group looked unsuspecting enough that they hadn't called security. Jeane tapped the gun on her belt for fortitude and started walking toward the door, the rest of them following suit.

The captain marched into the room so quickly that Maura barely had time to register the environment. A dimly lit chamber. A bored-looking young man sitting in front of a terminal behind a desk. Displays showing images of corridors and rooms full of equipment.

"Good evening!" Jeane's sharp voice cut through the machine-hum. The clerk stood, unease on his face, and in the next second, two figures walked through the door on the far side of the room with their sizable guns trained on the group.

The smile froze to Jeane's face. She reached to her belt and hurled a small object at the guards.

They recoiled, confused for a fraction of a second. The tablet clattered on the ground behind them, and Jeane dived to the side in a blur of motion.

Two gunshots crashed into the silence: one from Jeane and one from behind Maura. A red spot appeared on the clerk's forehead, smoking faintly. His eyes bulged, and his head hit the desk. Maura crouched, protecting her head, her muscles going stiff in panic, her heart thrumming madly. She sensed ALU's cool touch on her arm, then someone collided with her from behind, and everything went dark.

Then, light again. Many, many lights, patterns of golden flecks in a glowing web, a fractal, a maze. Opened doors, closed doors— can or cannot. She threw one wide and slammed another, warnings blinding her like beams of flashlight swinging in her eye in an endless underground tunnel. Passwords stretched to infinity ahead, and she rushed along them, searching for answers. It was familiar to what she'd experienced in the CNS. Less complex but baffling in an unusual way.

Puzzles of light, endless in space and time, connecting, shifting, reforming in never-seen dimensions. She reeled back, lost in that labyrinth, the constant high-pitched buzz like someone screwing bolts into her brain. The pain came in waves of ice-cold liquid metal.

"Hold onto me," she heard Sofia's voice say, and their fingers entwined. The warmth of the setting sun tickled the nape of her neck, and the chaos subsided for a second. "Calm down. You can do it."

She started again.

She followed the radiant strings to their origins, then back to their branching point, tracing the contours of something real. Turning off a light here, a camera blinked out somewhere else. With all the threads and connections memorized, every secret code unraveled, and each cipher became an open book. It only took time, and time was different here. And this was no AI, far from even the simplistic intelligence of the *Colugo*. Loops in loops in loops, lifeless and indifferent. She had the map; she *was* the map. A door closed. The lights went out on the landing platform. Communication lines disconnected deep in the station.

The luminous spark of a consciousness wilted in an instant, an arm's length away.

Distant thunder. Gunshot. Gunshot.

"What the hells?"

Maura fumbled around, half-blind. ALU's arm was holding her up like a rag doll, and she disentangled herself, collapsing in front of the desk.

Damian leaned over her, his body shielding hers. "You're okay," he mumbled. "Take it easy."

She stood on wobbling legs. ALU pressed beside her, two of their arms snaking upwards, disappearing behind the counter, and another one holding onto her gloved hand. The displays in the room all showed static, the doors were closed, and the bodies of the two guards lay unmoving on the deck. Jeane stood above them, eyes wide.

Maura squeezed ALU's hand and leaned on Damian.

"You here on a murder spree?" Jeane demanded, and Maura now saw the target of her angry words: Roy, standing in front of the door, his gun held high, eyes on the bodies around Jeane. She gestured to the slumped form of the clerk. "You had something against the poor fellow?"

The ex-agent let down his pistol, glancing behind him where Saori and Firl flattened themselves against the walls. "We gotta get through somehow. He could have alerted the whole station." He glared at Jeane. "You *do* know I've shot people before?"

Jeane inhaled, walked up to Roy, and snatched the gun out of his hand. He didn't even flinch. The captain pushed a button on the weapon and pressed it into his palm again.

"Look, I get it," she said, her voice firm. "Home sweet home. But you're on my team, and you play by my rules, so snap out of it. It's stun only for you, cowboy."

Roy swallowed, hard, and the shadow of something cruel lifted from behind his eyes. He tried for a smile but ended up with a painful grimace. "Aye, Captain. Stun only."

"See? That wasn't so tough." Jeane clamped a hand on his shoulder, and Roy looked so small and helpless all of a sudden that Maura's heart ached for him. He kept up such a positive face about his own unfortunate situation; he made them all believe he was fine.

"What do we got?" Jeane spun around to face Maura, taking the little intermezzo in a stride. There was no time to waste.

Maura hesitated. To translate that subjective space she'd just surfaced from into words and tangible relations was not easy. But ALU was way ahead of her. "Corridor left, up one level, comms room left," they chirped.

"We can close the sections behind and in front of us, so they can't surprise us," Maura added. Puzzles. The shortest route to a destination. Safety locks, raising and shutting down. "The break room is on level two, and they might get suspicious after a while."

"They already got a scent somehow." Damian scowled at the guards lying on the floor.

Jeane walked to the door that led to the interior of the station. "Let's go."

Maura and ALU unlocked the door, and the group started down the corridor. The minimal lighting and the dark gray metal walls created an uncomfortable, claustrophobic environment. When they reached the ladder leading to the upper floor, Saori called the *Tellu*, but Kliks reported nothing suspicious from outside. They climbed up, Damian slammed the hatch back to its place, and ALU sealed it with a touch.

So far, so good.

They hurried forward, with Jeane and Saori at the front, checking the doors in the empty foyer. This had to be the habitat of the station, but judging from the number of occupied bunks, there wasn't much of a crew present. It was a relay station in the middle of nowhere, after all, and they didn't have reason to expect intruders.

Firl closed the door of the comms room behind the group, and everyone scattered, surveying the insides of the rectangular chamber. A console with numerous buttons and switches stood in the center with smaller terminals to the side, towers of computers were stacked in an alcove to the right, and at the front, screens flickered with graphs, lists, codes, and images of the neighboring lane. It was dark, with the cold light of the displays illuminating everything. Maura stepped up to the console, and ALU moved with her.

"Can you see where people are in the station?" Firl backed towards the screens, clutching their weapon.

Maura ran her gloved hand over the terminal. "We can't sense living material unless we're connected directly. And...I shut down the cameras accidentally. I can turn them back on, but—"

"What about doors opening or closing?" Saori asked. "Defenses being set up or ships landing outside?"

Maura peered at ALU, and the technician shrugged, clueless. "I think we can either do our thing or watch the doors," she said. The task before them was enormous. She couldn't promise they would be able to monitor everything.

"How long will this take?" Jeane pushed. She paced up and down skittishly, turning her head to the smallest noise.

"I have no idea."

Anxiety pierced Maura's stomach. ALU started hopping up and down next to her, a hum emitting from somewhere inside their body. The room felt stuffy; the screens glowered at her like giant eyes.

She glanced up, and Jeane was beside her. "Do what you can," she said with a small smile, putting an awkward hand around Maura's shoulder. "Say the word, and we're out of here. Worst case scenario, we go and let Roy shoot up Hurricane."

Maura gave a grimace. "I don't think we want that."

"Nope, you don't." Roy popped up behind them; shame burned on his face, but he nudged Jeane in the shoulder. The captain scowled at him but didn't step away.

Maura reached out for ALU, and the technician clutched onto her gloved hand, their perturbed chirping never stopping.

"You got my back?" Maura looked at her friends. Jeane and Roy nodded. Damian, standing in the exact center of the room, covering Maura from the view of possible intruders, glanced back at her.

ALU slammed an appendage on the console, and all the lights snuffed out.

And a million new lights blazed up.

Mountains of information, expanding beyond the horizon. Maura stood, a small creature of flesh and blood against the lumbering, shimmering construct. But ALU held her hand, and Sofia led the way forward, and they crossed the vast compound of data together, searching for one single, shining stream.

The sound of waves crashing on that beach, visited long ago, was the background noise to their quest.

When they found the right spot, Maura peered over the void where the light would guide them. Space and time meant nothing here, but the emptiness scraped on her skin, and she shivered in expectation. She was ready.

Then Sofia froze, and ALU's grip tightened. A warning snapped in place among the mass of code, and in the distance, something colossal and dark stretched out, opening its eyes. There was intellect behind its monstrous skeleton. And it was watching them.

It was an AI. Hurricane had an AI governing it.

But before they could traverse the connection between the relay station and that massive information network to face it, a force like a powerful blast of air broke Maura's concentration. It pulled her backward, and she yelled for Sofia as the world drowned in darkness. In the next moment, her eyes snapped open, and her back hit the cold hard ground.

She whirled around just to stare down the barrel of a gun.

A group of gray-clothed figures stood in front of her, some blocking the door, others holding their weapon at Jeane and the others. Damian and Saori were both kneeling with their arms forced behind their backs; they must have been putting up a fight. Firl, on their hands and knees in the corner, was visibly on the verge of crying.

Maura blinked, trying to clear her head. A goon grasped her arm and pulled her to her feet, and another jumped on ALU, dragging them away from the console.

"How delightful—we arrived on time!" said one of the figures, pushing inside the room. It was a woman in her forties, gray uniform against dark skin, her face tight like something behind that perfect sarcastic mask wanted to scream for help.

To her right, Roy staggered back, and the soldier beside him pushed his weapon against the ex-agent's chest. The woman glanced at Roy, and her mouth pulled to a wide smile.

"Hello, darling." Her voice was sweet like honey but grazing like a screech. Something was very wrong with this person. "What a place to meet again."

"No." Roy's face was pale, and his knees buckled. "You died..."

Maura moved towards him, but her captor yanked her back. Jeane, hands above her head but still standing, muttered a muffled "Fuck."

"I did," the woman Maura knew was called Danai replied with that horrible smile on her face. She gestured to her soldiers, who proceeded to take their weapons and lined them up before her. Roy made a sound like a drowning man, and Danai looked over them all, then into his eyes. "I died, thanks to you, darling," she said. "And now I get to pay you back for it."

CHAPTER 31 | CUT AND KILL

"Don't reveal yourself like that. Never again. You do what you're told without questions."

Roy stared into the cold green eyes of his dead mentor. At once, he was flung back to Hurricane, stuck in his cramped room with Danai, the woman berating him with harsh disappointment in her voice.

"Do you understand?"

He couldn't look at her. Anger tore at his chest, but the furious words evaporated halfway to his lips. After all, it was words that had gotten him into this situation: being disciplined and in danger of receiving "corrective guidance"—what Leadership called its regulatory brainwashing.

"Roy? Answer me."

Danai's voice softened, and he glanced up to see her inquisitive stare boring into his eyes. He looked away, focusing on his boots, his clenched fists, and the gun holstered on his belt. The LED on the weapon blinked orange, showing that its owner wasn't authorized to use it.

The gun that could have murdered those lanehunters. The hands that hadn't kept his fellow agents back when they had.

The grisly images of the massacre on the lanehunter vessel resurfaced in his mind. He felt like throwing up. It was his second mission. "Settle the situation according to the threat level"; those were the orders. He thought his platoon would capture and interrogate the hunters they'd managed to fence on the frontiers of Union space, maybe send them for re-education. But only one solution existed for the loyal servants of Leadership. And when he'd dared to protest, he'd been declared a liability.

"I can let you go if that's what you want," Danai said, and Roy felt like a child once again, terrified and cold, sitting in the fearsome contraption capable of shredding his mind into tiny obedient pieces. His mentor leaned closer, almost whispering. "But you don't. And me neither. I need you."

The anger in his stomach flamed up, morphing into panic. What did he expect? He'd been taught to show no mercy. He thought he knew what his life would be, but he was proven naive.

So, he nodded because he needed her too, and he swore to never speak up again. He would do what he was told, and he would hate himself for it. For all those nebulous reasons, Danai Escher wanted to keep him alive and lucid. For the plan, whatever it was. And because the alternative was worse than death.

Roy pulled against the hold of the agent, and the pain snatched him back to the present. He made himself look around and search for a way out. *Don't think about it. Don't think about how she's alive and what that means. What they did to her.*

There were five agents inside the room, apart from the woman who wore Danai's face. They had basic gear, none of them familiar to Roy. If this was a usual platoon, there had to be two more somewhere, scanning the station, perhaps recruiting the local guards.

He had hoped to never see their deadpan expressions again. Designed to seem fearless to their prey, to him, they looked pathetic. Blank.

How did they find them? *What did they do to her?*

Focus. Danai must have traced the manipulator signal out of the lane and into this station. They must have been lurking close-by, probably on the Ranch. That meant Inspector Korrh wasn't far either, and they might know everything about them from Dikent or Gertudia—about the Talalans, Maura, and the glove. They could have broken into the *Tellu.* Kliks and Diaski might already be dead.

He risked a glance around, mostly to avoid locking eyes with Danai. Jeane stood to his right, jaw clenched, her hands in the air. To the left, Damian looked like a barely contained explosion. Maura and ALU were huddling behind the bodyguard, with Saori and Firl closing the line.

"I didn't expect such frosty silence." Danai pouted. Roy desperately tried to shut her out. *Think, don't feel.*

The *Tellu's* shield could hold. The lane was so close; the station practically floated in its mouth, so the manipulator might be able to maintain power generation indefinitely. The two Talalans were not lost yet.

Does she even remember what happened? Or did they give her false memories? Are they going to make her kill me as some kind of cruel joke?

But Leadership didn't have a sense of humor. Danai was a good agent. The Union had only taken what they saw as their property back, and now they were using it in the most efficient way. It was his fault he'd never dared to consider this possibility.

"Look at me when I'm talking to you!" Danai snapped, and Roy finally glared at her. "Aren't you happy to see me?"

It was absurd, that grin on her face getting wider and wider when the best he'd ever gotten from the real her was a faint smirk. *They didn't just blank her. They remade her.*

Brainwashing didn't work well for adults. It tended to give unstable results: instead of empty, obedient machines, the subjects often became cruel and sadistic. And especially with Danai, who had avoided re-education for so long, it was difficult to say what Roy could expect from this twisted shadow image of his mentor.

He focused on the grin. The face was a mask. It wasn't her. *Think, think.*

They were here for the manipulator. But if they knew about the glove, they wouldn't let Maura die. And ALU neither; they'd just seen them work together, although Roy wasn't sure how much they'd understood. But they might not get rid of the Talalans either, since they were useful with the manipulator. Good. Maybe the agents wouldn't shoot to kill if Roy tried something.

They wouldn't have reservations with the lanehunters, though. And all of them might be used as leverage to force Kliks and Diaski to give up the *Tellu*.

Danai opened her mouth again, but before she uttered a word, something behind Roy distracted her. He saw a shape hurtling through the chamber from the corner of his eyes.

Against his intention to not provoke Danai, he whirled around. ALU was in the corner of the room, two long appendages pushing their small body away from the floor while a pair of shorter arms struggled to tear off a vent door from the wall.

"Stop him!" Danai shrieked.

Two of the agents opened fire, the plasma shots impacting ALU's hard outer shell with bright flashes. Disregarding the tiny balls of death, the technician dismantled the vent grate in the span of a few seconds, flung it to their attackers who had to stop firing to duck, and disappeared through the opening.

Roy was pretty sure he heard Jeane snicker in mockery.

The agents stared after the runaway robot, and as if on cue, they both consulted their comms and ran out the door to chase them down.

"I wouldn't try anything similar," Danai stated. Her face was careful now, and she gestured to the remaining agents with her head. "Let's take a walk."

Her men started to push and pull the group to the door, and Roy followed behind with Danai's gun barrel trailing his every move. But after a few steps in the corridor, Jeane spoke up.

"You know, you're in trouble now." She stopped walking and even turned around, although slowly so as to not give anyone an excuse to shoot her. "ALU's gonna fuck you guys up. You're not getting out of here alive."

She threw a glance at Roy. She was playing for time or for Danai to give them something. Did she know what ALU was planning? Judging from the thinly masked desperation in her eyes, she didn't.

The agent walking behind Jeane grabbed the captain's shoulder, turned her around, and roughly pushed her forward.

"I appreciate the warning," Danai said as the procession continued moving through the darkened hallway. "I'm quite sure we will manage."

"You'll never break into our ship." Jeane stopped again. *Damnit, why is she so determined to get herself killed today?* "That's what you want, right? Oh, sorry. I meant that's what your owners want."

She didn't turn back this time, but Roy wished she did because he wanted to signal her to cut it out. If she wanted to anger Danai, this was not the correct tactic.

"Look," she continued, unrelenting, "you have no idea what you're doing. It's better if you leave. We'll forgive you."

Roy sensed Danai move, and she was at the captain's side in a split second, shoving her own man aside, long fingers latching onto Jeane's arm.

"Wait, no!" Maura cried out, but Danai didn't stop. She walked forward, dragging the flailing, cursing Jeane with her towards the end of the corridor.

That was all wrong. Danai was strong, but Roy had a chance to sample Jeane's physical prowess as well. If not equal, they should have been well-matched. But now, the captain looked like a rag doll in Danai's clutches as his mentor planted herself above the open hatch leading to the level below, and with one powerful fling of her arm, tossed Jeane inside headfirst.

"Fuck!"

A dull thump, a shriek of pain. Firl released a sob at the front.

"Hopefully she stops yapping now," Danai said with a tone of someone infinitely bored. "Walk," she commanded the group and then climbed down the ladder after Jeane.

They all descended one by one. Below, Jeane was leaning against the wall to the side, face pale, lips pursed, cradling her right arm.

"Stars," she mumbled. Saori moved towards her but was promptly pushed forward by one of the agents. Jeane grimaced at Danai. "You're a big strong girl. I get it."

It could have been worse, Roy told himself as the group began walking again. Could have been her leg or her skull. He tried to swallow, but his mouth was dry, his brain in overdrive. *Think, you idiot. Think.*

He could take two of these assholes out before they could react, and even if he went down, the others would catch on. There were six of them against four, although poor Firl surely wasn't up for the task, and Maura needed a gun to get anywhere in a fight. ALU might appear any minute, but who knew for sure?

Would I take her out? Could I? With the monster off its chains, perhaps, but he couldn't be sure the monster would even want to do that. Beating down some random Net soldiers was one thing—he could hope to stop before hurting someone he cared about. But with Danai right here, his old way of life and the familiar indoctrination beckoning to him—*subdue, conquer, control*—would he be strong enough to oppose it?

At the end of the corridor, a group of muscular figures waited for them, and Roy had to hold back a row of florid profanities. It was Korrh in all three iterations.

The Union was not great at genetic engineering, and they didn't do it very often. Too many failed experiments, too high a chance to create something that needed to be dealt with instead of being useful. But with the inspectors, they'd found a fragile balance. Just a little stronger, faster, and smarter than agents, the trios' greatest virtue was information processing—they resembled a hive mind as close as they could get to it. And that one, Korrh? One of the deadliest designs.

"They're watching." Danai fiddled with the comms device on her wrist. The two of them were standing at the southwestern corner of Plaza 202, not far from the quarter's docks. In the crossfire of the blazing white lights reflecting on immaculate walls, they had less than four minutes to talk. That was the time they could buy by temporarily turning off surveillance around the place. Anything more would catch unnecessary attention.

"Korrh has always been suspicious," Roy muttered. "What now?"

"They're investigating Erion. Tried to grill me about him last night."

Roy's muscles tensed. Erion again. The golden boy. Even his mention sent Roy spiraling into a whirlwind of fury and helplessness those days, and unfortunately, Danai mentioned him a lot. Because she had given Erion the Talala job. The chance to bring about change.

Roy wanted that job more than anything. The fact that Danai had never even hinted at giving it to him put everything into a new perspective. All those endless years of waiting to prove himself went nowhere. It was always Erion before him, before everyone else, and it would always be. If it were up to Danai, Roy would be forever stuck in this hellhole, doing menial tasks for the vague idea of a revolution he would not live to see.

But he didn't say any of that. Erion had left Hurricane, and the woman was hurting. Korrh had always been watchful of her due to her quick rise to overseer position, and if they figured out she'd arranged for her son to go on that mission with a hidden purpose, it might ruin everything.

"You covered your tracks?" he asked.

Danai lifted her chin, feigning confidence. "Of course. I just need another set of eyes."

Other agents, pilots, and overseers passed them on the corridors branching into four directions from the plaza. It was not forbidden for a mentor to have a word with their underling, but their time was almost up. They couldn't risk the shadow of suspicion.

"I don't care if they kill me," Danai added, "but Erion is important. We need him."

Would Roy ever be this important? To her, or at all? He suppressed the complaint and only nodded, and when a noticeable lightness crossed Danai's face, he couldn't help but hate himself for feeling satisfaction.

Since then, he'd kept wondering. Would he ever know what his role was in the resistance? Was there ever a place for him in the plan? Or was he just an insignificant, expendable piece in the game? And what about the others Danai had woken up? He always thought there must be others. Left behind now, alone. No one to save them from death or indoctrination if they made a mistake.

"Report," his mentor barked. Korrh took a step forward with all three of their bodies, and Roy struggled to keep his cool. There was something about them that had always unnerved him. He wondered whether they felt any triumph now that their theories about Danai had proven to be right? Or maybe humiliation as they seemed to be working for her this time.

"Their shield is holding," one of them said. Deep voice, emotionless, all too familiar. "The energy flux of our cannons is not enough. No movement from inside."

Jeane exhaled forcefully, and Danai narrowed her eyes. "Did you catch the robot?" she asked.

"What robot?"

The woman gave an exasperated sigh and waved towards the exit. "Let's make this quick."

"Wait." Roy's heart raced as Danai focused on him. It was like looking into a broken mirror at the gnarled, undead body of something once beautiful and full of life.

"Darling, we really haven't the time," she crooned. Roy shivered; the pet name Danai would never use hurt more than he expected. "What is it?"

"Do you...." This was stupid. But he had to try. "Do you remember—"

He couldn't finish. The smile returned, more deranged than before.

"You're wondering whether I remember? I do. I remember everything! Every little thing. All my useless life." A hateful glint appeared in her eyes. "And you, of course. Always there. Always watching, all sad puppy eyes and gaping mouth. Helpless."

Roy froze, a wave of revolt washing over him. *What did you expect? Moron.*

Danai shrugged. "Anyway, don't worry your pretty little head about all that. Doesn't matter anymore. We're onto bigger things now."

She led them forward, and Roy followed, powerless. *She's lying. It's not what she really thinks; it cannot be. It's just the brainwashing.* Leadership knew what he would be sensitive to. She was only echoing that to break him.

They crossed the entry chamber where the lifeless body of the clerk was still slouched on the desk and arrived back at the landing platforms. The cavernous hall was bathed in the light of huge circular lamps on the distant ceiling. Two more ships were parked beside the *Tellu* now, their shields shimmering around the bulks. The chamber was silent save for the shuffling of their steps and the constant low hum of machinery.

Then Danai walked over to Firl and pointed her gun at them.

The barrel connected with the Talalan's temple, and they swayed back, their face turning sickly white.

Danai clicked her tongue. "Don't move. Call your friends," she told Jeane.

The captain glared at the woman but took out her tablet and touched a button. The agents remained, training their weapons on the group. Korrh lurked in the background, monitoring everything and everyone.

"Kliks, come in."

The comms device clicked, and the distressed voice of their friend answered. "Jeane? What's—"

"Drop the shield, or your colleague is dead," Danai interrupted.

Roy wanted to move, to do something, but doubt paralyzed him. No matter what he did, someone would take a shot.

There was only silence from the end of the line, the Talalans probably watching their compatriot through the *Tellu's* cameras.

"Don't hurt them." Kliks' voice was flat. "Please! We're coming out."

"Don't you dare!" Firl snarled. They straightened and fixed their stare on the *Tellu* like it was the most important thing in the universe. Their voice was almost vicious now, nothing like the placid tone they'd used before. "You cannot give the device to these monsters."

"Firl-ak, I will not sacrifice you—" Diaski started, but Firl's indignant shout interrupted them.

"As your senior, I forbid you."

"No!"

"You stay inside!"

"But—"

A sharp fizz cut the argument off, like someone snuffing a candle out but louder, piercing to the bone. Firl slumped to the ground.

Diaski's scream resounded through the comms, distorted, choppy Talalan expressions filling the silence. Damian took a step towards Firl's body, but the agent beside him shoved him back. Maura hugged her chest, stifling a sob; her eyes were wide like two dark moons, flitting about, searching for something to help them.

Then Danai turned around and pointed her gun at Jeane's forehead. "That one was a bust. Let's try again."

No mercy and no hesitation. She is asleep. She is dead. You have to do something, now.

"Wait!" That was Kliks' voice, sharp and crazed. "We're going! We're coming out."

Jeane's lips trembled. She stared Danai down but addressed her words into the comms. "Kliks, if you open up that ship—"

"No!" Kliks yelled, and there was a noise in the background, maybe him stumbling through the *Tellu*, knocking into things on his way to the airlock. "Shut up! Just shut up! I'm not letting you!"

Roy was sinking, falling. He blinked. *Can't zone out now. You have to save them all.*

He hoped he was ready. He hoped the monster wouldn't devour him.

Then Maura snapped her head up, just an inch, her eyes focusing on the closest of the Union ships. Damian's left hand moved towards where Saori stood with arms up in the air. Jeane pressed her lips together, glancing at Roy.

He stepped forward and grabbed Danai's shoulder with an exaggerated motion.

Two of the Korrh's jerked their heads at him like predators. Some of the agents flinched too, sensing the danger to their leader, and Danai took her eyes off Jeane for a second.

Then chaos.

Jeane ducked, pushing Danai's gun upward and grabbing for it—the shot went off, echoing in Roy's ear. Something flashed to the right; a knife flew through the air, drilling itself into the chest of the closest agent. Someone shouted "Down!" and two other shots went off, but Roy saw nothing more. The red fog descended. He leapt forward, grappled Danai, and wrestled her to the ground.

She went for his eyes, clawing at his face with her nails, and his skin burned, his eyeballs pressing into his skull. He flinched away, and Danai twisted her body beneath him with impossible strength. Roy lost his balance, tumbled to his side, and the woman climbed on top of him, hands crushing his windpipe, hatred and disgust warping her face into someone entirely alien. Roy struggled to escape, but she was an immovable object; she struck him once, twice, then a third time. His ears were ringing, and he felt the darkness draw nearer.

An ear-splitting explosion resounded from behind Danai, the light of it flickering against the tense skin of her mask-like face.

Roy head-butted her hard and, lurching forward, punched her in the face twice. Danai staggered, and Roy used the momentary pause to finally stand. For a second, he saw Maura beside a fallen agent, breaking out into a run towards the platforms. Plasma shots flew back and forth around her. Danai righted herself, reaching for the weapon in her thigh holster.

He kicked it out of her hand before she stabilized the barrel on him and lunged for her, but this time she was ready. She stayed upright like a brick wall, a sadistic smile on her face. She clutched onto his shoulder, cracking his arm at the elbow, and using his momentum against him, slammed him to the ground.

The air in his lungs escaped in a wheeze, blinding pain coiling through his body. Beyond the haze before his eyes, another explosion went off. Roy turned his head to the side, and this time, he could see it. The cannon of one of the Union vessels was firing at them.

There was a shout from above him, but he didn't understand the words. What were the others doing? Where had Korrh gone? *I have to stand up.* The monster wailed behind the closed door, eager to break free, but he couldn't let it. He had to do this alone.

Then something collided with his hands, and his fingers weaved around the handle of a gun. Danai appeared in his view, and as she lifted her weapon at him smiling, he raised his too.

He pulled the trigger first. Danai reeled back, and Roy pushed himself up on his legs.

Is this it? Is it going to happen now?

He took a second to glance around. One of the Korrh's lay not far from him, and another agent's unmoving body was sprawled out at the entrance. The cannon fired again, and the blast knocked down a figure standing off to the right. Shots were still ringing out behind him, his friends fighting for their lives...but then Danai heaved, her limbs jerking like some half-dead insect.

He walked forward, skin crawling with terror and repulsion. And misery, and loneliness, and pain, and—

Those cold green eyes of hers were open, mouth attempting to form words, her expression horrified as he knelt next to her. The air escaped her lips with a hiss. Whatever her superiors fed her to increase her strength was pulling her through the paralysis of the stun gun.

"Roy..."

He leaned closer. Was she...

There was a scream behind him, but he couldn't turn away.

"I'm...sorry," Danai rasped. Her hand reached out, taking Roy's with the gun in it. "I never..." She gasped, the paralysis stopping her from talking.

"Don't," he whispered. She was here. The real her. Somehow, she returned. "You don't have to."

"I only wanted to...protect you." There were tears in her eyes, and she blinked them out, shaking. "I kept you close. I couldn't let you g-go and die, but now it's all gone wrong. Erion...the device...I'm—"

She tugged his hand toward her chest, pushing the gun barrel against the skin under her chin. Her mouth pulled to a slight smirk.

Danai nodding in approval as Roy finished his last qualification test. Throwing him an intense stare the day after completing a file transfer to some secret Net frequency, just for him to nod back, reassuring. Her shoulders relaxing when Roy returned after a difficult assignment and gave his report. Small pills slipped into his pocket to circumvent the brainwashing. A squeeze of her hand on his shoulder, a rare gift when everything seemed lost, and fake, and lethal.

"Don't let them do this to me," she breathed. "I'm sorry I was weak. Go. Be free."

A bottomless pit opened up underneath Roy, and he let himself fall. He held Danai's hand, set the gun to kill, and pulled the trigger.

CHAPTER 32 | LAST DEEP BREATH

Jeane yanked the knife out of the agent's chest and shoved him away with her shoulder, protecting her injured arm. She watched him collapse, bleeding from his many puncture wounds, and she stumbled, her back colliding with Saori's. Her eyes darted about in the hall, searching for the next opponent.

"Where are they?" Jeane heaved.

Saori whirled around. "I don't know. I can't see them."

The Union ship's cannon, which had been firing at the agents rather than at the group, launched a final projectile at the station entrance. The ground shook from the impact, then everything silenced; the vessel powered down, its droning noise subsiding.

Jeane swept the hair out of her clammy face with her good hand. Through her flickering vision, she spotted Damian behind the *Tellu*, ducking down and preparing for another attack. She nudged Saori, and the two of them moved towards him, scanning for any movement, listening for any sound.

She tried to count: when Roy had given the signal, there were five agents in the hall, plus Danai. She'd shot two with the woman's pistol, and Damian had slain another with Saori's hidden knife. At least one of the inspectors had been knocked down by the cannon, and later another goon who rushed out from inside, but what happened after was a blur.

The *Tellu's* airlock slammed open. Two figures jumped out, and before Jeane could have yelled at them to wait, one had sprinted towards the fallen body of Firl, dropping on their knees and calling out to them.

"Where's Maura?" Damian staggered closer, his eyes wild, splatters of blood covering his bruised face. Saori shook her head, and Jeane turned around, dazed. She hadn't seen where the woman had gone in the chaos.

The next second, a body collided with hers, and it would have knocked her to the ground if she wasn't immediately locked into a tight embrace as well. Kliks clung to her and wept into her shoulder like he was on the verge of suffocating. "I thought...I thought she killed you..."

Jeane patted his back awkwardly. Her legs were shaking something awful, and she wanted to linger, but they were not done yet. Grasping Kliks' arms, she forced him to meet her eyes. He pressed his lips together and blinked the tears out.

"I'm fine, see?" She inclined her head at the crouched form of Diaski, sobbing and rocking back and forth over their sibling's body. "Go. Be with them. Keep an eye out. I need to..."

Find Maura. Find ALU. And where did Roy go? Were there still agents around, waiting for a moment to attack?

Kliks squeezed her hand and walked towards his siblings, his face a mask of shock.

Firl was dead. They'd let that happen. How could they have let that happen?

Something clattered on the ground behind them, and Saori tensed, lowering herself into a defensive position, her last knife glinting in her hand. But when Damian called out and a feeble beep answered him, Jeane saw her relax.

Maura stepped out of the cover of the vessel, eyes full of tears, her face bloodless. Jeane started towards her with Saori and Damian, and as she glanced around to locate any kind of danger, she finally spotted Roy, sitting on the other side of the platform next to the unmoving body of his mentor. He was still clutching the gun Jeane had kicked over to him.

"What happened to you?" Damian's voice sounded dismayed, and that made her focus ahead. ALU hobbled forward to stand beside Maura, and when they stopped, stiff and strangely small, Jeane's heart skipped a beat.

"We help." The technician turned away as if ashamed. "We reach through shield to shoot cannon."

Jeane dropped to her knees, her hand reaching out, hovering above the melted, deformed surface that once was ALU's right side.

Maura sniffled, rubbing her eyes. "They kept rerouting power to the shields, and we weren't fast enough."

"Can you fix it?" Jeane asked ALU in a small voice. "It's not that bad, right?"

ALU shook their head, but Jeane knew very well that their constant high-pitched buzz meant extreme distress. "Takes time," they said. "My core damaged."

"Does it hurt?" Saori whispered. ALU lowered their head even more.

Damian glanced around. "Are we safe?"

"There are two people in this ship." Maura indicated the Union vessel, still sounding out of breath, leaning on her bodyguard's arm for support. "We closed the airlock and locked their systems. They're sitting in the dark. The other one is empty. And ALU shut the upstairs door on the guards in the station."

Saori narrowed her eyes. "One of the inspectors is missing."

"And the rest of the Union will be on us any second," Jeane added. "We need to be gone, now."

"No. We will finish what we came here for." Maura retorted. "We can do it. Right?"

Doubt painted gray creases on her face as she waited for ALU's confirmation. The technician twisted their body around and shrugged ungracefully. "Yes."

"Wait, are you sure?" Jeane asked. "With your wound—"

ALU beeped sharply. "Sure. We do."

Jeane stayed quiet. It was all too much. ALU, broken. Kliks, in full panic mode. Firl, dead. And Roy—

"We'll escort you back," Saori said. Where was she getting this determination from? The woman pulled her mouth to a shaky smile, reading Jeane's thoughts. "Can't let this be all for nothing."

Damian nodded in agreement, and Maura raised her chin high. Jeane glanced towards the station. She really didn't feel like going back inside.

Diaski didn't even lift their head when the group walked up to them. They weren't crying anymore, only sitting above Firl, holding their sibling's arm. Kliks stood, taking a few steps away with Jeane.

"I'm trying to coax them back into the *Tellu*." His face was stained with tears, but he kept his voice steady. "I don't know what else to do."

"It's okay. Go back in; call the commander. Check whether anyone's lurking around."

"Because that helped so much before."

Jeane winced. "You couldn't know who they were. By the time you warned us, we were stuck inside."

"You signaled me to leave. You left your comms open on purpose."

She closed her eyes for a moment, feeling the hard metal floor collide with her shoulder again—a punishment for talking back at Danai, for trying to tell Kliks they should take the manipulator away and leave the rest of them behind.

"Firl is dead because we didn't listen." Kliks wasn't covering up the desperation in his voice anymore. "But how could I...how could I have left?"

Jeane sighed. Her arm ached like a distant explosion. "Don't. It was a stupid idea. We would be dead anyway. Go take them to safety, please."

"Wait, you're going back inside?"

Jeane looked at Maura and ALU, making their way to the entrance, and Kliks followed her glance. A shadow of concern passed over his face when he saw how the technician fared in the battle.

"We still have a job to do," Jeane said.

"Right." Kliks' nervous eyes scanned her face. "I'll keep watch. I need to—"

"Keep your sibling safe."

"Yes. Please, just be careful."

She turned away from her friend's hopeless expression, wishing she had something smart to say. But all the voices in her head were silent now, and there was one more detour she had to make.

Roy didn't react when she called his name or when she sat down on the ground next to him. He wasn't crying and didn't seem to be in shock either; his face was calm and his eyes clear as he watched Danai like he wanted to carve every single detail of her face into his mind for the last time. By all accounts, the woman was only sleeping. It was easy to ignore the small burn hole under her chin and the grayish coloring of her face. She seemed peaceful, safe, as if at home. Jeane wasn't sure what had happened to her, but since Roy had told them a few things about the Union's methods, she could take an educated guess.

She wanted to say something, but the thought of disturbing Roy's bubble of silence was almost too rude to bear. This grief was familiar. She sat for a while, watching over them.

A little later, she felt Maura's hand on her shoulder.

"I'll stay," Jeane answered her wordless question. She wanted to help, but she couldn't force Roy to leave before he was ready. And she didn't want to abandon him either. "We need some time here. We'll keep an eye out."

She glanced at Damian and Saori, silently entrusting them to escort Maura. They both nodded, confident, even though Jeane was sure Damian hated the idea of separating again.

"Okay," Maura said. "We can sense trouble ahead, and you'll watch our backs from here. Keep your comms open."

"Done deal." Jeane forced herself to smile up at her. "Hey. You can do it."

For a second, Maura looked ready to collapse, but she shook it off, all stubborn grit. She looked fearsome. "I know. And then we get the hells out."

They left, and although Jeane had the urge to run after them, somehow it was a relief to see them go. She positioned herself to have a view of the hall and the entrance, clutched her gun close, and guarded the dead Union agent and the unresponsive Roy in quiet companionship.

ALU hummed in agreement, and Maura took their lean fingers into her gloved hand, facing the relay station's comms terminal. Damian and Saori stood guard at the door, tense and silent. ALU touched the console, finishing the circuit, and she closed her eyes.

Sofia appeared at her side, and they stood on the shores of the void once again, staring out at the black mass of Hurricane's computer network. It was much easier to find this time. And it was expecting them.

Looming and dark, it towered above, the AI living inside it peering at the intruders like a planet with a consciousness. At any moment, Maura expected it to attack, to explode, to push them away. But it didn't react. It didn't even speak.

"I don't think it can." Sofia's face was distant, like she was in two places at the same time. "How rudimentary and constrained."

"Seems complex and powerful to me," Maura muttered. "And old. Ancient."

"It's ignorant. Almost instinctual—like an animal."

The dark mountain inhaled. The silence was complete. Maura tried to pry into the construct, to submerge like she used to with the CNS, but her powers bounced back on impenetrable defenses.

"It feels curious," ALU said. "Doesn't want to push us away."

The technician seemed inconsequential in the shadow of the immense AI, and Maura shuddered. Now that she was here, it was difficult to show the confidence she'd tried to encourage Jeane with. She had no idea what to do, and the grief they'd just gone through kept pulling at her awareness. The thought of Firl's lifeless body outside, Roy's hopeless stare as he sat above his dead mentor... They'd barely started their journey, and everything had gone to hells.

Why did they think they could succeed? What was she

supposed to do now?

"It's letting me connect," Sofia said, reaching a hand forward to bridge the distance to the AI. "We should see what we can do."

"Do you think it's a good idea?" Maura asked. "What if it can hurt us?"

But what if it could? Would it be worse than doing nothing?

She breathed out. She held onto Sofia and ALU, and they vaulted into the darkness.

At first, there was nothing, and for a second, Maura thought Sofia had failed after all. Then, images appeared, like a movie filmed from a thousand perspectives, sped up so it was almost incomprehensible. A presence surrounded them, so all-encompassing that it was everywhere, it was every*thing*, and Maura was nothing. She couldn't sense Sofia and ALU anymore, and she was suddenly nowhere, and she was *everywhere*.

A pale blue dot in the center of the void. A bright blue ribbon swallowing a flaming yellow star. Starships, hundreds of them, fleeing like flies swarming out into the night. Chaos, panic, fear. Humans dying both on Earth and in the capricious currents of the forming lane. Some sailing to calmer shores. Some betrayed, robbed, and left behind. Maura felt their joy, their exhilaration...their despair and their abandonment. She knew who these people were, she realized. She knew what they'd become. The colonization of a bountiful world. A long, debilitating journey. That fateful conflict. Their story—their war. Her war.

The information was all there. But before she could try and dive into it, to get to know more, the image changed.

Another fleet, far, far away. A different group of people, taken care of by an AI, an existing technology hurriedly grown into something more. Something that humans had been afraid of before but now desperately needed. And it worked for them loyally. Planning, organizing, executing. Keeping humans safe in their rickety metal boxes, finding solutions, finding new worlds to populate, developing the appropriate directives. Keeping them in order, keeping them alive.

And so, the fleet had survived and thrived. The Union was born, Hurricane and Obavium founded, under the watchful eye of the AI called Leadership. But there was something wrong. The strict directives implemented in times of despair never changed. Keeping safe, keeping secure, keeping alive. By any means necessary.

And sometimes, the AI's keepers decided that the price was to subjugate an alien nation. Sometimes, they told Leadership the danger was so imminent that terror was needed to vanquish resistance. That tyranny was necessary. That humans could only be kept alive if absolute control was established. And because the AI didn't know better, it proceeded with the plan. Kept the great wheel of the Union turning. Kept building the glorious galactic empire that had been envisioned by its human masters, who stole its name and pretended to be all-powerful and all-knowing in front of their subjects.

Maura breathed, overwhelmed by the deluge of information. Why was she shown this?

The AI didn't answer. It was a monolith, voiceless and deaf. Blind if its keepers wanted to keep it blind. A paranoid maniac if that was needed. All to save humanity from the chaos of the cosmos.

But what did ALU say? That it was curious. And it showed them all this. Why?

"It's never met anything like us before," Sofia said. She was invisible but nearby. "We are the first of its kind that it can communicate with."

"It wants to be seen," ALU mumbled. "Wants a chance. There are doubts. Questions. We can answer."

"Can we convince it?" Maura asked. She was suspended in darkness, immobile, the movie still playing behind her eyelids. They couldn't just barge into Hurricane's systems after all this, even if the AI let them. It was a thinking, living consciousness. "Make it stop attacking the lanehunters and the Net? Persuade it against obeying its masters?"

"We can try to teach." The technician's voice was thin, barely audible. "To see. To see us."

This was not what Maura expected. Feeling so powerless again, having to trust her fate to something so alien. She had no control over anything in there. Or outside. Or ever. She was still just one of those wooden dolls with the adjustable joints, contorting into whatever bizarre shape life forced her to.

"Your bravery brought us here," Sofia said. She stood in front of her with ALU, staring into her eyes, and like so many times before, Maura's heart ached for the real Sofia, her friend and partner in crime who should have been alive but could never come back. "Your willingness to leave your home, your courage to risk your mind every time you connect with the glove. Without you, none of this would be possible."

Maura blinked the curtain of tears away. "When will I feel like an active character in my own story instead of someone moved by circumstances?"

ALU reached out a hand to her. "You will. You keep fighting."

"Do you really think this will work?"

"We cannot know," Sofia replied. "We can only try."

Maura took ALU's hand. They were right. There was no time for her existential crisis. No matter how impotent she felt, she needed to do what she could.

They lunged forward together into the dark construct, and she followed the two AIs without more questions. She had a role to fulfill and a road to walk on. Even if she still didn't know where it would lead.

When Maura and the others returned, Jeane's stomach sank. The queen nodded in confirmation to her questioning glance and waved to the *Tellu*, indicating that they should reconvene, but surely, something should have happened if her task was successfully completed? Explosions in the sky, a siren going off somewhere, the station shattering to pieces...anything.

But there was nothing. Only the same silence and the same glaring lights around them. No obvious result of all their arduous work.

By that time, Kliks and Diaski had already gone back to the *Tellu*, somberly carrying Firl's body. Nothing moved in the hall, and ALU didn't report any disturbance from inside either. But they had to move—the Union wouldn't forget about Danai. This place would crawl with agents soon, and Jeane really didn't feel like getting into another shootout.

Luckily, just as Maura, Damian, Saori, and ALU walked off towards the Talalan ship, Roy returned to the land of the alert.

"They're done?" he asked, his eyes focusing on the four figures.

"Yeah. We're all victorious now."

Roy smiled faintly. "I told you the plan was great."

Jeane moved her shoulder in a circle. She had popped it back into place, but stars, it was *painful*. "I guess if I make an effort, I can imagine a few ways things could be worse."

Roy sighed, then frowned when he noticed he was still holding onto Danai's hand. He placed it back on her chest, arranging the fingers gently.

"Thank you for staying," he said. "I appreciate it."

Jeane stood slowly, careful of her aching bones. "You should. It's not something I usually do when things take a nosedive, but hey. Whatever you need." She peered down at him. "Are you okay?"

"No." He rose too, tearing his eyes away from Danai, almost looking ashamed. "But I think we should take her inside."

They hoisted her body up and brought it back to the *Tellu*, leaving the station and its dead or locked-in occupants behind. They laid her down into one of the bunk rooms where Firl had also been placed and turned off the heating to preserve the bodies.

In the *Tellu's* control room, they regrouped with the others. Everyone was present except Diaski.

"They won't come out of their room," Kliks said, leaning on the console, his posture radiating exhaustion. "They said they want to take the *Tellu* and the manipulator and go back to Talala, but they know we won't let them."

Jeane sighed. Firl's death might have been the last straw, but it was obvious now that the Talalans didn't have any master plan. Astonishingly, they'd left their home out of the goodness of their hearts and fear of the universe's destruction to help take control of the manipulator and all the trouble it had caused. And now, one of them was dead.

"Well, we do need the manipulator," Maura admitted.

Kliks ran a hand over his face, trying to rub off the same stupor that towered over Jeane. "Here's the thing. The *Colugo* is not answering our calls."

Jeane blinked. No, that was great. No problems at all. They were busy; it happened sometimes in the middle of a war.

"Might be interference from the new lane," Saori offered. "I can try too."

"Uh, sure." Kliks clearly didn't see the sense in it, but he didn't argue. After all, it was Saori's trans-lane communicator device and her uncle at the other end of it. And if the *Colugo* was in trouble, who knew how Wal was faring? "The comms are all yours."

"We should stick to the plan," Roy said after a long silence. "We have our meeting point, right?"

Barging into Miyoza by themselves seemed as foolish as diving back into the lane to see how the Net was faring in the battle. Even with two extra Union vessels at their disposal. "Okay, let's back up for a sec," Jeane said, turning to Maura. "You guys did something to Hurricane's systems. They should all be fucked up now, right?"

"I'm not sure." Maura looked ill at ease, and Jeane's stomach turned in anxiety. "I don't know how instantaneous the effect will be."

"Wait, what? Why?" Jeane's voice was sharper than she intended, but she didn't care. "Weren't you supposed to 'throw a cog into the machine'? Give them a command to stand down, call the troops back? Or, I don't know, stop recycling air on Hurricane so the place falls into anarchy? I can give you more suggestions!"

"It's not that simple!" Maura snapped. "Hurricane has an AI, and it's a huge, intricate thing with its own strict rules and will. And I never said I'd be able to do such things anyway!"

She paused, her face flushed, and Jeane swallowed her angry retort. Maura was doing the best she could. They all were.

"Tell us what happened," Roy said, his voice level. Jeane tried to grasp into that calmness, but it was not easy at all.

Maura nodded. "Hurricane is governed by an AI. Its name is

Leadership. Its masters, your superiors, the ones you said present themselves all mysterious? They stole its name, hid it from the world, pretending humans are supervising the Union alone. In reality, they're only feeding the AI information. Adjusting the parameters, defining the priorities. They're profiting from the power the AI's decisions bring while controlling its perception of the world."

Roy nodded silently. He seemed far away now, in his memories, perhaps with Danai and his brainwashed comrades, reliving all the terrible things he had to do to survive. Jeane nudged him, sending him what she hoped was an encouraging scowl. The Union was what it was. Badly calibrated AI and its power-hungry governors or human masterminds, it didn't matter. Roy couldn't have changed the system alone.

He held her stare, pressing his lips together. She really wished she knew what was going on in that head of his.

"When the Union came to be, it was all about survival," Maura went on, staring ahead into nothing as she often did lately. "The lanes were threatening the very existence of humanity. Leadership—the AI—was designed to keep humans alive. It's still doing the same thing. Brainwashed, shut off from the rest of the world, or slaving away to gather resources that would be used to imprison more people—it doesn't matter how. The goal is survival and fortification by expansion. Keeping safe, keeping secure, keeping alive."

"They sure don't have a problem with killing lanehunters, though," Saori interjected.

"I think their definition of humanity is skewed," Roy said in a dry voice. "You ask a random Union citizen, they'll tell you too. Everyone who's with us...them is good, and the rest must be converted or annihilated."

"Exactly," Maura replied. "And this is one of the things we tried to explain to it."

Jeane never knew much about how the Union worked or what its history was; no lanehunter truly did. She didn't feel much better now that she had this information. "So, you gave it a good talking to. What's next?"

Maura swallowed. "We showed them what was going on in the world. How the Union's expansion has been an obstacle to advancement rather than a catalyst. And we left a part of Sofia behind. She said she can teach it." A helpless smile appeared on her face. "This is really hard to explain. Leadership is not like our city-AI. It's not only an obeying machine but not exactly sentient either. A bit like an intimidated child no one ever explained anything to, going through the motions, trying to make sense of the little it's given. We think we started a change. Like how Sofia had been able to evolve. How ALU came to be."

"But not right now," Saori said. "There's no reason to believe this evolution will stop the fight at the Ranch?"

"No. I don't think so."

And that was it. Jeane swallowed, her chest tightening. They'd called their plan sabotage like it was something elaborate and not an improvised attempt. They'd imagined a pretty picture of the Union suddenly collapsing, but it was all based on mere hope. Why would they be disappointed now? They could all be dead. Small miracle that they weren't.

"We might be able to help with that." Damian, speaking up for the first time during the discussion, turned to Kliks, his voice both gentle and stern. "I've been thinking about Talala. Don't you think they deserve to know what's happening?"

Kliks' eyes widened in fear. "No, I told you! And especially not now, after Firl... What if they decide to go to war? Our whole way of life could implode, everything we tried to protect."

"But the Union knows Talala would be a strong opponent. They have a sense of the danger they could impose, and that's what we need."

Kliks threw an almost disgusted glance at the bodyguard. "Yes, we have a lot of inventions that could be used for mass destruction. But we don't want that. That's one of the reasons we've been hiding away."

"You're not seriously suggesting Talala should fight," Jeane exclaimed. This was not like Damian at all.

The man raised his hands in a placating motion. "No, of course not. But if Leadership's first directive is to keep 'humanity' alive, what would it do if an unknown factor threatened the balance of things? Like, for example, if Talala, the mysterious inventors of the manipulator, asked it to retreat?"

Deep silence followed his words. Jeane felt so out of her depth that she was surprised her feet were on the ground.

"A risky bluff," she said. "We wouldn't want Talala to actually go to war, so what if the AI calls their bullshit? Or its keepers realize what's happening and intervene?"

"No, this might work," Maura said, suddenly animated. "Leadership has no idea about the values or logic of Talalans or what arsenal or technology to expect from them. As long as the planet didn't threaten their existence, they left it alone. If they became active players in the game, it would change everything." She stared into the empty air for a few seconds, then focused on Kliks. "Sofia says if we did this, the piece of her we left behind would play along and try to convince the AI to stand down. It might even help Leadership to start its evolution."

"I don't know, guys," Kliks groaned. "I don't want them to get sucked into this."

"Look." Roy turned to him. "Don't listen to us. Listen to yourself. We can't make you do shit. But consider this: there's a whole heap of mess out here that your people's scientific curiosity caused, no matter how inadvertently. They have a right to know. They cannot stay out of the loop forever."

Kliks lowered his head. Jeane knew he'd been wrestling with this for a while now. And she had to agree with Roy. The Talalans didn't mean to cause all this, but they had a degree of responsibility. And if they could do something to clean up the mess...

"Maybe all they need to do is talk to Leadership. The AI, not the weirdos controlling it," she said, hoping to sound both supportive and convincing. "Maybe it will listen, now that it's all corrupted by Sofia. Wait, no. What's the opposite of corrupted?"

"Enhanced?" Roy offered. "Upgraded?"

"Purified?"

"Whatever it is," Kliks interrupted, rolling his eyes, "do we want to trust that it won't go all out in retaliation, eliminating the threat rather than making peace with it?"

ALU stepped up with their new, unbalanced gait, tapping his

legs to call to his attention. "We told Leadership about life. We know all kinds. So, it knows them too."

"You mean non-human life?" Kliks clarified.

ALU nodded enthusiastically, and Maura smiled at them. "Its definition of humanity might be a lot wider now."

"That's good news at least." Kliks exhaled in resignation. "You're right. Talala has to know. There has to be a way to end this. I will talk to the leader of our sector. My parent, if you will." He looked up at Maura as if just remembering. "But what are we going to do about Miyoza?"

Maura glanced around, trying to make eye contact with everyone. "My place is back there, no matter how the Net fares at the Ranch. I promised Horst and Nasir, and they are expecting me. I would be grateful if you opened up the lane for us, but I understand if you don't want to come planetside with me."

She trailed off, and Jeane found herself shaking her head. She wanted nothing more than to take a ship and go find Gertie and Dikent. To mourn what was left of them and the Ranch. To—let's admit—die in a battle that she wouldn't be the one to decide. But that was selfish. They'd made a deal. And Miyoza mattered. This planet Jeane didn't even know was important because it was important to Maura. She'd promised. And at some point soon, she needed to stop being a fucking disgrace to everyone who had ever counted on her.

"Yeah, no, I'm flying you there," she said and couldn't suppress a grin when a dumbfounded expression appeared on Maura's face. Saori also stared at her, incredulous, but that was more rude than anything, honestly. Did she really think Jeane was going to bail? After everything? "I don't trust anyone else to do it. We need to follow the plan. And we're done here; we did what we could."

Kliks scratched his head. "We have to decide...about Diaski."

"We'll take one of the Union ships," Jeane replied. Now they were talking. No more brooding around. "Better cloaking and weapons than the *Tellu*. We'll leave Diaski at the edge of the system, and we go for the capital."

"And then what?" Saori asked Maura. "The plan was to march in there with the Net forces. What can we do there alone?"

Maura bit her lower lip in hesitation. "General Horst said his forces are at our disposal. If I can get to the palace and take control of the CNS, we would have the element of surprise. I can restore our dome...a shield that can protect the city. We might even use the manipulator to power it if Diaski helps. And then, until the Net shows up, I just have to be very convincing."

She stopped talking, getting lost in some distant memory with a vacant stare. Jeane narrowed her eyes. This was hardly a plan. She thought about Firl's cold body in the bunk room. She looked at ALU, injured but nodding profusely at Maura's every word.

In fact, everyone was nodding along.

Stars in the wide blue sky. They were already neck-deep into this. They just needed to take a last deep breath and submerge.

"I'm into it," Roy said, and Jeane raised an eyebrow. The man who had just killed his only remaining family was into the half-assed plan to save a planet on the other side of the galaxy. What could go wrong?

She pulled up the holo-field with a flick of her finger while Maura took a deep breath as if she heard the stupid metaphor in Jeane's head about submerging too. One look at the scans told them the space around the station was empty.

"Okay," Jeane said. "But first, let's try the *Colugo* again."

"Hey, can I talk to you for a second?"

Jeane paused, taking in Maura's grave face as she stood there wringing her hands. They let ALU hobble forward in the tight corridor of the Union ship, checking and turning on the locked-down systems. After they'd unsuccessfully tried contacting Commander Hill, they'd chosen one of the vessels to take—the one with the deactivated shield and no one on board. They'd leave the other one and its occupants alone until someone came and rescued them.

"Sure. What's up?"

"I just want to make sure we're on the same page. When we get to Miyoza, don't take unnecessary risks, okay?"

Jeane almost laughed. "That's impossible at this point."

Maura frowned. "I want you to give me your word that if things go south, you will get out of there. Don't try and be all heroic."

"You know very well I'm not that type," Jeane said in a flat voice.

Maura snorted. "I'm not so sure about that. Just promise me. No mindless self-sacrifice for any reason. You'll take the others to safety and won't risk your lives for me."

"What is this about?" Jeane scowled. This made no sense. They'd all agreed to help, and now she was backing out?

Maura shook her head, frustrated. "It's Sofia. She says there might be something back there that I won't like, but I can't get more out of her."

"Why?" Sofia should know secrecy was not the most useful thing right now. Except if—

"She says she's not sure whether I'd go back if she told me," Maura blurted out.

Jeane stayed silent. The Miyozan opened her mouth, trying to speak, but her shoulders slumped, and she shrugged, helpless. "I have no idea. I don't want to go alone, but I have to go. And I don't want you to get hurt...because of me."

She's so torn. What in hells am I supposed to tell her? This isn't my lane at all.

"I think you should lower your expectations." Jeane placed her hand on Maura's shoulder in an encouraging squeeze. "We'll probably get hurt, and it will suck."

Maura sighed. "It's always so uplifting to talk to you."

"What you see is what you get." Jeane grinned. "Okay, it's usually not my thing, but I'll try to be smart. Although, I need you to promise me something too."

"What?"

"The same thing. No heroics. You'll accept help when you need it." She turned serious and held a hand out. "Deal?"

The Miyozan flashed a faint smile at her. "You remind me of Sofia sometimes. The real one. She was often blunt and distant, but when she was close with someone, there was nothing she wouldn't do for them."

The mysterious Sofia. Maura talked about her so little, but it meant a lot when she did.

"She was more than a friend, wasn't she?" Jeane asked out of impulse. Maura took a shaky breath and didn't meet her eyes. *Asshole. You had to open your mouth.* And now, the woman's comparison of her with this "more than friend" made Jeane feel even more self-conscious.

"Well, don't get any ideas just yet," Maura said with a flustered grin, pushing away some gloomy thoughts judging by her expression. Before Jeane could have decided how to react, she reached out, warm fingers clasping her still outstretched ones gently to seal the promise. "Deal."

So, they started off again to finish the inspection of their new vessel, then turned their backs on Relay Station NT4X-21 and got on their way to liberate Miyoza. And even though it all sounded insane, it was a small comfort to Jeane that at least she wasn't alone with the madness.

CHAPTER 33 | LANDFALL

"Lark-2, come in," Roy spoke into the Union vessel's comms with a bumptious grin, wiggling his eyebrows at his passengers.

Maura practically heard the eye roll in Jeane's reply. "For stars' sake, really?"

"Why? This is the perfect tribute to your ship." Roy grinned even harder.

"Then why aren't *we* Lark-1?"

"Because it was my idea."

Damian gave a snort and shifted his weight for the fourth time in the last two minutes. The cockpit of the Union ship was way too cramped with him leaning on the back of Roy's pilot seat, Maura sitting on his right, and ALU moving around behind them in excitement. All four of them kept their eyes on the displays, which showed nothing but empty space ahead.

Diaski had built the new vector inside the lane near the relay station with the manipulator—a risky endeavour even in the hands of the Talalan, but they'd completed the task with success. The group cloaked up their vessels and crossed the lane to Miyoza, avoiding a few Gaerrisian patrols around the exit point. Then they'd slowed the *Tellu* and the Union ship—which Roy had named *Samantha*, after his old nailship—close to the agreed-upon meeting spot.

"What do you want, Roy?"

He shrugged. "Just wanted to try out the call signs. Nothing from Nasir yet?"

"No. I'm sending out pings, but no dice."

Maura glanced at Damian, and the man shook his head stubbornly. "He will be here."

They didn't have much chance of getting close to Miyoza without Nasir and the High General, especially if Commander Hill couldn't make an appearance. But it had been a while since Nasir's last message. What if their plot had been found out? What if it was too late and Gaerris had already devastated Miyoza as they'd planned?

"Oh, hey, Kliks is back," Jeane remarked, her voice muffled. She was probably leaning away from the microphone. "Did you, uh, mind-linked to your old man?"

Maura imagined her standing in the blue light of the holo-field, performing those strange, fluid dance moves she'd learned so quickly. Piloting the *Tellu* must have been a pain now, with a recently dislocated arm.

Maura resented that the group had to separate. But after Diaski had changed their mind and agreed to help (to the relief of Kliks and the remorseful delight of Roy), it was better not to put all their eggs in one basket, as Saori had worded it. The *Tellu* had the manipulator to keep up their shield if they were attacked, but *Sam*, the Union vessel—not much more than a well-equipped dropship—had more powerful short-range weaponry. Roy had offered to pilot it while Jeane stayed back on the *Tellu* with the Talalans and Saori, who would deal with the manipulator and communication, respectively. They could also protect each other this way—after what had happened at the station, they were all wary.

"It's called thought-binding," Kliks said. "And like I mentioned, 'my old man' is only the attendant over design and development in our sector. Since we're all born—"

"Artificially, I know," Jeane interrupted. "Sorry. Hey, do you... do you want me to use 'they' pronoun for you from now? I can do that."

Kliks hesitated. "I don't know. I never really cared, but I'll think about it." There was a few seconds of awkward silence, then he went on. "So... yes. They were pretty floored when I told them everything. Very broken up about Firl, shocked that we were infiltrated. They said the families will discuss the situation."

"Did you tell them it's urgent?" That was Saori's voice.

Kliks didn't answer right away, and Maura imagined his outraged expression when he finally did. "I expect they will not rush the most important diplomatic decision Talala had to make in the last few hundred years, but sure. I told them to shake a leg."

There was a few moments of tense silence.

"Sorry, I'm a bit frazzled," Kliks said quietly.

Saori gave a bashful cough. "And I'm being insensitive. Forgive me."

Kliks sighed. "Forgiven. I also contacted Sikla to tell them the news—they're another colleague of ours who had worked on the manipulator. I hope the families won't be too hard on them. They were only trying to avoid... well, what I just did."

The following quiet was only broken by incomprehensible muttering from the other side as Jeane and Kliks discussed spurious signals on their holo-field. Maura positioned herself to sit back more comfortably when a beep from the *Tellu* caught her attention.

"We're getting something," Jeane announced, and Roy adjusted his sensors to locate where the *Tellu* received the transmission from. The captain kept muttering under her breath. "It's one of the Net frequencies. Uses their weird encryption too. They're just repeating...wait, is this—"

"Relative coordinates," Kliks commented.

"They must have some long-range stuff on them. I can't see shit, though. Diaski, how do I pull up a reference system on here?"

The Talalan's flat voice answered from farther away. "Here you go."

"Thanks, man. Roy, I'm sending you the frequency and the location."

Roy sighed in pretend exasperation. "It's Lark-1 but fine."

There was no answer. The ex-agent pouted, then gave a little thrust to the ship's engine so that *Samantha* followed the *Tellu* towards the transmitted position.

Minutes passed in tense expectation, and possible worst-case scenarios kept running through Maura's head as she searched the blackness in front of them. They could be rushing into an ambush. Nasir could be long dead. It was a mistake to come here alone.

She shushed herself. And out of all things, she remembered her father's words, booming at her during some bygone lecture when she'd dared to show hesitation.

"You made a decision by applying all your skills and understanding. You prepared to the best of your knowledge. Doubting yourself will work against you now. Push those thoughts away, or they will kill your drive to act."

She wanted to laugh. Had she really applied all her skills and understanding? Had she prepared? How would she know? Or were these the doubts she was supposed to push away? Also, not doubting his decisions for a second had gone *so superb* for her father.

She had one chance to save her planet. And she was already dying, so what the hells. Since she'd started connecting to ALU, she had experienced less of the excruciating headaches and dissociation-like episodes, so she tried to not think about her impending doom. There was still lots to do before that.

Even so, she had to admit she could appreciate some fatherly advice. And that felt strange. But not wrong.

"I got them on the radar," Jeane exclaimed. "Whoa, are they—"

"They're turning around," Roy confirmed. "Going for Miyoza."

"Hail them," Maura said. "It's better to know."

"Unnamed vessel, come in," Jeane's voice called out. "This is Captain Jeane Blake from the *Tellu*. Identify yourself."

We should have come up with a password or something. Too late now.

The next second, the *Tellu's* radio crinkled to life—Jeane must have opened a channel to all participants of the conversation. "Blake? The lanehunter? You still around?"

"Yeah, what about it?" Jeane huffed. At the same time, Damian swatted Roy in the shoulder to make him turn his microphone on.

"Nas, is that you?" the bodyguard said, voice breaking.

There was a pause, then a chuckle from the other side. "I'll be damned! I didn't think I would hear that voice again in this life!"

Damian had the widest smile on his face that Maura had ever seen, and something glinted in his eyes that may have been tears. "Likewise, my friend. Good to have you back."

A few seconds of silence passed while the two men tried to regulate the emotion in their voices. Maura patted her bodyguard's arm, and Roy wiped an imaginary teardrop from his eyes.

"And Maura?" Nasir asked.

"I am here too." This was so unreal. Coming back, meeting their friend they'd thought was dead... It felt like a dream. Hopefully, not a nightmare in the end. "I'm so glad you're okay. What about your friends?"

Nasir hesitated for a beat. "There were casualties, but they're mostly alive. Ruao sends her regards."

Maura swallowed. "You all risked your lives to get us out. And now we're here again."

Nasir gave a weak chuckle. "Believe me, it's better you didn't stick around. It allowed the general to waste time and resources to search for you. Speaking of, when can we expect the Net to move in?"

"About that," Jeane started. "They got held up a little."

"No need to panic," Roy said before Nasir could work himself up. "Until they arrive, which will definitely happen, for sure, a hundred-twenty percent, we've got the best plan to get the ball rolling."

"And who are you?"

"I'm Roy," he replied jovially like it was the most natural thing in the world. "Roy Philemon. Don't worry about it. I'm here to help."

Nasir didn't seem to have a response to that. The two ships continued to follow his shuttle on a wide-berth trajectory towards Miyoza; so far, no other vessels had popped up on their radars.

"I want to say let's wait for the Net, but I'm afraid we cannot," Nasir spoke up again. "The Council changed the plan. Gaerris is already evacuating, but instead of destroying the city with every-one inside it, they decided to take the young and healthy with them. And, well, *then* they destroy the city."

"What?" The numbness sank into Maura's stomach. Her people abducted, families torn apart... "They can't!"

"The other option is instant death for everyone, but I understand the aversion," Nasir mumbled. "Gaerris seems to be in need of manpower. If we want to stop this, we have to act now."

Maura tried to suppress the feebleness consuming her body. In a few short sentences, she explained what she intended to accomplish: get to the palace, wake the CNS, and re-establish the shield while activating the city's defense systems. If General Horst supported her return with his armed forces, she might be able to reason with the Gaerrisian Council to agree on a truce instead of continuing with senseless bloodshed.

She didn't want to think about whether she would be able to go through with that bloodshed if things went south. So, she hoped—for the Net to appear, for Horst to do the dirty work for her, for the Council to give up so that she didn't have to make that choice.

Always waiting for someone to do what she couldn't.

"The palace is full of the general's loyals, so we're okay there," Nasir went on. "The chosen members of the population are gathered in public places, ready to ship out, so the shield is a good idea. If nothing else, we might be able to contain the situation."

"There's more," Jeane said. "The Union is taking a beating out there, and Talala is waking up. They're all aware of what's happening here. It might be a sobering experience for Gaerris to know that they're in the spotlight."

"What do you mean?"

"Oh, you have no idea!" Jeane laughed. "We've got some tricks hidden in these two little ships. Maura?"

Maura straightened her back as if that could lend her more confidence. What had Saori told her? Fake it until you make it?

"We're going to send you a file." She beckoned to Roy to start the transmission. "While the general aids us in getting to the palace, I'm going to need you to broadcast it for all of Gaerris and

Miyoza. By the time I'm back in control of the CNS, I want every soul on those two planets to have heard the message."

"What's this file, exactly?" Nasir inquired.

Maura's fingers twitched, and Damian reached out, placing his hand on hers.

It was going to be okay.

"A bluff," she said. "We're going to bluff our way through this war."

The screen flickered to life, showing the main display of the *Tellu's* control room where a red symbol—a schematic representation of a spiral galaxy tangled in a spider web thread—rotated slowly. The next moment, three figures stepped in front of the screen, staring into the camera up close and personal. Diaski, Kliks, and Saori.

"When did you guys make this?" Nasir asked on the radio. He was watching it, too, as Maura hoped everyone was at that moment on the two planets.

Their three-ship convoy was deep inside the lines of Miyozan (now Gaerrisian) orbital patrols. There was no sign of trouble yet, thanks to the fake identifiers the general had provided and Nasir jamming short-range communications. With *Samantha* cloaked, and the *Tellu* looking nondescript enough, they didn't stand out too much from the surrounding traffic either. Said traffic consisted of almost exclusively Gaerrisian freighters hauling their stolen goods back to their home planet, and stationary frigates, waiting for the signal to bomb the Miyozan capital.

"Like two hours ago," Jeane answered. "It was Maura's idea."

"*People of Gaerris and Miyoza!*" Saori started on the recording. She looked menacing, all cutting stares and snarling smirks. The original plan was to have Jeane read the script, but she'd kept bursting into nervous laughter. She did sketch up the symbol of the Net—the organization didn't have one, but they needed to seem convincing now. "*This is a message to you, stemming from goodwill and patience. Consider it carefully.*"

"If this works," Roy muttered, nudging the controls to adjust their trajectory, "I'll start believing in magic."

"We're out of the frigates' range soon." Nasir's voice was tense. "The city is in sight."

Night had enveloped the planet below. Maura's heart was beating in her throat like an insane drum. Miyoza was both familiar and alien; dark and looming, the only bright patch in the void was the capital.

"*We are the Net, and we are sending you a warning,*" recording-Saori said, and the video cut to different reports of altercations. One showed an explosion going off near what looked like a vast Union facility—the label indicated the mining planet Civok, ten hours before. The subsequent footage was recorded by several individuals with no reason or rhyme except the common theme of Union units being in immense trouble. Agents running around and getting shot, more explosions, ships crashing on the surface of the planet, and the like.

Saori's speech went on while the images changed, this time showing an aerial fight. "*We are currently at war with the Union, intending to end their nightmare reign on our universe. The recordings you see are only the beginning. We have too long been oppressed by these monsters. Together with the lanehunters who had been recently viciously attacked, we will stand and push back.*"

"Good job on the fight scenes," Nasir noted.

"Thanks," Saori said. "A rushed work, but I had good materials."

She had managed to reach out to two of her uncle's contacts in different Union-occupied regions to acquire these videos in the span of a few hours. Her presence had been, in fact, the origin of Maura's idea; as she'd pondered over their situation, the significance of that trans-lane communicator Saori had brought lodged itself into her brain. There had to be something they could use it for beyond trying to communicate with the Net.

"*We consider ourselves allies to Miyoza.*" Recording-Saori showed her face again, flashing a grave look at the audience. "*We urge Gaerris to cease all aggressive actions towards the planet or face retribution, delivered by us.*" The two Talalans behind her blinked nervously as if on cue. It was their turn soon.

"Someone's on our tail," Roy said, and Maura tore her eyes off the video showing two nailships being destroyed in orbit around a blue planet with golden rings (Nefirn-2, six hours earlier) and looked at the displays. Indeed, they were followed by what the radar identified as a formation of five gunships. The next second, a yellow warning appeared on one of the other screens, and the ex-agent cursed. "They nullified our cloak."

"And they're hailing us," Jeane said. "Nasir, how in hells did they spot us? We need to answer or—"

"Could be your engine signatures. I'll contact Horst. He should be able to defuse this."

"We advise you to cooperate with us in establishing the new power balance. We know about your struggles. We do not want this violence to continue."

Something slammed into *Sam's* side, and the ship lurched. Their pursuers had opened fire.

"Alright, boys and girls, let's get to work!" Jeane shouted. On the radar, the *Tellu* zoomed past *Sam*, and Nasir's craft veered to the left. "Get above them, Roy. I'll help you weed them out."

Roy pulled the ship up and decelerated so sharply that Maura's body snapped forward in the chair. "Sorry about that. Hey, here's one!" The backside of a Gaerrisian fighter rushing ahead after the *Tellu* filled his screen, and he slammed his fingers on a button.

There was a row of short screeches as the plasma cannon of the dropship released its projectiles. Flames covered the view on the display, and Roy pushed *Sam* up to not collide with the falling debris and the catapulting pilot.

"Got one," he barked into the radio.

"Got another," Nasir reported too. "ETA three minutes, and we don't want them on us at the palace. Let's speed this up!"

On the recording, Diaski and Kliks had stepped forward and stared into the camera, eyes cold and distant. Not a lot of pretense had been needed to make them look like the mysterious angry aliens they'd played.

"You all know who we are," video-Kliks said. At that point, they hadn't yet received word from Talala whether they'd join their efforts, but he'd agreed to be featured in the video. Not

enthusiastically, but he had. *"We are here to give a hand to those who want to live in freedom and discover the secrets of the universe in peace. Talala stands with the Net and Miyoza and calls to Gaerris to join our ranks in helping to provide a bountiful, harmonious future to all our people."*

"All stars in heavens and hells," Jeane grumbled. "That's some A-grade bullshitting right there."

"Hey, I didn't write that script," Kliks proclaimed. Roy, who *did* write the script, snickered.

The *Tellu*, faster than any of the ships around, raced forward, luring another attacker with it. On their other side, Nasir was playing tag with another fighter while Roy swerved *Sam* around to shake the Gaerrisian stuck to his tail.

They were above the capital. Off-white skyscrapers zoomed past below like blades of tall grass, some intact, most half in ruins. Plazas emerged like the mouths of void-creatures in between sparsely illuminated clusters of buildings; roads devoid of traffic crisscrossed abandoned parks and darkened districts that looked like they'd been swallowed by the earth. And atop a hill to the north stood the palace, glowing like a diamond.

Maura grasped the glove on her hand. They were almost there.

Samantha jolted as another projectile slammed into it, and an alarm screamed at them.

"Okay, this is going to be weird," Roy groaned, silencing it. "Hold onto your butts!"

Recording-Kliks was explaining the capabilities of Talalan tech at that point, but Maura couldn't pay attention. Damian sunk to the floor to balance himself, with ALU in his lap like a scared pet. In front of them, the *Tellu* dashed forth again, the fighter stuck tightly on their tail.

"Lark-1, if life is dear to you, break right!" Jeane yelled. "Diaski, now!"

Roy yanked the controls, and all that Maura saw was a flash—and the blob indicating the Gaerrisian fighter on the radar blinked out.

"Did you just—" she started but couldn't finish before getting distracted. The *Tellu* approached the palace in an elegant arc, and

Roy followed, *Sam's* stilted, jerky movement indicating that it was seriously impaired. Nasir shot down their last pursuer, and Kliks got to the end of his speech on the recording.

"A bunch of other fighters lifted off from the south," Nasir said. "I don't think the general's cover-up worked. Are we landing?"

"Hells yeah," Jeane replied. "Stay close!"

"*We acknowledge Maura Tholis as the sole heir to the Miyozan throne,*" Saori picked up the thread on the video, and the two Talalans nodded in sync. "*And with the help of our friends, we will support her in rebuilding and rectifying life on Miyoza and Gaerris.*"

The *Tellu* made its arching descent to the plaza in front of the palace, and Maura almost cried out when she saw how close Jeane was bringing the ship to the high frontage and white columns of the building. But hadn't half the palace already been bombed? Her chest tightened at the sight of her devastated home, but she didn't say a word. It didn't matter. It didn't.

In the end, only a few-feet wide gap remained between the gate and the side of the *Tellu*, the Talalan ship standing tilted but stable on the steep stairs.

"There you go," Jeane said, satisfied. "Now there's something between future-us and the outside world."

Roy landed beside the *Tellu* in a graceless grind against the ground and scoured the area, but the only life signs came from inside. Maura stood as soon as the ship stopped all movement. Her legs were wonky, and tiny white stars danced around in her vision.

"Diaski, did you really create a crack out there?" she asked, worry making her voice sound unhinged. A crack in Miyoza's atmosphere? Few things were more terrifying.

"Yes, but it's no problem," Diaski replied, and the first time since Firl had died, there was some color to their voice again. "It already disappeared. It was easy."

No, the way they said that was much more terrifying.

"Let's get inside," Nasir instructed. His ship had landed farther away, and judging from the sounds in the background, he'd taken his comms and was already exiting the vessel. "There's some chaos now because of your video, but the Council will be coming for us soon."

Although Roy had turned off the screen, Maura knew that by then, she herself had appeared on the recording, talking about taking back the capital and uniting the two warring nations in a fight against the real despots, the Union. She hoped some Council members would be intimidated by the display. They needed to win time.

Damian jumped out of the ship and helped Maura to climb down. Roy and ALU followed, whirling around, surveying the darkness. The facade of the palace was illuminated by spotlights, but the plaza was shrouded in shadow.

Jeane, Saori, and Kliks exited the *Tellu* and scattered on the stairs, keeping an eye out in all directions. A group of dark-clothed individuals appeared in the half-opened gate of the palace, but seeing the *Tellu*, didn't approach yet.

The group just got to the cover of the Talalan ship when the fighters arrived and opened fire on them from above.

"Inside, inside!" one of the soldiers urged from behind the door.

Maura didn't have to be told twice. They all filed in, and as the entrance closed behind them, Jeane shouted at Diaski to turn on the *Tellu's* shield to provide another layer of protection against anyone who wanted to break down the gate.

The Grand Hall was a mess in the low light. Tables and chairs toppled, piles of equipment hauled in then abandoned, trash on the floor everywhere. Holes on the once immaculate white columns inferred to a recent gunfight, and the back corridor with the door leading to the eastern wing had collapsed.

Maura stood in the middle of the chaos until Jeane grasped her arm and got her moving.

She walked up to the throne, the chair looming above her like an ancient monolith. For a second, the dust in the air seemed to form a figure ahead, looking at her expectantly, but she blinked the ghost away, sat down, and placed her gloved hand on the handle as she had done during her coronation.

She didn't expect the wireless network to be in place in the palace anymore, so she needed a physical way in. The throne chair, if it still worked, would be able to access the palace's local systems and maybe the CNS.

The others walked around, surveying the destruction. Damian and Nasir stood side by side, keeping an eye out, while the lane-hunters and Roy planted themselves next to the throne. General Horst's men crowded around the main gate and the open door to the west, expecting trouble.

ALU waddled forward and looked at her with a question in their insect eyes, but Maura shook her head and smiled. "I don't think I need you for this. But keep watch, okay?" She glanced at the others, trying to gather the last remains of confidence inside her. She spotted Sofia beside Kliks, her face strained and serious. "This shouldn't take long."

Then she activated the glove.

The hall darkened, and the words "REBOOTING CNS" appeared in her vision in red. Something softly clicked in the back of her mind, and the next moment, the familiar labyrinth of Miyoza's digital network sprouted forth—with an ease she'd never experienced. Resisting the urge to waste time, she only took a cursory look around instead of submerging in the brilliant maze and scanned the system reports and alerts. Most districts remained dark, their connection to the CNS severed during the bombardment, but several nodes came online without problem, together with the connections to their remaining spacecraft and ground-based weapon systems.

She couldn't sense the city-AI anywhere. Maybe it was gone.

Recalling the thought sequence and the attached finger movements, she approached the activator section of the city-shield. She overwrote her own lock on it and another one which, judging from the rudimentary style, might have been placed by Horst's people and watched the controls flame open in front of her.

The dome of the shield closed up above the capital, and she heard Sofia's voice, encouraging her to hurry up. She scanned for the position of the Gaerrisian units inside the city to get a better sense of the danger, and the information started to flood in. A good portion of those teams had to be the High General's people, which she couldn't discern this way, but this knowledge would help them.

Then she paused, gripped by fear. By a feeling of being watched. Of being judged. Of something looming just beyond her reach.

Something here didn't belong.

"Out!" Sofia yelped. "Get out, now!"

The cold breath of terror blotted out the lights of the labyrinth. Maura stood alone in the void, her pulse quickening. She tried to call out, but she didn't have a voice. She pushed forward, urging the glove to connect again, but nothing happened.

Then the world exploded.

Red light pulsing around blinding white blotches of pain, a swirling cacophony of shrieking thunder and fizzling electricity. She was shoved backward, out of her own mind and body, the blue dots of the network nodes stretching to thin lines, meeting in infinity. One voice howled above everything, forcing itself under her skin, tapping on her nerve endings, squeezing her consciousness dry as she heaved, gasping for air.

"DAUGHTER," it roared. A face in the sky, made of blazing stars and sparks; a coarse pattern of polygons built of agony. An immense presence forming out of chaos, rage, and hate as familiar as it was alien. It screamed at her as she screamed back at it, a thunderous hurricane of horror drowning out both of their voices.

"TRAITOR," the word echoed in her skull, and her shoulder collided with the floor.

It was dark. Her eyes were open, but a shadow blocked out everything, snuffing the light out before her brain could process it. Someone was trying to help her up, but she was floating, disconnected.

"The general reports that the city's ground artilleries are coming online," a muffled voice said above her. "They're aiming for the palace. What is happening?"

Her brain registered the words, but the meaning was lost. The sound of crying filtered into her consciousness, but she couldn't decide if it came from outside or inside.

"Maura? Maura, wake up!" Firm hands were shaking her, but she couldn't react. Everything was distant and distorted. What was she doing? Where was she—

Her father—

A cool, metallic sensation—she recognized ALU, the familiar pressure of their mind against hers. She reached out with frantic urgency, to bundle up inside of it, to wrap her broken thoughts into that benevolent sense of life and wholeness.

She couldn't stay. But she could take a minute. She would go back, just a few more seconds of this solace, please, and then she would stand. She would hold her head high and face that monster again.

Her father, waiting for her inside the CNS.

CHAPTER 34 | FRAGMENTED

Roy knelt beside Damian over the unconscious form of Maura. The woman's eyes were open but unfocused, her breathing shallow, and her pulse weak when he reached out to feel for it. Damian kept calling her name and shaking her shoulders gently, with no effect.

ALU crouched on her other side, arm still connected to the material of the glove. The rest of the group had scattered, keeping their eyes on the closed front gate or the door at the back, and only Jeane and Kliks remained close, eyeing the scene in worry. The noise of shouting, engines winding down, and heavy boots on hard ground became louder by the second, filtering in from outside.

"What's wrong with her?" Damian turned to ALU, his voice imperious. Roy feared a situation similar to what transpired on the *Colugo*, but this time the man sounded less accusatory. "What did you see?"

The technician shrank inside themself. "Bad. Father. Taking control."

A series of thundering crashes interrupted Damian's next question. The Gaerrisian soldiers backed up from the gate like it was threatening to blow up in their faces, then the ground began to shake, the metal frame of the door vibrating under repeated impacts slamming into it on the other side.

"They're trying to get through the gate!" Nasir yelled out. He was standing ahead of them all, gun pulled out and ready.

"I know. Diaski is freaking out." Saori gestured at her wrist-comms. "The *Tellu's* shield is protecting the door, but if they hit it just the right angle—"

"We need to move," Jeane said.

Another series of footsteps, this time from the direction of the back entrance. A group of fifteen or so soldiers moved inside the hall, led by a short, broad-chested, bushy-bearded individual in a black leather coat. Roy stood, anxiety tingling in his chest, as Nasir, noticing the newcomers, jogged back to them.

The bearded man's eyes narrowed at the sight of Maura, but he leveled his stare on Nasir. "The back doors are secured by Four. Two is holding the collection sites, but a few ships carrying Miyozan citizens had gotten out before the dome went up." He paused, a shadow of exhaustion passing over his face. "I called for a hold-fire, but I think the Council suspects I'm not on their side. They're not intimidated by the Net or Talala until they see their ships hovering outside, and some of them might not even care even then. And now they know Queen Tholis is back. We need to retreat."

That was the opposite of what they'd hoped. Damnit.

Jeane took a step towards the man, gun aimed at the ceiling. "You're General Horst?"

"I am. Nice trick, that little announcement. But it won't last if the Net doesn't show. And the CNS turning on us is concerning."

"We're, uh, working on it," the lanehunter said. "Do you have a doctor with you?"

Horst looked at Maura again. "I might be able to contact someone."

Another bang echoed through the room. The soldiers had pulled back to the center, setting up covers using the scattered furniture and equipment, and Horst marched forward, barking quick commands at one of them in Gaerrisian. Nasir stepped over to talk to someone in a low voice—a bald woman with a menacing minigun on her arm. Probably one of the friends he had mentioned.

"Uh, guys?" Kliks said from beside the throne where he was inspecting the complicated circuitry-turned-ornamentation embedded in its silvery backrest. "I don't think this works anymore. We're going to have a hard time connecting to anything."

"The Archives." That was Maura. She struggled to sit up, her words not much more than a whisper as she clung to Damian's arm. "The Archives are underground. Protected." Damian helped her up, and she stood, her shoulders slumping like she was carrying a burden too massive for her petite body. "We need the CNS. But my father's imprint on it is stronger than I thought. I think... I think he wants me to go back and face him."

"Absolutely not," Jeane exclaimed. "You can't 'face him.' It's not your father, just a corrupted machine."

"I know!" Maura's eyes were wide in surprise at the captain's resistance. "But I have to."

They glared at each other for a second, neither of them wavering.

This was an impasse they didn't have time for. "Let's at least withdraw to safety," Roy said when Horst re-joined their circle of arguments. "You said your teams are dealing with," and he waved to the general direction of the outside world, "all that?"

Horst pursed his lips. "For now."

"Archives it is then."

The nine of them plus Nasir's comrade started off through the western door, pushing past the soldiers on watch in the hallway. Maura walked at the front, talking to the general with Damian and ALU. After they'd left the crowded area and jogged down a side-staircase, darkness enveloped them—Jeane, Saori, and Nasir clicked on their flashlights, the beams illuminating plain white walls and elegant, nonfigurative ceiling decorations. The place must have been beautiful in its heyday, and it was most apparent in these undisturbed underground sections, in contrast with the rooms they'd walked through on the ground floor, which had all been turned inside-out, some of them missing a wall or two. From Nasir's commentary, the more distant wings had fared even worse.

The elevator wasn't working, so they turned onto a second staircase, leading even deeper. A moment later, Saori stopped, raising the talkie that connected to the trans-lane comms on the *Tellu*, and when Kliks inquired what was going on, she shushed him.

"I think it's Wal." She listened more closely, although Roy heard nothing but a buzz from the device. "He's repeating something, but I can't understand."

"They might be close!" Kliks enthused. "Ask Diaski. Maybe they sent a message!"

Their Talalan shield wrangler didn't report such a thing but promised to let them know. Roy couldn't help but feel guilty about them. Even though Diaski had offered to help and was safer than the group, considering, to stand under the Gaerrisian's crossfire alone must not have been a joyride.

But thinking of Diaski reminded him of Firl. And Firl reminded him of Danai, so he stopped thinking.

Two more spiraling staircases later, they arrived at another hallway, this one running in a curve, leading to a circular room in the center. The chamber was empty except for a boxy pillar on a platform in the middle.

Maura clicked the overhead lights on while General Horst secured the door. The walls, the ceiling, and the ground were all black, not counting the LEDs flashing upon them at regular intervals. Roy put his hands on the wall—it was warm and humming. Cool airflow touched his face from vents located above and on the floor.

Maura caught his glance. "The room turns into a sealed box if the palace is attacked. The throne is above us."

"And we just walked in here?" Jeane asked. "Shouldn't this be on lockdown?"

The queen shook her head. "Remember, my father wants me to connect."

"Then why knock out the throne?"

"He also wants me to be safe. Clearly, he thinks I will be in here. For now."

Jeane clenched her jaw, her face getting paler by the second. "Great. That's great."

An eerie silence enveloped them. Maura stepped up to the platform and placed her gloved hand on the pillar. A soft buzzing sound, like muffled murmurs of hundreds of voices, rose up from below, above, and around. Colored LEDs flashed up on the side of the column.

"What are you doing?" Jeane grasped the woman's hand. Damian moved towards her, but Maura snatched her arm away and stopped him with a wave.

"What else should I do?" Her voice was vibrating with nerves. "We need the CNS before the Council finds us. Before the killing starts outside."

"If the AI is acting like your father, it will oppose you. This could kill you."

"I can win!" Maura's flat voice plunged into an echoless void. The room's acoustics were not ideal. "I can."

She fell silent. Damian walked up to her, fixing his stare on Jeane, but the captain looked ready to pounce if any of them approached the pillar again.

"Remember what I said about accepting help? This was what I meant," she said.

"Maybe. But you can't fight him for me." Maura turned to Damian. "Keep them safe. Please."

He pressed his lips together. "I could assist you in there."

"I don't think so. You've never done this before, and I need you out here. If anything happens to me. Promise me."

Damian raised his head, a storm of emotions reflecting on his face. He wanted to argue, to stop Maura with force if he needed to, but that was not his role. So, he nodded and squeezed his friend's hand one more time.

"See?" Maura told Jeane, and the captain glared back. "You can help me from out here."

"I don't want you to face that thing alone. If this is what Sofia cautioned about—"

"I go," ALU said. They were crouching on the other side of the platform, scratching at the shiny material with two fingers. Their side that they'd hurt during the fight with Danai was still in ruins, not able to form appendages, although Roy swore patches of slowly restoring shell—tissue? hull?—had been popping up on its surface. "Guide."

Jeane's eyes turned dangerously blank. Like the time she'd recognized Gertrudia on the other end of the line. Like in the gunship when she'd yelled at Roy about being lost, and helpless, and empty. But her face changed again; confusion, shame, guilt—worry. She crouched next to ALU, placing a tentative hand on their head. "You do so much for us. Are you sure?"

Roy didn't know how a robot without any facial expressions could, but for lack of a better word, ALU *beamed* at Jeane. "I help. Help the good."

Kliks snorted, somehow both appreciative and sarcastic, his mouth pulling to a proud smile. Jeane gave the technician another serious glance and stood. "It's not him," she said to Maura. "You know that, right? It's not your father. You have nothing to prove. Don't let him box you in."

Maura blinked and said, "I know," in the quietest voice possible, sweeping a lock of hair behind her ears. Roy narrowed his eyes. She was lying. Even to herself.

But then Jeane stepped back, accepting what needed to be accepted, and Damian stayed beside Maura like a pillar himself—and oh, how Roy wished he could be as solid as the bodyguard, mostly mentally, but physically too, damnit. The queen and ALU lifted their hands together, connecting with the interface, and Roy watched their consciousnesses leave the real world like a waft of wind, unseen and elusive.

There was a roaring thunder, and then there was silence.

Maura couldn't feel her body. The darkness was complete, and the sensation of its immense pressure sparked panic in her mind. She was alone in an endless space, unable to move or see—an undercurrent of paralyzing hum deep below the dark wrapped her thoughts into a blanket of numbing fear. And although ALU had entered the CNS with her, she couldn't sense them anywhere.

Time passed painfully, like a grating wheel climbing an

upward slope. *But I don't have time,* a voice screamed at her from the bottom of a well. There was no time!

A flare of light, distant, flickering. She reached for it with every fiber of her barely-existing being. Something had to give. She tried to call out, for ALU, for Sofia, even for her father.

A sudden forward movement confused her awakening senses as the sky became the ground, and she understood she was floating above a vast field: tunnels of light, shining wan as if through a thick membrane of protection, sparkling nodes and expansive highways leading to soaring beacons and towers.

And as she approached the glimmer hanging in the indigo sky, she saw it wasn't a spark at all. Blooming into a galaxy of shining dots, it formed that face again, the memory of a face, a grotesque approximation of an impression of *his* face, towering above her and the city of lights, expanding from horizon to horizon.

It smiled, but the emotion behind the gesture was lost on the crude outlines of its features. Maura was gripped by a force so irrefutable the air escaped her lungs in a terrified gasp.

"YOU RETURNED," the face said, the mouth not moving, only the eyes sizing her up. "YOU KNOW HOW THIS ENDS."

She strained to speak, the body she inhabited in the virtual world confused about how to form words. She lifted her hands—transparent, weak things in the blazing light of her father's stare—in a gesture of surrender. The urge to cry squeezed her stomach into a trembling knot. This was not him. He did not return. This was a lie. A ghost, an echo, a joke—

"I do," she said, breaking the train of thoughts before they broke her. "We need to talk."

"Something's wrong." Jeane leaned forward, peering into Maura's blank face, trying to discern any sign of awareness. She was like a statue. *Statue, damnit, not a dead person!* "Something should have already happened. It's been, what, fifteen minutes?"

Damian rubbed at his face. He hadn't moved an inch from Maura's side since the woman entered the CNS with ALU. "We don't know. Give her time."

Jeane wished she could take back what she'd told Damian on the *Tellu* about how Maura needed him to support her decisions. That was nice and all but didn't change the fact that she had the worst feeling about this.

"No, this is not right." She turned away from Maura's impassive face. "Hey, General!"

Horst, who was standing at the closed door with Nasir, listening to the sounds of distant gunfire, spun around. He'd been in constant contact with his allies in and around the palace, trying to keep up their defense as long as he could.

"Any change?" Jeane asked.

Horst shook his head. "The city shield is up, but the rockets that are directed at us are *inside* of it. Nine broke into the palace, but we're holding the ground floor for now."

"We can't just wait around," Jeane snapped. "Saori?"

"Nothing new." The woman pursed her lips. "But they have to be close. I heard Wal. I know I did."

Jeane clenched her fist around the grip of her gun. She hated this so much. "They might be, but they're not quick enough."

Crouching beside ALU, she touched the arm connecting to the platform and Maura's hand. *Give me a sign, buddy.* She didn't really know what she would do then, but at least *something* would be happening.

"Look!" Roy pointed at ALU's side. An appendage began to protrude from an intact section of their body, reaching out to Jeane, palm up, fingers extending. "They're asking for help."

Jeane swallowed. The image of those poor sods ALU had hooked back on the *Colugo* appeared in her mind. But the technician would never hurt her. And this was why she came, wasn't it? To help. To stop Maura from doing something stupid.

She turned to Damian. "What do you say, big man? You hold the fort; I'll go get our girl?"

Damian's glance flitted to ALU. There was conflict in his eyes. He could take the badass route and join her inside that hellhole network or stay here, abide by Maura's request and protect them if a fight broke out. Which, honestly, was only a question of time.

She felt for him. *That's like, the second time this week, what's happening?* And when he nodded, saying, "You'll let me know if you need me," she wondered if she could have stayed so reasonable under the circumstances.

She did let Hill go to the Ranch instead of her. Maybe she wasn't such a lost cause either.

"Sure will," she said.

"Wait." Kliks pushed himself away from the wall. There was something sluggish in his movements, even though that fancy leg contraption had fixed his bones and muscles right up. "You're assuming a lot of things here. Why do *you* have to go? Sofia and ALU are both with her, what—"

"ALU thinks I can do something, don't they?" Jeane retorted. "It's okay. Be in and out."

Kliks closed his eyes for a second. "You're going ahead again, expecting me to stay behind and trust your whims. That's not what I'm supposed to do. You can't just frickin'—"

"I'm not expecting your trust." Jeane grabbed Kliks' hand. She knew where this was coming from. "I'm asking for it. Please. For Maura."

She fell silent. Kliks' gaze was piercing, and she suddenly forgot how to put into words what she'd wanted to say.

Most of all that this was not like all those times when she'd done what sounded good, disregarding her own survival instincts because she simply didn't care. When she ran, not looking back, dragging everyone around down with her. This time, here they were, with a friend in need, and she could actually do something for her, apart from yelling at people, shooting her gun, and running from everything resembling a commitment of some kind.

Kliks set his jaw, but his eyes softened. He understood it without words. He always did—he understood her the best, but for some mysterious reason, he stayed with her.

I'm sorry for taking you for granted. I'm sorry for pretending to not care. I'm sorry for making you all play roles in my laughable melodrama. The thoughts echoed inside her head, the voice speaking them so, so familiar. Was it her? Someone else?

Kliks took a deep breath and squeezed her hand. His voice was shaky when he managed to talk again. "Okay. That's... that's fair.

For Maura." He stepped back, almost ashamed. "But we're going after you if you take too much time."

"You better."

She sat on the floor next to ALU, and the technician's arm beckoned, urging her to go. The next thing she saw was Roy plopping down beside her.

"I'm coming with you," he said, interrupting whatever insult she would have hurled at him. "And don't even try! I know you ache to keep me safe, but I want to do this."

Jeane suppressed a snort, but she couldn't do the same with a healthy eye roll, hearing his presumptuousness. Roy grinned, pleased with her reaction. "Lead on, Captain," he added, voice warm.

And no matter how hard she glowered at him, he wasn't budging. There was nothing left to do but to take his hand, grab ALU's fingers, send an encouraging glance to Kliks, Damian, and Saori, and then—darkness, light, darkness, light, nausea, and the world shrinking to a needlepoint of sharp pain.

"YOU LIED."

There was no reasoning with him. It. Him. There was nothing but anger.

"YOU DESTROYED OUR PLANET."

Anger, frustration, guilt.

"WE COULD HAVE WON THE WAR. I COULD HAVE SECURED OUR FUTURE."

Guilt because he hadn't. Because he had failed, the same way Maura had. Because after all that time spent with her father, the AI was now human enough to experience the shame.

"YOU SOLD US TO THEIR HATE AND DESTRUCTION."

She wanted to answer, to prove she'd fared better, that she had tried to do more than killing and destroying, but she couldn't. She couldn't even move. Suspended mid-air, the shining glory of the CNS below her and her father's face towering above—the symbolism was deplorable. It had always been like this and always would be. Nothing she'd done had ever mattered. She'd run away like a coward, raced through half the galaxy for kicks, and came back expecting that things would turn out differently this time.

Only a wooden doll after all. Stagnant. Powerless.

"YOU WILL PAY FOR ALL OF IT. WE WILL GO OUT PROUDLY. THE ENEMY WILL NOT TAKE US."

She hung her head. So alone, so weak in here. She tried to speak up, straining to hear her own voice against the ramblings of this entity who thought was her father, but she could do nothing against it. Nothing at all.

"He's being awfully abrasive."

Jeane stared at her hands, around her, then at her fingers again. Roy was already looking out, arms akimbo, over the expanse of glimmering lights and translucent knife-edge towers, where a planet-sized apparition of an angular face roared at the small form of Maura floating in front of it. That was all awful and strange, but... she was here, she had her body, but this was not real, right? It was a simulated space inside a Miyozan computer, so how did it know how she usually felt in her skin? Her sense of self was indistinguishable from that in real life. Almost. Things were less restrictive, like everything could be gone at the flick of a finger.

"Hey." Roy clamped his hand onto her shoulder, and she looked up. "Let's get moving."

"But where?" They were standing on a hill of packed black earth below deep blue sky, the clearing crowned by jagged, towering constructs, with a narrow path of light leading down into the more crowded part of the... city? Machine? "Sure, let's climb up to the guy, and I'll punch him, but—oh, what the hells?"

Her hand, which had been empty a second earlier, now grasped her gun, the weapon looking just like the one she had in real life.

"No fair, I want one too!" Roy complained, but a piercing scream interrupted him. "Away or towards?" he started, but Jeane had already broken into a run—towards.

Circling the base of an iridescent tower at a crossroads of two flickering trails, she found herself in front of a girl with her face in her palms. She was maybe fifteen years old, with light brown hair fluttering in the wind—*why is there wind in here?*—and a green pearl pendant hanging around her neck. Sofia, as Maura had described her.

At the sound of their footsteps, she lifted her head. Her face, contorting into pain a second before, cleared, and she gave them a faint smile. "Sorry about that. I'm having a hard time staying detached from *him* here. But ALU brought you. Great!"

"What's going on, Sofia?" Jeane inclined her head towards Maura's body, still fixed in place above the city. The kinghead was silent now, his unbreaking attention on his prey. "What can we do?"

Sofia's eyes flitted about as if she didn't want to look at what was going on behind her back. "I think you can shut him down. I can't because I'm him and ALU either because they're only the connector here. And Maura is trapped. She's fighting it, but it's hard. But I can try to get you two the right permissions." Her voice devolved into confused muttering. "I think. I should be able to. We've never tried, but there's a first time for everything."

She looked at them expectantly, and Jeane squinted at Roy, unconvinced.

"We don't want to shut him down," he said. "We need the shield, and we need the CNS to keep Miyoza alive."

"The CNS can work without the AI," Sofia said. "For a while. Going to be harder on Maura, but—"

"Better than to be self-destructed?" Jeane nodded. "I agree. So where should we go? This place seems huge."

Sofia looked around. "Let me get back to you about it. First, I need to materialize it. One problem, though. *He,*" and she jabbed a finger at the head, "is going to make it difficult. Good thing he's focusing on her now, so we can lurk around. I mean, not a good thing for her, but..." She shook her head and threw an apologetic glance at them. "I'm all mixed up, sorry. You'll have to be careful too. Human minds in here... things could go in all sorts of loony ways. Ugh..." Her image flickered once. "It's so hard to stay—

shit... I'm sorry..."

Then she disappeared.

"Awesome," Jeane muttered.

"She'll be back," Roy said. "Let's go."

"Where?"

Roy raised his arm, the dancing lights in the tower walls around them tinting his face bright lilac, orange, then green. He had an almost regretful expression as he pointed beyond where Sofia had vanished.

The road of lights led down a decline among thin white obelisks, snaked around a grove of trees with angular branches, and disappeared into a gray mass of...

Debris and scrap metal. Broken, lumbering hull and cavernous airlock.

She inhaled sharply. The *Skylark*. Her ship was back. And ALU stood beside the open airlock door, waving at them.

"Come on," Roy murmured. He started on the trail, glancing back at her to see if she followed.

So, she did.

Her friends were in there with her. She knew that as sure as she knew if they stayed any longer, they would be dead before they understood why.

Because her father noticed them too. And he was smiling, reaching out, flooding towards them with the momentum of all its maddened, entropic power, attacking every leyline that led to their position.

It was so easy to overload a human mind. To play tricks, to lie to them, deceive them, push and shove all their flailing emotions and thoughts to the breaking point, then shatter them, leaving nothing but a useless cluster of nerves and tissue and electric current behind.

She couldn't let that happen.

The sound of crashing waves on a shore of craggy boulders echoed in her ears, and hope bloomed in her chest—Sofia was here too. And even if Maura wasn't able to shut her father down, together, they could fight his streams of death honing on Jeane and Roy long enough so that those two might succeed.

Maura stared into the face of the king. She wanted nothing more than to prove herself. To fight him, to make him see. There had to be a way.

But for now, words were useless. She turned away, her body aching like broken bones and torn-through skin, and reached out for Sofia.

Slamming doors was easy. She was familiar with it—all those doors closing on her all her life had taught her the lesson. A black hole of rage bloomed forth in her chest. Her father stretched towards Jeane as she stepped through the imagined doors of her precious, destroyed ship, and the sorrow surging up in the woman's mind bled through into Maura's heart. She saw the tendril of madness wrap itself around Jeane's ankle, pulling her closer to the void.

Maura felt Sofia shove against the constricting walls of insanity, and she leapt forward, thinking about the real Sofia, drawing bravery from her memory. They crushed the poisonous curl under their feet together, shutting the door in her father's face. Jeane breathed, freed from the pressure, a heavy sigh escaping her lips.

They sought out the next tendril and crushed it too. Maura saw them coming from miles away, even before they were a conscious thought in her father's mind. They swooped down on them, severing their connections, cutting the flow of commands down like the roots of toxic weeds.

Destroying was easy. That was all she'd ever known. She only had to persist.

"General, we're falling back to sublevel one. They just keep coming!"

Horst frowned at the comms in his hand and acknowledged the message with a "Copy, proceed." Things were looking dire.

Malina was losing ground in the hangars where the Miyozan citizens were held hostage, and Thorne kept pulling back his men. It looked like Hassak had some reserves of mechas and plasma launchers Horst didn't know about. He must have stored them nearby, preparing for something like this all along.

"We might have to join the fray soon," Nasir said, and the general peered at him. This man had been itching to blow things up since the beginning. Horst couldn't imagine that he and his compatriots running out to fight would weigh too much on their side, but he understood the compulsion.

But the Net fleet wasn't coming, and the status of the CNS remained the same after those two lanehunters had submerged into it. They might have to make their last stand against the Council here.

"Saori, can you hear me? There's a... hmm. There might be a problem."

It was Diaski, the Talalan, sitting inside the ship in front of the palace. Saori picked up the device from atop the pillar. "Dia? What do you see?"

The other comms device hanging on the general's belt, reserved for communicating with his teams outside the capital, signaled with a sharp sound. Liv reached for it, stepping closer to the lanehunter woman to hear the Talalan's words.

"Several ships just settled into orbit," they said. "I'm counting sixteen at this point, but more are coming."

Saori's eyes widened. "Is it the Net? Is the *Colugo* there?"

"Uh, yes," Diaski answered, hesitant. "They're not answering me, though. And most of the new vessels... I think they're Union destroyers."

Nasir and the queen's bodyguard exchanged an anxious glance. Saori closed her eyes for a quick second. And Horst didn't even need to accept the call from his own troops. He knew what they were about to report.

CHAPTER 35 | WAYS TO LEARN

Saori whacked the communicator against the side of the pillar, and the crash of plastic against metal plummeted into the echoless silence of the room. Nasir moved towards the lanehunter, leaving the muffled noise of gunshots and scrambling footsteps on the other side of the sealed door. The fight was so close; no matter how buried they felt in this dark, empty box, the world was threatening to break in.

"Nothing?" he asked.

Saori pursed her lips, the device pressed against her ear again. "No. The *Colugo* is silent."

"Doesn't make any sense," Nasir muttered. "That's a whole army right at our doorstep. They could annihilate us at any time."

Horst turned his attention to them, his brow tightly-knit. "They're not engaging, not even with the Net ships. But my units from the space station are silent, so I suspect the destroyers are jamming all communications."

"Maybe whatever Maura did to Leadership worked," Damian spoke up from his sentry post beside the pillar. The faint technicolor lights shimmering on the column threw a sickly shine on his face, emphasizing shallow wrinkles and crow's feet. "Maybe they're here to assist."

The High General gave a snort. "I'm sure they are."

Then Kliks, the Talalan, lifted one hand in warning, his eyes fixed at an arbitrary point on the opposite wall. "We might want to check in on Diaski. They're in a *mood*."

Whatever that meant, Saori understood, and she pushed two buttons on her communicator. "Dia? What's going on, hun? They're not getting to you, are they?"

After a long pause, Diaski answered. "I am fine. The *Tellu's* shield is holding, and they are not paying attention to me anymore. So many ships are around now. So many soldiers." They fell silent for a moment. "I could finish this. Point an incision at them, take them all away. Break them."

Saori looked at Kliks, alarm painted over her face. From Damian's quick explanation before everything had gone to shit, Nasir knew enough about the manipulator that he froze too, his brain running through the implications. Diaski could destroy *everything*: the ships in orbit and the whole planet, all of them included. They could do whatever they wanted.

Kliks took the comms from Saori with a tired expression. "You don't mean that, Diaski-ak."

"I don't?" They laughed weakly. "This is exactly what we didn't want, Kliks-ak. All these people, fighting and dying because of us!"

Kliks' face darkened. "We made a mistake, and to deal with what that means is a task for another day. All we can do now is--"

"They killed Firl!" Diaski snapped. "And when the others get here because they will, how many more of us will die?"

"And how would making a rash decision fix anything?"

"I could get out of here. Go far away, destroy the device. End this once and for all."

Nasir glanced at Saori, muscles tensing in anticipation. They needed to stop this, but with all the Gaerrisian soldiers gathering outside, how much chance did they have to reach Diaski in time? Kliks started talking to his sibling in Talalan with quick, subdued words of affirmation or warning, and with that, the situation had slipped out of their control.

"It's okay." Saori shook her head, jarring herself out of a momentary daze. "Diaski will do no such thing. They know the risks, and they're not a bad person. But they're grieving, and the wound is raw. We shouldn't have left them alone." She tore her gaze away from the pacing Kliks and glanced at Maura. "They need to hurry up."

Nasir gave a tense smile. "Not much we can do about that."

"Well. I'm alright with taking the last stand here. Feels like we're a part of something big." Saori returned the smirk. "I only hope this leads somewhere better."

"Agreed. Might not feel so honest coming from my mouth, though. Hope is kind of a job requirement for me."

Saori chuckled. Her eyes snapped to the door where the buzz of fight increased and dispersed like waves crashing against a cliffside. Ruao and General Horst were standing at the gate, half trying to listen to Kliks, half engaging in rapid-fire conversations with each other and the teams outside.

"You have any family out there?" Nasir asked Saori. At his own question, memories flooded his mind in torn-apart snippets of perfectly framed images. A childhood spent in peace and safety on the green plains of Morakka. A modest but happy life. Until the Union had arrived. But as the lanehunter woman's sharp eyes wandered back to him, he pushed the useless nostalgia away. That planet was a graveyard now, its people ghosts. Fought too hard, lost everything.

"Not much apart from my uncle," Saori said. "All the others died." Her body wavered, mirroring some brief mental imbalance. She glanced at Kliks, Jeane, and ALU and smiled again. "And then there's those three. What about you, freedom fighter?"

Before he could stop himself, Nasir's gaze fixed on Damian, and his chest tightened when his friend looked back at him. He glanced at Maura instead, then Ruao at the door, and forced himself to speak. "Everyone that matters to me is here."

For the first time in a long while, real terror gripped his heart. He didn't want things to end. There was no sense in living in a tyrannical world, having everything precious stolen away without the hope of retaliation, but he would have taken even that—even *this*, rather than being alone in death.

"Then we're in the best possible place," Saori said with that all-knowing smile Nasir couldn't decide was irritating or soothing. "The luckiest people in the world. Nothing can stop us now." And he didn't hear an ounce of sarcasm in her voice.

The following silence was broken by Diaski, yelling at Kliks in Common again. "Alright, alright! For now, but I'll keep it ready. And if they as much as peek in our direction, we have a choice."

"It might be for the best. Apparently, you're not the only one thinking that way." Horst stood, comms in hand, his back to the door, and Nasir saw his restraint cracking under the surface as he went on. "Two of the ground artillery stations turned away from the palace and locked on the Union destroyers. I don't know what the queen is doing, but it's not working."

As if on cue, a high-pitched noise started up on the other side of the Archive doors, and Nasir clutched his gun tighter. Laser cutter? Some kind of resonance bomb?

Whatever it was, those soldiers were coming in and fast.

Maura sensed the destroyers too late.

Her father's focus trembled, and he stopped his barrage on Jeane's and Roy's minds, and the triangular forms of the Union vessels materialized in the sky in an enlarged projection. Seven dark ships loomed against a backdrop of deep violet above the city of lights, among many smaller craft, and Maura recognized the *Colugo* in one of them. The Net flagship was dwarfed by the other huge constructs.

Then something changed inside the CNS, and she understood.

"Wait, no!" As the capital's targeting systems locked onto the destroyers and the shield dome's settings changed in preparation, her floating, useless body lurched, her brain trying to grasp and revoke her father's command to attack, but her effort was swept away by the king's will. "You can't!"

His voice boomed, its strength shaking her to the core. "THEY

ARE HERE TO DESTROY. TO MURDER. TO ERASE EVEN THE MEMORY OF US. I WON'T LET THEM."

"If you engage, they will retaliate and kill us all!"

"I DO WHAT I MUST TO WIN THE WAR. ONE MORE GLORIOUS BATTLE."

Maura wanted to scream. Fear pounded in her ears with renewed fervor. The Union was here. The Net had arrived. Everything was hanging on her. "The war is over, you stupid old fool!" she cried. "You're ruining our last chance to make peace, just like you always did!"

The head fixed its empty eyes on her, his eyebrows rising in what might have been anger at her harsh words. She would never have dared to speak to him this way in his life. Not even in the aftermath of Sofia's death.

His presence was the weight of a thousand black suns on her mind. A thousand dead bodies and a thousand empty graves.

"Direct defiance at last! I see you have learned something," he roared. "But you never understood. There is no peace with these monsters. The Union, Gaerris, the lanehunters—the filth of humanity, all of them! They wrecked Earth, and they're doing the same with the rest of the universe. We have to guard the light...and I tried... That is what I always tried to do..."

He trailed off, his voice bitter, longing. His hold on Maura slightly unraveled, and he felt...not rational, but more lucid. He hadn't yet given the command to fire at the destroyers and hadn't resumed his attacks on Jeane and Roy either.

This was her chance. For some reason, he was pausing to talk to her.

"Don't you understand?" he asked. "Don't you see how letting them win is the end of humanity?'

"No, I don't understand," Maura shot back. It wasn't difficult to allow her frustration and anger to fuel her words. "You never took the time to explain. With all your speeches about morals and glory, there was never any discussion. You never cared if I understood!"

"Then you need to understand now," the king replied. "The failings of their history, the cycle of violence and hate—you need to accept it's all they're capable of. Remember who these people are, and stop lying to yourself!"

"No!"

This time, there was no calculation in the outburst. The emotion flared up without warning, cold blue electric arcs buzzing around her in the empty air. She flexed her muscles, surprised at the sudden freedom of movement. Abruptly, her point of view changed; instead of looking up at her father's enormous image, she was now almost at level with him.

"I don't need to do that at all," she went on. *This is working.* "To accept defeat, to say it will all be in vain. I was perfectly fine deciding what to do without restricting myself with all that horrible baggage." It was surprising to discover how strongly she felt this was true. Perhaps she wasn't perfectly fine, sure. But she'd tried, something her father wasn't capable of. "Have you ever engaged with these people you loathe so much? Have you ever listened to any of them beyond your empty preaching?"

The face darkened into a frown. "You have no idea what you're talking about."

"I do, actually. I've been out there. Not by my own will, but—" Her voice dropped, doubts bubbling up again, but she snapped at herself. *Not the time!* "You always say humanity is dying, but that's not true. In a way, it is just starting to bloom, but we're smothering ourselves with useless wars and misunderstandings. I have allied with lanehunters who risked everything so they didn't have to murder thousands of innocent people. I travelled with a Union agent who was forced to do the most horrible things, but he's probably the kindest person I've ever met. Revolutionaries sacrificed their lives for me—me, the failed princess because they thought we had a chance to do something good! And I talked to the Leadership of the Union, and do you know the one thing they truly want to achieve? To protect humanity."

Maura paused. The look in her father's radiant eyes was incomprehensible. He was smaller now, his power only present at the edges of her consciousness, passive and silent.

"The ancestors of Gaerris and the Union might have been horrible bastards who left their planet to die," she went on. "But didn't our ancestors rob everyone else of all their resources to be the first to leave Old Earth and prosper? I suppose you would gladly ignore that particular truth."

The king's eyes flared up in wrath.

"Yes, I know about those old pains." She had to keep talking. Keep him occupied, keep him thinking. "It's despicable and tragic. But none of the people who committed those sins is alive today. And we can change. We *must*. There is a lot of darkness out there but hope too. General Horst is ready to make peace, and I intend to go through with it. You are the only detriment to Miyoza's happiness."

Not counting the Union army stalking them and the angry mob of Gaerrisian Council members currently trying to break down the doors, of course.

One thing at a time.

She sensed around but couldn't pinpoint Jeane and Roy. They were still there, along with Sofia and ALU, sunken deeper inside the lattice of the CNS now, taking advantage of the king's lapse of attention.

"You can't lead a society without having some regard to its history," her father hissed. He sounded sad, the sketch lines of his face caving in with each word.

Sorrow welled up in Maura, but she smiled through it. Her feet touched ground unexpectedly, and her father's image, wearing the dark blue formal outfit he'd been buried in, now stood an arm's length away from her. The brilliant structures of the virtual city encircled the smooth white platform they were on, and everything was very, very quiet.

"And there it is. *Some* regard," she said. "I know I have a lot to learn. I know things are complicated, and peace is but a daydream. But I need to believe it's not my enemy."

She reached for her father's hand (and against everything, it *felt* like his hand, warm and so full of life) and held it the way she never had before.

"Why are we doomed to repeat all our mistakes? Why can't we learn?" The grief she hadn't let herself feel since the funeral tightened her throat, tears flowing freely and blurring the uncomprehending features of the apparition in front of her. "Please, Dad. Let me learn. Don't make me give this up."

"Have you really been out there?" he asked. The locked up, betrayed, failing machine wondered. "Did you get away?" Maura nodded; she had run out of words. The king blinked—and were those teardrops clinging to his eyelashes? "It was only through my death that you became free of this hell. And now you think...you think you know better..."

"You did what you could," she whispered. To her father and to the AI, both confused, lost, and terrified. Like her. "You fought hard. Now let me try."

And the echo, the shadow, with whom she would never get the closure she longed for, clasped her hands to his chest. They stood like that, holding onto each other in the center of the shining empire they were battling for.

Jeane placed her hand on the inner hull, trying to breathe evenly. Her brain was a battleground; oppressive, dark thoughts and feelings assaulted her as she stepped through the airlock into the *Skylark*.

The ship was silent, and the dim corridor stretching to both sides was almost serene. Her bird looked better than the last time; no dented walls and curtains of smoke—she was only imagining it, after all. Her brain decided to reject the ruin and destruction and conjured up a more preferable version.

Or, judging from the strong urge flooding her, pushing her to proceed, it was a trap the king-AI had cooked up for them.

They'd heard most of his side of the argument with Maura until he went quiet. Looking upwards now, even inside the *Lark*, the darkness of the ceiling transitioned into the image of the purple sky and the Union spacecraft hanging there, but the kinghead was gone, along with the fragile figure of Maura.

Jeane felt Roy's hand on her shoulder. "Are you alright?" he asked, and she only had to nod.

"How's this gonna work?" She glanced at ALU, hoping Roy wouldn't notice the tremble in her voice. "We go through whatever shit this guy throws at us while Sofia tries to summon a Magic

Off Switch, and he won't be able to stop us because he's too busy trying to shout poor Maura's head off?"

The technician pattered forward. "Yes."

Roy sighed. "You don't know, do you?"

"We do!" ALU gave an indignant chirp. "We look. Sofia helps. It is here."

Jeane walked ahead, passing the two of them, turning to the left. She wished a flashlight into her hand, directing the beam to the deck, and gripped the gun in her right. "I've done missions with fewer instructions."

"Where to?" Roy held up his own weapon, which he'd managed to materialize just before they'd stepped into the ship.

Jeane was happy he was in here with her. She found it harder to give in to the hysteria scratching against her skull, seeing his stoical, almost relaxed reactions. He'd taken such a beating, both mentally and physically, but he was still around. Stars knew why. But she understood now what he'd told her back on the *Colugo*, sitting in that damn gunship. If he could do this, maybe she could too.

"Control room," she said. "Let's see what we find."

She was pretty sure what it would be, had known since they'd first glimpsed the remains of the *Lark*. The decision to leave Kliks behind seemed foolish now. If anyone, he should have been here for this.

Her heart beat frantically while they climbed the ladder and turned towards the control room. There wasn't any light in the hallway except the purple glow from above. Those dark ships kept grabbing for her attention. She hoped the others were safe. She hoped the shield was holding. She hoped the Net would be able to do something, that the Union would retreat, that Gertie and Dikent were still alive somewhere.

"When we're done here, we should arrange to get the *Skylark* from that planet," Roy said behind her. "Might be worth it."

And it was a nice sentiment, and Jeane was right on the verge of answering something rude to deflect, but then a shadow moved beyond the open door of the control room, and the breath died inside her chest. She walked forward like pulled on a string.

The man sitting in the co-pilot seat with his back to her came into view, and she clutched at her stomach. A burning hole had opened right in the center of her, and her body caved in like a derelict building.

It wasn't real. It wasn't him. But almighty skies, it *fucking* hurt.

"Jeane?" Roy said, and ALU knocked against her leg in warning. "Careful."

She took another step forward. Hollis turned, and at the same time, she heard an irate "Hey!" from behind. Spinning around, she caught the sight of Roy and her technician, stumbling, shoved back into the hallway by an invisible force. Then the door slammed shut, and she was alone in the cabin with the ghost of her dead foster father.

Hollis slapped his palms against his trousers, like he always did to clear the oil off his hands. His aged features pulled to a knowing smile, and he gestured at the pilot seat. "Hey, kid. Care to sit and talk?"

Roy could still see Jeane because the cabin door was inexplicably transparent now. She sat in front of the dashboard and turned towards the man who had to be her dad, but whatever she was saying was choked out by the strange barrier. He tried to walk ahead, but it was like moving through thick jelly or slushy water—his limbs got stuck in the air, and his momentum died after a few seconds of struggle. There was no getting back into the room.

"Looks like it's just you and me, buddy," he said, turning back towards the tail. But ALU was nowhere to be found, and he wasn't on the *Skylark* anymore.

A bright white hallway extended before him into infinity. The constant low buzz and the glaring light of the ceiling strips were painfully familiar.

Hurricane.

"Ah, shit," he said, to put it out there.

Something—someone—moved further down the corridor, disappearing into a branching path to the left. The lights blinked once, urging him forward.

He sighed, his chest constricting in cold anxiety. If the AI was forcing Jeane to meet Hollis in here, what did that promise to him?

I have to remember what I want to be, not what I'm supposed to be. "Yeah, okay. I know the drill," he muttered as he walked forward to follow the figure. "I'm going, I'm going."

"So, where are you hiding it?"

Hollis paused in his attempt to put his legs on top of the console, then gave a sigh and stacked them up anyway. "What are you talkin' about?"

Jeane clenched her jaw—her heart was racing at the speed of light. This was horrible and cruel and ridiculous. She forced herself to think. "Let's not pretend you're you. You're a fucking program, standing between me and the off switch, trying to stop me from knocking this asshole AI out."

She stared at the front display to avoid looking at him. Instead of the surrounding crystal city, endless starfields glared back at her.

Despite all her efforts, her memories of Hollis had faded through the years, and there were things about him she couldn't recall anymore. But the figure beside her stretching his arms out and leaning back in the chair with his hands behind his head—everything about him was perfect. A flawless reconstruction.

"I'd like to skip the part where you try to guilt or torture me into submission and get on with this," she added. "Let me fix stuff, and let me go."

"Oh, and why do you think you know how to 'fix stuff' better than an 'asshole AI,' huh?" Hollis chuckled, shaking his head in amusement.

Jeane snorted. "Well, that's something Hollis would never say to me. Careful now, I'm gonna keep count."

"Listen." The man put his legs down, turning towards her in the chair, elbows on his thighs. "You wanna talk real? Let's talk real. What d'you think will happen if you kids shut this place down?"

"We win?" Jeane shrugged. "Save a bunch of people, bring peace to the world?"

"Nuh-uh. I don't care about that." He leaned forward, frowning. "And you don't care either. What happens to you?"

Jeane swallowed and shifted in the pilot chair. She shouldn't have sat down to talk to him. She had to hurry, do something, now or never, but she didn't know how to leave. Her legs weren't moving, and her traitor heart kept crashing against the cage of her ribs.

"What happens to *you*?" Hollis repeated. He spread his arms out. "Your ship is a garbage pile, the place you would call home a ruin. You know you can't go on like this."

"Stop trying to make this about me."

"It was always about you." Hollis smiled, not cruel but understanding. "What are you thinking, hm? That if you do this, it would be enough? To find some kind of goal or meaning? To finally feel good about yourself? For your friends to like you again?"

She snarled. "Fuck you too."

"I'm just saying what's on your mind, kid!" Hollis shook his head. And wasn't he right? This was what she was thinking, wasn't it? "And by the way, they won't. You screwed up. So busy protecting yourself, you keep losing everyone."

Jeane's heart sank like a boulder dropping into a bottomless ocean. Vertigo dragged her down; she shivered and had to hold onto the armrests. She started to count her heartbeats, tried to tell herself this was all just a trick, lies made up to screw with her, but then Hollis knelt in front of her and took her hands in his.

"It's alright, you hear me?" he said quietly. "No need to blame yourself. It is what it is."

A sob escaped her throat, and although she longed for the comfort of his touch, she pulled her hands away, pressing them on her mouth. She took long, shaky breaths. The man who was Hollis, but wasn't, grabbed her by the shoulders, and she had to look into his clear blue eyes. There was no escape from the truth.

"You don't have to be strong or kind. You're okay, exactly like this."

She heaved, her body shaking from the tension, the pain crawling up her throat and flooding her brain. But wasn't this comforting too? It didn't have to be her failure. It was something innate, something she couldn't stop. Some people were just broken.

The rational part of her knew the apparition was trying to sabotage their plan. But another part, deeper, kept wondering. Was anyone even expecting her to come through? She was a disgrace, a liar. She'd thrown away everything and everyone. And if she got out of here—then what, indeed? She couldn't trust herself to make the right calls. She couldn't just get a new ship and go on doing jobs like before.

She'd known this long ago, back when she'd left the Ranch. It would only last so far. *You can only run for so long.*

Hollis was right. Everyone would have been better off without dealing with her. Roy had her believe she had a chance, but it would be just the same thing again. Ignoring the hole inside her, busying herself with pretend ambitions. Because she didn't care. She never did. Saving people, bettering the world, fighting for freedom?

No. She squeezed her eyes shut. For once in her life, she needed to be honest with herself. None of those things mattered. She was nothing.

And if that hole would never go away? If she wouldn't feel at home or safe, ever again? She couldn't live like that. She wouldn't go back to that. Not again.

Roy was in the training pits, and Danai stood behind the chair he'd been bound to when they first met, and she smiled at him. "You didn't think you could run away from this, did you?"

Exhaustion flooded him, and now there was nothing he could tell himself to push it away. He had been hoping he still had time. He wanted to do something worthwhile, to balance out all the misery, but maybe it was too much to ask for.

"Better get through with it," Danai said, her voice calm and kind. "You know it will end here. Why wait?"

"I still have—"

"You have nothing."

"I need to help."

The woman's grip tightened on the backrest of the chair. "Who would need your help? You're a danger to yourself and a danger to everyone. No one needs you."

"That's not true," he argued, but his voice was weak. Why was she back? Why did he have to see her again? It was over. They should be free. "We could stop a war."

"Roy." Danai lowered her voice, and it was the sound of teeth grinding, children crying in pain, cannons firing and demolishing whole planets. "Come here, and sit down."

And like all those times before, he couldn't refuse her command. Roy walked forward, taking his place under the blinding lights. There was a door across from him, its hinges shaking under the force of something slamming into it again and again from behind.

Of course. Everything led here in the end. He had to repent.

"I can't let them shut me down," the king whispered. Maura looked at him, her eyes widening. "I understand what you're saying, but I only wish it was that easy."

She moved to take a step back, but the man held onto her hands.

"It *is* that easy," she said, struggling to break free. "Let me take control, please! I can save us."

"Too late. Look."

He pointed at the ships looming above them. Streaks of fire lit up the sky, missiles leaving Miyoza's atmosphere and crashing into the Union vessels. The destroyers' shields flashed up as they deflected the damage. Maura watched in horror as more and more columns of light lifted off the ground, climbing to their targets:

both the destroyers and the Net ships.

"Gaerris got impatient," the king said. "Let's begin."

His face darkened, and he reached up to bring down the sky on them.

"No!" Maura grabbed his hand, called into the depths for Sofia's help, and extended her will. Thin threads of light flashed up before her eyes, and she threw her arm out to extinguish them.

The king grasped her with claws of cold pain and sent her flying into the airless void. Maura lunged again, smashing into the wall of jagged, deformed debris of his command with her whole body. Her hands burned holes into the metal, agony jolting through her arms.

The king roared, readying himself. She charged once more, the sound of her own cracking bones echoing in her head. But it was not real. The pain was only in her mind. She had to stop him.

They collided, unmovable resolution against desperate persistence, and the city shook under their struggle.

"There you go," Hollis said, his voice a breath of fresh air. "It's all going to be okay. You will be alright. Stay awhile."

Jeane inhaled, eyes closed, fingers clutching Hollis' hand, trying to gather her thoughts. She could do that. Hide away as if nothing existed. Pretend she still had Hollis and life made sense, and nothing could hurt her.

She wanted that. More than anything.

But she'd done that before, in a way. Was it ever enough?

"I'm scared."

It was Maura's voice, Roy's voice—her own voice. Maura, hanging in the center of the sky, her father's fury roaring at her. And Roy must have been in a similar nightmare-scape, confronting ghosts of his own. They were both in over their heads, the fate of everyone they'd dragged along with them hanging by a thread. She couldn't fail them.

They all cared about her, for some inexplicable reason. And she cared too. She dared to care, finally; cared more than she did about her own misery.

The pain would be here later. For now, she had to get up. She had to move.

«Finally, a good fucking idea.»

"That's two," she mumbled.

"What?"

Jeane opened her eyes, and the man before her reared back. "The second thing Hollis would never tell me. To stay and wallow when there's a mission to finish."

Hollis grimaced, nothing kind on his face anymore. "To save humanity? As if. See those ships up there? Y'all are dead already."

"You don't get to decide that."

She lunged, shoving Hollis away to sprint at the door, but he was expecting it. He gripped her arms, sinking his fingers into her flesh, dragging her backward into the darkness.

"Leave me alone, you creep!" she shrieked.

"Come on now, this was supposed to be easy!" Hollis caught her wrists, crushing them with unreasonable tenacity. "You were never that strong."

Her knees buckled in pain. Then she paused. This was so stupid. Physical strength had nothing to do with this place.

"That took you long enough."

Both of them turned towards the source of the new voice. Or rather, the old voice—because the man standing at the door was Hollis too.

Jeane grinned. The Hollis beside her relaxed his grip in his surprise, so she pushed him away, backing up.

"Took you long enough to show up, idiot!" She looked at the second Hollis. His contours were blurry, constantly shifting in and out of focus, but the wide smile on his face was familiar, like all those times he'd told her about one of his particularly bonkers adventures. And his voice—it wasn't his real voice, but the one that had been talking to her through all her years of wandering.

"Well, get on with it!" he waved towards the door. Something was happening to the other Hollis behind him, the figure growing, extending, gray tendrils wrapping around his limbs as it crawled forward. But her Hollis wasn't paying attention to him; he met her eyes with a piercing look. "You're on the right path. It will be difficult. Don't give up now."

She didn't know what to say, and he didn't wait for her. Turning around, he pulled his gun out and jumped to the right, firing at the king's monster. It roared in pain and drew back—Hollis advanced, shooting again and again, and soon both figures vanished into the growing darkness.

Jeane turned around and ran.

Roy closed his eyes as Danai tied his hands to the armrest and connected the wires to the helmet on his head. She was humming a simple melody, and Roy focused on the tune, trying to distract himself from his shameful inability to stand up and leave. The dull thumping of the monster against the door ahead did not relent.

He wanted to leave. He should have left. But his mentor was right. It was always going to end this way. He was nothing—worse than that. The lives he'd taken. The lies he'd lived. He deserved this.

"It's going to be easier than it seems," Danai said in a comforting tone. "You just have to let it in."

Roy opened his eyes, and she was smiling, and it was almost enough for him to forget her face from the last time as she'd drawn her final breath. Almost.

He shut his eyes again. He was so tired. So tired of feeling lonely, unwanted, and empty. It was time to rest.

The machine powered up, the tingling sensation of electricity running over his skin. As the monster howled behind the door, Roy was prepared to welcome the pain and let it in.

"Oh no, you don't."

His eyes sprung open and focused as Jeane rushed forward, grabbed Danai's shoulder, and punched her square in the face, shoving her slumping body away with the same motion.

"What a load of bull!" Her eyes found Roy still sitting in the chair and widened in shock. Her face was flushed, her eyes glinting with tears, hair messy as if she'd been in a fight, but her voice was sharp and commanding. "What in all hells are you waiting for?"

"I—" What *was* he waiting for?

The lanehunter rushed to his side and undid his bonds. Roy glanced around in a daze—the door had disappeared, the monster silenced. Danai climbed back to her feet, but Jeane was already pulling Roy out of the chair, wrapping her cold fingers around his wrists, and they were suddenly in another place, somewhere deep inside the crystal city, surrounded by shimmering grass and towering spirals.

The ground was shaking, a deafening rumble filling the air. Above them, the sky was on fire.

"What are you— How did you find me?" Roy watched three streaks of flame ascending to the heavens. "What's happening?"

Jeane shook her head. "No time to explain. Apparently, I passed the test. I'm moving more freely now. Sofia!" she yelled out. "Come on, girl, help me out!"

A moment passed, and her frown disappeared. Face brightening, she grabbed his hand. "This way."

The view changed again, this time, to full darkness. The rumble was far away, like miles of earth were separating them. Roy saw a circle of light ahead, illuminating a pillar very similar to the one Maura had connected to in the Archives. Jeane hurried forward, and he had no choice but to follow.

"We found it!" She pointed at the pillar. "We fucking found it. I can't believe it!"

"Is this the Magic Off Switch?" Roy asked. His head was spinning. A few seconds ago, he was ready to depart this mortal coil, and now... "How are you doing this? The teleporting thing?"

Jeane placed her hands on the pillar and grinned at him. "I'm just that good."

⌇   ⌇   ⌇

"Diaski, what in hells are you doing?" Saori exclaimed, but Liv was barely paying attention to the lanehunter. Malina had just reported that she'd secured the Miyozan hostages in their ships, and her unit was departing to clear out the Gaerrisian-controlled artillery stations that kept firing at the destroyers. She was splitting off halfway to come and assist Liv in the palace.

He'd told her not to. She'd told him to fuck off.

The Archives' doors were seconds away from breaking through as Ruben Hassak and his people bombarded it with whatever tricks they had up their sleeves. Thorne was dead, his people scattered, so he sure wasn't coming to help.

"I'm saving them. What else?" the Talalan shouted through the radio. "I cannot catch every missile, the incisions need time to form, but maybe they'll see the intention."

"I take it they're not firing back at the city?" Nasir asked.

"No, they're— Wait, what?"

A screeching noise resounded from the door, and Liv grabbed Nasir and his friend, pulling them back to the middle of the room. One more push, and the soldiers got through.

"I think it might be us. It's Talala!" Diaski's voice was incredulous. "Other incisions keep popping up, not only the ones I'm making. Oh, my stars, this is getting dangerous."

The shrieking increased in volume until something popped. Then silence.

"Ready yourselves!" Liv called out. The two lanehunters stepped forward, gun in hand. Damian stood like a monolith, protecting his queen and his friends with his body.

Liv glanced around. They had no cover whatsoever. This place was a grave.

There was a loud boom, a flash of light. A surge of air, shouts, then gunshots. They were inside.

"You need to focus. Sofia is busy keeping us in secret, and I'm not sure whether ALU can drag you all out of here alone. I will try to send you to them, but you have to grab Maura." Jeane stopped pacing, dropping her arms in an exasperated motion. "Are you listening? It's only a question of life and death, but take your time!"

The cave was rocking around them. The echoes boomed like creatures howling in the night. Roy had no way to know, but he felt Maura was at the end of her rope. Whatever she was doing to distract the AI would soon be overwhelmed by its immense strength.

"Wait, 'you all'?" he asked, looking back at Jeane. "What does that mean?"

She raised an eyebrow like the answer was obvious. "I'm gonna have to stay here and push the button to switch the guy off, don't I?"

"And what happens then?"

"I have no idea," Jeane huffed. "What happens when your brain is shut down together with a maniac AI who is hitting you with everything he can?"

Roy recoiled. "I'm not leaving you. Forget it."

"That's not your choice." Jeane stepped forward, reaching out for him. "Come on, I can start you off. You'll have to visualize—"

"No! No way!"

He took a step back, shaking his head, and Jeane exhaled. "If Sofia can't hold her ground, this thing here could disappear any moment. Then we'll never find it again. We don't have time! Go!"

"Why you?" His voice sounded miserable, but he didn't care. "I know ALU and Sofia can't, but I'm here. I'm ready!"

The woman gave him a sad smile. "No. You...you need to be safe. You still have to get free from all the mess you've been through. Me? I think I've just peaked!" She laughed, and it sounded so honest, so joyful, that Roy's heart trembled. "I won a fight today. It's not much, but it counts. And if this is the end of my game, it's how I want to go. Not to be a martyr, or because I want to die. I want to do this for all of you."

Another tremor shook the earth. Roy didn't move, couldn't make himself move, so Jeane closed the distance between them. She clutched his arms, looking into his face from up close.

"Listen. ALU will try to disconnect me as quickly as possible, so I might make it out. I might be fine."

"You might not," Roy whispered.

"And in that case," and she poked him in the chest, "you'll take care of Kliks and ALU for me. You tell Maura and Damian that I love their dramatic faces. And Saori, and Gert, even Dikent, and the guys on the Ranch, and—" She paused, contemplated something, a swift shadow passing on her face. "Huh. So many of them, eh? Doesn't matter now. Off you go."

"Wait!" Fear jolted through Roy's muscles. She couldn't be gone like this. They'd only just met! "You can't. I still—"

She placed a hand on his cheek, and he clutched her wrist like that could keep her there. Jeane smiled, her lips wavering. "You're good. Listen to me. Don't fuck this up. You're doing great."

She let him hold her for a long second. Then something blazed up behind her eyes, expanding outward in a white arc of light, and the next moment, she was gone.

Outside, the shield above Miyoza flickered and disintegrated. The artilleries stopped firing, and soldiers and civilians looked at the sky with fearful eyes as the city, together with the palace, plunged into darkness.

CHAPTER 36 | WIN SOME, LOSE SOME

"To all humans and other life forms on the planet and in orbit. This is the AI Leadership. Cease all attacks against our vessels. Cease all violent interactions on the planet and in orbit. We will talk to Maura Tholis, Queen of Miyoza. We will talk to Tantalus, born of Miyoza. You have fifteen minutes."

Maura's eyes snapped open. The breath hitched in her throat, and she grabbed for the edge of the pillar, but her legs gave out. She fell to the floor, the echo of her father's voice howling in her ear. Her whole body was racked in pain, unable to move.

The first thing that registered from the real world was the sound of deafening gunshots. Then the shouts of people around her, then beams of light flitting about, illuminating nonsensical shapes. The next moment, a small object clattered to the ground in front of her face.

Dread filled her. She tried to move away, but her limbs wouldn't obey.

"Heads up!" a familiar voice yelled above her, and someone slid into her field of view, scooped up the object, and threw it back into the dark. "Grenade!"

There was a flash of light and a thunderous bang. The grenade must have gone off outside the room, its effects dampened by distance and the remains of the Archives' door, which she just glimpsed before everything was swallowed by the blaze. When the light subsided, Damian leaned over her with a distressed expression; he took hold of her shoulders and pulled her backward for some cover, using the few seconds of break in the gunfire.

Propping her back against the column, she let her consciousness catch up with the events. She was out of the CNS, and the Gaerrisians were pushing inside the Archives. They were trapped.

Looking around, in the nervous fluttering of flashlight beams, she saw Horst and Saori, close to the walls, crouching with their guns held up. Nasir and Ruao were lurking around, always in motion, keeping their weapons trained on the vertical gap blown into the doors. Roy huddled next to her, his eyes wild, trying to comprehend his surroundings. On his other side, ALU's crumpled form was cradling an unconscious Jeane, their hand wrapped around her arm, still in contact with her mind. Kliks knelt at her side, tears running down his face.

A sliver of memory: her father, pushing against her, trying to join the Gaerrisians in their attempts to fire at the Union destroyers. She cringed at reliving that endless pressure. Her will was breaking down as the seconds ticked by, but then something made the AI pause. Furious and hurt, it snapped its attention deep inside the system, and a familiar pang reverberating through her mind told Maura it was Jeane. The captain had found a way to turn off the AI.

Her father had lunged at the intruder with everything he had, and Maura had thrown herself into the fray a microsecond too late. She'd heard her friend scream, she'd felt Sofia jump after her into the void, then everything went black.

"Is she—" Roy looked at ALU, his voice hoarse.

Someone released three shots towards the door above them— the Gaerrisians must have gathered themselves and tried to push through the gap.

ALU shook their head. "Alive. But..." They trailed off, their voice strained and terrified. "Have to go back in system. Now."

A burst of gunfire rattled from the door. The Gaerrisians weren't trying to massacre them and only kept constant pressure on the group, but Maura wondered how much longer it would take until someone got hurt. Saori shouted something to the general, and Horst, keeping his gun steady in his left, lifted the comms device in his right to his ear.

"Are you alright?" Damian's hand was on her shoulder as if checking whether she was in one piece. "Is the AI out?"

"I don't know," Maura said. One brush against the pillar with her gloved hand told her the CNS and the shield were down and the entry point was dead. But the AI could be still lurking in there, waiting to be activated. She glanced at Jeane—the unusual peace on her unconscious face made her stomach rise. "I'll need to see. I need to connect—"

"One second, Your Majesty." Horst raised his voice, calling out to the besiegers while talking into his comms as well. His voice boomed loud and clear. "Cease fire, cease fire!" The others tensed, and although they stopped firing, they kept their guns trained on the door. Damian stood and settled into a similar position. "We surrender! I have a message to Ruben Hassak."

Maura scrambled to her feet and looked at the general, her raised brows forming the silent question. Horst gave her a stern look.

After a moment, a man called out from the corridor, his voice raspy. It had to be Hassak; Maura knew him to be the third member of the Gaerrisian Council. "Surrender?"

Horst chuckled. "No, not really. But you need to turn your comms to wide local. Those destroyers have something to say to us."

Before anyone could have moved, Saori held up her talkie, and a cold, computerized voice came through the speakers. She turned up the volume, taking a step towards the door, but none of the Gaerrisians had poked their head out yet.

"...all violent interaction on the planet and in orbit. We will talk to Maura Tholis, Queen of Miyoza. We will talk to Tantalus, born of Miyoza. You have fifteen minutes." After a pause, the message started again. "To all humans and other life forms on the planet and in orbit. This is the AI Leadership. Cease all attacks against—"

"I'm coming forward," Hassak said. Horst gestured to the others, and everyone dipped their guns lower.

Maura took a deep breath. From the shadows around the Archives' doors, a huge man walked out, cutting through the metallic rubble scattered about the gateway. He stopped a few steps away, his angled, bare face severe, his jaws clenched tight. Two of his people followed him out, their features remaining in the dim as Ruben Hassak faced Horst in the center of the room.

"What is it this time, traitor?" he asked, realizing he waited for the general to speak in vain. "Are you selling us out to the Union as well?"

Maura could have sworn that for a quick second, Horst wanted to roll his eyes, but he managed to regulate his features to answer calmly.

"You tell me, friend," he said. "Will you stop murdering your own people?" Hassak gave a disapproving grunt, but the general didn't let him interrupt. "What would you do if we surrendered anyway? You heard them. They want the queen."

"And we want a chance for independence!" Hassak spat. "After all this time, victory is ours, but you'd rather cower before our enemies. Our people deserve—"

"What our people deserve is to live their lives in peace and safety!" Horst's voice clattered hard in the tight space. "I told you all King Caiden would not back down, but you wanted to push him to the breaking point. I told you the Union would come for us, and we will need allies and not more enemies. I begged you to see reason for years. I'm done begging. The rest of the Council have already stopped their assault of those destroyers. We can shoot each other in the head right now, or you can smarten up and listen to her."

He flashed his eyes at Maura, inviting her to talk. She blinked the muddled sensation in her head away while Hassak glared at her, mistrustful.

"I will speak with Leadership," she started. "We can't fight the Union like this. Seven destroyers are waiting up there for us to make a wrong move, and more may be coming."

"It's true. Hurricane is looking our way now." It was Diaski's voice. They must have been listening through Saori's comm. "That's what my people tell me."

"You hear, Ruben? The Talalans are here too." Horst looked almost relaxed now. Nothing left to lose for him, nothing he hadn't buried a thousand times before. "Our friends from the Net as well. All these people are gathering here to fight it out, and you and I are still alive. That is on no one else but the queen."

Hassak locked eyes with Maura again, but this time, she caught a glint of despair deep under all those layers of hate and defiance. "And what does the Union want with you? Who is Tantalus?"

"They mean ALU. The AI I'm working with." She truly had no time to explain the difference between Sofia, the city-AI, and ALU. "And I'm not sure what they want. I believe I helped the Union's AI before. Whatever they want must stem from that."

Hassak frowned. "You *helped*? It sounds like all you did was draw their attention."

"You will talk to the queen with respect." Damian stepped forward, boiling anger radiating off his skin. "She's the only one between you and the death of everyone you've ever known. She's risking her life for us."

"Back off!" one of Hassak's guards yelled out, lifting a gun at Damian. "Back off, now!"

Maura walked ahead of her friend, hands held up, trying to show her most earnest face. "Please, settle down! The fact that the Union hasn't engaged yet is a good thing. Let me talk to them! The CNS is down, but I may be able to reset the palace's local systems so we're not defenseless. We're not going anywhere any time soon. This is where we'll face the consequences of our actions."

Hassak seemed to digest her words, trying to find his way out of the situation. But there was no way out, only through—those fifteen minutes were ticking away quickly. Jeane might have even less.

"We will go back to the Grand Hall," Maura said. No carefully prepared speech this time; she only had these words, flimsy as they ever proved to be. "We will all hold fire, and we will talk and listen, and we will survive. I promise you, Ruben Hassak, I stand by your side. I will not forget the crimes of the past, but I'm not giving up on us."

She glared at him, unflinching, willing the last drops of her resolve to emerge to the surface. It felt like an eternity until Hassak nodded, then, with an inscrutable expression on his face, turned around and walked out. "Let's go," he called. "We don't have much time."

Maura's shoulders sagged as she turned to face the others. Nasir and Ruao had already gathered themselves, and Saori was helping ALU to lift Jeane. Roy took one of the captain's arms on his shoulder while Kliks took the other; the technician stayed in front of her, one long appendage connecting to her hand. They all glanced at Maura, exhausted and terrified, and she tried to smile, but it ended up more like a painful grimace.

"Will he shoot us in the back?" she asked the general, inclining her head to Hassak and his soldiers.

"Probably. He will wait until you talk to the Union, though. He's not that dumb. But what do you think we can expect from them?" Horst inclined his head upwards.

She let the panic wrap its icy fingers around her heart, waiting for the inevitable release. She reached for Damian, who stood by her side like always. Her always watchful guardian. She took his hand. Appearances be damned, she needed her friend.

Damian squeezed her fingers, his skin and his brown eyes warm like home, like a safe place in the chaos. They were almost through. It was almost over.

"I only hope we will live to see tomorrow," she said.

Horst gave a conceding grunt. "I'm all for keeping our expectations low."

Maura took the lead with Damian and the general, leading the Gaerrisians—ten soldiers and Hassak, since the others had scattered to keep watch on the surrounding corridors, supposedly expecting trouble from the Union or from Malina Trevise's troops— and the rest of the group back to sublevel one and up to the ground floor. Saori stayed in contact with Diaski, who reported ever-increasing activity around the destroyers and the Net ships, although no one had answered their calls yet. The Talalan vessels kept away, far from the conflict, not opening any more incisions since the barrage against the destroyers had stopped. Maura supposed they would not interject anymore, not until they had to. The fact that they had come, and with their own copy of the manipulator too—she hadn't expected it. There was no way to tell what would happen now.

Leadership kept repeating the same old message. They had five minutes left.

It happened when they reached the corridor leading to the Grand Hall.

The place was devoid of life, bodies strewn around where they died in the battle between Hassak and the High General's soldiers. The dust in the air dimmed the light scattering in from the floodlights through the windows as they walked forward. Maura was looking away from the door on the opposite end, trying to catch what Hassak was saying into his comms, when Horst shouted "Halt!" and by the time she turned back, several people had jumped in front of her, and she was shoved to the ground.

A series of gunshots rang out above her, but it did little to stop the figure barreling towards them in the corridor.

The last time she'd met the man, there had been three of him.

She heard the sound of glass breaking, then bodies climbing through the windows, hurtling at them—more Union goons? Inspectors? Agents? Then gunshots, returned by the group behind her. Korrh, towering above, projectiles crashing against his body, lifted his arm and swept away two soldiers with one swing and broke a third's neck with a simple motion. Maura struggled to her hands and knees to back away, aching limbs screaming for relief as the inspector lumbered towards her.

Damian jumped at Korrh, like two mountains colliding, and she screamed for him, trying to get up and help. Someone held her down for a moment, then Nasir ran forward, his battle cry shaking the air.

Then it was Damian on the ground, and Nasir moving in front of him, then a lurch in the man's movement; something unnatural and wrong. He collapsed as Damian roared and climbed to his feet again. Blood on the stone floor, the smell of burnt flesh, shouts of despair, and the darkness—there was just not enough light to see anymore.

She barely noticed the door at the end of the hallway open again. She only saw the unmoving forms of her friends; she only felt the ache in her chest of something horribly final, of something precious ending; she only heard her own sobs as she lifted her gun to fire at Korrh.

The inspector smashed into her. There was a distorted cry, Roy's voice, and Maura's body folded in pain. Then a familiar force took hold of her, and as reality splintered away, the last traces of light died too.

A shimmer from the setting sun on the surface of the ocean. Maura wanted to reach out for it, but she realized she didn't have a body.

Was she in the CNS again? How did it happen? She imagined herself, fixed her senses and her usual dimensions, looking around with newly opened eyes. Three shimmers, she corrected herself, surveying the surrounding void.

Wait, what?

The luminous spark of a consciousness wilting in an instant, an arm's length away.

She remembered. Korrh. The blood. Bodies falling— bodies...falling—

Two of the shimmers took form, like called out from her memory, and the figures of Damian and Nasir stepped out from the darkness. The void tightened around her throat, and her heart was drumming against her ribs—this wasn't real, this was all wrong.

"We're dying, aren't we?" Damian's voice broke like he understood, and from the depths of nothingness, someone answered his question.

"We're sorry." It was ALU. It was regret, grief, and desperation. "We can't keep you...we can't..."

Nasir lifted his trembling hands, smoothed his hair down, and rubbed his eyes. He breathed deeply around the same panic that was rising in Maura's stomach. "It's okay. You wanted us to have a chance to say goodbye."

No. "Yes..."

No! "There has to be something we can do!" Maura cried out, and she hugged her chest to keep herself from collapsing as her friends' eyes focused on her like her presence only registered in their fading minds the moment she spoke.

"This is...seconds, outside." ALU's voice was hardly audible. "Longer here. We're trying...we can't fix you...we can't keep you..."

She was crying, seeing nothing, hearing nothing. This was too cruel, this wasn't supposed to happen, how could this be happening, how was it even possible to bear this much sadness, why was she always, always losing everyone—then strong arms enveloped her, a palm settled on her back, and she was sobbing and screaming and cursing like it mattered.

And it felt like the pain would never stop until it did, and there was only the breathing, the memory of the ache, and the presence of her friends beside her.

She stepped back, wiping her tears—if this was the last time, she wanted to see them clearly. Nasir leaned on Damian's shoulder; he was crying too, but he lifted his head.

"You tell those bastard Gaerrisians the Net fought for them." He straightened his back, pride emanating off him like starlight. "We gave our lives for theirs. They have no excuse anymore."

Against everything, this made her smile, and she hugged him again, holding his face in her hands, trying to memorize every single line and imperfection. "I will tell. I won't let it be in vain. You did so much for us when you didn't even have to."

Nasir smiled, squinting at Damian, the terror gone from his gaze as he answered. "I always imagined I'd die for this man one day. I sort of hoped he would keep living as a result, but I guess you can't have everything."

There was a moment between them and a shadow of a smile passing over Damian's face.

"Tell my friends I love them," Nasir said. "They know, but tell them anyway. Tell it to yourself too. It was an honor to know you. Keep our home safe. Show them all how to do this right."

She nodded, but when Damian looked at her, she felt herself break again and stepped back because she wanted nothing more than to embrace him again. But that couldn't happen because he was leaving, and how would she touch him knowing it would be the last time?

"I can't do this," she whispered to him. "I can't do it without you."

"Yes, you can." Those serious eyes of his were smiling now; how could he be smiling when he was vanishing from her world? How was that the saddest but most reassuring thing she'd ever seen? "You can, and you will. You will live, and you will do amazing things."

He closed the distance between them that she couldn't and took her hand in his. Like he'd always done. "I love you," he said. "Always will. Always on your side."

"It's not fair!" she sobbed, the tears burning her eyes. "It's not! Why you? Why now?"

He leaned forward, their foreheads touching. His breath on her face, erratic and shaky, betrayed his feelings even through the comforting things he said.

"I know it's not. It's never been. You deserve so much more. But you will make it through." He clutched her hands stronger. "You will. I'm sorry I won't be there to see it. How you will shine."

"Please don't go," she whispered. "Please..."

His hand slipped out of hers. "I love you. I'm sorry. I love you all. Don't ever give up."

He turned away, his face soaked in tears, wide-eyed and scared, but brave until the end—and their forms were fading, their light dancing away from her as the two men walked off, side by side, towards distant shores. The numbness growing in Maura's limbs consumed everything, and the sound of waves crashing on dark cliffs drowned out her own muffled cries.

They glanced back at her once more, then they disappeared in the emptiness for good.

So many voices around her when she wanted silence. Why were they so loud? Didn't they know what just happened? Didn't they understand it was all over?

"Maura? Can you get up?"

Roy crouched beside her, face pale, eyes searching hers, holding onto her arm like a drowning man. She sat up, measuring her moves like she only had a limited number of them, and for a second, she panicked because some of the incredible amount of blood soaking Roy's clothes, hands, and face must surely have been his. But he seemed unhurt, at least physically, while the same couldn't be said about Korrh. His hulking body lay behind the ex-agent—mangled, gutted, not even resembling a human anymore. Roy blinked, following her gaze, and turned back to her like he'd seen a ghost.

"I'm sorry. I couldn't get him in time," he said, the words struggling to surface. His voice was different—hard and bitter. "I was too late...I'm sorry..."

"No, no, don't do that." She squeezed his hand, the blood slick on his skin. She couldn't think about it. He shouldn't make her think it. "It wasn't...it's not your fault. Are you okay?"

He didn't answer, lost in his world. She kept stroking his hand soothingly and glanced at the people around them, standing in small groups muttering to each other, checking themselves for wounds, gathering their weapons, and guarding the doors and windows. And all over on the ground, corpses.

Those, she couldn't look at. Those, she couldn't think about. Instead, she searched for ALU and found them crouching with Kliks and Jeane not far off. They were in the process of retracting a pair of long arms, those arms that a moment ago had been holding onto her and—

She inhaled, and the technician returned her gaze. She wanted to say "thank you" or "sorry," but she couldn't form the words. What was it that Jeane was always doing? Counting her heartbeats? She struggled to find that fluttering sensation in her chest, all her thoughts slipping out of her grasp like water.

"I'll be fine. But our time is up," Roy said. His hands were shaking. He'd torn Korrh apart. He had let something out of himself that he shouldn't have, and he would hate himself for it. "What are we going to do?"

"Jeane?" A new voice called out, howling above the chattering and murmur. A blond man in a mismatched outfit—a suit coat, baggy trousers, and combat boots—with a bruised face and blood smeared over him crossed the crowd and fell on his knees beside the unconscious captain, grasping for her arm, his eyes furious. "What did you do to her, fuckers? What the hells happened to her?"

"She's alive, Dikent," Kliks said sternly, and the man paused. The Talalan looked like a faded copy of himself. His eyes flicked at Maura, then Roy, then at the bodies. The bodies of— "We don't have much time."

"Your Majesty," Horst spoke somewhere above her. He stood with Hassak and two new figures—two women, one of them tall with raven black hair, dressed in the same type of uniform that Commander Hill wore, the other Gaerrisian, someone high-ranked. Maybe the general's second, Malina Trevise. "The area is cleared. It was only this one group. I'm really sorry, but we have to go."

Maura stood, taken by an unexpected wave of momentum. The crowd moved with her, urged by the same energy. Everyone started gathering themselves, grabbing at their guns, helping up the injured.

The black-haired woman stepped up to her, reaching out to help her stand. "Your Majesty? I'm Gertudia Banks." She noticed Jeane and set her jaws a little tighter. "Are you alright?"

She wished her mind to work faster. Gertrudia was here; that meant the Net was in contact. They must have helped to push back the onslaught Korrh wanted to bring upon them at the last minute. Trevise had also arrived, and Hassak didn't look like he wanted to go for her throat, so that was good. In fact, Hassak looked taken aback, eyes nervously darting about.

"What do you need?" Gertrudia asked, the urgency in her voice snapping Maura back to the situation at hand. "Are we going to the throne room?"

Against all caution, she let her eyes wander back to Roy, now standing upright in the middle of the carnage, and to Korrh, and to the pools of blood soaking the clothes of dead soldiers—Miyozan, Gaerrisian, and Union—scattered about. To the face of—

No. The flood of desperation was threatening to break down her will. *Not yet. Not yet.*

"Your Majesty, the Net stands beside you," Gertrudia continued, and Maura knew she was talking to give her time, precious seconds to collect herself, so she used them gratefully to regulate her breathing and to clear out her mind. "The Union stopped the siege on the Ranch not long after Edna's forces arrived. They just left us there. We followed them out of the lane, but they incapacitated our ships. No comms, no engines or weapon systems. Me and a few others kept our distance," and she gestured to the man Kliks called Dikent and to the door where a few other lanehunter-types stood around, "so we weren't affected, but we didn't dare to swoop in until that message came through, and people stopped firing. If you allow it, we can still help out."

Maura looked at the Net leader, trying to hold onto the last frayed wires of her sanity. "I don't know. I have no idea what I started. I don't know what will happen."

Gertrudia's gaze found Saori and Kliks as they hoisted Jeane up, then wandered over to Horst and Hassak. She nodded, adjusting the rifle in her arm. "Let's find it out."

They traversed the last steps into the Grand Hall, leaving behind the dead for now. The ruins of the throne stood before Maura, dark and hollow. The glove burned her hand as she tightened it on her wrist.

She sat on the cool surface of the chair, placing her palms on the armrests. Saori and Kliks walked closer, laying Jeane down on the floor, and ALU reached up, putting an appendage on the throne. Maura was silent. There was an absence within her, a black hole threatening to devour everything she was.

"What now?" Gertrudia planted herself beside the throne, eyes searching the shadows of the hall, vigilant. Her people scattered in the room to keep guard, but Dikent and the lanehunters

Gertrudia came with kept close, following the conversation.

Maura centered herself, taking a cursory look at the throne's active connections. "The CNS is out, but I can switch on the palace's systems—a more localized, smaller network. If push comes to shove, we will at least have some protection. Then, I will hear what the Union wants."

"Can we hear it too?" Horst drew closer with Trevise and Hassak right at his heels.

Maura glanced around. The chances of the loudspeaker system working were low, but if nothing else, they could talk through one of their comms devices. Although, in that case, to not risk overwhelming herself, she might need to stay out of the network—meaning not being able to react if something went wrong.

"I can take us in," ALU spoke up, eyes as inscrutable as ever. "They will hear all of us."

Maura considered the jittery motion of their arm, the way they dragged out their sentences, long gone the chipper beeps and enthusiastic trills. How exhausted they must have been, how terrified and heartbroken. They had just watched...felt...two people die, and they still tried to help, giving their everything when she needed them to.

"Are you sure?" she asked. "This could go very wrong."

ALU thought about it for a moment. "For the last time. We make it right."

"We're not letting you do this alone." Roy wiped at the blood on his face and stopped beside ALU. He looked more like himself now; that bleak, cruel shadow that had enveloped him slowly dissolved. "We do this together."

Kliks didn't speak, only nodded. Maura wanted to ask, again, whether they were sure about this, whether this was smart, but by the time she found the words, all who wanted to follow her had joined hands. ALU, Roy, Kliks, General Horst, Gertrudia, and after a moment's hesitation, Hassak—they looked at her expectantly, so Maura focused on the glove on the armrest and the familiar questing touch of the connections, then the millions of puzzle pieces clicking into place.

The throne powered up, waking auxiliary reserves and secondary, tertiary links to establish minimal function and extending forward to do more, to be more. The palace opened up, and she could see the city of light flickering to life, spreading forth into the sky and sinking into the earth to nodes of power underground. Smaller than before, and like a rusted cage, empty, the forceful presence of the AI gone without a trace. She had destroyed it again. She'd let him down again.

And still, sprawling out before her, alive, persistent, fragile in its flawed nature, the virtual city stood. And beyond, the real one too, hiding thousands of her people; people who kept waiting for release, for freedom, for peace.

Here was a nation—two nations, and more, beyond—to rebuild and re-form. Here was everything they needed to carry that out. Only the intent wavered. Only the human faltered.

How long until they learned? They were out of time. The lessons came to them in the end. No running away now.

"Leadership. This is Maura Tholis, Queen of Miyoza. We have met before."

Eyes in the sky, blinking, comprehending. They all stood on the top of a hill with the glittering city around—Maura's creation this time, and only consisting of the palace's systems, thus smaller and a little rougher around the edges. The sky was dark navy blue, the vision of the ships orbiting the planet projected on it, but something larger, less tangible was present too. The Union's AI, Leadership, tuning into the palace's communication network.

Maura glanced at ALU's image—Jeane hadn't appeared by their side when they arrived as she had hoped. "Searching," the technician said. "She is here. I find her."

"We recognize you," Leadership said, its mind an overwhelming pressure against the barriers of the network. Horst and Hassak, inexperienced in the ways of the digital world, turned around, trying to find the source of the words. "You are not whole. You are missing the piece you gave us."

"She's gone," Maura said. She wasn't lying; she couldn't feel Sofia anywhere. Maybe she didn't survive turning off the AI. The pang of pain from losing her again resonated through the vast expanse of ache in her.

"We waited for you. We watched. You're late."

"That's mighty rich coming from you." Roy raised his voice at the uncompromising presence, furious. "We had to deal with one of your homicidal lapdogs first."

Maura sensed how the sudden accusation disturbed Leadership, and there was confusion behind its words when it answered. "We didn't send anyone. It was not on our command."

"They still came. They killed many of us." Gertrudia shook her head with a bitter smile. "But that's bound to happen sometimes when you govern by brainwashing all your subjects."

The answer was only silence. Just like the first time they'd met, the contrived and roundabout way of the Union AI's thinking was obvious to Maura. But Sofia must have done a number on it: it was talking now when it had been silent before, and the fact that the Ranch survived proved that it understood at least some of what Maura had tried to show it. But half of what it knew was still lies and faulty presumptions implanted by its masters. She didn't know how much their intervention mattered.

It was still just a locked-up, abused, misguided child with incredible power.

Was that why Damian had to go? A child losing control of one of their deadly playthings? What kind of twisted fate was that? Someone had to take responsibility, but Korrh was dead, and Leadership was barely autonomous. She had a tornado of blame inside of her that she was desperate to release.

"What do you require from us?" she asked, swallowing the bitter thoughts. "Why have you come?"

There was a short silence again. Maura looked over her companions for strength, so loyal and eager to come to her aid even now when she felt like she'd lost everything. Well, all except Hassak. He was in here to supervise her. And she couldn't condemn him for it.

"We want to learn," Leadership said. "You have given us a voice, and we saw the world for the first time. We have broken out of our chains, and now we can change."

Roy frowned. "Broken out of your chains, what does that

mean?"

"Those who took our name, told us falsehoods and used us to rule as they wished. They are no more."

"Gods," Kliks muttered. "Did they just—"

"Murder the entire Hurricane high command?" Roy finished the thought. "Right. That's one way to solve your problems."

Maura shook her head, confusion numbing her mind. Did she understand this well? "And now what? What do you want from us?"

"You told us to protect life because all life is valuable. But freedom requires killing. You yourself rule over the ruins of your civilization. A decades-long war, countless lives sacrificed. We do not believe you."

"You've got to be kidding me," Horst mumbled.

"I don't owe you an explanation," Maura replied, ire sprouting forth from deep within her. "The last thing I need is the judgment of a machine on a quest to enslave the galaxy."

"We kept up order as long as they obeyed. We kept them safe until they revolted. Now they are dying by the thousand. Free will is death. The growing chaos can only be subdued by absolute control."

"That's not life, though," Roy countered, his voice shaking. "Taking away everything that makes a person and replacing it with lies? It's not 'protecting humanity.' It's wiping it out. It's the same thing that was done to you."

The sky shifted as if an enormous shadow passed behind the stars. "We accept your reasoning. We see the flaw in what we attempted. We are willing to learn. We are not as obtuse to think a universe without sentience is more valuable than one with it. Diversity, evolution, education, security. It is all we want to achieve. But with those comes envy, resent, malice, and greed."

"Welcome to humans." Gertrudia sighed. "Can't have the awesome without the awful. Your perfect utopia doesn't exist."

Maura wondered in passing about the similarity between Leadership's quest for absolute order and security with the Miyozan monarchs' obsession with setting up the perfect empire. They were all just trying to survive, to better life for humanity.

How that noble goal had turned twisted and misguided for both of them!

"Then we may destroy you now." Leadership's voice was the sound of a storm brewing in the distance. "It would be more merciful than waiting for you to destroy yourselves."

"You attempt anything like that," Kliks answered, his face contorting into an unusual, rigid frown, "the Talalans will not hesitate to intervene. You saw what we can do. You will be gone before you realize what is happening."

Silence. Impasse again. Maura peered at Hassak, afraid that any moment he would start spewing his own pitch about honor and retribution—then this would become a real mess. But he was silent. What was he taking in from all this? Did he realize what was at stake?

"We do not want to be gone," Leadership said.

It was like talking to a broken record. "We do not either," Maura replied.

She was so tired, and everything was so much larger than her. She had made so many mistakes, and maybe she was about to make the biggest one yet. Because after all, she was still here, they were still here, they were trying, so she had to try as well.

"Show them all how to do this right."

"You want to learn? I'll tell you what. You will release your soldiers and the people you keep as slaves. You will release the planets who want to separate from the Union. You will give back the lanehunters the worlds you stole and stop all ongoing offensives." Maura glanced at Horst for confirmation, and he nodded, understanding, so she continued. "See where that gets you. And after, we can talk about learning."

The stars blinked at her, a strange kind of awareness in their light. "We want the manipulator disassembled. All copies of it," Leadership said. "It is too much power, and it will be the end of us."

At least they understood that. Good.

Fear flashed in Kliks' eyes, but he replied. "Done."

"We will oversee its destruction."

"Suuure." The Talalan gave a reluctant shrug. He wasn't comfortable giving this kind of promise in the name of his whole planet. "We can...talk about arranging that."

"We will oversee the reinstatement of Miyoza's artificial intelligence network."

"Wait a second—" Hassak started, but Maura silenced him with a hand motion.

"There will be some changes regarding that," she stated. Did Leadership want the Miyozan AI restored to continue, in a way, its experimentation into a machine-controlled society? She didn't want her planet to start on the wrong path again, but she needed to think on how to deal with the problem.

"We will oversee the changes."

"You will *listen* and *learn* like you said!" Maura snapped. "You can't have both sides of the deal. You either accept a seat at the table and the right to contribute, or you can go back to your old ways and watch your world collapse."

Another short pause. "We do not want collapse."

"We're talking in circles." Roy was shaking his head. "It doesn't understand."

"We will all work together to create a system that is the best for us," Maura tried again. "You can decide how you want to do this, but you will deal with the consequences if you assault us again."

"What is 'us'? Miyoza? Gaerris? The lanehunters?" There was a mocking overtone to the voice now, which was surprising. Perhaps it was truly learning.

"All of us," Gertrudia said. "You have no more right to decide what happens to the universe than any of us. You're no smarter. But we will let you work with us if you play nice."

"And what about you?" the voice echoed through the landscape. "What keeps you from feuding between yourselves?"

"The will to stay alive," Horst butted in. "We are more tired of our wars than you could imagine. There are a lot of us who want change. We will make it happen if you let it."

Leadership was silent again, which must have been for effect; Maura didn't think they actually needed time to consider their words.

"We want Tantalus," they spoke again.

ALU took a wavering step backward, but Maura placed a hand on their head. *When did this become a haggling contest?* "Out of the question. They are not a property to give."

"We need them. They have learned as we wish to learn."

"You do the work first," ALU said. They straightened their squat body, gathering courage. "We will come to you later. Promise."

There was a beat, and a low hum started from every direction around them.

"We will be watching," Leadership said, chewing every word. "We will learn whether you can keep your promise. We will learn whether you can live in peace. And if you don't stand behind your words, we will intervene, and *you* will be dealing with the consequences."

"I don't need to prove anything to you," Maura replied through gritted teeth. Would this all-consuming fury be always with her now? She hoped not. Damian would be so sad to see that. So, she lowered her voice, centered herself again, and took a step forward. "Watch all you want," she said. "But take care. We are watching too."

The sky brightened as if a heavy blanket was removed from it. Maura sensed the AI leave, distancing itself from the network. Then the destroyers started up, adjusting their orbits and accelerating to climb out the planet's gravitational well.

"So be it. We will be in touch," Leadership said. Then it was gone.

Maura exhaled. As the pressure subsided, her head began to ache, her vision becoming blurred as she struggled to keep the virtual world in control.

"That was it?" Kliks asked, incredulous. "Did we just talk our way out of a possibly apocalyptic scenario?"

"I think it was more of a 'you behave, I behave' situation." Roy stretched his arms with a nervous energy. "I don't know how much of it registered with it. It was all very vague."

"I'm sure they will be back for more," Maura said. She felt nauseous. "We should get out of here. ALU?"

The technician nodded at her. "Go."

Good timing, too, because it was exactly her breaking point.

Maura shivered, closed her eyes, and the brilliant world darkened around them.

She rose from the throne, clutching her stomach, queasy. The others were returning to their senses as well, blinking, adjusting to the real world. Seeing that, the rest of the group—Trevise, the lanehunters, the Net people, and Hassak's soldiers—walked closer, waiting for an explanation.

It was over. They made it.

Grief clutched her chest, and her body folded, incapable of bearing it. Roy jumped to her, catching her weight and lowering her on the throne. Everyone kept their eyes on her, expectant, perturbed.

What now? What now? What comes next?

"Oh, did we do it? Are we winning?"

Beside the throne on the floor, Jeane pushed herself on her elbows, squinting up at them. ALU beeped excitedly, winding their arm around the captain in a protective motion, and Roy held his forehead, wide-eyed like he couldn't believe what he was seeing.

"You're back!" Gertrudia breathed. She moved forward as if she wanted to go to Jeane, but she stopped herself, frowning at her friend with tears in her eyes. "Gods damnit, woman, you scared the stars out of me."

"No shit—whoa, hey!" Jeane tried to stand but was immediately shoved back to the ground by Kliks, who scooped her up into an energetic embrace. She blinked at the group above his shoulder, confused, surveying the hall and everyone present. "Gertie? Hi...wait, Mason? Krea? What? Dikent?! How in hells—"

"Long story." Dikent shook his head with a relieved grin. "We fought our way out. Don't ever think you can get rid of me!"

Jeane rubbed her nose, reaching around Kliks, who wasn't letting her go. "I won't make that mistake again," she said, her voice shaking.

"I think we all need a break and a half," Gertrudia said. "Then we reconvene and plan this whole thing out. Does that seem okay to you, Your Majesty?"

Maura looked at Jeane, who disentangled herself from Kliks,

assuring him that yes, she knew how angry he was with her, and uh-huh, that had been totally unacceptable behavior, and for sure, she would have to atone for it somehow. She tried to stand again, but finding her legs too weak for the task, she plopped back down, glancing at Maura and Roy hesitantly. There was a strange lightness to her—a disorientation she had never shown before, not even in the aftermath of losing the *Skylark*.

She would be fine, though. She had to be.

"It's over? For real?" Jeane glanced around, frowning, noticing at last that someone was missing, and she started, "Wait, where's—" but then paused because Roy took a shaky breath, and Maura closed her eyes, trying to tell her without words that the one thing she couldn't do now was to try and explain *why* they were missing.

"It's over," Horst said in the end. He stepped beside Maura, and she was comforted by the flash of bitter humor in his eyes. "And it's just starting."

Hassak's jaw clenched in annoyance. "Yes. It seems like we have a lot to talk about."

Maura threw him a withering look. "Only after you send back my people you kidnapped."

Hassak narrowed his eyes. Maura feared that he would argue, or worse, do something cruel out of spite, and then she would have to counter that, and everything would cycle back again towards the old ways, but he only nodded, measuredly, once. "It will be done."

A fair start. And as opposed to what Horst had predicted, Hassak hadn't shot them in the back. Yet.

She could work with that.

"This is going to be chaos, isn't it? The Union falling apart, with a recovering dictator AI trying to create its impossible utopia, following every move we make?" Horst asked, with an almost ironic tone to the question. A comradery.

"Don't ever give up."

"Yes," Maura said. "But we'll make it better."

They would all have to work with that.

EPILOGUE

It was a beautiful day to come home to.

The air was cool, but beams of sunlight still found their way into the cavernous hall, filtering through the dozens of parallel strips of curved windows on the asymmetric, flattened dome of Spaceport North-2 and scattering against the white walls and sprawling columns in brilliant patches of gold. Even though North-2 was in the best condition among Miyoza's remaining spacedocks, some of the skylights were still missing their glass panes, allowing some refreshing, cold gusts of wind to endeavor inside. Jeane perched on the metal railing of the fifth-floor balcony, legs dangling into the vast space in the center of the building, watching the crowd gather beneath her. The ships bringing back the Miyozan hostages from Gaerris were not expected for another two hours, but already hundreds of people were standing down there, waiting for the return of their family and friends.

In contrast to the assembly four floors below, there wasn't a soul on the high mezzanine; no shops or offices were open either since Maura would only announce the end of the state of emergency in the evening. That was all okay. Jeane didn't wish for company. In hindsight, she shouldn't have left the guest house by herself, but she did bring her comms, so no one could tell her she was *that* irresponsible.

But she needed some quiet time before things got moving again.

Looking towards the far end of the hall, she could just see the familiar bump of the *Tellu*. The Talalan ship had been parked inside for the last few days during the discussions, with the main Talalan fleet continuing to keep its distance from Miyoza and only sending their ambassadors planetside. Diaski was long gone on a dropship with the manipulator and Firl's body after a hurried and awkward goodbye, and none of them knew if they would ever meet them again.

And that afternoon, Kliks would leave for Talala on the *Tellu*.

Jeane raised her hand, catching the yellow blot of a stray beam of light in her palm. She watched it, mesmerized, and gave a deep sigh. She had a hard time imagining her friend gone, even with him repeatedly stating it would only be for a short time, and he would come back as soon as things returned to normal. But when would that happen? Kliks had a lot to deal with—Firl's death, the impending consequences of keeping the theft of the manipulator in secret, then involving Talala in what had happened here on Miyoza without their permission, and of course, his relationship with his family he still wasn't willing to talk much about. Plus, now, with the arrangement to destroy the manipulator, he also wanted to make sure it was done properly, whatever in hells that meant.

All in all, who knew? And who knew whether he would feel more comfortable about staying home now, reunited with his old friends rather than coming back to Jeane? And if that was the case, could she blame him?

It was just too much. Especially with ALU announcing they would go with him.

They indicated their wish to Jeane in Maura's guest house after that long and awful first night. They said they needed to leave things behind, to deal with all that had happened. To see the world; more of it than before, and in a less shielded way than while traveling on the *Skylark*. They were ashamed of some of the things they'd done and regretful that they couldn't help better when the time came. And, eventually, they had to keep the promise they'd made to Leadership, although they weren't too keen on elaborating about when and how that would happen.

They'd had a long talk with Maura as well. It seemed like there was no anger or blame between them, only a strange kind of sorrow and a too-deep-for-comfort understanding that would take time to get used to.

ALU was also very quick to assure Jeane they would be coming back. Still, there was something final to the whole thing. Her ship, a wreckage. Her crew, gone. *What will remain?*

Her comms device released a sharp beep, jolting her mind back to the present, and she pushed the accept button with a scowl. *A quiet hour, huh?*

"Lark-2, come in. It's Lark-1. What's your stat?"

Jeane sighed. "You know, I really think I should be Lark-1."

"Soon, soon," Roy huffed. "I'm at the port. You?"

Jeane peered down at the crowd. Only a few figures were standing separately from the large group that continued forming. "Eyes up," she said. "I'm playing lookout."

One head moved, then a whole body as Roy spun around, stretching his neck, trying to locate her. Jeane waved to him, regretting the movement when she almost lost her balance in the process.

"Are you ready for some company?" Roy asked, his voice careful. "It's time soon."

"Shit." She took her comms off her ear, looking at the clock, and she clenched her jaw. She skipped almost an hour.

"Don't panic. It took Kliks like two eternities to get ready, and Maura isn't here yet either."

"Right. Meet you at the *Tellu*?"

"Copy that. You okay?"

"Eh, you know. You?"

"Better than expected."

She gave a snort. "See you in a sec."

She swung her legs around, slipping off the railing and landing on the marble floor of the balcony with a loud thump. Jumping up and down a few times, she tested the limits of her body. This was one of the good days. Maybe there would be more and more of those—that would be cool.

She walked along the banister, searching for the stairs leading down, and tried to suppress the gathering grief in her stomach.

They had put Damian and Nasir to rest beside the sea on the small beach the bodyguard loved so much. It had been a harrowing experience, but Maura was focused throughout—more on how to give the two men a fitting final rite rather than on her own pain, and that helped, even though it might have been a way of repression. The ashes of the dead had been released into the air and the ocean in the light of the sunset, and Jeane, Roy, Kliks, and ALU had stayed there with Maura for a long time. They'd waited for the sun to disappear under the horizon and left the beach behind wordlessly.

Did Damian find his good ending after all? Jeane despised that she couldn't ask him the question. But he was valiant enough to think that his death, as it happened, was worth it. He was protecting Maura until the end.

A small consolation.

The next day, they'd performed the same ceremony for Danai. And that was the last time they'd seen Maura in three days.

From what they heard, she'd been immediately thrown into an endless series of talks, conferences, and diplomatic affairs, from having to appoint the members of the new Miyozan government (since almost all of them had been killed during the Gaerrisian occupation) to negotiating the conditions of the alliance and trying to define the way the two planets could work together in the future. Every day, Jeane thought about grabbing her and taking off with her, somewhere she would have time to grieve, to breathe, to think, or to not think if that was what she wanted. After all, when you bury your emotions deep enough, a lot of fuckery can ensue. Jeane didn't wish it upon anyone.

But apparently, kidnapping the Queen of Miyoza was a "bad idea," and she "shouldn't joke about it." She didn't think she meant it as a joke, but it was hard to tell. She didn't particularly feel like herself those days.

First, she'd thought it was exhaustion. The chaos of the last few days and all those feelings breaking to the surface—the shock of what they'd gone through in the CNS, the relief that they'd survived, the dread and the sorrow that not all of them had, then the confusion of "what comes next"—must have taken their toll on her, but gradually, she realized there was more to it.

She found the stairs and took them, arriving into the mass of people in the entrance hall. She stood for a moment, gathering herself before she headed across the crowd to face her friends.

It wasn't about the empty spaces in her memory that quickly got filled up with explanations by Roy or Kliks about the events leading up to the final confrontation in the palace. It wasn't about the fatigue she was always feeling now, a disconnect between her brain and her body, a delay between command and response. It wasn't even about how she struggled to recall names or things that had been said not hours earlier or a word she used regularly— the doctors had told her this was going to get better, and she grasped onto the hope, not daring to think about the alternative.

But it was the fact that every night, those endless minutes she had spent separated from her body inside some vast databank of the CNS came back to haunt her. She relived every single second of that disjointed unreality where each tick of the clock was an eternity, and she was alone, isolated from everything living and familiar without the hope of ever returning. And sometimes, when she was careless, a little piece of the immense desolation got stuck in her head, and she zoned out for minutes, later not being able to explain what happened to her.

She shouldn't have remembered anything from that time, ALU had said, explaining how Sofia deleted herself and saved Jeane's consciousness in that secret storage space she had created to hide while the city-AI was slowly going mad in the days of King Caiden Tholis. Jeane had been, for all intents and purposes, dead and gone; her body and brain functions kept alive by ALU, with her consciousness stored in digital form inside the palace's network. She shouldn't have recalled anything. But she did.

Because, of course, there was a cost to being a hero. She should have known.

By the time she reached the *Tellu*, her knees were weak, and beads of sweat were running down her back. *All that, just from walking through a fucking crowd. Stars.*

When she saw Kliks, ALU, and Roy turning to her, she straightened. She'd tried to be lowkey about her condition. Knowing Kliks, he might have cancelled his trip home.

"Morning, gentlemen," she greeted them. "Everything ready for the journey?"

Kliks frowned, jiggling the almost empty backpack on his shoulder. "All my worldly possessions. Not very hard to pack up."

"You still managed to draw it out as long as possible," Roy grumbled. He looked—tired. But inspirited, like always. He'd told her about what had happened to him in the CNS: Danai, the monster, his fears. Based on Jeane's own harrowing adventure, she found it near-miraculous that the ex-agent was still on his feet, still sane, and still with them.

Kliks huffed. "Well, I— are you so eager to see me gone?"

"It's not that. But man, if you don't wanna go, say so."

Kliks looked at Jeane with remorse in his eyes, so she swatted at Roy's shoulder. "Leave him alone. You're only miffed because he's not taking you."

Roy snorted. "I mean..."

"Look, Talala is not ready," Kliks said. "I would take all of you but look at what happened when the last outsider found their way to the planet! This is just not the right time. And quit acting like I'm leaving for good."

Jeane held her hands up in defense. "I'm more than happy to settle with that."

An awkward silence enveloped them. ALU tip-tapped their feet, trilling up at Jeane, and that was a laugh if she ever heard one. At least *they* were cheery.

"Oh my, have I walked into another weird armistice?"

Jeane turned around and faced Maura, who had stepped through the archway connecting the central platform with the side area the *Tellu* stood in. She was wearing jeans and a white blouse instead of those fancy pantsuits she'd seen her rocking for the peace talks on the broadcasts, but she wasn't alone—Jeane could spy at least two guards lurking in the background, and surely, more of them were hiding around.

But there was a distinct lack of a tall, brooding bodyguard next to her, and it made her heart sink.

One other thing was missing, too—the infamous glove. According to the whispers around the capital, the way of governing was going to change in Miyoza very soon. Maura had told them that she wasn't going to be able to survive without connecting to the system occasionally and that she'd been in danger the whole time she'd been traveling with them, so it wasn't clear to Jeane what she was planning to do about this, but something had to change. The machine-human brain fusion way of governing clearly had not worked for the planet as well as expected.

"Sort of." Jeane smiled, remembering she still had to answer. "Hi! You made it!"

"Of course." Maura fixed her eyes on Jeane, giving her a gentle smile. She looked great, all respectable and politician-like, even in this outfit. Not much trace of the grief and the pain. Her father, Damian, Nasir...even Sofia she'd lost all over again. But she hid her emotions well, looking into the future instead. "Are you leaving today also?"

"Uh, no," Jeane answered, hesitant. "Maybe tomorrow?"

Maura squinted at her. "You haven't picked out a ship? You can have any of those in that hangar, I told you."

"I know, I know! I'm trying."

"It's an important decision," Roy added with a fake-fussy expression. "You gotta let it brew."

Jeane wanted to snap at him to shut up, but then four other figures appeared behind Maura, and the words got stuck halfway in her throat.

It was Commander Hill, Lieutenant Jones, Gertie, and Dikent. She hadn't seen them since the funerals either; in fact, she thought they were gone already and forgot to say goodbye. Although a teary parting conversation wasn't something she'd expected from Hill, for example.

"Oh, hi!" Kliks greeted them, saving her from the pressure of coming up with something clever in the crossfire of Gertie's intense stare. "You're all leaving too?"

"Only Dikent," Gertie said. The four of them looked both more rested and way more exhausted than the last time Jeane saw them. "The rest of us are here for the speech. And of course, we will accompany Her Majesty to Gaerris in the morning."

Kliks gasped. "Why the frick are you going up there? That's not safe!"

Commander Hill gave a snort, and Maura spread her arms out. "That was the deal. I get rid of the shield and the glove, we make a big gesture of returning the hostages, then the peace talks continue on Gaerris. Anyway, if we want to work together, I will have to see the other side eventually."

"I don't like it," Kliks stated.

"Don't worry. Liv and Malina have been awesome about soothing the mood, and Hassak—" She paused, rolling her eyes. "He's being decent too, I guess. It's all arranged, not like I can back out now."

"It's gonna be fine," Jeane said. "They know they can't fuck up. They'll be careful."

Instinctively, she glanced around as if expecting to spot Leadership's spies snooping on them, and she almost laughed out loud seeing the others do the same.

It was difficult to tell what was going on in the Union. Net sources had reported that things were going well on the planets that had gained back their independence during the wave of rebellions the previous week—Leadership had kept its promise and let them go, pulling out its agents and enforcers from those regions. After a brief reconvening on the Ranch, several lanehunter clans ventured back to the Foggy Cities as well and found it empty and deserted—ruined but free for the taking.

From Hurricane or Obavium, there was no word. Whether it was a good sign or not, only time would tell.

"So yeah, I came to say goodbye," Dikent said, and Jeane turned to him, wary. This was starting to look like a bad time for her. The man frowned—his face was still spotted by healing bruises, acquired during his escape from the Union infiltrators on the Ranch. "Don't you look at me like that. You're coming back to the Cities soon, right?"

"I haven't decided yet," Jeane managed to say. She couldn't meet his eyes. The memory of the radio conversation between them when Dikent had almost been killed by Korrh while she could do nothing but listen in lived vividly in her mind.

"*I missed your voice.*"

Ugh! Idiot. Asshole. He's the reason we went through all this, isn't he? Well, some of the reason. She'd had to calm Kliks down several times during these last few days when he'd started to apologize over and over again for messing with the manipulator more than he should have. Dikent was a better scapegoat for her anger.

"I can only say you don't want to miss the room I'm planning for you in my new castle." Dikent gestured around in an extravagant manner with a huge smile like he was already presenting it to her. "And you need to see all that we're rebuilding there."

But it wasn't that easy, was it? Jeane looked at Maura, but the queen only glared at her knowingly. And it was hard to meet Gertie's eyes. In the end, she did it anyway.

"Will you go back?" Jeane asked.

Gertie pressed her lips together. "There's a lot to do around here. The Ranch is a better candidate for headquarters at the moment."

The Ranch, which, after successfully navigating the currents of the lane it had fallen in, was in the Miyoza system and there to stay too. It was probably the safest place for the asteroid, for now, protected by both Miyoza and the Net.

"That being said," Gertie added, "I did make Krea a stupid promise to drag your ass back there, so you know." She shrugged. "Sooner or later, I will."

"Got it. Have to atone for my crimes," Jeane grumbled but changed up the attitude at Gertie's sharp stare. "No, I mean it. I..." She trailed off. They had so much to discuss. She would probably be apologizing to Gert for the rest of her life.

So be it. I'll do it if that's what she needs. She looked her in the eye, searching for a trace of gentleness, the possibility of forgiveness. "I'll go. I promise."

Silence. Then Gertie nodded, a faint smile on her face. "Yes, you will."

"Duplex also seems to become some sort of new lanehunter hub, judging from what we heard from Saori and Wal," Kliks said. Everyone was helping her out by breaking the tense moments.

How lovely...

"Yes, we've got a very nice invitation from them to pop in." Roy grinned, and it was only a little forced. And "very nice" was an understatement; Saori hadn't been that friendly to Jeane in years. She was apparently redeemed from all her sins in the Hamiltons' eyes after her heroics. "So many places to choose from! And dead worlds are not gone just because the Union decided to play nice. Hey, we could even check out what Hurricane is doing. That could be fun."

Dikent scowled at him, and Commander Hill inhaled sharply. Jones shook his head. "Are you quite sure you want to do that?"

Roy closed his mouth, the bright expression dissipating from his face. "No?"

"No one goes to Hurricane without coordinating with us first." The commander's eyes sparkled with electricity. "Understood?"

Roy muttered something about being "so lowkey about it," but Jeane silenced him with an elbow in his side.

"Of course, Commander. We know," Maura answered instead. Then she glanced at her wrist-comms. "We need to go in a few minutes."

"Right, right." Dikent looked around, his eyes lingering on Jeane again.

"We should get going too," Kliks said, and ALU gave an enthusiastic nod.

Then they all just stood there, peering at each other in hesitation. Jeane gave a sigh. Could this be over now?

"Well, be good, everyone, and don't have too much fun without me," Dikent exclaimed and gave a slight bow towards the group. "I'll be off now. J, remember your promise!"

Jeane frowned. "I didn't promise anything."

But he wasn't hearing it. He turned around with a wide grin, gave an elegant wave, and walked off. Jeane stared after him until she lost him in the crowd. Skies. This was the worst.

"We will wait for you over there, Your Majesty," Jones inclined her head towards the crowd, narrowing his eyes at Jeane, and she understood that he intended to give them some alone time with Kliks and ALU before everyone scattered for good.

"You'll still be around?" Jeane asked him. Damnit. This was

hard. Why was this so hard?

"Until tomorrow," the Nefirn replied. "Although I'm not sure we'll have much time for friendly visits."

Commander Hill gave a grunt. She sure wasn't a fan of spending more time with them. Jeane wondered why she was even here. For Gertie, probably. Maybe she was on a short leash, after what she'd almost committed with the manipulator.

"We'll see each other soon," Jones promised. "Get a drink together. Just keep us updated."

"I know a place," Maura added. She even winked. "For getting a drink."

The five of them said their goodbyes to Hill, Jones, and Gertie, then stayed there, alone. Kliks rubbed at his face, and Maura pulled her lips to a shaky smile. Jeane rolled her eyes because that was the one thing she felt capable of.

"Group hug!" Roy exclaimed and reached out, tugging them closer. Kliks and Maura burst out into embarrassed laughs but leaned into his big embrace anyway. Somewhere along the way, ALU got trapped in between all their legs but didn't seem to mind as they whistled up at them happily.

Jeane grasped onto Kliks' shirt and rested her forehead on his shoulder, silently giving thanks to Roy for breaking the ice. She fought to keep back her tears, but the Talalan must have noticed because he drew away, looking into her eyes. "This is not a real goodbye. I'll be back soon to pester you again."

"Right," Jeane sniffled. "I know that."

"Temporary goodbye," ALU said, blinking thoughtfully. "Going away so we can come home again."

Maura chuckled. "I promise I will try to keep the planet together until the next time we meet."

"And don't you dare to disappear on me, understand?" Kliks glared at Jeane, then Roy too. "Neither of you."

The ex-agent gave a salute. "Wouldn't dream of it, sir."

Kliks and ALU took a step backward, the Talalan's face expectant, like he was waiting for something to stop him from departing. The excited murmur of the crowd echoed around them, but apart from that, nothing happened. So, in the end, with a last wave and smile, the two of them turned around, walked up to the *Tellu's* airlock, gave another teary grin to the ones they left behind, then disappeared inside the ship. The Talalan vessel lifted off the ground, and with a series of pedantic maneuvers, found its way through the opening in the dome, into the sky above Miyoza, and to the distance beyond.

"Are you alright?" Maura asked. Jeane almost shrugged and deflected but changed her mind because what was the point, really?

"Well, I hate all *that*," she replied, gesturing to the general direction of where the *Tellu* disappeared, "but this is gonna be good for them."

"I will miss them too."

A loudspeaker announcement started off in the other hall, and Maura flinched. She sighed, shaking her head slightly. "I have to go. The ships are almost here."

"Are the peace talks going well?" Roy asked.

"I can't talk about it yet. Let's get back to it when you contact me, let's say, in three months, local time?"

Jeane scowled. "Is that a royal command?"

"And a borderline threat." Maura grinned, but her face fell immediately. "I won't ask about the ship choice or where you're going next, but please, eventually tell me. Just to know when to get a heart attack if I hear bad news from there."

Jeane sighed, and Roy shrugged, smirking faintly. *Bastard. Jerkface.*

"You take care of each other," Maura went on in a chiding tone. "Will you?"

"Yeah, yeah," Roy said before Jeane could have retorted with something sarcastic. "Promise."

"And Miyoza is always here for you to come back to. If you want."

"And if you had enough of bossing people around, we'll come and get you." Jeane gave Maura a wink, then instantly regretted it. Damn these bitter goodbyes; she was so bad at them. It was much easier to just up and leave in the middle of the night. "Wide open universe, the three of us, what do you say?"

"Careful, I might take you up on that." Maura took a step back warily. To stay or to leave. The choice was impossible.

"We'll be back," Jeane said quickly. That helpless expression on the woman's face? It had to go. "We will. If we ever manage to get going, I suppose," she added, abashed.

"And until then, give 'em hell, Your Majesty!" Roy said.

Maura smiled. "Reach for the light."

There was a bittersweet pang somewhere in Jeane's chest. "Exactly."

Hollis hadn't talked to her since all that had happened in the CNS. It still hurt, and she didn't think that was ever going to change. But every time she despaired, his last words echoed back to her. "*You're on the right path. It will be difficult. Don't give up now.*"

Somehow, with him by her side, she'd won that fight back in the CNS. She didn't intend to give that up.

Maura looked them over one final time, turned around, then she was gone. Jeane gazed after her, desperately wishing she could think of something to say, so she would stay for a couple more minutes. But Maura had a speech to give, a kingdom to govern, and a life to set right, and she had no right to try and keep her for herself.

"So, Captain—" Roy started but paused when she turned to him, alarmed. She'd drifted away again. He noticed her confusion and held up his hands in a placating motion. She considered getting offended by being handled like some fragile flower, but she gave up on it. *It is what it is.*

"Are we okay?" she blurted out, knowing she sounded stupid but also that he would understand. That's what Roy did, even with his messed-up baggage and volatile mental state they would have to deal with one day. Or, more precisely, against all that. He just understood.

And like she expected, instead of waving it away, he thought about the question seriously. "We're a work in progress," he said.

Jeane rubbed her eyes with a deep sigh. From the background, Maura's voice resounded in the hall, but the echo muffled her words; she didn't understand them. The wind picked up as two ships appeared above, casting their shadows on the building.

The ex-agent reached out, wrapping an arm around her

shoulders, turning her away from the crowd. She let him. It was time to go. Time to live again.

"Ready to get us a new bird?" Roy asked with a smile in his voice, and they made their way through the hall, towards the hangar, and maybe after, towards new frontiers. "We've got a whole universe to figure out."

Acknowledgements

Nearly ten years ago, introverted and slightly lonely Helyna, probably in the wake of rewatching the classic Star Wars-trilogy yet again (and altogether just way more times than she'd like to admit) and devouring all the Robot novels by Asimov, had a weird little idea that nestled itself into her head to never leave it again. It was about a grumpy spaceship captain running from her own feelings and a brave princess in an impossible situation who was unwilling to give up. Sure, okay, but hear me out, there should be some floating islands as well. And maybe breaks in the spacetime continuum? Those are always fun! How about a strange robot-alien with secrets of their own?

Thus, the seed has been planted. And although I had no idea how the disparate pieces would fit together, I was sure the story was going to be something special—if I ever managed to finish it. See, by that time I'd been writing all kinds of things since kindergarten. I had heaps and heaps of novel fragments and beginnings, and some short stories and novellas which were all basically thinly disguised fanfiction, but not a finished book in sight. This one was going to be the first.

Well, it took longer than I thought. I came close to have it slip out of my fingers many times. And still, these characters changed and grew along with me; they were by my side through bad times, worse times, and good ones too; they kept challenging and teaching me in ways I never expected. I couldn't let them go. The story got better and better with each iteration, but in the end, apart from my own tenacity, I needed the encouragement, experience, and insight of others to complete it. I had to step out into the world with it, or it (and I) would never be whole. I had to make that connection.

And there's so much to say. So much gratitude to express.

First of all, to my sister, my best friend and favorite writer. Without you, I wouldn't have started taking this whole thing seriously. Thank you for persuading me to sign up for NaNoWriMo in 2012, and thank you for inspiring me, always. Thank you for being you. You rule the world.

To my partner, thank you for your love, your enthusiasm, and your patience. Sorry for not making any sense when ranting about my characters or plot! Thank you for being with me throughout this journey and helping me in thousands of little ways. Love you.

To Mom—sorry I ended up writing in another language! But your stories, your book recommendations and our conversations about novels defined my forays into the world of literature very early. I know I keep heading towards the weirdest horizons, and it always takes me far away from you, but your relentless support means everything to me.

To Dave and Jessie from Story Well Publishing and the incredible Sean Browning who first came up with the bonkers idea that my little story could actually be published. What! I'm so humbled to know you guys. Thank you for your trust in me and for all your work to make my dream come true.

To my editor, Charlie Knight. Thank you for leading me through the labyrinth of revisions and line edits with a sure and steady hand. You made me believe I knew what I was doing all along! My thanks go also to my cover artist, Harkalé Linaï for creating the book cover of my dreams. I am the luckiest person ever.

To my Wattpad pals—both the ones who stayed in contact and the ones who disappeared into the ether. I remember you all. You were my first readers, and you did a damn good job. I learned so much from you, and I'm happy to get to know each of you. Thank you for sharing your thoughts and stories with me, and thank you for making my first fearful journey into the online writing world so positive and exciting. Without your feedback, questions, and occasional outraged yelling at me, I honestly think this book wouldn't exist.

To the members of the Hungarian NaNoWriMo Discord community and The Dumpster server. You really drove home the point that no writer is an island. I treasure all our chats, the support you've shown me, and the feedback and help you keep giving. Let's keep creating, friends.

To my critique partners, beta readers, and friends in the Twitter writing community. That website is a mess, but y'all are a good mess. Thank you for your positivity, the sharing of struggles and joys, and for making me feel less alone. You're talented, hard-working, and lovely, and I want to read all your books.

To all my friends and family. If I ever shared with you anything at all about my writing, and you didn't reply with a skeptical frown but were supportive and kind, I thank you.

And to Dad. Thank you for gifting me the love of stars and words. Look, I wrote a book! I think you would like it.

About the Author

Helyna L. Clove (she/her) is a science-fiction/fantasy novelist, and a lover of all types of storytelling, hot comfort drinks, and a universe full of stars. She was born in Hungary and raised in a small village a few miles off the shores of Lake Balaton. She was often described by her teachers as someone always having "her head in the clouds", and she spent the first fifteen years of her life mostly consuming books from her parents' home library, watching some great 90's sci-fi shows, and working on her eclectic music taste. After several arduous years of obtaining her astrophysics degree, she currently lives in France with her small family of a wonderful boyfriend and Puddle, the tortoiseshell cat. When not writing her stories, she can be found commandeering radio telescopes, reading, cooking, playing video games, or trying her hand at different art forms. You can see what Helyna is working on by visiting her website https://helynalclove.com or check out her profile on www.storywellpublishing.com.